COUNTDOWN T

by the same author
Disappearer
Colin Cleveland and the End of the World
Girl's Rock
The Eternal Prisoner
Rogue Males

Mark Hunter series
Beautiful Chaos
Sixty-Six Curses
Trouble at School
Mysterious Girlfriend
The Beasts of Bellend
Countdown to Zero

Countdown to Zero

Chris Johnson

Samurai West

Published by Samurai West
disappearer007@gmail.com

Story and Art © Chris Johnson 2025
All rights reserved

ISBN-13: 979-8292056683

The film called *The Earth Dies Screaming* featured in this story is completely fictitious and, apart from having more or less the same plot, bears no resemblance to any actual film called *The Earth Dies Screaming* living or dead.

PART ONE - THE COUNTDOWN BEGINS

Chapter One
The Old How Did That Get There

Unbuttoning her blouse, the woman exposes a left formidable breast (the right one, although not seen, doubtless equally formidable) and offers an erect pink nipple to the swaddled baby cradled in her arm. Instinctively, the infant's small toothless mouth locks itself around the nipple and commences sucking, taking in its mother's warm milk.

This operation does not pass unnoticed in the conference hall and many a male head turns to admire this charming *vignette* of mother nature at her most motherly.

'Plenty of milk in those cans,' says one man to his neighbour.

'Pillock,' says the other. 'It's subcutaneous fat that makes tits big, not how much milk they've got in them.'

The speakers are two young businessmen; Jensen and Brunner by name, they are two of a kind: both tall and handsome, impeccably groomed and attired. Jensen and Brunner are both firm believers that it is what's *outside*, and not what's inside, that counts, and as such are both tremendously pleased with themselves confident that *their* outsides are immaculate.

'Any idea who the daddy is?' proceeds Brunner.

'I doubt she cares,' replies Jensen. (For all he knows it might be one of his own.) He glances at the dial of his Journe wristwatch. 'Should be starting soon.'

'You reckon this is going to be about Zero, then?' asks Brunner.

'*Of course* this is going to be about Zero. Everyone on the payroll getting called here; the big boss herself taking the stand. What else is it going to be about?'

'A lot of 'em are Zero's been our baby all along, but top secret, only a privileged few in on it, and that's today's going to be the big announcement, where we all get to hear what it's all about.'

'I don't buy that one,' says Jensen. 'Yeah, the boss might've found what Zero is all about, but it won't be because it was our project all along.'

'Bettya it *does* turn out it's our project,' says Brunner.

'You're on. How much?'

'Ten grand suit you?'

'Suits me fine.'

Jensen looks at his watch again. 'Come on, come on…'

'You're impatient.'

'Aren't you? We're actually going to see the boss lady face to face.'

'If you call being in the same conference hall with her face to face.'

'Well, you know what I mean. She doesn't usually condescend to show her face to us junior execs at all.'

'So what? It's not like we don't know what she looks like. We've seen pictures of her; just your average snooty bitch in a business suit.'

'Yes, we know what she *looks* like, but that's not the same as actually *seeing* her; seeing how she moves, hearing how she talks—and there's nothing *average* about her, either. She's got to be a lot more than *average* to have climbed to the top of the tree the way she has. Do you know why they call her Flat-Sol Park?'

'Because it's her name?'

'Yes, Einstein, it's her name; but it wasn't the one her mummy and daddy gave her. Maybe the 'Park' bit, yeah. From what I hear, every other person in South Korea is called Park; but the Flat-Sol, that wasn't always her first name. So, do you know what Flat-Sol means? The clue is in the question.'

'Okay… Because she comes from Seoul and she's got small tits?'

'Wrong. I mean yes, she does come from Seoul and she is pretty flat-chested—a lot of Asian women have small tits—but no, 'Flat-Sol' comes from the shoes she wears. She only ever wears flat-soled shoes, see?'

'And so do all the women around here!' protests Brunner. 'It's the rule, isn't it? No heels in the office. Company policy,'

'Yes, but you ever wonder who came up with that rule and made it company policy? In most office places it's the other way round. *She* did it; Flat-Sol made it the rule.'

'She did? Seriously?'

'Seriously. When she took over the company from old Hurst.'

'Oh, yes; he had some kind of a breakdown, didn't he? They had to put him in the funny farm.'

'Right. And from what I hear, *she* was the one who sent him there.'

'What? You mean Flat-Sol Park sent the old fart off his rocker?'

'That's what I hear. I don't know the details; the higher-ups all kept shtum about it; but she did *something* to him. The office rumours are hazy on the details, but she did something to the old man that drove him doolally. And with him out of the executive chair, she just slid her own sweet Asian tush into it.'

Brunner whistles. 'But her promotion had to have been approved by the board of directors; I mean, you can't just move up the ladder automatically like that.'

'*Of course* the board approved her; they knew where their bread was buttered—and so do I. That's why I want in.'

'You want in what? Flat-Sol's knickers?'

'Her office will do for a start. She's looking for a new personal assistant; I've applied for the post.'

'You never told me!'

'Well, I'm telling you now, aren't I?—Ah, here we go!'

The lights drop in the conference hall. The room falls silent, and all eyes are drawn to the stage where a cinema-sized LCD screen has come to life, displaying a static image of the Parkhurst Corporation logo.

A woman appears, stage left, and makes her way towards the rostrum, which is placed slightly to the right of centre-stage to leave the audience's view of the flatscreen uninterrupted. Flat-Sol moves with an unstudied grace and confidence in the sensible footwear from which she allegedly takes her name. In stature she is tall for an Asian woman, and the lines of her body are strong. She wears a tailored business suit, dark grey in colour, skirt snug and short, jacket unbuttoned, a white silk blouse, charcoal grey tights, and the aforementioned black loafers.

Taking her place at the rostrum, Flat-Sol Park stands facing the audience, pausing before speaking. Her head is a soft rectangle, the hair cut short with a broken fringe carefully arranged. The exposed ears are large without being ungainly. Her nose and mouth are well-defined, her jawline powerful, even heavy. Her eyes, by contrast, are small and narrow, but brought into prominence by a pair of full-frame rectangular glasses. Her complexion is a natural deep tan, the colour of honey.

All eyes are fixed upon Flat-Sol, none more avidly than those of Jensen.

The image on the screen changes. Stark and white against a black background, a single word in bold, chunky capitals:

ZERO

Murmurs from the audience. Nearly everyone was expecting it, but this sudden silent confirmation still creates a stir.

'Zero.' Flat-Sol's first word, two syllables, crisply enunciated, spoken with the perfect elocution of a second language comprehensively mastered. 'This is the subject I have gathered you here to brief you upon today.'

Her tones, clear and compelling, appeal to the ear of the listener. His eyes fixed on her, Jensen smiles as he feels his rapidly-tumescing penis crawling down his inside leg.

'First, I wish to quash a rumour that I know has been circulating amongst you: Zero is no project of ours. It has not been instigated by the Parkhurst Corporation or any of its subsidiaries and affiliates.'

Another hushed wave of sound, a mingling of surprise, satisfaction and disappointment, as the audience variously hears the confirmation or refutation of their suspicions.

Jensen's smile broadens. 'That's ten grand you owe me,' he breathes.

'Smartarse,' mutters Brunner.

'Yes, Zero is not our project,' repeats Flat-Sol. 'But I intend to *make* it ours. You all know how it began, how overnight the advertisements started to appear: on television, on the internet, on billboards. The adverts all displayed the same image you see behind me now: the word "Zero" in white lettering against a black background, and below it, in smaller text the words "Coming Soon."

'The advertisements are completely unauthorised and attempts to block them have either been fruitless or short-lived. No-one that we know of has been able to trace them to their source.

'But just what is Zero? There has been no elaboration as to its nature thus far. Is Zero a brand name or a specific product? Is it a service or provider of some kind? Some have hypothesized that the entire advertising campaign is an enormous practical joke, others have postulated that it is intended as an act of terrorism or of psychological warfare. Speculation is rife but tangible facts are lacking. Speculation is risk and can result in huge profit but also in heavy losses. Tangible facts yield certain and immediate profit. Therefore, we must ascertain the facts; we must ascertain the facts about Zero.

'But how do we go about obtaining these facts? Our own intelligence and information gathering networks have so far failed in their efforts; therefore we must outsource, and we have calculated that the best available resource for obtaining the information we require is *this* man.'

A new image appears on the screen behind the speaker, a head and shoulders portrait of a man. The photograph appears to have been taken in the street without the subject's knowledge. The man appears to be in his mid-thirties. He is wearing a brown suit, his eyes are hazel and his hair is dark brown, neatly cut and parted on the left. The expression of the face, humorous and affable, suggests a calm, good-natured man.

'His name is Mark Hunter. He is a senior operative for British Counter-Intelligence. Some of you may have heard of him. As a public sector employee with no additional sources of income, his fiscal worth is too negligible to even be mentioned. His entire income and savings are held in a high-street bank account. He lives in rented accommodation. His suit, as you will have observed, is ready-made. Financially, he is worthless, but viewed in terms of job performance he is a tremendous asset to whomever he serves. Several times now he has interfered with projects instigated by the Parkhurst Corporation and its subsidiaries, and his interference has cost our organisation millions of pounds. We have learned that Mark Hunter has been given the assignment of tracing the Zero campaign to its source and his performance record suggests to us that of all available resources he is the one most likely to lead us to the information we require.

'There is, however, one major drawback: Mark Hunter is incorruptible.'

Gasps of disbelief ripple across the auditorium.

'Yes, incredible as this may sound, he is as impervious to bribery as he is to either threats or coercion. A leftwing, humanitarian worldview blinds him to the obvious advantages of accumulating wealth. He cannot be bought, and if he cannot be bought, then he must be used. He must be kept under the closest possible surveillance, and as we are dealing with a man adept at detecting and eluding surveillance, this will be no easy task. But it *must* be done. Wherever he goes, whatever he does, we must be one step behind him. In the past, Mark Hunter has been known to work in association *with* this person.'

The picture changes. Another head and shoulders portrait, this time a woman with short black hair wearing a silk blouse. Head cocked on one side she smiles at the camera, displaying strong teeth. Her eyes are grey in colour but warm and friendly in expression. She is strikingly beautiful, this woman, and there is strength and confidence about her, evident even in this static image.

'This is Professor Dorothea Dupont, a psychologist and media celebrity. Many of you will know her by reputation. Her net worth is admirable, amounting to tens of millions. The foundation of her wealth was an inheritance from her mother, a fortune she has enlarged by the judicious exploitation of her academic learning in the arena of mass-media. In spite of a predilection to dissipate a large percentage of her annual income in unprofitable charity donations, her personal expenditure is commendably extravagant. However, in spite of her wealth she hypocritically shares the same altruistic worldview as her friend Mark Hunter, as is demonstrated by the very fact that she often assists him on his assignments, expending her time and energy, often endangering her life, and all for absolutely no financial remuneration. Therefore, as with Mark Hunter, she is not amenable to bribery.

'Although she often assists Mark Hunter, it is unclear if she will be doing so on this particular occasion, as we know that he will be liaising with *this* man, who is due to arrive in the UK very soon.'

Another new picture, a semi-profile shot of a man in his early thirties wearing a dark grey suit. The man's hair is prematurely grey, cropped at the back and sides, and with a waved side-parting on top. A cigarette smoulders in the corner of his mouth. The man's eyebrows are knit and the mouth is set and he is directing a look at someone off-camera that suggests he would very much like to favour that someone with a knuckle sandwich. But we shouldn't prejudge him: the camera probably just caught him at a bad time.

'This is Richard Bedford, field agent for the CIA. Born in the city of Tyler, Texas, his financial worth is moderate but he makes absolutely no effort to invest and increase his wealth, being content to subsist entirely on his government salary. Add to this a doggedly stubborn sense of duty and of loyalty to his country and we have yet another subject woefully inaccessible to bribery and corruption.

'The fact that Richard Bedford is flying to the UK in his quest to locate the instigators of the Zero campaign is significant. The CIA, having access to captured alien technology may have been able to succeed where others have failed and have traced the source of the Zero transmissions, and have traced them here to the British Isles. It seems unlikely they have pinpointed the precise location, or the CIA would be arriving in force; but they might have been able to determine the general location. Regardless, it is a fact that Bedford is coming to the UK to liaise with Mark Hunter and Dodo Dupont, and their assignment is to find the headquarters of Zero, the source of the transmissions.

'Next picture.'

The next picture proves to be a picture of Flat-Sol herself, and a very candid picture at that. In fact, aside from her designer glasses and trademark loafers, she isn't wearing a stitch. Bending forward over a straight-backed wooden chair, she has her left leg raised, the foot planted on the seat of the chair; and she has posed herself thusly with a view to presenting to the camera as much as is humanly possible of her raised buttocks and her foam-flecked vagina into which is inserted the immense erect penis of the male companion, muscular and naked but anonymous, head and upper torso out of shot, standing immediately behind her. That this male companion conjoined with Flat-Sol has just achieved sexual climax is evinced by the copious discharge of semen issuing from the purple-lipped mouth of Flat-Sol's vagina, and streaming down her inside leg. Simultaneously (she can multitask, you see), Flat-Sol is fellating a second male companion (likewise muscular and naked, with head and upper torso out of shot), his penis (immense like his friend's) gripped in her right hand, the glans inside her mouth. And that this second male companion has, in synchronicity with the first male companion, also achieved sexual climax, is demonstrated by the flood of semen streaming from between Flat-Sol's lips and falling from her chin in thick droplets.

This is the picture now filling the conference hall screen.

Stunned silence in the auditorium.

Flat-Sol looks round at the screen, and then, raising a thoughtful forefinger to her underlip and her eyes to the ceiling, says in a voice totally deadpan:

'Oh dear. How did that get there?'

A pause, and then the conference hall erupts into helpless laughter. Everybody just laughs and laughs and laughs (baby included.)

Chapter Two
At the Sign of the Jolly Tar

Waddaya say, Mark? Waddaya say?

That's how it will be. Mark knows it. Waddaya say? It's the only greeting the fellow seems to know. Waddaya say? Waddaya say? Yes, he'll walk in through that door over there looking like someone who's gotten out of the wrong side of bed so many times it's become part of his daily routine, and he'll walk across the room, and when Mark rises from his to chair to greet him, his surly face will light up with that 'sudden generous smile' of his and ignoring Mark's outstretched hand, he'll punch him not-so-playfully in the arm and utter the words: 'Waddaya say, Mark?'

Richard Bedford, Rick for short. Mark Hunter's CIA counterpart, his 'opposite number' in American Intelligence. The Felix Leiter to Mark's James Bond, as Dodo Dupont had remarked this morning in her usual bantering tone. ('I'm not laughing *at* you, sweetheart, I'm laughing *with* you!') Mark has no objection to working with Rick Bedford. Not at all; he likes the fellow, likes him in spite of his 'waddaya say?' and his tendency to fly off the handle at the tiniest provocation. No, he has teamed up with Rick Bedford on a number of occasions now, and the only real complaint he has about the man is that he has his own particular brand of bad weather which he never fails to bring along with him.

You see, there's a very good reason why Rick Bedford's hair is prematurely grey. *Your* hair would be prematurely grey if you'd been hit over the head as many times as Rick Bedford has been hit over the head. Wherever he goes, whatever room he walks into, there will invariably be someone hiding behind the door waiting to clobber him over the head with a blunt instrument the second he walks through it. And the worst thing is that it's contagious, this microclimate that accompanies Rick Bedford; and whenever he has teamed up with him, Mark himself always finds himself getting hit over the head by people with blunt instruments hiding behind doors.

Mark looks at his wristwatch. He should be along any time now.

The name of the pub is the Jolly Tar, and located in a Bermondsey backstreet a stone's throw away from St Katherine's docks, it may well have once been the rendezvous for thirsty sailors its name suggests. The room is low-ceilinged, its oak beams adorned with antique nautical paraphernalia. On the walls hang framed mezzotints depicting the docklands in their Victorian heyday: the roadsteads with their forests of masts, the swarming wharves with bales of goods being loaded and unloaded…

But that was then, and the docks have long since closed for business and the pub's seafaring clientele are a thing of the past. These days, if tonight's turnout is anything to go by, the pub has become a rendezvous for middle-aged solitary drinkers. Male of course, as solitary drinkers invariably are.

And there's something very odd about these solitary drinkers that has not gone unnoticed with Mark Hunter: not one of them has his smartphone in his hands. In this day and age there are many people who, even sitting in convivial company and engaged in conversation, will not be able to leave their smartphones alone for more than five minutes at a time; and yet here are all these men, nursing their pints in lugubrious solitude, and not one of them turning to the solace of their smartphones in order to find relief from their maudlin thoughts.

Curious.

But what about Mark Hunter himself, I hear you cry? He hasn't got *his* smartphone out either. True, but Mark is a spy, and nobody is more conscious than a spy that to be walking around with a smartphone is tantamount to walking around with a tracking device planted on yourself.

In addition to this Mark is no internet junkie, belongs to no social media platforms and likes to keep his digital footprint to the barest minimum.

There is, however, one person in the room absorbed in her smartphone screen like any self-respecting twenty-first century citizen should be: to wit, the barmaid. Slowly chewing the gum in her mouth, her eyes are fixed on the glowing screen of her device, scrolling and typing with nimble fingers. This barmaid, a young black woman, stands out not only on account of the normalcy of her present occupation, but also on account of her hair, which is mauve in colour and styled in a tousled bob, which gives her the look of a *UFO* Moonbase girl fallen on hard times.

And the look might be intentional as well, thinks Mark, observing the oversized t-shirt the girl wears. It is emblazoned with the logo of the television series *I'll Be in My Cabin if You Need Me*, the late-night sketch comedy series which specialises in sending up vintage cult television, is much beloved by fandom (or at least by that section of fandom blessed with a sense of humour.) Characters include the 'Excellent!' Cyberleader; the 'Holy Expletive!' Batman and Robin; the Starsky and Hutch and Bodie and Doyle who keep gatecrashing each other's action scenes; and of course the on-going mini-serial *Carry On Tenko,* with the comedy Major Yamauchi always popping up out of nowhere and scaring the bejesus out of everybody. The show's title comes from a much-used line from *Voyage to the Bottom of the Sea.*

The girl seems oddly out of place in a dive like this, muses Mark, idly wondering whether the mauve hair-do is just a wig or actually her own hair straightened and dyed. He wonders what her backstory is: is she a temping student, or does she work here fulltime?

The door opens and a man, grey-haired, black-suited, carrying a suitcase, enters the pub. The newcomer pauses in the doorway, scans the room and, catching sight of Mark, crosses the room. His movements combine the light-footed grace of a dancer with the squared-shoulders bellicosity of a quarterback. Mark rises to greet him.

'Hey, Mark! Waddaya say?' says Bedford, bringing that 'sudden generous smile' into play and thumping him in the arm.

I knew it, I knew it. 'Nice to see you, Rick,' extending a hand.

'Likewise. How's it going?' pumping Mark's hand.

'Not too bad.'

Bedford drops into a chair, puts his suitcase (a real antique; it doesn't even have wheels) down beside him and loosens his tie.

'Man, this place is off the map! Even the taxi driver had a hard time finding it. What're you drinking? Scotch?' Calling out: 'Say, bartender: two scotches on the rocks!'

'English pub, Rick,' Mark reminds him. 'You have to go up to the bar to get your drinks. Allow me.'

Mark goes to the bar, where the black girl has put her phone aside and is filling two glasses with measures of scotch whisky from the row of upturned bottles bracketed to the wall behind the bar.

She places the glasses before affably smiling Mark.

'Anything else? That'll be eleven-ninety,' proffering the card reader. The girl's voice and expression are toneless, her whole aura one that seems to actively discourage any attempts at small talk on the part of the customers.

'Thank you,' says Mark, making the payment.

He returns to Bedford with the drinks.

'So, did you choose this place, or your stool pigeon?' inquires Bedford, after the usual pleasantries about general health and the comfort of international flights have been gone through.

'My stool pigeon chose the venue.'

'So where is the guy?'

'He'll be along in about ten minutes,' says Mark, checking his watch.

'And he's found out where those Zero transmissions are coming from? For sure?'

'It's more like he's found someone who claims they know where the transmissions are coming from. Perfect is acting as the go-between; he's going to introduce us to his source.'

'So how's it going down? Is your man gunna bring the guy here, or take us to wherever he's holed up?'

'That, I don't know. Perfect will tell us that when he gets here. But before he does, there's been a new development I'd like to bring you up to speed with.'

'Sure. Fill me in.' Bedford reaches into the inside pocket of his jacket, produces a packet of cigarettes, deftly shakes one filter-tip loose from its brethren, and extracts it with his mouth.

'You can't smoke that here, Rick,' Mark tells him.

Bedford frowns. 'What, isn't this the smoking area?'

'There *is* no smoking area. There's a complete smoking ban in pubs in the UK.'

Rick Bedford erupts. This simple piece of news, and very old news at that, is all it takes.

Snarling 'Well, that's just *beautiful!*' he springs to his feet and kicks the table over, nearly taking Mark with it and sending two perfectly innocent glasses of whisky tumbling to the wooden floor, where they shatter on impact.

The silence that follows is palpable. Everyone is looking at them.

Sighing, Mark gets to his feet and sets the table back on its legs.

Well, that didn't take long.

'Rick, I'm sure I've told you about the smoking ban before,' he says patiently.

'Yeah, I guess I forgot,' confesses Rick, his anger having passed as quickly as it came. 'Sorry about that, man. I'll get us some more drinks.'

'No, no, allow me,' says Mark. He returns to the bar where the girl is already filling two more glasses with measures of scotch.

'That'll be fifteen-ninety.'

'Really? A minute ago it was only—oh, we're paying for the broken glasses, are we?'

'Yes,' flatly. 'We are.'

Mark returns to the table, sets down the replacement drinks and resumes his seat.

Bedford swallows a generous mouthful of his drink. 'So, what's this news? This new development? How come I haven't heard about it?'

'I only got the word this morning,' answers Mark. 'It's something very odd; something that might add a whole new dimension to this already puzzling—'

He breaks off. The barmaid, armed with long-handled dustpan and brush, has arrived to sweep up the two broken glasses, which she does in silence, eyes focused on her task, jaws working as she chews her gum.

The glass duly swept up, the girl retreats and Mark resumes, keeping his voice low: 'We've received a report from one of our radio telescopes in Wales. As you know, radio telescopes pick up signals from space, the kind of natural radio waves that are emitted by stars, planets and nebulae, etcetera; but recently this telescope has picked up these signals emanating from the star system Vega, signals that have a distinct pattern to them, and do not seem to be natural emissions.'

'Now hold on a minute! You're not gunna tell me these phoney commercials are coming in from *outer space*? That's crazy, man!'

'Keep your voice down!' hisses Mark, casting an anxious look around the room. 'We're not certain about anything yet, but the pattern of the signals suggests they might be compressed encrypted transmissions. And what's more,

23

these signals were first detected around the same time the Zero commercials first started hijacking the airwaves.'

Mark pauses once more as the barmaid returns, this time with a mop. She cleans up the spilled whisky on the floor and then returns to her place behind the bar.

'Look man, those broadcasts are coming from someplace here on *Earth*,' says Bedford, dropping his voice to an urgent whisper. 'We *know* that much. And they're in *English*, for Christ's sake! You seriously think aliens from the other side of the universe are gunna use the same language we do?'

'I know it all sounds wildly improbable,' says Mark patiently. 'And by the way, Vega isn't exactly on the other side of the universe; in fact, in astronomical terms—'

'I don't give a rat's ass where the Goddammed star is! The place we're looking for is right here on *Earth*, man! Right here in the British Isles! We *know* this!'

'Yes, and as I've already said, we've yet to confirm that there is any connection between the signals from space and the Zero commercials; but it could be that the broadcasts are just being *relayed* from somewhere here on Earth, after being received from space.'

'Well, it sounds crazy to me,' declares Bedford.

'I know it does, but we—Ah! Here's Perfect.'

Perfect's entrance into the Jolly Tar is unobtrusive, going all but unnoticed by the clientele. Now, for many of those afflicted with it, this lack of personal presence can be a crushing handicap, especially when it comes to acquiring a circle of friends; but if making friends isn't really your thing, and earning a precarious living by listening in on other people's conversations *is*, then possessing this dirty raincoat of invisibility is a positive asset—people tend not to lower their voices when they don't even notice that you're there.

And with him being so forgettable the gentle reader has doubtless forgotten that we did briefly make Perfect's acquaintance back in the first in this series of books which aiming to please aficionados of both literary and genre fiction, probably fails to please either, so allow me to reintroduce him to you.

Having been born within earshot of Bow Bells, Perfect is of course short in stature, his growth stunted by one of his Victorian ancestors having been spoon-fed laudanum and gin as incentives to quiet repose. His face is thin, with prominent eyes and a prominent nose, and his demeanour shifty and nervous. In dress he is invariably turned out in a seedy raincoat over a seedy suit of clothes, a flatcap on his head and fingerless gloves on his hands. As well as being a useful source of underworld information, Perfect also serves as Mark's occasional chauffeur, and earns a salary ferrying him around the metropolis in a black cab. (The choice of vehicle by way of being urban camouflage.)

Touching his cap in greeting to Mark, Perfect crosses to the bar and orders himself a pint of bitter. With this in hand he makes his way to Mark's table.

'Evenin', Mr 'Unter,' greets Perfect, placing his glass on a beermat and seating himself on the table's third chair.

'Evening, Perfect. How are you? Let me introduce my American colleague, Rick Bedford.'

'So, you've brung 'im, 'ave yer?' eyeing the American warily.

'You got a problem with that?' inquires Bedford threateningly.

'Rick will be working with me on this assignment,' says Mark quickly. 'I told you about him, remember?'

'Yeah...' unenthusiastically.

'So, what's the drill?' inquires Mark. 'Is your contact coming here, or are you taking us to them?'

'Neither. It's off,' replies Perfect. He takes a noisy swig of his pint.

'Waddya mean "it's off"?' demands Bedford angrily.

'Calm down, Rick. Why is the meeting off, Perfect? And is it off for good, or is it just a postponement?'

'Well, I reckon I can fix something up, but it's off fer tonight, tha's definite.'

'And why is that? Did they give a reason?'

'Well, Mr 'Unter, my contact, y'see, they's very particular, they is. Won't talk to just anybody, y'see?'

'But we're not just anybody,' says Mark. 'We're both accredited representatives of our respective countries' security services. Didn't you explain that to your source?'

'Yeah, but tha's just the problem, ain't it?' says Perfect. 'This person, they don't like people ooz like what you just said, people what's puppets of the establishment.'

'Puppets of the establishment,' echoes Mark, smiling. 'I take it that was your friend's description, not yours?'

'Yeah, tha's just what they said, they did: puppets of the establishment, they said.'

'And of course, working for the establishment, I must inevitably be a Tory voter and Brexiteer? Couldn't you have explained to your friend that we're not actually all like that?'

'I did, Mr 'Unter, I did! I told 'em 'ow you was diff'rent like; 'ow you was a straight-up bloke an' not like all them White'all stuffed shirts! But, like I says, they's very particular, this contact o' mine; suspicious like. An' then you 'ad to go'n bring 'im along, din't yer?' nodding his head at Bedford.

'What's that supposed to mean?' flaring up again.

'Well, I mean: you're with the CIA, aincher? An' tha's even worse, innit?'

'Now listen, buster—!' snarls Bedford, grabbing Perfect by the collar and this time dragging him to his feet.

''Ere! Gerroff!' protests Perfect.

'Let go of him and sit down, Rick,' sighs Mark. 'A lot of people are wary of the CIA. You don't exactly enjoy the best of reputations, do you?'

'Who is this turkey, anyway?' demands Bedford. 'This pigeon of yours: is he part of this Zero outfit?'

'I don't think so…' answers Perfect cautiously. 'They ain't told me much…'

'But they do know the location of the source of the transmissions?' Mark prompts him.

'Yeah, they knows that alright…'

'Oh yeah, and *how* does he know?' demands Bedford. 'You say he's not an inside man, so how's he managed to track down something even my people and Mark's combined haven't been able to track down?'

'I dunno *'ow* they know! They just do!'

'What puzzles me, Perfect, is if your contact is so opposed to the establishment, why is it they're offering to share their knowledge with us in the first place?'

'For the dough! What else?' says Bedford.

'But they haven't asked for any money, have they, Perfect?'

'No, they don't want no money; but now yer mention it, I could do with a couple—'

'Yes, yes, you'll be reimbursed for your services, Perfect. But this friend of yours, what's their motive for passing on what they've found out about Zero?'

'Cuz iss too big for them, tha's why! Iss too big for them to 'andle by theirselves! An' I mean *really* big, Mr 'Unter; *really* big!'

'In what way, Perfect? Do you know?'

'Well yeah, somethink they *did* tell me: it's to do with… *up there*,' pointing solemnly up at the ceiling with a dirty fingernail.

'Up there?'

'Yeah, up *there*,' still pointing. 'An' I don't mean up there as in 'eaven an' the pearly gates an' all that; I mean up there as in *outta space.*'

Mark and Bedford exchange meaningful glances—glances that are promptly misread by Perfect, who insists:

'No, iss the truth, I swear it is, Mr 'Unter! This 'ole Zero thing, iss to do with outta space!'

'We believe you, Perfect,' Mark assures. 'In fact, what you've just told us ties in with something my department discovered only today—and the fact that your contact already knew about it makes it seem all the more likely that the information they have is genuine. When can you set up another meeting? Tell your friend we'll agree to any terms they choose to stipulate, but try and arrange it for as soon as possible.'

'I'll do me best, Mr 'Unter, an I'll give you a bell tomorrer. But about that money—?'

Mark reaches for his wallet.

'All things considered,' he says, counting out the notes into Perfect's eager palm, 'it's probably just as well our informant has cried off this evening…'

'Why'd you say that?' asks Bedford.

Mark nods his head towards the adjacent tables and their solitary tenants.

Bedford casts an eye over them. 'You think one of these bozos is keeping tabs on us?'

'I think they *all* are.'

Chapter Three
What Do You Fantasise About When You're Masturbating? (If it's Not a Personal Question)

It can be seen at a glance that the recumbent Japanese woman in the photograph is a tennis player. Although she has discarded most of her clothing, the trainers and white sports socks on her feet, the sweatbands on her wrists and the sun visor on her head are suggestive of her vocation, as is the tennis racket she holds between her open legs, and with which she is engaged in pleasuring herself. The woman's physique is wiry and athletic, the muscles of her upper arms and of her abdomen visibly taut. That she has successfully brought herself to a climax by her efforts with the tennis racket is evinced by the expression on the woman's face: the closed eyes, the knotted junction of the eyebrows, the flared nostrils and the open mouth with its proud overbite, expressive of a pleasure so intense and overwhelming as to verge on pain.

'This is Hiromi Kimura, Japanese tennis pro, national champion and Olympic gold medallist. Hiromi is an old schoolfriend of mine.'

The speaker is Mayumi Takahashi, the location the Elysium Art Gallery, Bond Street, London. Tonight is the evening preview of Mayumi's latest photographic exhibition, which officially opens tomorrow morning. Her subject this time is the orgasm (female of course) achieved through self-manipulation; each of her models being captured at the very moment of attaining those fleeting few seconds of physical ecstasy that the human race is forever making such a huge fuss about.

Mayumi dressed in one of her business suits *sans-culottes*, with matching fedora (Mayumi is rarely seen in public without a hat), black tights and buckle shoes, is a Japanese woman of average Japanese height, a deep tan complexion. She wears glasses with large round lenses and her straight black hair is long and abundant. In age, she looks to be about twenty but is actually thirty. As she conducts the group of guests around the exhibition, her expression is characteristically impassive, as is her voice, which is sharp and clipped yet oh-so-sweet.

Impassive and taciturn is the exterior Mayumi may present to the world, and people who don't know any better might assume that this is how she always is, but in fact Mayumi possesses a smile that can light up a room, recessed laterals and fang-like canines notwithstanding, but it is a smile she generally reserves for her lover, Dodo Dupont, as likewise she will shed her taciturnity when in Dodo's company.

The rooms housing the exhibition are art-deco in design, the enlarged prints of the artist's photography displayed on large bulky boards and mounted unframed both on the walls and on a number of freestanding display panels. Numerous other guests mill around the rooms viewing the pictures for themselves or stand in groups, talking and sipping glasses of the complimentary champagne.

Mayumi and her tour group have arrived at the next picture. The subject here, another Japanese woman (to cut a long story short, they all are), lies sprawled on a polished metal floor, her elevated posterior presented to the viewer, as she pleasures herself with an electric clitoris stimulator, while to further intensify the experience, she has a second battery-operated device inserted into her anus. A set of pale blue overalls with patches and insignia are bunched up around her knees. Having attained the dizzy peak of self-inflicted pleasure, the woman, with disarranged tresses falling across her face, bites the joint of the index finger of her disengaged hand to stifle her cries.

'This is Lieutenant Midori Yamura, astronaut for JAXA, Japanese Space Agency. Midori is an old schoolfriend of mine and she is currently in training for the International Jupiter Space Mission. The vibrator up Midori's butthole is an astronaut joke: means Uranus Probe.'

A ripple of appreciative laughter from Mayumi's listeners; the refined, erudite laughter you would you would expect to hear from members of the intelligentsia in response to a particularly humorous erudite remark at an after-dinner speech.

Mayumi, allowing herself a brief smile, leads the way to the next picture. The model here is a professional-looking woman, bespectacled, hair elegantly-styled, face carefully made-up. She sits spread-legged on the floor, back against the office desk behind her, wearing a white blouse and the jacket of a stylish lilac suit (whether a skirt or trouser suit is anybody's guess.) Her breasts, large for those of a Japanese woman, have been freed from the unbuttoned blouse, allowing the woman to manipulate her erect nipples, in order to enhance the climax she has just attained and which is demonstrated both by the snarling curl of her painted lips and by the jet of clear liquid arcing up from her vagina.

'This is Atsuko Sakaguchi, news anchor for the NHK television network. She is an old schoolfriend of mine and as you can see, she ejaculates when achieving orgasm.'

And if you are starting to think that it seems like just about every notable Japanese woman around the age of thirty is an old schoolfriend of Mayumi Takahashi's, you will not be the first person to have thought this. This new exhibition of Mayumi's, entitled *Afternoon Dreams* from Yoko Ono once having used the expression as a polite euphemism for female masturbation fantasies, has already attracted a degree of criticism before it has even opened— but Mayumi is impervious to criticism of her art, tending to look upon it as you would upon the buffoonery of some not-very-amusing circus clowns. And when righteous individuals hurl epithets like 'exploitation' and 'objectification,' she does not deny them; merely stipulating that hers is the nice kind.

Her supporters have argued that in the case of this new exhibition that Mayumi has, capturing her models at the very moment of climax, challenged the conventions of traditional female beauty in that the expressions contorting the faces of these women would be considered unflattering by many. Not that Mayumi herself would agree with this appraisal; possessing in full as she does the refined and all-embracing Japanese aesthetic sense, Mayumi sees the beautiful in everything, and to her the savage, pleasure-distorted features of her models are visions of beauty.

And that's not the half of it.

What we are witnessing here in this gallery is only Mayumi's contribution to a joint project, a collaboration between herself and her lover Professor Dodo Dupont! And this collaboration takes the form of a book. Sharing its title with the exhibition, *Afternoon Dreams* is an oversized (and suitably overpriced) glossy hardback, featuring Mayumi's photography, interspersed with quotes from the featured models in which they describe their own 'afternoon dreams.' Dodo's contribution is a scholarly essay (which shares its title with this chapter) exploring the realm of women's sexual fantasies.

In short, *Afternoon Dreams* is a triumphant marriage of art and psychology! (And it goes on sale tomorrow.)

Trina Truelove, Mayumi Takahashi's loyal apprentice, is dolled up in her posh frock, her one and only posh frock, which she keeps especially for formal occasions like this evening. That she is not generally a posh frock wearing kind of person is evinced both by the number of tattoos visible on the exposed portions of her body, and by her bright pink hair, which is gathered in girlish bunches. Trina, never one to turn her nose up at free booze, has already been helping herself liberally to the complimentary champagne, and she mills around the gallery, glass in hand, her head buzzing agreeably.

From a shrewd evaluation of the male talent gathered in the room, she has decided that there's nothing worth trying to get picked up by tonight. Trina is always in search of her latest boyfriend, someone with whom to remove the sour taste of her previous relationship disaster. One of those disasters (and their numbers are large) is here tonight in the form of that smarmy, pretentious modern artist (con artist more like!) Roy Hucklebuck. A particular grievance Trina has with Hucklebuck is the fact that while they were going out, he had told Trina that he was pals with the elusive artist Banksy, and that Banksy's real name was actually David

Banksy and he used to play a Cyberman in *Doctor Who*. But it turned out Hucklebuck had just been winding her up—a fact she had only discovered after she'd already passed on her hot titbit of news to other people! (There *is* an actor called David Banks, and he *did* play a Cyberman in *Doctor Who*, but he has bugger all to do with the artist Banksy.) Well, after that little stunt, soon she'd sent the bastard packing—and had taken great pleasure in telling him just what she thought of his so-called 'art' in the process!

And just think, tonight he's had the nerve to greet her as though he never even pulled that humiliating stunt on her! Trina had given him the full benefit of her cold shoulder in order to make it quite clear that all was *not* forgiven. (And what was Mayumi thinking of even inviting that twat? Just whose side is she on here?)

The alcohol has done its usual trick of boosting her confidence in herself, her creative talent and her prospects; and as she drifts around the gallery admiring the work of her mentor, Trina dreams of the day she will be hosting her own photo exhibition and Dodo Dupont and Mayumi Takahashi, the most ardent admirers of her work, will have their names at the top of the guestlist.

And where is Dodo—ah, here she comes!
One thing that was not manifest about Dodo Dupont from the image we saw of her at the corporate briefing is her stature: she is six foot tall and possessed of one of those robust hourglass figures of the type to which descriptions like 'Junoesque' and 'Amazonian' are frequently applied (and I think I may have been guilty of using both of those myself on different occasions.) Tonight she is dressed in an unaccustomed evening dress, black in colour and cut just below the knee, and even less-accustomed high-heeled sandals. Dodo generally prefers the kind of footwear Flat-Sol Park would approve of, although you'd think she wore heels all the time from the way she walks across the room,

moving with her usual fluid grace, exchanging smiles and greetings with the guests.

Just look at her! thinks Trina. Elegance, style and total sex on legs! She's like one of those larger-than-life big-arsed, big-titted women in the erotic Japanese comics Mayumi has shown her. (The text being in Japanese, Trina hadn't been able to actually read these stimulating publications, but the pictures had told her all she'd really needed to know.) And to think that Dodo's actually a dress-size sixteen! But then, when you're as tall as Dodo is, it's all sort of stretched out a lot more, isn't it?

Catching sight of Trina, Dodo favours her with a wink and a smile. Trina grins back at her.

After watching Dodo's tightly-sheathed rear out of sight, Trina proceeds with her stroll, stopping before one of her favourite pictures in the collection, which has been hung on one of the freestanding boards. In this image, the camera looks down upon the model, a woman lying upon tatami mats; spread out around her are the silky folds of an open kimono whose polychromatic design really ought to look garish but somehow doesn't. The woman's hair is arranged in the traditional Japanese style, held in place with those knitting-needle hairpins, and adorned with decorative pins and combs and artificial flowers. Her face is elaborately painted over a foundation so white that the bared teeth of her open mouth look yellow by comparison. In the tumult of her manually-induced orgasm, the woman's left leg is raised in the air, so that the sole of her foot fills much of the frame on the righthand side of the picture. The toes, clenched in ecstasy, compress the surface skin of the sole, from the ball to the heel pad, into a pattern of soft, fleshy ripples. By using deep focus, the foot in the foreground is in as sharp focus as its recumbent owner.

Trina considers this picture to be one of the masterpieces of the exhibition and she never tires of admiring it. There's just something about that clenched-toed foot, raw and visceral as a gaping vagina...

'I'm surprised there aren't any pictures of Professor Dupont amongst this lot,' says a sudden voice at Trina's side. 'I thought she was the only person Mayumi Takahashi deigned to photograph these days.'

Trina looks round. The speaker, a tall woman curiously dressed in a buttoned-up black raincoat, is a stranger to her. She has a mass of frizzy chestnut hair that can't seem to decide whether it's an afro or a mop and is probably wig. Her face, already diminished by the abundance of surrounding hair, is further obscured by a pair of large sunglasses. Only the lower part of her face is visible, the skin a mid-brown in colour, the features giving Trina no clue as to the woman's ethnicity; neither does the voice, which tells her only that she is English.

'No, she doesn't just photograph Dodo,' says Trina. 'That was mostly back when they first met. Yumi does most of her work in Japan, so her models are mostly Japanese.'

'Really? I thought she'd emigrated to the UK.'

'Well, she's got dual-citizenship, so she sort of comes and goes, really.'

'You seem to know a lot about her. Are you a friend?'

'I'm her assistant, actually,' announces Trina proudly.

'Is that so? How impressive. What's your name?'

'I'm Trina Truelove; and you're...?'

'Delighted!' says the woman, shaking Trina's hand. (She's wearing black driving gloves.) 'So, tell me, were you with her when she photographed this geisha girl?'

'Yeah, I was there, but she's not actually a geisha girl: she's a dancer. She does this traditional Japanese dancing, I forget what it's called. Her name's Yayoi and she's an old schoolfriend of Yumi's. We watched her doing her dance while we were over there and it was like really nice to watch; all slow and delicate... sort of soothing, y'know...?'

'Really? How fascinating. So I suppose, being Mayumi Takahashi's assistant and going off to Japan with her all the time, you don't get to see much of her partner, Professor Dupont?'

'Dodo? No, I see Dodo all the time.'

'Do you? What do you think of her? Do you like her?'

'Like her? Course I like her! Everyone likes Dodo! What's not to like about her?'

'Well... she's a bit full of herself, isn't she? That's what I've heard.'

'Who told you that? No, she's not full of herself at all. She's very modest.'

'Yes, but a very affected modesty, isn't it? That kind of false modesty that's really just vanity fishing for compliments...'

'No, she's not like that, either. Dodo, she's... well, she's perfect, really!'

The woman's face twitches. 'Perfect? Oh, come now: *nobody's* perfect, are they?'

'Well, if they're not, then Dodo's about as near to perfect as it gets,' avows Trina.

Another twitch, this time accompanied by a nervous laugh. 'Now, *really*—'

'No, honest! She's kind, she's understanding, she's always got time for you, she never gets snooty, never does anything mean or petty, she's smart, she's strong, she's funny, she's she's got bags of charisma, she's beautiful, she's sexy; she's like the alpha woman plus a hundred zillion; the perfect role-model: an inspiration to us all! Here! You should meet her! She's only over there with Yumi. Come on: I can introduce you! We can—'

Trina breaks off. She is issuing her invitation to thin air: the woman in the raincoat has vanished.

When I said before that Mayumi only really opens up when she is with her lover Dodo Dupont, I was forgetting the one other person in whose company she will also shed her Oriental reserve: and that person is called Alcohol-san, or in English, Mr Alcohol. And it always seems to be when she is with her protégé Trina Truelove (who really is a terrible influence on her!) that she becomes particularly prone to spending just a bit too much time in the company of Mr Alcohol.

And so it comes to pass that by the end of the evening Mayumi and Trina are completely hammered. The invited guests have departed, having been duly lectured, laughed at, and mooned at by both the artist and her assistant, and only the intervention of Dodo Dupont has prevented the photographer from demolishing her own exhibition.

The three of them now stand on the Bond Street pavement, waiting for their ride home. Actually it is Dodo who is doing most of the standing, being the one in the best condition to perform that useful office, while Trina hangs onto her left arm, and Mayumi hangs onto her right. A dispute is in progress. Trina having been invited by Dodo to crash in one of the spare rooms at her place tonight, has vetoed this plan, declaring that she does not want to sleep in the spare room because she wants to sleep in Dodo and Mayumi's room with Dodo and Mayumi. Dodo responds to this by telling Trina that she cannot sleep in hers and Mayumi's room, she can sleep in the spare room; to which Trina replies by reaffirming her original statement, to wit that she does *not* want to sleep in the spare room and would much prefer to sleep in Dodo and Mayumi's room with Dodo and Mayumi. Dodo informs Trina that this preference of hers is unfortunate, because she bloody well *isn't* going to be sleeping with them in their room.

It is at this point Mayumi intervenes in the dispute. 'I have a suggestion,' she announces importantly. 'Listen. *Listen.*'

'I'm hanging on your every word, sweetheart,' Dodo assures her.

'Good. My suggestion is this: Trina *can* sleep in our bedroom—listen. *Listen!*'

'Still hanging on your every word.'

'Good. Trina, *Trina* can sleep in our bedroom, and we, you and I, *we* shall sleep in the spare bedroom!'

Dodo, more in love with Mayumi than ever, is just about to further open her widely-smiling mouth to inquire as to what precisely would be bloody point to this swapping of rooms, when a sudden sound directs her attention skywards, and looking up, she sees against the orange-smudged night sky the silhouette of some unidentifiable bulky object teetering on the brink of the rooftop directly above them. Even as she watches, the object tips over the edge of the roof and plunges downwards.

'Move!' yells Dodo.

The injunction is a formality, as it is she who does the moving for all three of them, grabbing her two drunken charges, first dragging and then, when this doesn't answer, throwing both them and herself out of harm's way.

They land in a confused heap on the paving stones; and behind them, where they were just standing, a heavy object slams into the pavement, impacting with a cacophonous crash in which the discordant death of eighty-eight musical notes reverberates amidst the sound of splintering woodwork.

A piano. Someone has just tried to drop a piano on them.

Chapter Four
In Less-than-Perfect Condition

It is on the third floor of a modest apartment building in Pimlico that Mark hangs his metaphorical hat, and if we look in on him this morning, we find we find him sitting in his shirtsleeves at the dining table in his front room, breakfasting on unsweetened coffee and buttered toast while watching the television news. Mark favours television or radio broadcasts for his daily digest of world events, the newspapers a) being too partisan and b) taking too long to read. (Although of course it is only after he arrives at work that Mark gets to hear the *real* news.)

The news. That which is new is news. News, the plural of new. Back in the nineteenth century they used the plural and would say 'these are the news,' today we are even less grammatical and say '*this* is the news.' Mayumi Takahashi had once told Mark that 'NEWS' was in fact an acronym and that it stood for 'Notable Events, Weather and Sport.' Mayumi had imparted this information with such a perfectly straight face, and in such a deadly-serious tone of voice, that for a moment Mark had thought that she actually believed this to be true; nay, for one insane moment, he had started to wonder if it *was* actually true—but then he had remembered that Mayumi always spoke in that straight-faced, deadly serious tone, even when she was pulling your leg. (Dodo had later confessed that even *she* couldn't always tell when Mayumi was being serious and when she wasn't.)

Mark's is a neatly furnished and neatly maintained apartment. The first thing that would strike the visitor upon entering is the abundance of bookcases; they line all four walls of the room, wherever there is space for one. Bibliophile, scholar and voracious reader, Mark's collection embraces the authors of antiquity, philosophers and historians of all ages; but by far the most shelf-space is taken up by his chief interest and 'guilty pleasure,' nineteenth-century fiction.

You might think that someone as thorough and meticulous as Mark would keep his book collection alphabetised: but you would be wrong. To apply such an unnecessary system to one's personal belongings would be the sign of an intractable mind, a mind too rigid in its thinking, hedged in by order and convention, a mind incapable of thinking outside the box, and this Mark Hunter is not. Instead, it is with a view to aesthetics that the books are arranged on his shelves: antiquarian hardbacks on some shelves, modern paperbacks on others, books of the same size arranged together.

Vladimir Putin on the news. Putin is one of Mark's oldest enemies and they have crossed swords many a time—quite literally on one never-to-be-forgotten occasion in the hidden chambers of the Winter Palace.

Well, whoever's behind Zero, it isn't him, muses Mark. It's completely lacking in his trademark complete lack of subtlety.

But then, from what they now know, the perpetrators behind Zero might not be anyone from Earth at all.

An advertising campaign from outer space? Why is it he always ends up with the science fiction assignments?

Mark starts. The face of his friend Mayumi Takahashi has just appeared on the television screen. She has become a Notable Event!

'…And in other news, the controversial photographer Mayumi Takahashi had a close brush with death last night when a grand piano was dropped from the roof of the Elysium Art Gallery in Bond Street in an apparently deliberate attempt on her life. According to reports, Miss Takahashi was standing on the pavement outside the gallery, which is housing her latest exhibition, when the attempt took place. With her at the time was her partner, the famous Professor Dodo Dupont, and one other person. All three of them were able to avoid the falling piano and are understood to have sustained no serious injuries. Police are now trying to determine how the assailants were able to gain access to the roof of the building with a grand piano…'

Well, I'll be…! thinks Mark. I hope they *are* alright. I'll have to give Dodo a bell later. I wonder if that 'other person' they mentioned was Trina Truelove…?

But an actual attempt on Mayumi's life? And just because someone doesn't like her art! Sadly, not at all improbable in this day and age, but it's never happened to Mayumi before. Up until now her opponents have only attacked her verbally or in print, and that sort of thing is water off a duck's back to Mayumi. This sudden escalation, if that's what it is, is disturbing to say the least...

The next story pertaining to a Love Island contestant, Mark picks up the remote and switches off the TV. He takes his cup and plate through to the kitchen and washes up. Returning to the living room, he looks out through the window. Mark's flat is situated at the front of the building, and his windows look out on the residents' carpark and the busy thoroughfare beyond.

Yes, he's still there: the man watching the building from across the street. Mark spotted the man the moment he'd opened the curtains this morning—spotted him and identified him as one of the solitary drinkers from the Jolly Tar.

Why is he standing there out in the open in such an obvious manner? The logical inference would be that Mark's observer wants him to know that he is under observation. On the other hand, it could just be that the man is very bad at his job. Mark has long since given up being surprised at how many people there are in the world who are totally unsuited to their chosen vocations.

The phone rings. He answers it quickly, thinking it might be Perfect, announcing he has set up another meeting with that mysterious contact of his.

But it isn't Perfect on the line, it's Special Branch, informing him that Perfect has been beaten half to death and is now in hospital.

The day is warm but overcast. Mark Hunter and Rick Bedford make their way across the hospital carpark towards the entrance to the main building.

'They must have either worked him over to *make* him talk, or to *stop* him from talking.'

'That figures. And if they wanted him to talk, your man must have held out a long time to get beaten up so bad. I'm kind of surprised: I wouldn't have thought the little guy had it in him.'

'He *doesn't* have it in him. If it was information they were after, Perfect would have told them all he knew with very little physical encouragement. So unless they beat him up anyway *after* he'd spilled the beans, it might be that he just didn't know whatever it was they wanted him to get from him.'

'You think it was one of those bozos from the bar who worked him over? But how did they get to him? We shook them off when they tried to tail us.'

'Yes, but if any of them knew who Perfect was then they probably also knew where he lives, and the alley where the attack took place is not far from there. The question is, *who* got to him: was it the people behind Zero or was it some interested third party? Those people watching us at the pub weren't all working together. If it was Zero who attacked Perfect, then most likely they did it to stop him from talking.'

'Yeah, but the guy didn't know anything! He pretty much told us that himself.'

'They may have thought he knew more than he did. Or they may have put him out of circulation just to prevent him from arranging that meeting between ourselves and his contact.'

They enter the hospital. At the reception desk they are told to take the lift to the third floor. Having the lift car to themselves they continue their conversation.

'This guy of yours,' says Bedford; 'Why's he called "Perfect," anyhow?'

'It's his nickname.'

'Yeah, but *why's* it his nickname? What's so damn perfect about the guy?'

'You know, I've often wondered about that one myself,' confesses Mark.

The lift stops, the doors slide open, admitting the usual antiseptic smell of a hospital ward. Before the doors stands a young woman with a polished pageboy haircut dressed in a smart trouser suit. She smiles at Mark, extending a hand.

'Hello, Mark,' she greets him. 'I thought you might be interested in this one. This way.'

'I'm glad you contacted me. Sheila, this is my colleague Rick Bedford from the Central Intelligence Agency. Rick, this DS Sheila Staffel of Special Branch. We know each other on account of Perfect, whose services Sheila has also had occasion to use.'

Greetings are exchanged.

'It was the local CID who gave me the word. A friend of mine was there and she knew that Perfect was one of my snouts.'

'So, how is Perfect?' asks Mark.

'He'll live, and the doctors say he *will* make a full recovery, but he won't be going anywhere anytime soon. He was worked over by professionals, at least that's what it looks like, and they broke just about every major bone in his body.' To Mark: 'You say he was involved in something for you at the moment?'

'That's right,' confirms Mark. 'Rick and I were with him only last night, at the Jolly Tar in Bermondsey. We're investigating the Zero business and, well I can't give you the details, but Perfect was in touch with someone who claims to know something that may help us crack the case. He was going to arrange a meeting... How is he at the moment? I mean is he conscious? I really need to talk to him if I can...'

'Yes, he's conscious, but I doubt you'll get much out of him. He's heavily sedated, so he's groggy, and on top of that, he has injuries to his face that make it hard for him to talk... Here we are.'

Sheila leads the way into the room, a private room with a single bed, and on that bed lies Perfect, although you wouldn't recognise him at first glance. Wrapped in bandages from head to toe, his arms and legs are encased in plaster, and elevated by the bed's hoist apparatus, and the general effect is of a lumbering reanimated mummy suddenly rendered *in*animate mid-lumber and fallen over on its back. A young black nurse wearing a surgical mask kneels beside the patient. She rises quickly to her feet and turns to the newcomers.

'How is he, nurse?' asks Sheila.

'Still the same,' is the muffled answer.

The nurse steps aside and Mark takes her place at the bedside. Perfect's head is swathed in bandages, just one eye visible through an opening in the wrappings, the other being covered by a patch. Another opening has been left for his bruised and swollen mouth. Two tubes disappear into the bandages at the base of his nose.

Mark sighs. Perfect has been beaten up before—in his line of work it would be a miracle if he hadn't been—but never this badly.

'Hello, Perfect. It's Mark.' The one eye swivels to focus on Mark. 'I'm sorry this had to happen to you, Perfect. But can you tell me who did this to you? Was it anyone you know? Was it one of the people who were in the pub last night?'

A sound, a single syllable, rasping and indistinct issues, from Perfect's swollen lips.

'What was that?' Mark leans closer, turning his ear to the injured man's mouth. 'Say it again, Perfect.'

The sound is repeated.

'Hurts? Is that what you said? I'm sure it does hurt, Perfect, but who did it? Can you tell me who it was?'

The sound comes again.

'Hearse…? Oh, *nurse!* You want the nurse, do you?' Mark looks up from the bed. 'Nurse—Where is she?'

'She just stepped out,' reports Bedford.

Mark springs to his feet, galvanised by sudden alarm. 'Was that nurse just now the same nurse who's been here all the time?' he asks Sheila.

'The same one? I'm not sure… Since I've been here there have been several nurses coming in and out…'

Mark erupts into the corridor, eyes scanning in both directions. There is no sign of the black nurse.

Bedford comes up behind him. 'What's up, Mark? You think that nurse was a phoney?'

'Yes. The way she stood up when we came in: it was like she'd been caught doing something she shouldn't have been doing. We need to find her. Rick, you go that way, I'll go this. Sheila: hit the emergency button. She may have injected Perfect with something. Stay with him till the doctor gets here.'

Mark sets off, taking the corridor to the right. Dodging patients on the gurneys, on crutches, in wheelchairs, he barrels along. Angry voices yell at him to stop running.

That nurse! Could she have been the purple-haired barmaid from the night before—the one person in that pub he *hadn't* suspected of being a spy?

He bursts through a pair of doors. The end of the corridor: stairs up and down, two lifts, neither in operation—and adjacent to the lifts, a door marked 'emergency.' Mark grabs the bar, pulls the door open. A narrow stairwell and yes, the sound of running footsteps echoing up from below. He looks over the banister and catches a glimpse of a white dress and brown limbs.

Mark takes the stairs two at a time. As a spy, Mark has had a lot of experience of running up and down emergency staircases in his time and he's become rather good at it. He closes the gap between himself and his quarry who, not stopping at the ground floor, takes the final flight to the basement level. Mark, now close behind her, bursts through the doors and finds himself in the inevitable dimly lit underground carpark.

There is no sign of the girl. Mark pauses, listens. No sound of running, but she can't have outdistanced him so soon. She's hiding somewhere.

Mark unholsters his automatic, steps cautiously forward, scanning the likely hiding places. The parked cars offer cover and so do the concrete pillars, the nearest of which is just in front of him. Handy things to hide behind, concrete pillars. Gun at the ready, Mark approaches it slowly.

Behind him, the sound of a lift coming to life. He spins around. One of the lifts has started to ascend. The girl? Did she come down all those stairs and then duck straight back into the lift to give him the slip?

But then the blunt instrument comes into violent contact with the back of Mark's head and tells him that no, the girl did not get into the lift: she was hiding behind that bloody pillar.

He should have seen this coming; he should have realised that teamed up with Rick Bedford, he was under the influence of that headache-inducing microclimate he carries around with him, and that it was only a matter of time before he received a dose of the bad weather.

Such is Mark's last thought before he stops thinking at all.

Chapter Five
The Great Heathrow Baggage Mix-up - Part One

Brunner, following Jensen's lead, has also applied for the post of Flat-Sol Park's new assistant, and to cut a long story short they have *both* been accepted. Provisionally.

This was how they received the tidings: they had been summoned to Flat-Sol's *sanctum sanctorum*, her office on the top floor of the Parkhurst Building, accessible only by a private lift, the other lifts going no higher than the floor below. To be summoned to Flat-Sol's office is a rare occurrence, and if it happens to you then it is either your lucky day or else you are in very deep shit. (It has been rumoured that some hapless offenders, employees whose professional incompetence has led to significant financial losses for the corporation, have stepped into that executive lift never to be seen again.)

Assuming that all of the applicants must have been summoned for the announcement of the result, Jensen and Brunner had been surprised to find it was themselves and themselves alone who had found themselves standing before Flat-Sol Park in her corporate eyrie.

'I have studied your records at great length and I find you both to be admirably suited for the position for which you have applied. You are both young, tall, handsome and well-groomed male specimens; you both work out on a regular basis and maintain your bodies excellent physical condition; you both possess penises of above-average dimensions and have great sexual stamina and high sperm-counts—and you both understand the importance of accumulating and possessing wealth and of its attendant obligation to conform to a lifestyle and personal expenditure commensurate with your financial worth.'

Well, being endowed with all these attributes so essential to the function of a personal assistant to the chief executive officer of a financial corporation, naturally Flat-Sol had accepted them both—albeit on probation. She would make her final decision in due course.

The sexual tension in the air you could have cut with a knife as Flat-Sol had made the above announcement, standing before the two applicants, cooly surveying them with those narrow predatory eyes of hers. Both men had felt it, Jensen visibly. But then it was well-known around the office that Flat-Sol Park liked sex almost as much as she liked accumulating money—a quick look at her photo album would tell you that much.

You would have thought that with the two men being effectively in competition with one another for the coveted position, that Flat-Sol would have assigned Brunner and Jensen separate tasks the better to judge between them; but no, for reasons of her own she has been keeping the two men together.

And their latest joint task is as undemanding as all their other assignments have been: they have been sent to Heathrow Airport to pick up Flat-Sol Park's kid sister Yu-Mi Park, who is arriving today at Terminal 2, on ANA Flight 257 from Narita, Japan. With a sinecure at the Parkhurst Corporation waiting for her, Yu-Mi Park's move to the UK is to be a permanent one. (Just what her sister has been doing in Japan, is something Flat-Sol has not deigned to explain.)

Brunner and Jensen stand outside the Burger King in the terminal's busy food court, the place designated for making contact with Yu-Mi Park. The flight from Narita has arrived on time, so their charge should be with them any time now.

Watching this unending flow of bustling humanity Jensen and Brunner now see before them, can provide much food for thought, can be conducive of much philosophical reflection. Men and women of all ages, all races, creeds and colours, this endless influx, coalescing and then dispersing, the cycle repeated over and over, an endless kaleidoscope; all these lives, these existences brushing against each other, perhaps to be forgotten as soon as glimpsed, perhaps to be remembered forever; the chance meetings, the fateful encounters, the lost opportunities, the might-have-beens; those who travel for business, those who travel for pleasure, those who travel in hope, those who travel in despair; the selfish desires, the noble aspirations, the searchers and the lost; the consciousness of that trite but oh-so-true saying that no-one is more lonely than in a crowd; the human casualties of a technology spiralling out of control, the annihilation of time and space, the poisoned, overburdened ether, endlessly crisscrossed with lines of communication, the electric crackle of information overload…

Yes, no more than here, at this conflux of humanity, the international airport terminal, can these thoughts be brought home to the minds that have time to ponder them.

Brunner and Jensen however, are not thinking about any of these things: they're just eyeing up the passing talent.

'Now *she's* not bad. I'd fuck her. How old d'you reckon she is?'

'Oh… twenty-three, twenty-four…'

'Oh, what about her? Nice perky arse she's got.'

'Black girls usually do have perky arses; it's because of the shape of their pelvises.'

'Is it?'

'Yeah. Different races have different shaped pelvic pones. That's why Asian girls have the saggiest arses and black girls have the perkiest arses.'

'What about white girls?'

'About halfway between.'

'I still say this is just a put-on,' says Brunner, having paused to digest this information. 'I reckon she's just gunna hire both of us.'

'So you keep still-saying,' replies Jensen. 'So you've been still-saying since last fucking week. And *I* still say I'm not so sure.'

'Why not? I mean, it makes sense, doesn't it? A woman like her: she can do a lot more with two personal assistants than she can with one!' chuckling.

'Yeah, and if she hires two personal assistants then she'll have to *pay* two personal assistants, won't she? Double the salary, basically.'

'Well, so what? She's not a skinflint, is she?'

'No, she's not a skinflint, but she doesn't throw money down the drain, either. She only pays out if she knows she's getting value for money; and paying two people to do one person's job: that's not value for money, is it?'

'Yes, but like I just said: she can do a lot more with two—'

'She doesn't need to pay two executive salaries just for *that*. Sexual partners she can get whenever she wants, and without paying a penny for 'em. So don't get your hopes up. She's only going to keep one of us, I'm pretty sure of that.'

'Okay, genius: how is she going to decide which one of us is best when she keeps sending us out on piddling jobs like this? *Anyone* could have picked her fucking sister up!'

'I know. I don't get it, either...' admits Jensen. 'She'll have a reason, though. She never does anything without a reason. Maybe she's just getting a sadistic kick out of keeping us both guessing...'

'Sadistic? You mean because she's Asian? I thought it was just the Japs who were meant to be sadists...?'

'No, they all are in that part of the world,' says Jensen, that careful sifter of racial stereotypes. 'Yeah, she'd probably made her mind up before she even called us up to her office; and she's just keeping us hanging on for the pleasure of it, like a cat—Head's up: Asian totty at two o'clock! Is that her?'

A young Asian woman, towing a suitcase is coming along the concourse in their direction.

'I dunno...' says Brunner. 'Looks like she's heading this way... Short hair... No, wait! It's *not* short hair; it's long hair in a ponytail!'

'Well, maybe she had long hair in a ponytail in the picture we saw, and we just assumed it was short hair because her sister's got short hair. Look! She's coming right towards us: it's got to be her!'

Jensen smiles and waves. The Asian girl stops in her tracks. She points first at herself and then at the two men, an inquiring look on her face. Jensen and Brunner nod their heads in eager confirmation. The girl breaks out in a smile and comes up to them.

'*Ahn-young-ha-say-yo!*' greets Jensen. (His single sentence of Korean, prepared in advance.) 'Welcome to London!'

Both men bow their heads. Smiling, the girl bows in return. Her expression is lively, a wide grin and sparkling eyes evincing an affable, cheerful nature. Not at all like her cool, clinical sister, thinks Brunner. In fact, she doesn't look much like her sister at all.

'Are you sure this is her?'

Jensen groans. 'Oh, give it a rest. Who the hell else would it be?' To the girl: 'Yu-Mi? Yu-Mi?'

The girl nods eagerly, repeating the name.

Jensen, turning to Brunner: 'There, you see! Yu-Mi. And if you're still not satisfied, why don't you check the label on her luggage?'

Brunner does so. 'Yeah, it's her,' he reports. 'Yu-Mi Park.'

'Well, I'm glad we've cleared that one up,' says Jensen. To the girl: 'My name is Jensen. *Jensen,*' indicating himself; 'and this is Brunner,' indicating Brunner. '*Brunner.*'

'Jen-sen,' pronounces the girl, pointing at Jensen. 'Brunner,' pointing at Brunner. She pauses, searching her mind for her next words. 'You… you are meeting me?' pointing at herself.

'That's right,' confirms Jensen. 'We are here to drive you,' making car-steering motions, '*drive you* into London.'

The girl seems puzzled by this. Another pause to leaf through her internal English lexicon. 'Where… where is woman?'

'Woman? Oh, you mean your sister? Your sister sent us, *us*, to pick you up. We *work* for your sister. We are here to *drive you* to meet her, yes? *Drive you.*' More mime acting.

The girl renews her smile, nodding her understanding.

'We *go* now,' proceeds Jensen, pointing in the general direction of the main entrance. 'We go to where car is parked, yes?'

'Yes!' concurs the girl, and then, taking hold of her suitcase, walks resolutely past the two men and into the *Burger King*. 'Eat first!'

They must have really starved Yu-Mi Park on that flight from Narita, because she ordered just about everything on the menu and consumed it with gusto. And apparently even this is not enough to appease her appetite, because she is all ready to sample the menus of every other eatery in the food court, and it is only by the two men urgently pointing at the dials of their designer watches, that they are able to convince her that time constraints rendered this plan unfeasible.

Having conciliated their charge with a selection of *Subway* sandwiches to go, the trio make their way across the airport carpark.

In spite of the language barrier, Jensen has already managed to strike up a rapport with the girl, much to Brunner's private annoyance. Look at him, he thinks. Already worked his charm on her, so that all those sunny smiles are aimed squarely at *him*. And he doesn't even speak the same language as her…! But then don't need words to make *that* kind of connection; all you need are the right pheromones. This is just like Jensen. Not that Brunner is exactly the opposite of Jensen when it comes to picking up women: Brunner's sex life is an active one. The two men often go out on the prowl together, and whenever they happen to both find something to chat up, everything goes swimmingly. But if it's only the one eligible female they come across, then Jensen is guaranteed to be the one who takes the prize. Every time. Because Jensen just always has that slight edge over Brunner when it comes to accumulating belt-notches; he always has and he always will.

They arrive at the car; Jensen's car, a black Porsche Taycan, newest model. Yu-Mi's eyes goggle at the sight of it.

'This your car?' she inquiries, pointing at the car and looking at Jensen.

'Yep,' confirms Jensen. 'Pretty sweet, isn't she?'

'Wow…!' says Yu-Mi, gazing at Jensen with renewed admiration. 'You must be super rich!'

'Can't complain,' says Jensen, smiling complacently.

While Brunner silently wishes they could have come in *his* car, Jensen takes the girl's suitcase and stows it in the boot. He opens the back door for her.

'Step inside,' he invites her.

Yu-Mi, about to do so, stops and starts sniffing Jensen, leaning in close to his face.

'Mmmm…!' she says. 'Nice fragrance!'

Jensen looks at her. His expression becomes intent, his breathing hard.

'Oh, to hell with it,' and he grabs the girl, drags her into the car, and slams the door.

I knew it, thinks Brunner. I just bloody knew it. He wonders whether he is expected to get behind the wheel and start driving or to just wait out here until they've finished. Preferring for the latter course he reaches for his fag packet.

Two cigarettes later Jensen emerges from the back of the car, clothing dishevelled, zipping up his fly.

'Whew! That's better! Okay, let's get going.'

What is wrong with this woman? Three times she's forced them to stop, insisting on visiting restaurants that had caught her eye. If she always eats like this, how does she stay so slim? She must have a bottomless pit for a stomach!

They arrive at the Parkhurst Building and park in the basement.

'She live in penthouse?' asks Yu-Mi, pointing to the roof as they cross the parking lot to the doors of the private lift (to which Brunner and Jensen both now have access.) She seems confused again. When they got out of the car, she wanted to bring her suitcase with her and Jensen had a hard time convincing her that this wasn't necessary, that they were taking her to meet her sister in her office, not her home.

'Yeah, I Flat-Sol's got a penthouse,' replies Jensen. 'But it's not here, see? This is where she *works*, not where she *lives*, right?'

'Not on top floor…?' still perplexed.

'Yes, it is on top floor, but it's her office, her *office*, not her apartment. Yes?'

'Off-ees…?'

'Yes, she—look, you'll be with her in a minute. She can explain things to you better than I can.'

The girl still looking doubtful, they file into the lift and the lift takes them up to the top floor where they make their way to Flat-Sol's private office, which while it may not actually *be* a penthouse apartment is pretty much the size of one. Her voice bids them enter. She sits at her desk at the far end of the room, behind her the window wall and its view over Canary Wharf.

'You have arrived. Good.'

She rises from her desk, makes her way towards them. As she draws closer, the smile she has assumed for greeting her sister vanishes, her expression darkens. She stops, glares at Jensen and then at Brunner.

'What is the meaning of this?' she demands, her voice chilly.

'What's the meaning of what?' asks Jensen, bewildered. 'We've brought your sister here, just like you asked us to…'

'*That*,' pointing a denunciatory finger at the alleged Yu-Mi Park: 'is *not* my sister.'

Chapter Six
The Great Heathrow Baggage Mix-up - Part Two

Trina Truelove is both seriously hungover and seriously pissed off.

Last night she had narrowly escaped being flattened into the pavement after someone had decided to drop a piano on her employer—and what did the news on the telly have to say about her own participation in that close brush with death?

'One other person.'

Yes: Mayumi Takahashi, Professor Dodo Dupont and 'one other person'! That's what the newscasters are all saying! 'One other person'? She's got a name, you know! And it's not Chopped Liver, either! It's Trina! Trina Truelove! Truelove spelt with an 'e' after the 'u'! Why can't those stupid hacks at the news offices do their homework? There were *three* people nearly killed in that attack; *three*! They should have found out the names of all of them! Her name is Trina Truelove, and she happens to be Mayumi Takahashi's senior (as well as only) photographic assistant! Calling her 'one other person' makes it sound like she was just a bystander or something! Some chance passerby who just happened to be there at the time!

Drunk as she was, Trina still recalls the incident. At least she recalls being suddenly swept off her feet by Dodo and all three of them landing in a heap and then deafening sound of the piano hitting the ground—she remembers it all, and what's more she has a torn pair of tights a badly grazed knee as a souvenir of the incident. Of the events leading up to the piano-dropping, the latter stages of the preview party, her memory is much more patchy. (And from what she *does* remember, she feels this is probably for the best.)

But who would want to drop a piano on Mayumi? It must have been one of those bonkers anti-porn activists! They're always coming down on poor Mayumi. Seriously, what's with those people? As far as Trina is concerned, people can be as anti-porn as they like, and for that matter she isn't particularly fond of the stuff herself—but Mayumi's work isn't porn, it's art, *art* for Christ's sake! And art is art and porn is porn! Can't those idiots see that? Art is art and porn is porn!

(You can't help feeling that, if you were to get into a debate with Trina on the subject, that she would keep returning to the charge with 'Art is art and porn is porn!' until you would find yourself compelled to concede that art is indeed art, while porn on the overhand, is indubitably just porn.)

Yes, Mayumi has always had her detractors, but none of them had actually tried to *kill* her before! All they'd ever done was wave banners and shout slogans and bitch about her on their blog pages… Dropping pianos on her: that was taking things to a whole new level. It had to be a man, didn't it? A woman wouldn't do something like that.

But on the other hand, what about that suspicious woman at the gallery? The woman in the trench coat and hat who'd been asking her all those questions…? Trina recalls the incident clearly, it having taken place in the earlier part of the evening, and therefore before she got completely sozzled. After her abrupt departure, Trina had looked around for her but couldn't find her anywhere and neither Dodo or Mayumi or anyone else she'd asked had any idea of just who she was. Could *she* have been the one behind the piano attack? She'd been suspicious alright, but from the questions she'd been asking, she'd seemed more interested in Dodo than in Mayumi…

Well, whoever was behind it, Dodo is taking no chances today and she's sticking close to Yumi while she attends the official opening of her exhibition. Trina would have liked to have been there as well (because for one thing she could then have spoken to one of the television news reporters who were bound to be there and told him or her in clear and ringing tones what her bloody *name* was!), but instead she has been sent on an important errand by her employer: to wit, to pick up a friend of hers who is arriving on a visit today from Japan. The friend in question is Yuki Kinoshita, the well-known competitive eater (and inevitably, an old schoolfriend of Mayumi's), whose flight, ANA Flight 257 from Narita, Japan, is arriving today at Terminal 2, Heathrow—and it has been arranged that Trina will meet up with her outside the *Burger King* in the food court of the terminal building.

(Sounds familiar? The perceptive reader should be starting to get a glimmering as to where this is heading.)

Swigging bottled water (because it's important to rehydrate!) Trina wends her way through the crowd with the purposeful stride of someone who knows that she's late. Mind you, she's not *late* late, just a *bit* late, and this state of slightly-lateness is one for which she is in no way to blame: she had set off in what she firmly believed to be ample time in which to reach Heathrow in time to meet the two o'clock flight, and it *would* have been ample time as well, if there hadn't been any other motorists on the road—and Trina can't be held responsible for the state of the roads, can she?

Reaching the food court, she homes in on the familiar *Burger King* signboard, and sure enough, there waiting beneath it is a young Asian woman with a suitcase beside her. Trina hurries up to the woman, who, seeing her approaching, looks at her with an expression of vague inquiry.

Trina pauses. Hang on a minute, is this actually her? Is this Yuki Kinoshita? She doesn't look much like the picture Mayumi showed her. Right age, right ethnicity, but this woman has short hair; the woman in the picture had long hair… Well, yeah, long hair can be cut short, but then there are also the features: in the picture Yuki had been all sunny smiles and bright eyes but this woman looks all doughy-faced and gormless.

Well, she *is* the only Asian woman standing here outside Burger King, and she's standing here like she's waiting for someone, so who else can it be?

Only one way to find out for sure…

'Hi there!' she greets, assuming a cheerful face. 'Are you Yuki? Sorry I'm a bit late!'

The woman looks at her. Her face remains expressionless.

'Hello? You're Yuki, right?' says Trina, her smile wavering.

Still no response, either verbal or nonverbal.

Hang on a mo. Mayumi said her English isn't too good. Speak more slowly. 'Are… you… Yuki…? Yu—ki…? Yuki…?'

The woman continues to look at her blankly.

Trina's lips tighten round her by now very strained smile. She's beginning to feel like she's being stonewalled here.

Wait a minute: her luggage! The label on her luggage!

Trina looks at the label on the suitcase. And there it is: Yuki Kinoshita! It's her! But what's with the doughy face…? Of course: jetlag! She's just jetlagged! Makes sense: after all, she's just flown halfway round the world…

Trina's smile returns with full force. 'It *is* you! *Konnichi wa*, Yuki!' bowing Japanese style. 'Welcome to London! I'm Trina! *Tri-na!*'

The woman looks at her. She now speaks. Two syllables, intoned colourlessly: 'Yu-mi.'

'Yumi?' echoes Trina. 'Oh, you mean *Ma*yumi! No, Yumi couldn't make it! She sent me to meet you instead! Didn't she send you a text? I'm Trina! *Tri—na!* I… take… you… to… Yumi…!' miming driving movements. 'I… take… you… to… see… her…!'

58

Now the woman smiles, nodding her head. 'Sis-ter...?'

At last! thinks Trina. 'Yes, see her! See her!' eagerly, pointing to her eyes. 'I take you to see her! Come on!'

Trina turns, starts walking. She looks back. The woman, blank-faced again, hasn't moved. Trina, gritting her teeth, turns back, grabs the woman's wheelie luggage and sets off again. The woman follows.

In the carpark they stop before a Toyota C-Pod, the compact two-seater looking particularly compact compared to the much more substantial vehicles parked on either side of it.

'Well, here we are!' announces Trina.

The Asian woman, who has been silent during their passage across the parking lot, now smiles, pointing at the car.

'Funny car,' she says, grinning and nodding her head appreciatively.

Trina's own smile vanishes. 'It's *my* car!'

And so saying, she takes the other woman's suitcase (of which she still has custody) and deposits it, defiantly and none too gently, in the boot of the car.

Her challenging eyes meet those of the Asian woman, whose expression, as much as it registers anything at all, now registers incredulity.

'We go in this?' pointing at the car.

'Yes, we go in this!' snaps Trina, and she gets into the driving seat.

With obvious reluctance, the Asian woman joins her. She turns questioning eyes to Trina as she straps herself into the passenger seat.

'This is joke...?'

Muttering, Trina starts the car and they set off.

'I'm very sorry if my car doesn't meet with your approval. It might not be a Jaguar—Oh! Is that it? Did Yumi tell you about Dodo's Jaguar and you were expecting to get picked up in that? Well, fair dos: if you like those sporty models then I s'pose my C-Pod is a bit of a letdown; but it's good enough for me! It's economical and good for getting around in. I live on my own, y'see, so I don't need a family car. And anyway, it's Japanese, isn't it, this car? Toyota: that's Japanese! Where's your whatsit, your national pride? Jaguars, they're not Japanese, are they? They're… what *are* Jaguars, anyway…? Are they British or American? Well, whatever they are, I could never afford anything like that even if I wanted one; but then Dodo, she's rolling in it, isn't she? You should see her flat—I mean, you *will* be seeing it, cuz that's where we're going. Big swanky penthouse it is; you'll like it there. Still, Mayumi—omigod, Mayumi! You won't have heard, will you? You've been stuck on a plane since last night! Or did she tell you when she texted you? No? Well, I'll tell you what's happened to Mayumi, not to mention me and Dodo as well, cuz we happened to be standing next to her at the time: someone went and dropped a piano on her! Well, tried to, anyway. I mean, we got out of the way in time, obviously, or I wouldn't be here talking to you now. Yeah, it was outside the gallery where Yumi's got her exhibition. Last night it happened: someone went and dropped a piano from the roof! Ker-bang! They don't know who it was that did it yet, but it's bound to be one of those anti-porn nutcases. Feminists, they call themselves! That's a laugh, isn't it? I mean *Dodo*'s a fucking feminist, pardon my French, isn't she? And so am I, and in her own way, so's Yumi! But *they* won't have that, would they? Those cows think they own the copyright on the word, like they think it's some kind of exclusive club, and anyone who doesn't think the same way they do, doesn't get accepted as a member! Stupid cows! It's people like them that give feminism a bad name and *that's* why you've got all these women around who basically *are* feminists, right? but they don't like to *call* themselves feminists, cuz they've got this negative idea of what a feminist is like! That's what I say—well actually it's what Dodo says but I agree with her—and as for the *men*, those male feminists, Christ, they're even worse! You ever met any of them? They're just like that new man version of Rimmer in that *Red Dwarf* episode! Seriously: that's what they're really like! Walking fucking stereotypes, pardon my French. But then, at least those ones are harmless; I mean, it won't be one of them who dropped that piano on us: it'll be one of the completely loony psycho ones! Yeah, it's bound to be a bloke. I mean, it was a bloke who shot that American porno guy, wasn't it? What was his name? Not Heffner, the other one—anyway, it was bloke that shot him and put him in a wheelchair; it wasn't a woman! Think they've got a mission to rid the world of porn or something, these nutjobs, and that porn's so bad it's alright for them to kill the people who make it! Not that what Yumi does *is* porn! Course it's not! It's art, isn't it? And art is art, and porn is porn, right? But trying telling *them* that! No aesthetic sense at all, these people! But Yumi; well, you know Yumi: she's Japanese—like you are, really—and so she's got that Japanese sense of beauty, hasn't she? She's an artist! She makes art! Photography's art when it's done well, isn't it? I mean, yeah, some porn is photos as well, but it's not art, is it? Or if it is, it's bad art; 'pends how good the photography is, I suppose; some of it might be alright, but a lot of it, it'll just be total amateur stuff, won't it? Smartphone pictures! And anyway, these days most of the porn you get online is videos not images, isn't it? Videos of people on the job! And that's not art, is it? That's just home movies or reality TV or something; not like proper films, right? And these people think what me and Yumi do is no different to that, for Christ's sake! And they go on about it being degrading to women, turning them into lumps of meat, blah, blah, blah; I mean, yeah, you've *got* men, like that arsehole Donald Trump, who just see women as lumps of meat, but it's not because of them being in photographs, is it? I mean, there's *always* been men like that, and a long time before they ever *had* photographs! And then they have the nerve call Yumi a gender traitor, for fuck's sake and pardon my French! *Yumi* of all people! No-one likes women more than Yumi does! I mean, I don't need to tell you, do I? You know her. It's *men* she doesn't like! That's why she doesn't have them in her pictures. With her it's all about her connection with the woman she's photographing, y'know? Her "emotional bond with the subject.' And when she ties them up for the bondage stuff, she does all the tying herself; that's very important, right? Yumi's art's about *her* as much as it is about her models. Same as with painters—'

A sound like snort interrupts Trina. It sounds suspiciously like derision. She glances to her left. But no, it isn't derision so much as complete inattention, the snort being actually a snore. Her passenger is fast asleep and has been fast asleep for some time.

And when they get back to Dodo's apartment, what does she do but go straight back to sleep: and not even in the bedroom that's waiting for her! After one appraising look at the living room (she seems more impressed with the apartment than she was with the Toyota) she just kicks off her shoes, stretches herself out on one of the sofas and is soon fast asleep again.

Dodo and Mayumi are still out when they arrive, but Trina, sitting on the loo, hears the sounds that announce their return. Answering in the affirmative to a called-out inquiry from Dodo as to whether or not she, Trina Truelove, is there, Trina hurries to 'complete her toilet' (to misuse a bygone expression) and joins them in the living room.

For those of you not familiar with Dodo's apartment (in other words anyone who either hasn't read or doesn't remember the first book in this series) the apartment is dominated by a vast, studio-like living area, with one wall entirely glazed and offering a panoramic view of the Central London skyline and all of the apartment's other rooms, master bedroom and spare bedrooms, kitchen, bathroom and study, leading off from this room. The living room's furniture is arranged mostly on the window wall side of the room and it is here Dodo and Mayumi stand looking down at their slumbering houseguest. And as Trina approaches them, she sees they are not regarding her with the indulgent smiles she would have expected to have seen.

'Who's this?' is Dodo's first question.

The question, the last one she was expecting, stops Trina in her tracks. 'What do you mean? It's Yuki, isn't it?'

'No,' says Dodo, firmly. 'It isn't.'

'Not her,' confirms Mayumi.

'Bu-but it *must* be her!' insists Trina; and in a trembling voice that belies the certainty contained in the words. 'It-it… well, it's her bloody suitcase! Look at it! It says Yuki Kinoshita, clear as day!'

Dodo looks; and the luggage label does indeed say Yuki Kinoshita, and with the advertised pre-sunset clarity.

A ring at the doorbell. Dodo suspends whatever she was about to say to go and answer it. She opens the door and voices an indignant cry of protest as a woman, Asian, in a business suit, sweeps past her and into the room. The woman is followed by two men, Caucasian, also in business suits, and they in turn are followed by a second, also Asian, woman, in casual attire.

'I have something that belongs to you,' announces the first woman, 'and I believe that you have something that belongs to me,' and catching sight of the sofa's still-slumbering tenant. 'Ah, yes. I see there has indeed been a mix-up of property. I suggest an amicable exchange of goods.'

'Yes, and you are…?' says Dodo pointedly. Accommodating though she is, Dodo does not care for complete strangers barging into her apartment uninvited.

'Of course: introductions are in order,' agrees the woman smoothly. 'My name is Flat-Sol Park, President of the Parkhurst Corporation. You, of course, need no introduction,

Professor Dupont. These two men are my associates Mr Jensen and Mr Brunner. It is through their error that Miss Kinoshita here was misappropriated. They mistook her for my younger sister Yu-Mi Park, who you currently have in your custody—or perhaps you had already ascertained her identity?'

'No, we hadn't got that far, actually.'

Having spotted Mayumi, Yuki crosses the room to join her. They first bow to one another and, all smiles, embrace and launch into an animated conversation in Japanese.

Says Flat-Sol, addressing the former: 'It is an honour to meet you, Mayumi Takahashi; I am an admirer of your art. On the behalf of the Parkhurst Corporation, I would like to apologise for our temporary misappropriation of your friend; and I can assure you she was in no way misused during her time in our custody.'

(At this Brunner glances sideways at Jensen, who suddenly finds himself strangely fascinated by the ceiling.)

'It seems to have been a luggage mix-up that was the original cause of all this,' says Dodo.

'This is true. But nevertheless, I still accept responsibility on the behalf of my employees, and apologise for their part in this regrettable transaction.'

Flat-Sol now walks over to the sofa where her sister has woken up and sitting up is rubbing her eyes. Groggily, she fixes these orbs on Flat-Sol.

'She's a bit jetlagged,' says Trina.

'Not at all. My sister is always like this,' reports Flat-Sol. 'You must be Trina Truelove, Mayumi Takahashi's esteemed photographic assistant. It is a pleasure to make your acquaintance.'

Recognition at last! 'Thanks!' says Trina, blushing. 'It was… it was me who picked your sister up from the airport…'

'Then I must thank you for having taken such great care of her,' says Flat-Sol, bowing. To her sister, switching to Korean: 'Come, sister. We must be leaving.'

Listlessly, Yu-Mi rises to her feet. She reaches for the suitcase.

'Leave it; that is not your suitcase. *I* have your luggage and it is quite safe back at my office.'

Yu-Mi accepts this seemingly miraculous transposition of her belongings with a brief shrug of the shoulders.

Addressing Dodo: 'Professor Dupont, before we will take our leave, I would like to inquire as to your wellbeing. I have heard that yourself and your two associates were the victims of a murderous attack last evening. Also, I am curious to know if there is any lead as to the identity of the perpetrators?'

'As you can see, we're all okay. No leads yet, but considering where and when the attack happened, it seems most likely it was some crackpot activist who doesn't like Yumi's photography.'

'Really? Have you not considered the possibility that you yourself were the primary target of the attack?'

'I *have* considered it, yes, but it doesn't seem likely.'

'No? I would have thought your work with the intelligence agent Mark Hunter would be a possible source of danger to you.'

Dodo's eyes widen. 'You're very well informed. How did you know that I sometimes work with Mark Hunter?'

'Perhaps you forget, Professor Dupont: the Vernon Grange research establishment in East Anglia belonged to the Parkhurst Corporation. Your felonious nocturnal visit to the establishment in the company of Mark Hunter was recorded by the closed-circuit television system. The destruction of that facility cost us a great deal of money. We lost many valuable test subjects'

'Well, it wasn't us who blew up the place,' says Dodo. 'It was a gas mains explosion, and probably caused by one of your "test subjects."'

'True, but your presence in the locality did serve to aggravate the situation.'

'Yes, our presence usually has that effect.'

'Quite so. I understand that Mark Hunter is presently investigating the Zero advertising campaign, and that he is attempting to trace it to its source; could the attack on yourself perhaps have been related to this?'

'You *do* know a lot, don't you?' says Dodo. 'But no, as it happens, I'm not helping Mark with his current assignment. He's working with someone else.'

'The CIA operative, Richard Bedford. Yes, I am aware of this as well. But enough of this: we have imposed upon your hospitality for too long, Professor Dupont. We will now take our leave. Good day to you all.'

Flat-Sol bows to the room and she and her entourage exit the apartment, Yu-Mi pausing in the doorway to wave a vague goodbye to Trina.

Chapter Seven
The Mark Hunter Fanclub is Accepting New Members

'…Either they took it from his person when they beat him up or they took it from his apartment when they searched it—assuming these two acts were committed by the same people, which of course they might not have been. Either way, someone's got hold of Perfect's phone, which presumably has his contact's number on it, and depending on who these people are, they will either want to get hold of this contact themselves or to stop us from getting hold of him. Here we are. Let's hope the landlord's arrived.'

'You still say that nurse who clobbered you was the girl working the bar here last night?'

'Yes, I do still say.'

They walk into the pub. It is midafternoon and there are no customers, but a man, small of stature and sullen of expression, stands behind the bar, polishing glasses with a tea towel.

'Good afternoon,' greets Mark. 'Would you be the landlord?'

'I would,' is the reply. 'Are you the two blokes what was asking for me lunchtime?'

'We are. We want to ask you about the young woman who was barmaid here last night.'

'Yeah? What about 'er?'

'We'd like to know where to find her.'

'Oh, yer would, would yer? An' you reckon I go around giving out my barmaids' contact information to any geezer what comes along askin' for 'em? Get out of it!'

Bedford slams his fist down on the bar counter. 'Now, listen buster! We're not just anyone! This is official business! Now spill it!'

'Now, now, Rick,' says Mark. To the landlord: 'He's telling the truth, though: we are officials. Here are my credentials.'

The landlord scrutinises the proffered identity card. 'Mark Hunter... So *you're* Mark 'Unter!'

'You've heard of me?' asks Mark, surprised.

'Oh, I've 'eard of yer alright!' says the man in a voice that suggests he doesn't consider the knowledge to be an asset to him. 'Yeah, I've 'eard of yer... Perfect, he was always goin' on about you, 'e was!'

'Oh, you know Perfect, then?'

''Course I does! We goes way back, me an' 'im! So you're the 'igh an' mighty Mark 'Unter, are you? Gor, the way ''e used to go on about you: thought the sun shined out o' your bloody arse, 'e did! Mark 'Unter, the famous spy, an' 'ow 'e'd always come to little ol' Perfect when 'e wanted hinformation about somethin'! "Mark 'Unter did this, Mark 'Unter did that! Mark 'Unter stopped the 'ole bloody universe from blowin' up cuz I put the finger on this geezer wot was 'idin out in Peckham!" Well, a lot o' good knowin' you's done 'im! Lyin there in bloody 'ospital, beaten arf ter death, every bleedin' bone in 'is body broke!'

'Oh, come on, man: you can't blame Mark for that!' protests Bedford. 'The guy's a stool pigeon, for Christ's sake! Getting worked over's an occupational hazard for guys like him! It comes with the territory!'

'And it's partly on Perfect's account that we need to get hold of that barmaid,' says Mark. 'We think she may have had some involvement in what happened to him last night. So please, who is she and where can we find her?'

''Ow should I know that?' retorts the landlord.

'Well, you employed her! You must have her contact information!'

'Yeah? Well, 'appens I don't 'ave it, do I? An' that's that! She ain't one of me regular staff, see? She only worked 'ere last night. Just a one-off, it was, cash in 'and. Din't Perfect tell yer about that?'

'Perfect? He's not in any condition to tell us much at the moment—but how should he know about your barmaid?'

'What you on about? It was 'im what arst me to let 'er work 'ere in the first place! 'E *musta* told you about that! 'E said it all 'ad to do wi' what 'e was 'elpin' you with, 'e did! Said you was comin' 'ere last night, an' that this girl 'ad to be the one workin' the bar when you come!'

Bedford looks at Mark. 'What the hell? I don't get it!'

'I think I'm beginning to,' says Mark. 'When she came to Perfect's hospital room in disguise this morning: she wasn't trying to kill him, she was trying to talk to him! Don't you see: that girl is the contact! She's the one who knows about Zero!'

Chapter Eight
Counselling, with Extreme Prejudice

'...I mean, you get to my age and you stop and you look back over your life, and you see that you haven't really *achieved* anything; you haven't done any of the things you wanted to do; you haven't achieved any of your goals...'

'What sort of goals are we talking about here, Peter? Career? Relationships?'

'Well, both, I suppose. I had *plans!* There were so many things I wanted to do: I wanted to be an author; a properly published author, I mean; not just self-published. And television: I wanted to write for television! All these ideas I've had; things that would have made great TV dramas. It's just so frustrating! I feel like I've had so much to offer, so many ideas... But I've just never had that lucky break. Always rejection letters...'

'Yes, I can see how frustrated that must make you feel.'

'Yes, it's... it's luck of the draw, really, isn't it? You meet the right people and they support you; they help you along; that's how it goes. But then some people, they go through their entire lives and they *never* meet the right person, the right people... And that's how it's been for me. I'm one of the unlucky ones... I've *never* met the right people, *never* met that right special person; the person who'd come along and set me on my feet. I've never had a truly meaningful relationship with anyone; *never!*'

'You've never had a long-term relationship?'

'No, not really... Nothing that ever really worked out...'

'You must feel very lonely, then.'

'I feel so lonely it's killing me. Here I am; I'm fifty, and by the time you get to that age it's so much harder to go out and make new friends. I mean, you know that Smiths song

'How Soon is Now?' Well, I can't even do *that*: I can't even stand on my own at a nightclub all night, because I'm way too old to be going to nightclubs! I can still sit on my own in pubs, of course; yes, I can do that whenever I want to make myself feel really miserable... You see, I've always had this idea that if I was successful with my writing, that I'd make new friends that way; but I *haven't* succeeded. And now I'm wondering if it's worth it; if it's worth still chasing after those dreams, or if I should just resign myself to having failed...?'

'Well, the best thing to do is to look at those goals, those dreams of yours, and decide whether they fall into the category of *achievable goals* or *unachievable goals*. Most of us have dreams of fame and fortune, especially when we're young and optimistic, but often those dreams *are* just dreams; they are not goals that we could realistically achieve. You have to look at yourself and decide if you have the necessary talent required to achieve your goals or if actually you haven't really got that talent...'

'Well, I know I can write! I know I'm good enough!'

'But, are you? You say the work you have submitted has always been rejected; and this has been going on for what, several decades now? Perhaps it's time to face the fact that perhaps you aren't as good a writer as you think you are. When it comes to things like this, none of us can really judge our own abilities; it's just not possible: only other people can judge our work accurately and impartially...'

'So you're saying I should just give up...?'

'Well, at your age, and considering your complete lack of success, it might be for the best, yes.'

'Bu-but aren't you supposed to be encouraging me...?'

'I'm here to help you to face facts, Peter; to help you see your situation clearly. It would be cruel of me to encourage you with false hopes that might still be able to realise your dreams of fame and fortune, when the chances of that ever happening are below infinitesimal. Unachievable goals,

Peter. You have to stop deluding yourself with unachievable goals.'

'Yes… Yes, I suppose you're… I suppose you must be right, then…'

'I *know* I'm right, Peter. You can trust me in this.'

'Yes… Well… what are you saying I should do, then? Just carry on as I am, plodding on, living this lonely life one day at a time…?'

'Well, of course you *could* do that…'

'Well what *else* is there for me to do? I don't seem to have any choice…!'

'There's always a choice, Peter. Having accepted that you are never going to achieve your goals, you can either resign yourself to living out the rest of your mundane life, or…'

'Or…?'

'…Or you can resign yourself to *not* living out the rest of your life. You did say you'd been thinking more and more about suicide recently, didn't you? Of just throwing yourself into the Thames and ending it all…'

'Well, yes, but you can't be saying I should—! I mean, aren't you supposed to talk people *out* of doing that?'

'Usually, yes. But in your case, Peter, I really don't think it would be a kindness to dissuade you from what is really the only logical course of action left open to you. You've lost the few friends you ever had; you've never had a lasting, meaningful relationship with another human being; and it's certainly not going to happen now, is it? Not at this late stage; like you say, when you're over fifty it's very hard to change your life; almost impossible.'

'But things might get better! I might still find someone! I-I've been looking online…!'

'Online dating? And how long have you been looking? How many years? And during that time how many women have you even matched with and started talking to, let alone gone out on a date with…? And of course you will have been setting your sights on women younger than yourself: that's always the way with men of your age and your lack of relationship experience; men who've never really grown up... Isn't that right? You've been hoping to find some younger woman who will take pity on you and coddle you...?'

'Well... if I'm completely honest about it, yes...'

'Yes, and you see, you really must see that that is another *unachievable goal*. No reasonably good-looking young woman is going to tie herself down to a man your age, not unless you're wealthy enough to make it worth her while. You do see that, don't you, Peter?'

'But-but there might... I thought that *you* might... that you might...'

'Me? No, no, no. Out of the question. It is strictly forbidden for a health worker to form any kind of relationship with a patient; and if I ever *were* to make an exception to that rule... well, it wouldn't be for you, Peter. I'm just not attracted to you; quite the reverse, in fact.'

'Y-you can't say that...!'

'I'm only being *honest* with you, Peter. This is our last session together and our time is nearly up. *Your* time is nearly up. So you see, you've really got no-one to turn to, nowhere to go...'

'...the river's that way...!'

'Ah, there you are, Professor Sunnybrook.'

The woman in the doorway spins round, a picture of startled guilt.

'Doctor Garner! I was just... seeing off my last patient!'

Let us look at this startled woman. Rajni Sunnybrook is a tall, beautiful woman, short-haired, thirty years old and she holds a professorship in psychology. Sounds just like Dodo, doesn't it? And indeed, ethnicity aside Rajni does bear more than a passing resemblance to our paragon protagonist. However, when placed in direct comparison with Dodo, everything about Rajni Sunnybrook is just a little bit *less* so:

she is tall, but not quite as tall as Dodo; and her hourglass figure is admirable but not quite as admirable; she has (when not looking like a startled rabbit caught with its paw in the cookie jar) poise and composure, but not quite as much poise and composure as Dodo; and the clothes she wears are stylish, but not quite as stylish as Dodo's... And so on and so on; from the breadth of her knowledge to the length of her foot, everything about Rajni is just that little bit *less* so.

The man addressing her is Doctor Garner, chief psychiatrist of the mental health outpatient clinic in which we presently find ourselves: Doctor Garner is a rumpled, tweedy man of bald-headed middle age, who conceals his efficiency behind an amiably absent-minded exterior. He is the director of this clinic, housed in this converted Victorian townhouse.

Says Doctor Garner: 'Heading off home now? Well, er, before you do, I was, er, wondering if I could have a quick word...?'

'Yes of course, Doctor Garner! What is it?' says Rajni, now all smiles.

'Er, well... could you, er, come along to my office...? I won't keep you too long...'

'As long as you like, Doctor Garner!'

'Er, yes... splendid...'

Rajni follows Garner along the hallway to his ground floor office. He has made this room very much his own, importing ponderous mahogany furniture, and generally imposing an air of comfortable, absentminded disorder.

'Come in, come in... and, er, take your coat off...'

'I'm not wearing my coat.'

'You're not... er, jolly good... Well, take a seat, take a seat...'

Rajni lowers herself into the chair indicated.

'Actually, no *don't* take a seat...'

Rajni stands up again.

'Come over here, come over here...'

Rajni joins Garner standing before a bar chart pinned to the wall.

'You... er, you see this bar chart...?'

'Yes, Doctor Garner. I'm looking directly at it.'

'Splendid... Well, this chart represents the clinic's performance figures over the past fiscal year...'

'Performance? In what sense'

'Well... er, in the sense of losses... of, er, the number of patients we've lost... er, you know... the, ahem... suicides...'

'Oh, I see!'

'Good, good... Well, er, these bars reflect the er, performance record of each clinician on the staff here... You're with me...?'

'Oh yes, Doctor Garner. Please continue.'

'Good, good... Well, these er, these smaller bars, these ones indicate suicide rates of half a dozen or so, yes...? And er, figures of this kind are to be expected, these, er, are what we refer to as "acceptable losses" yes...? You know, try as hard as we might, we... er, we will always lose one or two patients *per annum*... Regrettable, regrettable, but just can't be avoided, yes...?'

'Yes, I understand you perfectly.'

'Yes... Well, er... *this* much higher bar, this one here, this bar represents *your* performance record, Professor Sunnybrook... Now, er, do you see the discrepancy here...?'

The bar indicated, placed in the centre of the chart, towers above the others; defiant, derisive, like an extended mid-digit.

'Yes, I do seem to have suffered a few more losses.'

'A few...? A few...? Professor, this bar represents ninety-seven patients lost over the past fiscal year... *Ninety-seven*, Professor. *Ninety-seven* suicides...'

'Ninety-eight, any minute now.'

'Pardon...?'

74

'Oh, nothing. So, what are you saying, Doctor Garner? Do you consider this figure to exceed acceptable losses?'

'Well, I'm afraid it does, Professor; I'm afraid it does... Yes, I... I mean, the work we do here... hacking our way through the human jungle, doing our best to help those poor souls who've lost their way... Well, er... sometimes we can start to lose our way ourselves, can't we...? And we, erm... we can even come down with a spot of jungle fever every now and then, yes...? It can happen to even the best of us...!'

'If you're suggesting I need some time off work, Doctor Garner, I can assure you that that is not the case; I am in good physical and mental health. I am willing and able to continue with my work.'

'But the figures, Professor; the figures: ninety-seven patients lost... It won't do, you know... No, it really won't do...'

'Well, if it will set your mind at rest, Doctor Garner, I shall do my best to improve my performance record for the remainder of the fiscal year,' promises Rajni, and she places a reassuring hand on the Doctor's tweedy shoulder for good measure.

He looks uncomfortable. 'Well, er, that... that er, won't actually be, erm, necessary...' he says, addressing his words at the hand of the shoulder. 'You, er, you see, I'm er, letting you go...'

The hand is removed. 'You mean you're giving me the sack?'

'Well, er, that's a, that's a rather blunt way of putting it... But, er, in essence, er, yes...'

'But you can't fire me!' protests Rajni. 'I'm the most qualified person on your staff!'

'Well, er, yes, yes you are, you are...! Somewhat *over*qualified, in fact... A job like this... outpatient clinic... NHS... overworked and underpaid and all that... I'm sure, er, with all your accolades, Professor... you know, you could, you could do much better for yourself... Have you ever thought about setting up shop as a private practitioner? Plenty of demand for that sort of thing these days... All those self-obsessed rich people with their neuroses, eh...! Yes...er, much more remunerative, and you er, you can work at your own pace...'

'Thank you for the suggestion, Doctor, but I've already tried that: the profession has become so overcrowded I just couldn't get enough patients to make it pay.'

'No? Well, er... well, it doesn't have to be *that*... There are plenty of other career openings for someone with your qualifications... Why er, look at Professor Dupont...!'

Rajni's face freezes over.

'I beg your pardon?'

'Professor Dupont! You er, studied alongside her at Cambridge, didn't you...?'

Rajni's face starts to twitch on the left side. 'I attended the same course at the same time as her, yes.'

'Well, there you go! Just look at her: done famously for herself, hasn't she? Books, television documentaries and, erm... all sorts of things... Made a tidy sum of money for herself... Now, you er, you could do something like that... Yes, take a leaf out of her book! Are you, er, are you still in touch with her...?'

The left side of Rajni's face is by now twitching madly. (It rather looks like Doctor Garner was a bit wide of the mark with that allusion of his to *The Human Jungle*: it is another Herbert Lom character entirely that Rajni seems to be taking her cues from!)

'No, Doctor Garner. I am not in touch with Professor Dupont.'

'Well, then: it might be an idea if you were to look her up! Yes... old college friend, she might be able to put you in the way of something... Er, is there something wrong with your face, Professor...?'

'No, there is nothing wrong with my face, Doctor Garner; and I thank you for your kind advice, which I will certainly give all the consideration it deserves,' says Rajni. 'Just to be clear, am I to take it then that my dismissal from this clinic is not open to any discussion?'

'Well, er... no... I er, I'm afraid it isn't...' uncomfortably, scratching the back of his head.

'Then I shall bid you goodbye, Doctor Garner.'

And ignoring Doctor Garner's awkwardly proffered hand, Rajni turns her back on him and makes her face-twitching way to the door.

'Well, er, best of luck for the future Professor erm... Sunnybrook... Oh! And don't forget to give Professor Dupont a call!'

The words freeze Rajni in the act of opening the door. For a moment she stands motionless; and then, vouchsafing no response, she resumes her departure, closing the door carefully behind her.

Chapter Nine
The Countdown Begins

It happens the next morning, at precisely 07:00 BST. It cuts in on all television broadcasts, cable, satellite, terrestrial; it appears on every billboard the length and breadth of the British Isles; on the internet it multiplies rapidly, overriding all preprogrammed advertisements.

It is a new commercial from Zero, an announcement, brief and succinct:

ZERO

Coming 1st June 202-

And that is it. The commercial is in all other respects like its predecessors: the synthesised sting, ominous, a sustained single note, as first the Zero logo fades onto the screen and then a second line of smaller text beneath; but now Zero is no longer just 'coming soon': a release date has been announced:1st June 202-! (The suppression of the final digit is not featured on the actual commercial, I hasten to add: this is just your cautious narrator not wanting to consign the events of this story to the past before it even sees the light of day.)

June the first! Zero is coming on June the first! But *what? What* is coming on June the first? There's still no hint as to what Zero actually *is!*

Unless... unless the clue is in the date itself! June the first! What's so special about June the first? Well, obviously it's the first day of the summer season: but what else? Is there anything else happening on that particular day the release of Zero might be designed to coincide with? People with nothing better to do (and many who *do* have better things to do) search furiously online, dredging up the statistics, facts and figures: all the anniversaries, births and deaths, religious festivals, etc that fall on June the first, analysing them for any significance, and when significance is lacking, inventing it.

Corporations draw up exhaustive lists of all the new products, projects, initiatives, etc scheduled for launch on June the first; anything the simultaneous launch of Zero might be designed to undermine, overshadow, compromise or conflict with; astrologers, mystics and fortune tellers consult the stars and planets, nearly all of them discovering a portentous cosmic significance attached to the date of the first of June (its precise nature varying) that had somehow managed to escape their attention until now.

Meanwhile Mark Hunter, with his knowledge of Zero's possible extraterrestrial origins, focuses his attention on the possibility of any astronomical, rather than astrological, events that might be due to take place on June the first (Earth Time). But according to the experts nothing of any note is forecast to take place on that particular date.

And as for the deciphering of the signals, those mysterious signals picked up by the radio observatory in Wales; the task is going to be no easy one. The recording has been sent to the codebreaking experts at Turing Grange, and they are now having to resort to more traditional codebreaking techniques to crack the code—because the AI codebreakers refuse to have anything to do with the transmissions. It seems almost as though they are actually *scared* of them.

The long and short of this latest development is that Mark is now working to a deadline. He has to find out the truth about Zero before June the first, because something very bad might be due to happen on June the first. He has just forty-five days to trace the Zero campaign to its terrestrial source, a source known to be on the UK mainland.

And the only solid lead Mark has, the only person who might know precisely *where* on the UK mainland Zero has established itself, is an elusive young woman whose name he doesn't even know.

And the only solid lead Mark has to *that* solid lead is a badly-injured hospitalised man.

They've had a round the clock guard put on Perfect. Mike Collins and Daisy Fontaine, two of Mark's strongarm operatives, have been on duty all night and they have already thwarted three attempts by imposters in various disguises to gain access to the injured man's room.

Perfect's attackers come back to finish the job they started? Or other interested parties hoping to get information from him?

Mark sits at Perfect's bedside. The informer, still cocooned in bandage and plaster, said to be in satisfactory condition, is more alert this morning, but with the injuries to throat and jaw, his allocation of words has been strictly rationed by the doctors.

'That barmaid at the Jolly Tar,' says Mark; 'the black girl: she was your contact, wasn't she? And it was her who was here yesterday, wasn't it? The girl dressed as a nurse? Tell me if I'm right, Perfect. Just a yes or a no.'

He leans close to Perfect's mouth, picks up a rasped affirmative.

'Good. That's good, Perfect. Now I need to speak to that girl very urgently. Where can I get hold of her?'

'Phone...' wheezes Perfect.

'Phone? You mean your phone? You've got her number on your phone? That's no good, Perfect. We've looked for your phone and we can't find it; it must have been stolen. I don't suppose you'd have the number committed to memory, would you...?'

Perfect wouldn't.

'And you don't know her address?'

He doesn't.

'What about her name? Can you tell me that?'

Perfect rasps a name.

'Anna...?'

Not Anna.

'Oh, *Amber*?'

Yes.

'What about her second name?'

The reply sounds like Dillon, but on repetition solidifies into 'dunno.'

'You don't know? Pity. Well, one name's better than none at all. I'd better get onto this,' says Mark. He stands up. 'Thank you, Perfect. I'll come back later, but if there's anything you need to say to me in the meantime, a couple of my people will be just outside the door.'

Perfect says something.

'What's that?' Mark leans in again.

'Twenty...' rasps Perfect.

'Twenty? Twenty what?'

'Quid… For the… info…'

'Oh yes, of course. Business is still business, isn't it?' Smiling, Mark reaches for his wallet. 'You know, this reminds me I haven't replenished my supply of ready cash since that last payment I made to you the other night. I hope I've got—'

Mark breaks off, stopped by the sight of a folded slip of paper nestled in the billfold of his wallet. He extracts the slip and opens it. A brief message, unsigned, scrawled in urgent capitals, the last word vehemently underscored:

> MEET ME AT THE CULT CAFÉ TONIGHT
> COME <u>ALONE</u>

'Oh, that stupid girl…!'

Chapter Ten
I Caught the Sun in a Bucket

The two Japanese women sit upright on the sofa, politely formal, knees together, hands resting on laps. The woman sitting on the right is our friend Yuki Kinoshita, the competitive eater. Her hair is now loose and has been carefully arranged, as has her makeup. Her clothes, plastic sandals, denim shorts, t-shirt, are as vibrant as her smile. The woman sitting beside her also smiles, but with a more businesslike smile to match her more businesslike attire, a neat light grey skirt suit and a white blouse. Her hair is cut in a prim East Asian bob and she wears gold-framed spectacles; her name is Shizuka Todoroki.

Their hosts, Ruth and Jordan Kendal, the thirty-something husband and wife who present *Morning Live*, own the company that finances it, and who of course come complete with their own personal soap opera, are seated on the sofa opposite. The Kendals, more relaxed in posture than the Japanese women, both wear stylish casual suits. Jordan Kendal is tall and rangy, handsome and square-jawed; Ruth Kendal is smaller, more compact, artificially blonde.

The two sofas have been arranged at oblique angles with a coffee table placed between them. On the wall directly behind is a large flatscreen for the video link interviews and which presently just displays a static image of the *Morning Live* logo.

Jordan Kendal is addressing the camera. '…And joining us in the studio now all the way from Japan, we have Yuki Kinoshita, reigning world champion of that unusual sporting phenomenon, competitive eating. Good morning, Yuki!'

'Good morning!' sings Yuki, bowing her head.

'Now, Yuki's English isn't very strong, and so we have sitting next to Yuki, Shizuka Todoroki—and I think I've pronounced that correctly!—who will be acting as her interpreter. Now Shizuka, I believe you actually work for the Japanese embassy here in London, don't you?'

'That is correct.'

'So, Yuki, is this your first visit to the UK?' asks Ruth.

'It is,' confirms Yuki via the formal tones of her interpreter, 'and I am very happy to be here.'

'And will you be seeing all the sights while you're here: the Tower, St Pauls, Westminster Abbey…?'

'Yes, I plan to do this and I am very much looking forward to it.'

'Now, a little bird tells me,' says Jordan, 'that you went to the same school as a certain Mayumi Takahashi…'

'Would that be Mayumi Takahashi the erotic photographer whose name we've been hearing in the news?' inquires Ruth archly, swapping smiles with her husband.

'The very same,' confirms he. 'Yes; Mayumi Takahashi, the woman whose controversial, some might say completely outrageous, photography has been the subject of fierce debate. In fact, her latest exhibition angered somebody so much that they tried to drop a *piano* on her! Mind you, no-one has claimed responsibility for this as yet and sceptics are suggesting that the whole thing was in fact just a huge publicity stunt!'

'Yes, but the police do say that they're taking the matter seriously,' Ruth reminds him.

'They do. Let us not forget that, and here on *Morning Live* we're certainly not indorsing these rumours—and that is all they are: unsubstantiated rumours. But as for the subject matter of this exhibition: well, we've been asked not to go into too much detail about that here on the show as it does involve a subject that's not exactly daytime television friendly—the exhibition, and is called *Afternoon Dreams* and there's a book along with it that literally poses the question "What Do You Fantasise About When You're, ahem, Pleasuring Yourself (I've been told not to use the M-word)—If it's Not a Personal Question!" which is a Monty Python reference, of course. *"If it's not a personal question? How much more personal can you get?"*'

'Not much more, I'd say,' says Ruth.

'Now, I haven't been to this exhibition myself—'

'Because I won't let you go, darling.'

'Because you won't let me go: yes! But it involves pictures of women, ahem, pleasuring themselves and from all accounts pictures that don't leave *anything* to the imagination... But is it Art? Is it Art?'

'Sounds more like smut to me, but there you go, I'm old fashioned.'

'Well, they have put an age-registration on admission to the exhibition: no under-eighteens allowed. And apparently, *apparently*, the photographer herself only agreed to this age restriction under protest! Seems she thought that *everyone* should be allowed to come in and have a look at her naughty pictures! Because they're *Art*, apparently. Well, we'll leave it to *The Culture Show* to thrash out the debate on that one, because they will be having not only Mayumi Takahashi, but also Dodo Dupont, the one who wrote the book, live on the show this week. And that will be happening… tomorrow night…? yes, tomorrow night, here on BBC1—and of course it'll be after the watershed so they can mention the M-word as much as they like. But now!—back to our guests.'

The camera returns to the two Japanese women, who have sat patiently through this lengthy digression, smiling with polite attention on the part of the interpreter and polite incomprehension on the part of Yuki, who has barely understood a word of it. (The conversation not having directly related to Yuki, Shizuka has deemed it unnecessary to translate it for her.)

'So, is this true, Yuki? You went to school with Mayumi Takahashi?'

'This is correct. We were in the same class.'

'And so, is the main reason for your visit to the UK is actually to see her?'

'Yes, I am here by Takahashi-san's invitation and I am staying as her guest.'

'Well, well, well. And could it be then, that you've actually come here to do some *modelling* for her? Click, click, nudge, nudge, wink, wink; say no more. Oops! Another Monty Python reference!'

'Second-hand humour.'

'You're right; second-hand humour. But tell us: *have* you come to the UK to model for Mayumi Takahashi? And of course it would be *nude* photography we're talking about, because that's pretty much the only kind Mayumi Takahashi does!'

Yuki's reply, via Shizuka: 'No, I have not consented to model for Mayumi-chan, nor do I have any desire to model in the nude. However, it is likely I will ultimately do so in any event as Mayumi-chan can be most persuasive and is able to convince almost anyone she desires into disrobing for her photography.'

'Well, if she does get you in front of the camera in the altogether, you've certainly got the figure for it—which brings me to my *next* question: just where do you put it all, Yuki? Here you are, the reigning champion of competitive eaters, gobbling down huge amounts of food in record time. Now, all those calories, all those carbohydrates: where do they go? How on earth do you manage to keep your figure so slim?'

'Yes, what's your secret?' says Ruth. 'Because I'd certainly be interested in knowing what it is!'

'Yes, because you have been putting on a few extra ounces of late, haven't you? The old bathroom scales have been sending you warning messages.'

'I thought we weren't going to mention that one, darling,' tightly.

'Whoops! The cat's out of the bag: I've said something I shouldn't have. Well, slap my wrist!' playfully miming the action. 'So, tell us: how do you do it Yuki? How do you stop yourself from piling on the pounds after those eating binges of yours? I *thought* perhaps you might have been doing as the Romans do, or *did*, when they had *their* eating binges. Orgies, they used to call them, although that's not orgies in the sense most of us understand the word to mean these days! So, is that what you do? Do you bring it all straight back up again? Fingers down the throat?'

'Oh no,' is the translated reply. 'It is forbidden to vomit during an eating contest. Any participant who did so would be immediately disqualified.'

'Yes, but I wasn't thinking as much of *during* an eating contest, as immediately *afterwards*. You know, as soon as the show is over and you've left the stage... Do you rush straight to the nearest ladies' room and bring it all back up again?'

'No, I do not do this.'

'Then how in the name of all that's holy do you stay so slim when you're always stuffing yourself to the gills like that?'

'Do you go on a starvation diet before you have an eating contest?' inquires Ruth.

'Not at all. Eating frugally shrinks the stomach and diminishes the appetite, and this would only have an adverse effect on a contestant's performance.'

'Then do you work it all off with exercise?' asks Jordan. 'Burning off those calories at the gym?'

'No, I am not fond of exercise.'

'What? You don't diet, you don't exercise and you don't just bring it all back up: well, frankly I'm flummoxed; I am completely flummoxed. You must have hollow legs. Well,' turning to the camera, 'however she manages keep down her waistline, there's no doubt that Yuki Kinoshita *is* Japan's reigning competitive eating champion, and she has agreed to give us a demonstration of her talents here in the studio.' To Yuki: 'Isn't that right, Yuki?'

'Yes, I am greatly looking forward to it.'

'Good! Well, it looks like they're just getting things ready over there…' looking off camera.

'Yes, I can smell it,' says Ruth.

'Mm! It *does* smell good.' To the camera: 'Our chefs have been busy preparing this behind the scenes and what they've put together for our visitor from Japan is a selection—'

'—a very *large* selection.'

'A very *large* selection of good old British grub, and which we're going to be calling *The Great British Eat Off!* So, Yuki, do you like English food?'

'Yes, I like it very much.'

(Actually, and in common with most Japanese people, Yuki considers English food to be very boring—but also being possessed of Japanese good manners, she is far too polite to say so.)

'And what's your favourite English meal?'

'Fish and chips.' (The standard response.)

'Ah, yes! Good old fish and chips. And yes, I think they're ready for us over there, so if I can just ask our guests to come with us across the studio, we'll have a look at what they've cooked up.'

Presenters and guests rise from their sofas and, tracked by the cameras, cross to the far side of the studio where a large screen has been placed, bearing the logo *The Great British Eat Off*. The screen is now wheeled away by studio hands to reveal a large white food-laden table. The logo is repeated on the front panel of the table.

'And here we are!' says Jordan. 'Just look at that spread! It looks like we've got everything here: there's your fish and chips, and we've got bangers and mash, shepherd's pie, toad in the hole, haddock casserole, steak and kidney pie—'

'—with more mash,' says Ruth.

'With more mash. And there's a Sunday roast, roast beef, roast potatoes, Yorkshire pudding, all the trimmings…'

'And I see a full English breakfast there.'

'Yes, look at that, we've got everything: sausages, bacon, fried eggs, fried bread, baked beans, mushrooms, grilled tomatoes…And oh, look: they've got desserts as well! "What's fer afters, mam?" Well, for afters we've got sticky toffee pudding, apple crumble, bread-and-butter pudding, treacle tart, and even bananas and custard: yes, the humble bananas and custard!' Turning to guest and interpreter: 'Now, Yuki, will you please come round here and take the chair of honour…?'

Obediently, Yuki sits herself in the chair behind the table, Shizuka placing herself attendant-like at her side.

'Now, are you ready, Yuki? You've got your knife and fork—are you okay with a knife and fork, or would you prefer chopsticks?'

'I am proficient in the use of knife and fork.'

'Excellent! Now, you're going to be on the clock of course, and you've got just three minutes to polish off everything you see on this table; just *three minutes*! Think you can do it?'

'I shall do my best!' (The exclamation mark is Yuki's, and unfortunately lost in the deadpan translation.)

'You'll do your best! I'm sensing a lot of confidence here! Well let's see if that confidence is justified as we now commence the *Great British Eat Off*!'

The buzzer sounds and Yuki Kinoshita goes into action, attacking first the plate directly in front of her, which happens to be the full English breakfast. Sausages, bacon, fried eggs, fried bread, baked beans, mushrooms, grilled tomatoes: all of them disappear into her mouth and apparently just slide straight down her throat. The plate emptied she picks up the next, the Shepard's pie, scooping it straight into her mouth. Then comes the bangers and mash, the pie and mash, the Sunday roast, the toad in the hole, the haddock casserole, and the fish and chips: all are vanquished and destroyed! And after the main course, the dessert: spoon in hand Yuki attacks the apple crumble, the bread-and-butter pudding, the treacle tart, the sticky toffee pudding; Yuki is unstoppable! The final plate, the bananas and custard disappear into the maw, and Yuki puts down the plate, still with five seconds to spare.

The buzzer rings, the applause erupts, and Yuki, smiling through food-smeared lips, distributes peace signs all round.

The presenters turn to the camera.

'Well, she did it!' announces Jordan. 'I wouldn't have thought it possible, but she actually did it!'

'She certainly did,' agrees Ruth.

'And with five seconds to spare! Now, how does someone so small put away that much food? I still just can't believe it!'

'Like you said, she must have hollow legs.'

'She must!' To Yuki: 'Now Yuki, can I ask you to come back to the sofa with us? If you can actually get up after putting away all that food!'

Yuki has no problem ambulating. Hosts and guests return to the sofas.

'Now, Yuki, how was it?'

'It was delicious. All of the food was very well prepared and very flavoursome.'

'But you must be feeling completely stuffed after eating all that nosh and in less than three minutes!'

'I'm feeling fine, thank you.'

Yuki now addresses some words directly at Shizuka.

'Miss Kinoshita inquires whether she may leave the studio now,' reports the latter.

'Oh-ho! You want to leave the studio, do you?' There is a note of triumph in Jordan's voice, and he exchanges significant looks with his wife. 'Perhaps to visit the little girl's room...? But weren't you just telling us that you *didn't* do as the Romans did? That after one of your eating binges you *don't* just bring it all back up again to stop yourself from piling on the pounds?'

'Yes, this is true.'

'Well then, we'll just give you a chance to prove that it's true by having you stay right where you are, where we can all see you. But,' standing up, 'if it turns out you really *can't* hold it in, then allow me to present you with *this*.'

And from behind the sofa Jordan Kendal produces a bucket, a traditional floor-cleaner's metal pail, and he places it with emphasis down on the coffee table in front of a bewildered-looking Yuki. 'There you go,' he says, resuming his seat. 'It's all yours, Yuki. Feel free to use it if you need to.'

'You wish me to use this bucket?' asks Yuki, via Shizuka.

'Well, we don't *want* you to use it,' says Jordan. 'But it's just there for you if you absolutely *need* to use it.'

Yuki shifts uncomfortably in her seat, exchanges a rapid flow of words with Shizuka. 'Miss Kinoshita would rather withdraw from the studio,' reports the latter.

'Well, I'm afraid Miss Kinoshita can*not* withdraw from the studio. We want her to stay right here where we can keep an eye on her.' To his wife: 'Don't we?'

'Yes, we insist on it!'

'But the bucket's there if you really can't hold it in…'

Another rapid exchange of Japanese.

'Very well. This seems rather unorthodox, but if it must be so then Miss Kinoshita will comply with your wishes and make use of the bucket.'

Yuki, looking uncomfortable, rises from the sofa, climbs onto the coffee table and, pulling down her knickers and shorts, lowers herself onto the metal bucket. The bucket echoes with a series of heavy thuds.

And the mystery of how Yuki Kinoshita manages to keep her weight down is very publicly solved.

Chapter Eleven
Cult Times

The feature film *Dr Who and the Daleks* holds a unique place in the history of the motion picture for being the only film in cinema history of which it can be said that the best thing about it is the sound that automatic doors make when they open and close. And it is to the accompaniment of this iconic sound effect that the sliding doors of the Cult Café, Camden High Street NW1, open to admit Mark Hunter.

The sign above the door, featuring the words Cult Café in bold letters against a background of a vista of outer space tightly packed with planets, comets and nebulae, announces the café's area of interest while carefully avoiding using any copyrighted images. When you walk inside you will find the serving counter is on your right, with the drinks menu on a board affixed to the wall behind it, and on your left a row of booths running the length of the wall, the remaining space occupied with tables and chairs. The walls above the booths are hung with large framed prints of vintage horror and sci-fi B-movies. One particular poster catches Mark's eye: *The Earth Dies Screaming*. He remembers watching that film once, back when he was a kid; he'd stayed up late to watch it one night on the black and white portable he had in his bedroom.

After discovering the letter in his wallet, Mark has made his way to the appointed meeting place as fast as London Transport could take him.

That girl! She conks him on the head and then writes a message saying she wants to meet him! Why did she have to hide it in the billfold of his wallet? Why couldn't she have put it somewhere he would have found it straight away? For that matter, if she wanted to talk to him, why couldn't she have just spoken to him down there in the carpark instead of hitting him over the head with a blunt instrument?

Mark considers it just as well he hasn't been able to get hold of Rick Bedford this morning; because he cannot help but feel that that underlined injunction in Amber's letter for him to 'come alone' was made with particular reference to Bedford. That his display of temper at the pub the other night might have been a factor in putting the girl off talking to them seems very easy to believe.

(The reason for Rick Bedford's absence, as Mark will discover later, is that his hotel still under surveillance, Bedford had decided to take the bull by the horns and wring some answers out of the man on duty; and that man, seeing the burly American marching purposefully towards him, had turned and ran—and two hours later he is still running.)

The rendezvous was set for last night and Mark knows it was too much to hope that the girl might be in the café this morning; and a quick survey of the room reveals that she is not: there are just two customers at present, both men, both at work on their laptops.

An obese Princess Leia stands on duty behind the counter. Mark walks up to her., vaguely wondering if her side buns are the real deal or not.

'Morning,' says she. 'What can I get you?'

'I'm looking for someone, actually,' replies Mark. 'Do you work here often?'

'All the time, pretty much. I own the place.'

'Oh you do, do you? Well, it's a nice little place you've got here. Been in business long?'

'Three years now.'

'And you run it all by yourself?'

'Apart from a couple of weekend part-timers, yes.'

'Would one of those part-timers happen to be a black girl called Amber?'

'No, but I can do you a black girl called Amber who's a regular customer here.'

'Ah! I knew she had some connection to the place; I just wasn't sure what. You see, I was supposed to meet her here last night.'

'Oh, it was you, was it? I thought she looked like she was waiting for somebody.'

'Sitting on her own, was she?'

'She *always* sits on her own, but last night she was sitting on her own and looking like she was waiting for somebody. Why did you stand her up, then?'

'I didn't; not intentionally; due to an unfortunate chain of circumstances, I didn't actually receive her message until this morning.'

'Well, it's a bit late you turning up here now, isn't it? Or did you think she'd still be here waiting for you? I'd say you better get in touch with her and start doing some serious apologising.'

'I would dearly love to get in touch with her, but unfortunately I don't have any contact information.'

'Well, just message her on the dating app! Or has she already blocked you? Wouldn't blame her if she has; no-one likes getting stood up.'

'Erm, you seem to be labouring under a misapprehension here: we weren't meeting for a blind date—which by the way, I would say I was a bit old for in this particular case.'

The woman shrugs. 'She might have been after a sugar daddy.'

'Well, it wasn't a date. We had some… business to discuss. Do you happen to have her contact number or know where she lives…?'

'No, I don't,' says the woman, now frowning with suspicion. 'And even if I did, I wouldn't tell you. How do I know it really was you she was meeting up with?'

Mark reaches for identification. 'I can understand your suspicion, but I am here as an official. My credentials.' He shows her his card.

The woman's eyes widen. 'Jesus Christ!' She looks from the card to its owner. 'Is Amber in trouble?'

'Not with me, she isn't. I just need to speak to her because I believe she is in possession of some information I urgently need.'

'What kind of information?'

'I'm afraid I'm going to have to be very clichéd here by telling you that I'm not at liberty to say. But it really is important that I talk to that girl and as soon as possible.'

'Well, I'm sorry, but I really *don't* have her phone number or anything. She's a customer here and we say hello, but that's about it. She doesn't say much, that girl; a quiet one; a lot of them are who come here. Usually sits on her own.'

'I see. Are there any particular times she's more likely to be here?'

'No,' shaking her head. 'She just turns up whenever: daytime, evening, weekday, weekend. You can't set your clock by her.'

'Hmm. Well, I can't really sit here all day just on the off-chance… Could I leave a message with you? I could write her a note and you could pass it onto her the next time she comes in.'

'Sure, I can do that for you.'

'And if I may, I'll also give you my contact number, just in case something happens and you need to reach me,' says Mark. He reaches into his breast pocket for notepaper and pen.

'No problem,' says the woman. 'And what would you like to drink while you're writing your letter?'

Taking the hint, Mark orders a latte.

Chapter Twelve
The Boardroom Jungle

You may recall Jensen relating to Brunner back in chapter one that Flat-Sol Park was so named on account of her having bravely challenged the then-existing company rule that all female employees must wear only high-heeled shoes in the workplace—well, Jensen was completely wrong about that because it just happens to be the case that the name Flat-Sol was the one given to her by her parents and has nothing whatsoever to do with her preference for sensible shoes.

But the rest of the story is true.

When Flat-Sol had first come to the UK to work for the Parkhurst Corporation she had worn three-inch heels because high-heeled shoes were part of the established uniform of the corporate woman; she didn't particularly like them but she had worn them because she had no desire to jeopardise her career prospects by challenging the status quo. But as she had made her rapid progress up the corporate ladder, she began to find that in wearing high-heels the ascent was starting to hurt her poor feet more and more.

What was so good about shoes with high heels? By keeping the foot in an unnatural position, they strained muscles and tendons, they affected your posture and caused you to walk in a way that was likewise unnatural, leading to aches and strains that could reach all the way up your back. The only points in favour of high heels seemed to be entirely on the aesthetic side; they were good because they were deemed look good—and even that was a matter of opinion.

And so Flat-Sol decided she would switch to wearing flat-soled shoes. She felt that she had now risen high enough, made herself valuable enough to her superiors and respected enough by her inferiors that she would be able to commit this minor infraction of the rules without incurring any risk or opposition.

And at first it seemed that she had gauged the situation correctly. She had begun to walk the carpeted corridors of financial power wearing flat-soled loafers and while it had not passed unnoticed, it had passed without reprimand.

Until the man at the very top had seen them.

Old Jaundyce Parkhurst (first name pronounced 'Jaundiss' as in 'Jarndiss'—and anyone who says otherwise, you send them to me) was, when CEO, rarely seen in person by the lower echelons, as is now the case with his successor. But in the hierarchy (or *higher*-archy) of the Parkhurst Corporation, to climb the corporate ladder is literally to climb to the higher storeys of the building—and nearer you come to that top-storey seat of power, the more likely you are to come under the direct gaze of the big boss—and one day Flat-Sol Park had come under that executive gaze and, said gaze settling on her feet, Jaundyce Parkhurst's face had darkened with a frown. It was not just the infraction of the rules flaunted under his very eyes that had caused Jaundyce Parkhurst to frown; no, there were other factors at work, first and foremost that Jaundyce Parkhurst happened to be a shoe fetishist. And in common with most members of this fraternity, it was shoes with heels that tickled his fancy; the higher the heel the more was his fancy tickled. As far as Jaundyce Parkhurst was concerned all professional women ought to wear high-heeled shoes, whatever that profession might be: firefighters, mountaineers, track runners and tennis players; all women in all walks of life, without exception, ought to be doing that walking wearing high-heeled shoes. Flat-soled shoes on the female foot were not just a sexual turn-off for Jaundyce Parkhurst; they were offensive to his sight, an obscenity, a hideous spectacle, a blot on the landscape. And now here was a woman, and a woman in his own employ, having the unmitigated gall to parade around in flat-soled shoes!

Jaundyce Parkhurst, after having been forced to accept that what he was seeing was not some hallucination or trick of the light, had turned to his personal assistant. 'Who is that woman?' he had asked her, pointing an accusing finger.

'Flat-Sol Park, Mr Parkhurst,' had been the reply.

'Park? Park? Is that the Park I've been hearing so many good things about?'

It was.

'And you say her first name is *Flat-Sol*?'

'Yessir.'

'And that's *really* her name?'

'Yessir.'

Flat-Sol? *Flat-Sol*? How had someone with an offensive name like that even been employed here in the first place?

He approached the owner of the regrettable name and coughed politely. Flat-Sol found herself for the first time looking into the liver-spotted, shaggy eyebrowed, wrinkled *roué* visage of her septuagenarian CEO.

'Miss Park,' he said. 'I presume you know who I am?'

'Of course, sir. And it is a great pleasure to finally meet you in person.'

'Quite so, quite so. I have been hearing good things about you, my dear. But, erm, there is one teeny-tweeny problem…'

'And what would that be, sir?'

'Well, it would be, erm… those… things on your feet…'

'My shoes, sir?'

'Yes, your shoes. Office regulations clearly state that all female employees must wear shoes with heels of at least… what is it, three inches…?' turning to his assistant.

'Two-and-a-half, Mr Parkhurst.'

'Heels of at least two-and-a-half inches in length, and your shoes… do not appear to have heels at all…'

'Yessir; that is very observant of you. I wear these flat-soled shoes because I find them to be more comfortable. I can assure you they do not impair my efficiency with respect to discharging my duties.'

'Well, that's not really the point, is it? You might be able to discharge your duties walking around on your hands, but you still wouldn't do it, would you? These… these *things* you're wearing are a violation of company policy. Didn't you know this? Because if you didn't know, then fair enough, we can just—'

'Oh no, sir, I am fully conversant with company regulations, and indeed up until recently I complied with them in regards to footwear and wore three-inch heels; but as they began to cause me increasing physical discomfort, I made the decision to switch to these flat shoes and discomfort has eased.'

'Well, I'm sorry my dear, but that's just not on, is it? You can't just make decisions like that willy-nilly, off your own bat. There's protocol to be followed. No, no, you must go back to wearing high-heeled shoes, and you must do so at once. And as for that discomfort you spoke of; well, I'm afraid you'll just have to put up with it, won't you? We all have our crosses to bear.'

'What if I were to acquire a medical certificate from my chiropodist, sir?' suggested Flat-Sol. 'A certificate stating that for health reasons I must be allowed to wear flat-soled shoes?'

'A medical certificate? Well, of course you could get a medical certificate, yes of course you could; but we'd be very sorry to lose such a valuable employee…'

'Lose me, sir?'

'Well, yes; we'd have to let you go, wouldn't we? A certificate like that would mean you were medically unfit for work, wouldn't it? An invalid, a cripple. We'd have to pension you off.'

'But I am fit for work—'

'My dear, if you are unable to function in the required office uniform, you are *not* fit for work in this office. Simple as that. If you wish to remain here—and you *do* wish to remain here, I take it?'

'Yessir, I desire very much to remain here.'

'Good. Then I expect to see those lovely feet of yours out of those monstrosities and back where they belong in three-inch heels when next I see you.'

And Jaundyce Parkhurst had taken his leave, blithely assuming that his request was as good as already carried out. But it was not carried out and when next he saw Flat-Sol Park she was still wearing flat shoes. Parkhurst couldn't believe his eyes. Surely this time he just *had* to be hallucinating! He had to turn to his assistant for confirmation of his visual clarity.

Another polite clearing of the throat. 'Miss Park. Perhaps we didn't understand each other last time? I said that you were to stop wearing those… things, and return to wearing the prescribed regulation footwear, this being shoes with heels.'

'No sir, I did understand you,' was the calm reply.

'And yet you persist in wearing those abominations?'

'I'm afraid I do, sir.'

Jaundyce Parkhurst was flabbergasted. So accustomed was he to having his every wish obeyed without even having to so much as raise his voice, he found himself at a complete loss as to how to deal with this act of unruffled insubordination.

'Bu-but why?' he stammered.

'They are more comfortable to wear.'

'And I told you that was neither here nor there! I *did* tell you that, didn't I?' To his assistant: 'I *did* tell her, didn't I?'

'You did, Mr Parkhurst,' replied the assistant.

'You see? I told you! I told you that you just had to put up with the discomfort!'

'True, but it seems needless to have to endure the discomfort when the situation can so easily be remedied by wearing sensible shoes.'

'Sensible…! Is that what you call them? Well, as I have repeatedly told you, those so-called "sensible" shoes of yours are a violation of the Parkhurst Corporation regulations, and therefore to persist in wearing them is a flagrant act of insubordination!'

'Perhaps.'

'Perhaps? *Perhaps?* There's no "perhaps" about it!'

'Perhaps not.'

'Per—' With a handkerchief he mops his flurried brow: 'Now look here, Miss Flat-Sol Park!—and you really should do something about that first name of yours—You will either start conforming to the established dress code or else you will find yourself in front of a disciplinary committee! And let me tell you, this is no idle threat! Do we understand each other?'

'Perfectly, sir.'

'Good!'

And not wishing to prolong the debate, Jaundyce Parkhurst took leave of Flat-Sol Park (whom he just did *not* understand) and took refuge in his *sanctum-sanctorum*, where he spent a consoling afternoon with his private secretaries and his collection of high-heeled shoes.

But if he hoped that the matter was now closed, he hoped in vain. With a display of indomitable passive-resistance that would have done Mr Bartleby proud, Flat-Sol continued to arrive to work wearing her flat-soled loafers. These unassuming shoes, these sensible size sevens were becoming legendary throughout the Parkhurst Building. And as for the person whose feet they adorned, what could she be thinking of? Defying an order to cease and desist that came from the CEO himself! What were her motives? What was she hoping to achieve?

The inevitable result came at last, Jaundyce Parkhurst carried out his threat and Flat-Sol's first trip in the executive elevator to the top floor of the Parkhurst Building came when she was summoned to appear before a disciplinary hearing. She obeyed the summons punctually and without demur, to all appearances completely unconcerned.

The lofty portals were opened and she walked into the boardroom. Before her, dominating the room, was the long table with the members of the board seated on either side; and in the big chair at the head of the table sat Jaundyce Parkhurst himself, his assistant standing at his side. Calmly, she took her place at the foot of the table, where there was no chair because she was expected to stand, and she quailed not under the gaze of all those eyes. But then, murmurs of surprise started to make their way along the long table, from one end to the other, until they reached the ears of the president himself. He looked staggered. A hurried consultation with his assistant and the latter quickly crossed the room, had a good long look at Flat-Sol's feet and returning to the CEO, whispered her report.

Said Parkhurst: 'Miss Park, it appears that you have finally relented, and that you are now wearing high-heeled shoes as you should be! I'm pleased, of course I'm pleased, overjoyed in fact; but why couldn't you have done this sooner? It would have saved us all a lot of trouble, you know.'

'And for this I apologise most humbly, sir. It was my desire to express my respect and gratitude for you by adorning my feet with the most presentable pair of high-heeled shoes that money could buy, and as the search for these took some time and the shoes had to be imported from overseas, their arrival was delayed until only the early hours of this very morning. And now my only desire is to present them to you personally, that you may inspect them for your approval, and I trust, your approbation.'

'Well, if that's all you want to do, then come here, Miss Park, come here! I can't *wait* to see them!'

'I shall come at once, sir.'

And, much to everyone's surprise, instead of walking round it, Flat-Sol climbed up onto the table, doubtless the better to display her new shoes to all the members of the board. The shoes were a pair of five-inch stiletto heels that were a fetishist's wet dream. She now began to traverse the length of the conference table, and she moved with a catwalk poise and confidence that made it seem hard to believe she hadn't been wearing five-inch heels since she first learned to walk.

And she came to a halt before Jaundyce Parkhurst, and she towered over him as she turned and posed herself to display her new shoes to their best advantage; and old Parkhurst literally drooled at the mouth, his bulging eyes fixed on the gleaming black shoes with their blade-like heels.

'I trust my footwear meets with your approval, sir?' inquired Flat-Sol.

'Oh yes! Oh yes! They're exquisite! Yes, my dear, absolutely exquisite!'

'Perhaps you would care to examine them more closely?'

'Oh, yes, yes! By all means! Let me see them, let me see them!'

With the provocative, deliberate movements of a redlight performance artist, Flat-Sol dropped to a sitting position in front of her aroused CEO and placed first one foot and then the other on the arms of his chair. She brought first one foot, then the other for Parkhurst's eager inspection.

'Oh yes, oh yes…! Simply divine, my dear; simply divine…!' enthused he, quivering with delight, fondling and caressing the shoes with his hairy-fingered hands, devouring them with his eyes.

And it was to be the last meal those eyes ever had because Flat-Sol then drove her spiked heels into them.

Parkhurst screamed like a strangled peacock, hands clawing at his eyes. He tried to rise from his chair, stumbled to the floor, and here he floundered around, tears of blood pouring from his ruptured eyes. And the board members, after a moment of stunned silence, the board members started to laugh. Yes, they started to laugh at the screaming man crawling helplessly around the floor, and they got up from their chairs and started to push him, kick him and trip him, laughing and jeering, the pack turning on the injured member of the group. And pack-like they instantly accepted as their new leader the one who had vanquished the old.

Flat-Sol Park was triumphant. Jaundyce Parkhurst, driven completely insane by his downfall was pensioned off to a lunatic asylum, his name reduced along with his status. Henceforth he was merely Jaundyce Hurst; his shares and his position as CEO transferred to Flat-Sol and with them a portion of the company name, it now being understood that Parkhurst Corporation now stood for Park and Hurst.

And Flat-Sol Park's first mandate as president was to declare that high-heeled shoes were to be banned entirely from the offices of the Parkhurst Building, and that henceforth flat shoes only would be worn by all.

Cut to the present and Flat-Sol Park, opening the doors and walking into the boardroom, is greeted by the unexpected sight of a body stretched out at full length on the conference table. Lying perfectly straight in the exact centre of the table, the recumbent form has the appearance of a freshly laid out corpse—except that this corpse is snoring.

It is Yu-Mi Park, dressed in her crisp new business suit, sleeping peacefully on the hard surface of the boardroom table. She hasn't even taken her shoes off.

Flat-Sol shakes her sister by the shoulder. Yu-Mi's eyes open blearily, focus on her sister as, with the back of hand, she wipes away the drool that has trickled from her open mouth.

'What are you doing, Yu-Mi?' inquires Flat-Sol.

'Having a rest...' mumbles Yu-Mi, sitting up on her elbows.

'Well, you cannot rest here,' Flat-Sol tells her. 'I have an important meeting. Go back to your office if you need to rest. Or better still, why not do something? Have you checked your email yet? Some of your new colleagues will be sure to have sent you messages.'

'I already looked...' says Yu-Mi. 'They just keep sending me porn.'

'Of course they do; that is just their way of welcoming you. I had the same experience myself when I first began working here. You must remember to send them thankyou messages.'

There comes a knock on the double doors.

'Enter,' says Flat-Sol crisply.

The door opens and in walk Brunner and Jensen.

'I will be with you shortly,' says Flat-Sol. To her sister: 'Come, you must leave now.'

Yu-Mi shuffles herself off the table. Flat-Sol takes her by the arm and escorts her to the door. 'I will see you later.'

'What should I do...?'

'Return to your office and view some of the pornography you have been sent. It will be educational for you.'

'Okay...'

Yu-Mi departs. Flat-Sol closes the door and turns to face Brunner and Jensen. A rare smile forms on her face as she regards the two men.

'You can perhaps surmise why I have summoned you both here?' she says, walking over to the table and leaning back against it.

'You're going to tell us which one of us has got the job?' says Jensen.

'Correct,' says Flat-Sol. 'Or rather, that will be decided upon shortly, once you have taken the final test. Remove your jackets.'

Exchanging puzzled looks Brunner and Jensen obey.

'Place them on the table here.'

They do so.

'Now stand before me.'

They stand before Flat-Sol. She approaches Jensen, runs her hand along the sleeve of his shirt, across the chest, feeling the muscles of the arms and torso, taut and unyielding beneath the thin material, all the while looking him squarely in the eye, undaunted by his superior height and physical strength.

She moves onto Brunner and subjects him to the same lingering inspection.

'Excellent.' She returns to her place at the end of the table. 'As I have already told you, I find you both admirably suited for the position for which you have been accepted on a trial basis. You are both fine physical specimens and possessed of the drive and business acumen which I demand of my subordinates. You both understand that sentimentality has no place in the corporate arena; that frailties such as compassion and mercy must never be allowed to interfere with performing your duties and achieving your goals.

'During your period of probation, you have been working together and performing tasks that may have seemed trivial and undemanding; however, this was the necessary preliminary to the final test before you now. Being young men of similar age, similar background, similar proclivities, you have naturally bonded since working for the Parkhurst Corporation; you are friends as well as colleagues and mix socially as well as professionally. But only one of you can become my personal assistant and of that one I demand a greater allegiance to myself than you owe to any other individual. Therefore, your final test will be to compete in a test of physical strength to determine which of you displays the greater loyalty to myself.'

Brunner and Jensen look confused. 'A test of strength…?' says Jensen. 'What kind of test…?'

'I thought that would be obvious,' replies Flat-Sol. 'You compete against each other; you engage in hand-to-hand physical combat and the victor is awarded the promotion.'

'You want us to fight each other…?' Brunner smiles uncomfortably. 'You mean, right here and now…?'

'I mean precisely that. And please remember, this is not a sporting event: there will be no rules, no intervals. You simply have to fight one another until one has been vanquished by the other.'

'You're kidding, right…?'

'No, Mr Brunner, I am not "kidding." The unarmed combat I have just outlined is your final test. You must fight to earn your promotion. And as a further incentive—' Flat-Sol stands up, unbuckles her belt, unzips her skirt and steps out of it. She folds it neatly and places it on the nearest chair. The two men stare at her. Although partly concealed by the length of her blouse, it is apparent she is wearing no briefs of any kind beneath the translucent sheath of her tights. Flat-Sol now sits on the table-edge, parts her legs, places her feet on two chairs, and taking hold of the crotch of her tights, pulls and tears the fragile material, exposing the brown lips of her vagina and its nest of rampant pubic hair.

'And as a further incentive,' she repeats, still cool and businesslike, 'the victor will be rewarded with immediate access to myself.'

Brunner laughs hollowly. 'This is crazy! If you think me and Jensen are going to—'

Jensen's fist smashes into his jaw.

Brunner staggers back, his face a picture of disbelief. 'What the fuck—?'

Jensen punches him again. 'Oh, come on; don't look so surprised,' he says irritably. 'I told you it was never going to be both of us. There's only room for one, and you're in my way.'

Jensen hits him again and again. At first Brunner, stunned by the sudden onslaught, fights only a weakly defensive fight, but his shock at Jensen's abrupt treachery soon turns to rage and he takes the offensive.

And now the fight begins in earnest, the two men punching, dodging punches, grappling, wrestling. They seem evenly matched, sometimes one man having the upper hand, sometimes the other. But as Brunner knows too well, Jensen has always had that slight edge over himself. And right now it is Jensen's determination that gives him that edge—Jensen is determined to win the fight, while Brunner is only determined not to lose.

Slowly but surely, Jensen starts to gain the upper hand. He redoubles his attack, and Brunner is back on the defensive, dodging and deflecting punches but throwing none of his own. And now Jensen *knows* he is going to win. He throws punch after punch, and Brunner starts to weaken. He staggers, his eyes clouding over, his movements become sluggish, his efforts to fend off his opponent's punches steadily less and less effective. And Jensen keeps on hitting him and finally Brunner's eyes roll up in their sockets; he collapses to the floor and down he stays.

Drawing a deep breath, Jensen swings round to face Flat-Sol Park, sitting spread-legged on the table, one hand working at her crotch, the narrow eyes behind her designer glasses enflamed by the spectacle of the combat. Jensen, dripping sweat, his shirt torn open, face bruised and bleeding, walks up to her, smiling, confident. He knows he looks a mess right now but he's not concerned: it's fine to look like you've been in a fight if you're the one who *won* the fight.

'I guess this makes me your new personal assistant,' and he unzips his fly, pulls out his penis. It quickly grows to tumescence.

Flat-Sol places a restrained flat of her hand against the urgent member.

'You forget yourself, Mr Jensen.'

'What? You said if I—'

'I said if you vanquished your opponent, the situation is yours. You have yet to do this.'

'What are you talking about? Look at him, he's out for the count, he—!'

'Yes, but he is still *alive*, Mr Jensen. Therefore he is not yet vanquished.'

Jensen stares at her. 'But you—you never said it was a fight to the death…'

She shrugs. 'Perhaps I did not; but nevertheless it is so. You must extinguish your opponent before you can take up your new position in the corporation. Finish what you have begun, Mr Jensen,' gripping his penis. 'Only then will you have earned your promotion.'

'But, I can't just—!'

'The matter is not up for discussion, Mr Jensen. If you concerned of possible consequences to yourself, set your mind at ease: there will *be* no consequences. The body will be efficiently disposed of; no crime will be laid at your door.' Tightening her grip on his penis, her eyes bore into his. 'Now be the man I know you to be and *kill your opponent*, Mr Jensen. He is an obstacle in your path. *Kill him.*'

Boiling with rage, Jensen bunches his fists, eyes glaring hatred at his employer—then he swings round and marches up to Brunner, who is just beginning to stir. Groaning, he weakly raises his head—and Jensen kicks it. He kicks it again and he kicks it again and he keeps kicking until Brunner's head has become a bloody pulp.

And now Jensen turns back to Flat-Sol Park, aroused, and with eyes full of hate and resentment.

She smiles.

Chapter Thirteen
The Second Piano

Media whore though she undoubtedly is, one thing Dodo Dupont draws the line at is appearing on debate programmes. She considers them to be a complete waste of time: you have your two opposing factions assailing each other with their conflicting opinions, with neither side ever convincing the other one that they're wrong; so, aside from any entertainment value they may provide, a complete waste of time. So thinks Dodo; and this is why although she is happy to appear on talk shows, she will always decline invitations to appear on debate programmes.

Tonight however, Dodo is appearing on a talk show that is already fast deteriorating into a debate.

It wasn't supposed to be this way, not originally. Mayumi and herself had been invited onto *The Culture Show* to talk about their *Afternoon Dreams* collaboration, and originally it was to have been just the two of them in conversation with the programme's affable host, Melvyn Sucrose. It was only when they arrived at Television Centre that they discovered they would be sharing the interview with an additional guest.

And the additional guest happens to be Joanna Fairbright, cultural correspondent for the *Observer*, and caustic critic of Mayumi Takahashi's art—and the last-minute addition of a third party who can only be expected to be antagonistic towards the other two guests is in no coincidence; as an embarrassed and apologetic Melvyn Sucrose explained to Dodo and Mayumi before the show.

'Look, I'm dreadfully sorry about all this; I don't like it any more than you do, but I really didn't have any choice! You know what they're like these days,' ('they' being 'the people upstairs' at the BBC); 'and they're worried that viewers will accuse the station of endorsing your photography, Mayumi, which as you know is not everybody's cup of tea... And so, they felt that the only way to avoid any negative viewer reaction would be to have "both sides of the argument" as they call it represented on the show...'

'And they had to go and choose Joanna Fairbright of all people?'

Dodo Dupont considers Joanna Fairbright to be a royal pain in the arse

Yes, reader: even Dodo Dupont, the easy-going, always-affable, takes-people-as-she-finds-them consummate 'people person' Dodo Dupont, considers Joanna Fairbright, cultural correspondent for the *Observer*, to be a royal pain in the arse.

And the reason for this is simple enough: because Joanna Fairbright *is* a royal pain in the arse.

'Oh, "celebrating the beauty of women," is it? Is that what you call it, do you? Masturbation fodder for men, is what *I'd* call it!'

'Look if Yumi says her art is about celebrating the beauty of women, then that's what it is. It's *her* art, isn't it? It's not for you or anyone else to say what her intentions were when she created it.'

'Oh, it's not for me or anyone else to say, is it? So I'm not even allowed to *speak* now, aren't I? Is that what you're saying?'

'Of course that's not what I'm saying...!'

'Oh, of *course* that's not what you're saying! I just imagined it, I suppose!'

See what I mean.

Four tube-framed swivel chairs arranged in a semi-circle comprise the spartan interview set; sofas are strictly for daytime talk shows. Even the dark blue colour of the wall panel behind them is somehow suggestive of weightier, more serious discussion. No cosy, pastel shades here. From left to right, the first chair is occupied by Dodo. Dressed in her regular casual attire of t-shirt, cargo pants and aggressive boots, she sits with one leg resting on the other. Next to her is Mayumi, who wears a broadbrimmed hat, burgundy in colour, a waistcoat of the same colour over a black satin blouse, flared trousers and platform boots, also in burgundy. She sits with legs close together, arms on tubular armrests, pivoting herself back and forth in her swivel chair (which as Dodo knows is Mayumi's way of expressing irritation.)

In the third chair sits our genial host, Melvyn Sucrose. Victorian scholar and *Doctor Who* aficionado, he is a mild-mannered, academic-looking man with gold-framed glasses and a dark suit. The Beeb's hair stylists have done their best to tame his unruly brown hair into some semblance of manageability.

And in chair number four sits wheel number five: the gate crasher ruining the party for everyone else, Joanna Fairbright. Dressed in black jacket and ankle length skirt, she has mid-length black hair framing a thin oval face which, with its hawkish nose and her horsey teeth, admirably caricatures its owner's temperament. That nose whose length is so well-suited as a viewfinder for looking down on people; and those cavernous nostrils are ideally formed for emitting derisive snorts; and the teeth whose equine plenitude is so perfect for emphasising curled-back scornful lips.

Says Dodo: 'Look, all I'm saying is that an artist's intentions *are* whatever the artist says they are and to dispute them is basically calling either the artist a liar or telling them you know what they're thinking better than they do. It is only how the art is perceived by others that's a subjective quantity.'

'Oh, perception's a *subjective* quantity now, is it? Well, silly me for not realising that! So you're saying we can't even believe our own eyes now, can we?'

'No, Joanna, I'm not saying that; I'm talking about how your mind judges these things, and that when you say that Yumi's photography is just masturbation fodder for men, then that is the judgement *your* mind has made; therefore, it's a subjective opinion and not an empirical fact.'

'Oh, it's just my subjective opinion, is it? And I suppose all those men queueing up to see her exhibition of Japanese women with their legs spread aren't just there to look at something they can jerk themselves off to?'

'No, they are not!' speaks up Mayumi, crossly. 'Jerking off is not allowed in art gallery!'

'Er, yes, she does have a point there,' speaks up Melvyn Sucrose. 'They don't allow that sort of thing at art galleries and they never have. Now Mayumi, I believe you, in common with many people in your country, see erotic art as something that can be relaxing, rather than arousing, to look upon. Isn't that right?'

A valiant attempt to turn the conversation on the part of our host, but one sadly doomed to failure, because the moment Mayumi opens her mouth to reply, Joanna Fairbright jumps in and beats her to it. 'Oh, it's *relaxing* now, is it? Pornography is relaxing, is it? Oh yes, it's not intended for sexual arousal at all, is it? It's designed to *relax* you! Yes: put your feet up, pour yourself a cup of tea, and open up a dirty magazine! Of *course*! Now why didn't I realise that before?'

Dodo: 'We're not talking about dirty magazines, for Christ's sake. We're talking about Yumi's photography—!'

'Which is essentially the same thing!'

Mayumi: 'No, it isn't! My art is not porno! Woman is beautiful and my art captures that beauty, and to look at beautiful things is soothing the soul—'

'Oh, it's soothing to the *soul* now, is it? Soothing the *soul* is it, to have women put on display like that, reducing them to lumps of meat—!'

Dodo: 'I'd like to remind you that I've posed for Yumi myself, and I did not in any way feel like I was being reduced to a lump of meat, as you call it.'

Mayumi: 'It is not just body, it is mind also that I capture in my photographs! When I take picture of beautiful woman, I show her mind as well as her body!'

'Oh, you manage to take pictures of their *minds* as well as their bodies, do you? How very clever of you! Well, you'll have to show me where exactly in those pictures of yours I'm supposed to look to see their minds! Because all I see is a lot of naked flesh.'

'Then you're not looking properly. Get some glasses'

'Look, can we just get this interview back on track?' says Dodo, controlling her temper with an effort. 'This was supposed to be about *Afternoon Dreams*, about Yumi's intentions behind the project, but you're not letting her get a word in edgeways—'

'Oh, I'm not letting her get a word in edgeways, am I? So, I just have to sit here quietly, do I? Oh, wonderful! So now I'm not even entitled to express my opinions!'

'Of course you're entitled to express your stupid opinions! But Mayumi's entitled to express herself through her art, isn't she? And she—'

'Oh yes, and of course *everybody*'s trying to stop poor Mayumi Takahashi from expressing herself through her porn—sorry, her *art*, aren't they?'

'Well actually, some people do seem to be very determined to stop her,' steps in Melvyn Sucrose. 'It was only three days ago there was an attempt on her life—'

'Oh yes, the attempt on her life! Let's not forget that! The grand piano that fell from the roof of the Elysium Gallery! And of course, that *certainly* wasn't a put-up job, was it? That *certainly* wasn't a carefully arranged publicity stunt, was it? Oh no, not at all!'

'No, it bloody wasn't!'

'Yes! If it wasn't for Dodo, I would be dead now! Squashed!'

'Oh yes, *of course* you would! If it hadn't been for your dear, sweet Dodo, who just *happened* to hear a noise and look up at just the right moment—!'

Dodo hears a noise. She looks up. She sees an object detach itself from the gridwork of the studio ceiling high above.

'Look out!' she yells. Springing from her chair, she grabs Mayumi and dives from the set.

Says Joanna: 'Oh yes, *of course!* Look out, look out! Everyone run for cover! There's another piano about to fall—!'

CRASH!

It smashes into the ground with a shattering impact. The fallen object is not actually a piano, but a studio floodlight. Less spectacular perhaps, but it has done just as thorough a job of crushing Joanna Fairbright to death as the most robust of grand pianos would have done.

Pandemonium in the studio.

'Cut transmission!' somebody yells.

Camera crew and studio hands converge on the interview set. Melvyn Sucrose picks himself up. Dodo helps Mayumi to her feet. All eyes are on the impact area.

Only Joanna Fairbright's legs project from beneath the buckled form of the huge floodlight—her legs and a rapidly spreading pool of blood.

Melvyn Sucrose, on seeing all this blood, discovers for the first time in his life that he suffers from acute hemophobia, and he faints in Dodo's arms.

Quickly passing her burden onto one of the cameramen, Dodo looks up at the ceiling. Shielding her eyes from the glare of the lights, she descries two figures running along one of the catwalks.

'They're still up there!'

She runs for the far wall, where a wooden staircase zigzags its way to the upper regions of the studio.

The room suddenly plunges into total darkness.

More swearing and cries of alarm.

Dodo listens. She hears footsteps clattering down the stairs. She runs towards the sound. Someone barrels into her, knocking her off-balance. She makes a grab for whoever it is but misses. Moments later a rectangle of light appears off to the left. The doors! They're escaping from the studio! Dodo makes a beeline for the spot, and such is her unerring sense of direction that in spite of the darkness she hits them head on—but unfortunately the fleeing assailants having taken the precaution of locking the doors behind them, and instead of yielding to her they knock her flat on her back.

By the time the lights come back and the alarm raised, the assailants have made a clean getaway.

Chapter Fourteen
The Professor and the Avoidants

When, a few chapters ago, I introduced the reader to Professor Rajni Sunnybrook (her 'official' introduction, having previously appeared incognito), if I gave you the impression that in pursuit of her duties as a mental health practitioner she was, by dispensing words like lethal injections, systematically sending all of her patients to their self-inflicted deaths, then I have done the good Professor an injustice: because I know of at least two of her patients who still very much alive and (physically) well. Rajni has put these two survivors of her counselling technique to good use, having turned them both into her slaves. (Whether she spared these two expressly with a view to making them her slaves, or if the idea only occurred to her later, I couldn't say.)

Two deeply troubled teens, their names are Jenny and Ian. Both of them suffer from, amongst other things, avoidant personality disorder, a variant of schizoid personality disorder and which indeed some experts argue is the same condition trading under a different name—and let me tell you, Rajni with her expert's eye for the symptoms of these disorders, gets a real kick out of watching them suffer! Indeed, with judicious application of verbal pokes and prods, she does all she can to aggravate their conditions (it not being in her best interests to have her slaves showing any signs of improvement, as this might lead to insubordination.)

What cracks Rajni up the most is that Ian and Jenny clearly fancy the pants off each other. Or rather, to be more Thomson and Thompson, the fact is clear to *herself*, expert observer of their behaviour as she is, but it is no clearer than mud to the young people themselves. Both are very much aware of the feelings each possesses for the other, but neither has the least idea that those feelings are in any way reciprocated or that they ever could be; and being afflicted as they are with avoidant personality disorder with its inbuilt terror of being rejected in any way, both are far too scared of rejection to ever even *hint* at the feelings each has for the other, let alone to boldly confess them out loud. So there they both are, these two love-starved youngsters, literally within arm's reach of each other, each yearning for the other with every fibre of their repressed beings—and neither one can bring themselves to take the plunge and make that first move.

As you can imagine, Rajni has hours of fun laughing up her sleeve as the two of them silently pine away with feelings unuttered, suffering endless torment, close in physical proximity, but forever sundered by the yawning abyss of their own inhibitions.

What a hoot!

(Rajni, you see, considers herself to have been dealt a very unfair hand by life, and as such she finds she derives a measure of consolation from observing, and indeed exacerbating, the miseries of other people. And why not? Whatever gets you through the day, right?)

'...CCTV footage shows what is believed to be a man and two women as they flee from BBC Television Centre shortly after the attack. It has been suggested that Mayumi Takahashi might have been the intended target after having been the victim of a previous attempt on her life on Monday evening—'

'Switch it off, switch it off!' screams Jenny, clawing her hair.

APD, in common with most personality disorders, comes with a range of add-on extras, the most common of which are depression and anxiety—so when it comes to worrying, both Jenny and Ian are premier league. This morning, knowing that they are wanted felons and are all over the news, their anxiety has gone into meltdown.

'What does it matter if it's on or off?' demands Rajni. 'It doesn't change the fact that it's there, does it?' Nevertheless she picks up the remote and switches off the television.

'They'll catch us, they'll catch us!'

'They *won't* catch us! Just calm down and examine the facts: what have they got to go on? Some CCTV footage of three people in hoodies running down a street at night! We weren't wearing our normal clothes and no-one saw our faces, did they? There's no way they can identify us!'

'Yeah, but what about at the hostel? They'll know that I was out all last night!'

'And so bloody what? You've stayed out all night lots of times! They're not going to connect you with one particular murder just because you happened to be out when it happened!'

'They will, they will!' insists Jenny. 'They'll be after us!' (I should probably mention here that paranoia is another one of the add-on extras that can come with APD.)

It is morning, and we are in the modestly-sized front room of the rented terrace house that Rajni Sunnybrook calls home. Rajni sits calmly on the sofa, while Jenny stands fraught and at bay. Jenny is a thickset, powerful-looking girl, her hair a dishevelled bob, black with blue streaks. A riot grrrl, she wears the regulation t-shirt, PVC mini-skirt, ripped fishnets, and big boots, all in black. Her warpaint emphasises a pair of restless haunted eyes and pouting lips reminiscent of Courtney Love. (Thanks to the immortal legacy of Kurt Cobain, even a girl as young as Jenny knows who Courtney Love is.)

Ian, the second of the avoidants, is cowering in a corner of the room, out of sight of the two women. The same age as Jenny, he is slighter in build and has a boyish face and mother-me eyes (which at the moment is pale with fear.) His hair is bland in style and cut, and he wears bri-nylon trousers and a knitted V-neck jumper over a striped shirt; an ensemble which puts you in mind of a middle-aged golfer with dubious aesthetic sense. He sits in his corner, knees drawn up, rocking himself back and forth in an attempt (clearly not working) to induce calmness.

Altogether Ian and Rajni are two people who, outside of a young people's therapy group, would have been unlikely to have ever crossed paths; and if it seems unlikely to you that two such dissimilar people could ever have fallen for each other, then you can begin to understand why it might also seem so unlikely to *them*.

'Listen, you two,' proceeds Rajni. 'You need to have more faith in *me*. Professor Sunnybrook knows best, remember? I planned this thing, didn't I? And I planned it *well*. I got us safely in, and I got us safely out. In fact, the whole thing went off like clockwork, didn't it? Exactly according to plan.'

'Yeah, except that we killed the wrong person!' snaps Jenny.

'Except for that, yes. But at least we killed *someone*, didn't we? That first time we didn't get anyone. You see? That shows that we're improving, doesn't it? You need to look at the *positive* side of things. I've told you time and again about your negative thinking, haven't I? It's your negative thinking that causes you both all this needless anxiety. It's all in your heads, this constant fear of danger.'

'It's not all in our heads! There's a fucking manhunt out for us!'

'But they're not going to find us!' insists Rajni. 'They're on completely the wrong scent. They still think Takahashi was the intended target and they will be looking for someone who has motive to want to kill *her*. There's no way they can trace it back to us! So just listen to me Jennifer, Ian—come here, Ian, where I can see you.'

There is no response.

Rajni, standing up: 'I said come here—'

She breaks off. Ian is not in his corner.

'Where's he gone—?'

Banging sounds from the floor above.

'That sod! He's at the bloody medicine cabinet again!'

Jenny at her heels, Rajni charges upstairs. Making straight for the bathroom, they find Ian, sobbing piteously while ineffectually battering with two puny fists at the doors of a sturdily-built medicine cabinet secured with bar and padlock.

'The pills! The pills!' he sobs.

'You're not having any pills!' says Rajni. 'I've already given you twice your usual allowance this morning! Are you trying to kill yourself?'

'Yes!' screams the boy.

'Oh, so *that's* it! Want to take the coward's way out, do you? Not on my time you're not! We've got work to do, remember?'

'But the police are going to find us!'

'No, the police are *not* going to find us—'

'They will, they will!'

'They will *not*, because as I just explained to Jennifer, and if you hadn't snuck off like the little worm you are *you* would have heard as well, the police will be on completely the wrong scent! Now come back downstairs.'

Rajni forcing Ian to lead the way, they troop back down to the living room.

'Now sit down you two,' pointing an imperious finger at the settee, 'and I will explain.'

She stands before them, subduing them with her aura of power and authority. Ian sits awkwardly upright, pigeon-toed, arms like he doesn't know what to do with them; Jenny slouches, affecting nonchalance, gnawing at enamelled nails.

Rajni picks out a cigar from the humidor on the sideboard, unwraps it. 'The police will be looking for people with a motive for wanting to kill Mayumi Takahashi, right? And that's not us, is it? *We* don't hate her stupid photographs, do we?'

Begins Jenny: '*I* do! They're—'

'Yes, yes, we all know about pornophobia, Billie Eilish. Serves you right for looking at the stuff when you were too young to understand it.' She pauses to light her cigar. 'Well, regardless of any private opinions we might have, there's nothing to actually connect us with Takahashi; we do not number amongst her known opponents. And furthermore, there's no way they can identify any of us from that CCTV footage: we were too far from the cameras and too well disguised.'

'But we killed someone!' whines Ian.

Having taken a drag on her cigar, Rajni's reply is stifled by a violent fit of coughing. To judge from Ian and Jenny's lack of reaction, it would seem that this is a common occurrence. They patiently wait for the fit to pass.

'Well, so what if we did?' she finally manages to gasp. And then, having recovered her voice: 'We were *trying* to kill someone, weren't we? That was our objective! It's just that we unfortunately killed the *wrong* someone, that's all. These things happen. And as I keep saying, this actually this works out well for us, because the authorities still think Takahashi was the intended target—'

'I thought you was pissed off about them thinking it was Takahashi and not Dodo Dupont we were after?' says Jenny.

'I was *before*, yes: but *now* I see how we can use this to our advantage. Yes, if Dodo Dupont thinks it's her precious Mayumi somebody's out to get, we can use this as bait to lure her out into the open—and this time, *this time* we'll get her!'

Chapter Fifteen
The Perfect Set-Up

Is a team as strong as its strongest member, or is it only as strong as its weakest member? Flat-Sol Park in her indomitable self-confidence would probably assert the former—and for her own sake Jensen prays that she is right, because otherwise the future looks bleak for the Parkhurst Corporation.

That job description 'personal assistant' had seemed to carry with it the implication that the owner of the coveted title would be permanently at his mistress's side, her righthand man; but in actuality Jensen hasn't seen that much of his illustrious employer since that memorable afternoon of his promotion. She has put him in charge of the Zero Project and as such he has been coordinating with

Parkhurst's intelligence department—and a right Mickey Mouse outfit they have turned out to be! No wonder they hadn't made any progress. Well, he's been doing his level best to whip them into shape.

If Jensen had believed that the consummation of his promotion, that caveman sex session on the boardroom table was going to be the first in a regular series, he was soon disabused of that notion. Having one afternoon, instinctively, without really thinking, grabbed Flat-Sol's arse as she was bending over her desk, she had turned around and floored him with a rabbit punch that proved the story about her Thai kickboxing skills was no idle rumour.

(When he had regained consciousness Flat-Sol had explained to him that although she didn't object to having her arse spontaneously groped *per se*, it nevertheless depended on not just whom, but when and where and if she happened to be in the right mood at the time. Jensen had inquired as to how he would be able to determine precisely when it *was* the right moment, and had received the discouraging response that the only way to find out was the hard way. And then, when he had hesitantly suggested that he should perhaps request her permission before going in for the grope, Flat-Sol had dismissed the notion with all the contempt it deserved, pointing out that it would hardly be spontaneous then.)

Jensen hasn't been too put out at learning he's not going to be his boss's regular bedroom partner. It's not as though he was ever a one-woman man; quite the reverse in fact: he soon gets bored with sexual partners and is more than ready to move onto the next one. True there are those more adventurous bedroom partners you sometimes get; the ones who go that extra mile or two and you who don't get bored with in a hurry—and Christ knows his boss would be one of the women who fall into that category—but in the end its quantity over quality that matters.

And as for killing his friend Brunner, well Jensen has managed to come to terms with this. He never asked Brunner to compete with him for the promotion; it was his own decision and he knew the risks. And as for that decisive battle: it was a fair fight between men who were evenly matched, wasn't it? It could have gone either way; but Jensen was just the better man and victory always goes to the better man. True, he had been compelled to finish him off by kicking him to death when he was already down; but hey, this is a dog-eat-dog world, and sometimes in this dog-eat-dog world you *do* have to kick a man to death when he's down if it means that you get what you want; it may not be nice, but it's how the world goes, and the ends always justify the means.

Jensen likes to think that Brunner would have seen it this way himself.

Emerging from the executive lift, Jensen makes his way to Flat-Sol's office, knocks on the door. A voice bids him enter and he walks into the room. It is night outside and the lighting in the office is subdued save for the corona of light surrounding Flat-Sol Park's desk at the far end of the room. The light throws the reflection of the desk and its occupant against the window wall behind, partially obscuring the geometric pattern of light and shadow that forms the nocturnal skyline. Jensen approaches the desk. Flat-Sol saves her work and looks up at him inquiringly. He notices that her swollen cheek, one of the injuries she sustained during their horizontal warfare, is almost back to normal now.

'What have you to report?' she inquires. 'I trust you have made progress?'

'Yes, I just got a hot tip from my inside woman at the hospital.'

'Ah yes, the nurse with whom you have formed a relationship.'

'Yes. She's found out that Mark Hunter's people are moving Perfect out of the hospital. It was supposed to be secret, but word's got out amongst the staff, the way these things always do.'

'And does she know to what location they are moving him?'

'Nope, but it'll most likely be some private clinic or safehouse somewhere. Somewhere where it'll be easier for them to keep him under wraps.'

'So the man is now well enough to be moved… Your informant has proved a valuable resource; we must reimburse her for her services. What was her name again?'

'Alice. Alice Kincaid.'

'Ah yes, Alice Kincaid. Let me draw up her file…' consulting her laptop. 'Age twenty-seven, lives in rented accommodation… Engaged to be married, I see. When is the event to take place?'

'This weekend actually. She's looking forward to it. They'll be honeymooning in Spain.'

'Then we must give them a wedding present.'

'Erm… I've kind of already done that…'

'You have given her money?'

'No, I've given her their first kid.'

'I see. And is Miss Kincaid comfortable with this situation?'

'Oh, she's over the moon. Seems her fiancé said something that pissed her off a while back; probably just some stupid thoughtless comment he forgot the moment he said it, but it really got under her skin. You know; the way these things can.'

'Quite so. Then she has adequately revenged herself for the annoyance: good. Even so, in addition to the child we must still tender her due financial remuneration for the information she has provided. Business is business.'

'Sure; I'll see to it.'

'Back to the case in hand: you say the informer Perfect is about to be transferred from the hospital; when is this to take place?'

'Tomorrow morning, 0830 hours.'

'Tomorrow? This is short notice. We know this man Perfect to be a valuable source of information and as such it is imperative that we acquire him. Have you had time to prepare your strategy?'

'Yes, I've got it all planned.'

'I assume you plan to take possession of him while he is in transit?'

'Actually, no. My plan is for us to take him from the hospital just when he's due to leave; that'll be the best time to do it. I know he's well-guarded; and I know that all the attempts to spring him by us and by others have failed: but there will be that window of opportunity, that one moment when the guards aren't going to stop anyone from walking into that hospital room and taking the patient: and that's the moment he's supposed to be leaving anyway.'

'I see… Yes, that might work…'

'I'm sure it will. Here's the set-up: the ambulance that's taking him away is due to arrive at ambulance bay six at 0820 hours…'

Act XV Scene II: The Hospital. Morning.

(Establishing shot: hospital exterior. Up-tempo incidental music (library.) Cut to: ambulance bay. An ambulance pulls up. Ambulance crew emerge from the ambulance, wheeling an empty gurney. They move quickly and efficiently; all of them wear masks. They wheel the gurney in through the doorway.)

JENSEN (voiceover): Our own ambulance will pull in at bay seven five minutes before this. Our team, dressed as ambulance crew, will enter the building wheeling a gurney. I will be leading them myself. In the event of our being stopped and questioned, we will have papers of authorisation explaining the last-minute change in plans regarding the transfer of the patient. We will make our way to the elevator…

(The ambulance crew wheel the gurney into the elevator. The doors close. Camera zooms in on floor indicator; the light moves from ground floor to third floor. Camera pulls back; lift doors open and ambulance crew emerge, wheeling the gurney.)

…and up to the third floor. From there we go straight to room twenty-seven and announce to the guards at the door that we're here to collect the patient. The same papers of authorisation will be produced in the event of our being challenged by the guards, but the chances are we *won't* be challenged; after all they're expecting the man they're guarding to be taken away at around this time. Once inside we will quickly secure the patient…

(Cut to: room twenty-seven. The ambulance crew enter the room. In the room are the patient and two nurses. The patient is sitting up in bed, wrapped from head to toe in bandages, arms and legs in plaster casts, a flat cap on his head. The nurses help the ambulance crew lift him out of the bed and onto the gurney.)

Having done this, we will exit the room and make our way back to the elevator. The genuine ambulance crew will by this time be on their way up, but there will be no risk of a collision with them because they will be using a different lift. Back on the ground floor we return to the ambulance…

(Cut to: ambulance bay. The ambulance crew exit the building and lift the gurney with the patient into the back of the ambulance; two of them stay in with the patient, the other two get into the front of the ambulance.)

…and then we just drive away and the informer and all the information in his head will belong to the Parkhurst Corporation.

(Cut to: hospital entrance. The ambulance passes through the barrier gates. Cut to: road. Incidental music rises to crescendo as van drives down road away from camera. Fade to black.)

A warehouse of course.

The ambulance is parked close to closed doors and all around are the usual stacks of wooden crates and cardboard boxes. Three of the ersatz ambulance crew are relaxing over a bottle of whiskey and a poker game, crates serving as both chairs and card table. Further off, the liberated patient has been propped up in his gurney against a stack of crates. The fourth ambulance man sits on another crate beside him. The ambulance man is Jensen.

Opening a gold-plated cigarette case, Jensen extracts a cigarette, lights it then, standing up, he transfers it to the mouth of the bandage-swathed patient.

'Cheers, Mr Jensen!' says a gruff cockney voice in a cloud of cigarette smoke. 'Bin dying for one o' these, I 'as.' Confidentially: 'Y'know, they wouldn't let me smoke at all in that bleedin' 'orspital! Not once!'

'Shocking,' sympathises Jensen. Having lit a cigarette for himself, he resumes his seat, returning the cigarette case to his breast pocket.

'Bloomin' nicotine patches is all they'd gimme! Well, I mean: not the same thing, is it; them nicotine patches?'

'Not the same thing at all,' concurs Jensen. 'You must be glad to be out of that place.'

'Too right I am! Very obligin' of yer that was, Mr Jensen! Nice one…! Mind you, I was bein' discharged anyway…'

'Well yes, you were, but that was only to move you to some other place, wasn't it? And anyway, we wouldn't have been able to have this nice little chat together if we hadn't come along and sprung you, would we?'

'Well, no, thas true enuff... You wants to 'ave a chat with me then, does yer?'

'Yes, yes, I do, Perfect,' contemplating the tip of his cigarette. 'I *would* like to have a chat with you. In fact, it's very important that we have this little chat, very important indeed.'

'And... is it like a general conversation you wants, or is it somethink spercific?'

'It's something specific, Perfect; it's about that very valuable information you've got stashed away in that head of yours.'

'Important infermation? 'Oo says I got any important infermation?'

'Oh, come on, Perfect! Let's not play games here. Why have you been so heavily guarded? Why have so many people been trying to get at you in your hospital room?'

'Well, that was just your mob, weren't it? 'Ere! Come ter think of it, 'ow do I know it wasn't your lot what put me in the 'orspital in the first place?'

'It wasn't my people who put you in the hospital,' Jensen assures him. 'There are a lot of other interested parties who are eager to get their hands on you. Now why would that be?'

'Beats me.'

'Oh, come on. Those people who worked you over: they didn't just break your arms and legs for the fun of it, did they? They weren't just doing it for a bet. They wanted information from you, didn't they?'

'Well... Yeah, they did...'

'Yes, they did. It was information about Zero, wasn't it? You know something about Zero, don't you, Perfect?'

''Oo sez so?'

'I sez so. MI5 agent Mark Hunter and CIA agent Richard Bedford have both been assigned to track down the source of the Zero commercials. They met you at a pub in Bermondsey called the Jolly Tar. Later that same night you were attacked and hospitalised. I'm assuming you didn't tell your attackers what they wanted to know: but did you tell Hunter and Bedford? I don't think you did. Maybe the price wasn't right. Are you holding out for more money, Perfect? Is that it? Well, if you are, then I'm the person you want to be talking to. The company I represent can offer you a lot more money than the CIA or MI5 ever would.'

'Oh, yeah? An' what outfit's that then, what's got so much money ter throw around? 'Oo do you work for?'

'The Parkhurst Corporation. Maybe you've heard of us?'

'Parkhurst, eh…? Can't say I 'ave… Doin' well fer yerselves then, are yer? Turnin' a tidy profit, eh?'

'Pretty tidy, yes. We could make you a millionaire just like that,' clicking his fingers, 'and we wouldn't even feel the loss.'

'A millionaire? Geraway! Yer 'avin' me on!'

'Nope, I'm deadly serious. At Parkhurst we always pay value for value, and if you can tell us where the Zero campaign has its headquarters, that would be information well worth a million. So, Perfect, how do you fancy being a millionaire? I can make you one right now, and you won't even need to call a friend.'

'Well, tha's 'andy, that is; cuz I ain't really got any friends to speak of…' and sliding his hand out of its plaster cast, he takes the cigarette from his mouth to tap off the ash.

'Well, there you go, then! Once you're a millionaire you can buy all the friends you'll ever want! You can—' Jensen stops midsentence. 'Wait a minute: how did you do that?'

'Do what, mate?'

'You just pulled off your plaster cast like it was a glove and now you're using your hand to hold your cigarette like there's nothing wrong with it. What the hell's going on here?'

'Well, y'see, I reckon you just bin too clever by arf, Mr Jensen, that's what I reckon.'

Jensen springs backwards as the alleged invalid steps calmly from his slant board, reaches under his left arm, and then comes the sound of a hidden zipper in action, the bandage suit falls away and out of it steps Mark Hunter in his usual brown suit.

'Hunter!' snarls Jensen.

'In person. I'm afraid you've been the victim of a little deception, Mr Jensen,' says Mark; and swiftly drawing his Walther automatic from its shoulder holster, he levels it at Jensen and the by now alerted poker players.

Next moment an explosion rocks the warehouse, the doors crash inwards, and from the clouds of smoke several armed figures come running, one of them a grinning Rick Bedford with a rocket-launcher cradled on his shoulder.

'Okay you turkeys, hands up! Now!'

With lips compressed, Jensen raises his hands. The ambulance men follow suit.

Chapter Sixteen
Crisis: Help a Homeless Spy!

Night has fallen when Mark Hunter steps out of Pimlico underground station and makes his way home to his apartment building. It being a dry, mild evening he pauses to light a cigarette, standing on the pavement just in front of the resident's carpark.

'Can I trouble you for a light?' inquires a female voice, crisp and formal but still pleasing to the ear (or the two Mark possesses at least.)

Mark turns and sees a face and form as agreeable as the voice; a beautiful Asian woman, tall above the average, wearing a corporate grey skirt suit. Her hair is cut short and she wears small, rectangular glasses. Her age could be anywhere between thirty and forty, thinks Mark, studying the face illuminated by the flame of his lighter as she leans forward to ignite her cigarette.

She takes a pull on her cigarette, exhales.

'I am much obliged, Mark Hunter.'

'Oh, have we met? I'm usually very good with faces, but I—'

'No, we have never met, Mark Hunter,' returns the woman. 'Although I did have the pleasure of becoming acquainted with your good friend Dodo Dupont recently. Perhaps she has mentioned me: my name is Flat-Sol Park.'

'Oh!' says Mark, studying her with renewed interest. 'Yes, she *did* mention you. To what do I owe the honour?'

'I just happened to be passing,' is the casual reply. 'However, I am glad of this opportunity of making your acquaintance.'

'Really? I thought you'd be more likely to be somewhat annoyed with me. I had a run-in some of your employees this morning and they've been detained by the authorities.'

'I know, but please do not concern yourself. I had them released on bail this afternoon.'

'Did you? That was quick work.'

'Time and money are both commodities that should never be wasted or ill-used. I must congratulate you on your ingenious ruse; your reputation as an efficient counter-intelligence operative is not undeserved. But I have to ask you: did your actions really achieve anything?'

'Well, yes, I think they did, because I now know that the Parkhurst Corporation is very interested in learning the secret of the Zero campaign, but that you are not the people behind it.'

'You thought that we were?'

'You were on my suspect list.'

'But now you know better. And now I too have learnt something: your words have told me that you yourself have yet to discover the authors of the Zero campaign. So, what *do* you know, Mark Hunter? How much have you learned?'

'You don't really expect me to answer that, do you?'

'It would be in your best interests to cooperate with me.'

'That sounds like a threat.'

'Merely a statement of fact. Any information you were to share with myself would be amply remunerated.'

Mark smiles that wry smile of his. 'Oh, I see. Your colleague this morning offered to make me a millionaire; are you about to renew the offer?'

'It can be renewed if you wish it. It can be substantially increased if you wish it. My colleague's offer was directed at one whom he thought to be a lowly underworld informer; the cooperation of a man such as yourself, Mark Hunter, would be of considerably higher value.'

'You talk about "value," but how do you know if there's any value at all in all this? Here you are, willing to expend all this money to find out the secret of the Zero campaign, when the information might prove to be completely valueless, if the campaign turns out to be nothing more than an elaborate practical joke and that "Zero" is quite literally nothing.'

A frown creases Flat-Sol's brow. 'This I refuse to believe. Millions must have been invested in propagating the Zero publicity campaign; no-one would sacrifice such a sum without hope of a return.'

'Oh, I don't know about that,' replies Mark, smiling again. 'You'd be surprised how many people there are in the world with more money than sense. I've run into quite a few of them myself. In my line of work, you meet all sorts of people.'

'And what about yourself, Mark Hunter? I know you pride yourself on your unworldliness, but do you really not appreciate the value of money? You perform duties vital to the security of your nation, duties in the execution of which you endanger your life on a daily basis; and for what are you remunerated for your services? A miserable pittance.'

Mark shrugs his shoulders. 'I make enough to live on; that's all I want really. Unlike yourself I'm not a capitalist; I'm not in it for the money.'

'Then tell me, what are you "in it" for, Mr Hunter? Patriotism?'

'Well, "patriotism" is a bit of a dirty word in this country, thanks to a flag-waving far right and a colonial heritage. No, I just do my little bit to try and make the world a safer place—or at least to prevent it from becoming any *less* safe than it already is.'

'And isn't that fighting a losing battle, Mark Hunter?'

Another shrug. 'I just do the best I can.'

'You're an idealist, then.'

'Really? I've always considered myself a bit of a cynic.'

'A cynic, Mark Hunter? A cynic would not be content to squander his abilities working for an ungrateful Establishment for a pitiful wage; a cynic would not be content to live in a tiny apartment like *that*,' pointing across the carpark. 'A cynic would seize any opportunity to enrich himself that presented itself.'

'Yes, but what if I'm cynical about money?'

'To be cynical about money is to be an idealist, Mark Hunter.'

Mark laughs at this, shaking his head. Flat-Sol remains impassive.

'What do you find so amusing, Mark Hunter?'

'Oh, just how adroitly you won that argument. You're a very good talker, Miss Park. You'd make a good politician.'

'I have no wish to pursue such a career. Now that we have established your idealism, am I take it that it would be fruitless for me to continue to negotiate with you for information in return for cash payment?'

'I'm afraid it would.'

'I thought as much when I first approached you with my offer—'

'Even though you just happened to be passing…'

'—But I nevertheless wished to give you the chance to be cooperative. Your response is the one I anticipated, but is disappointing nevertheless. A will bid you goodnight, Mark Hunter. It has been a great pleasure to make your acquaintance. I have enjoyed our conversation and I am sure we will meet again.'

'I'm sure we will. It's been a pleasure to meet you too, Miss Park.'

Flat-Sol bows formally, turns on her heel and vanishes into the darkness. Mark, a thoughtful expression on his face, watches her out of sight; then, stubbing out his cigarette in his portable ashtray, he sets off across the carpark. Ahead of him welcoming light shines through the glazed double doors of the apartment building's main entrance.

The sudden explosion dazzles him, while the roar of a detonation rips through the night sky, a savage sound, proclaiming calamity. A shower of debris descends on the roofs of parked cars. Mark, staggering, blinks his eyes, recovering his night vision. He looks up. A plume of black smoke spirals upwards from the angry flaming eye of a second-floor apartment window.

His apartment window.

Dodo answers the door, dressed in black lingerie. Before her stands Mark, listless, subdued. He offers her a weak smile.

'Sorry for the short notice.'

'Never mind *that*.'

Dodo looks at him for a moment, eyes brimful of compassion, and then she folds him in her sweet-smelling embrace.

'Come in, come in, sweetheart. We're all here waiting for you.'

Mark follows Dodo into her apartment. Mayumi, Trina, Yuki Kinoshita and Shizuka Todoroki, are seated in the living room area, in a similar state of semi-dress to Dodo.

Music plays quietly on the surround-sound stereo, one of Mayumi's Japanese bands.

'Oh,' says Mark. 'I hope I'm not keeping you all up?'

'Not at all,' says Dodo. 'We were just having one of our girlie sitting-around-in-our-underwear nights in.'

Mayumi, dressed in white, rushes forward to hug Mark, her embrace smaller but equally heartfelt.

'Thank you, Mayumi,' says Mark.

Tattooed Trina, dressed in blue, now steps forward, blushing, eyes questioning, hands behind back.

'You'd like to offer me your condolences as well?' suggests Mark helpfully.

Accepting the invitation, Trina hugs him.

'Thank you, Trina,' says Mark.

'I hug you too,' says flower-patterned Yuki Kinoshita, and promptly suits the action to the word.

'Thank you, Yuki,' says Mark.

And lastly, burgundy Shizuka steps forward and hugs him.

'Thank you...' Mark stops, studies her. 'Erm, who are you?'

'Oh, this is Shizuka Todoroki,' says Dodo. 'Yuki's interpreter.'

'Oh, of course... When she was on TV...'

Introductions are made. (Shizuka, an employee of the Japanese embassy, was only supposed to have served as Yuki Kinoshita's interpreter for the duration of her now world-famous morning television appearance, but for reasons unknown, she never went *back* to the embassy, and has remained by Yuki's side ever since.)

'Well, sit yourself down,' says Dodo. 'I'll get you a drink.'

'A drink would be very welcome right now,' says Mark.

He sits down on one of the sofas. Trina resumes her seat on the armchair and Yuki and Shizuka on the rug. Mayumi hovers around, contemplating Mark with compassionate curiosity.

Dodo returns from the mini-bar with a Southern Comfort on the rocks.

Handing it to Mark: 'Here you go, sweetheart.'

'Thank you,' says Mark, gratefully swallowing a generous mouthful of the liqueur.

Dodo seats herself on the sofa beside him. Mayumi, subsides cross-legged onto the rug, still studying Mark.

'How are you feeling?' asks Dodo.

'Oh, I'm alright,' answers Mark. 'It's not the first time I've been uncomfortably close to an explosion. Happens all the time in my line of work.'

'Yes, but it isn't usually your own home you see getting blown up in front of your eyes,' insists Dodo. 'And you're *not* alright: you're in a mild state of shock and that's only to be expected. You don't have to put up a front with us, Mark. You say the place is completely gutted?'

'Yes. It was an incendiary device, burnt up the whole place in no time. Fortunately, the fire brigade arrived in time to stop the fire from spreading. The flats adjacent to mine were damaged and have had to be evacuated, but the building's been declared structurally sound, and the rest of the tenants have been allowed back in.'

'But you, you've lost everything, haven't you…?' says Dodo. She squeezes his hand.

Mark shrugs. 'Didn't have that much to lose, did I? Just the furniture, my books… I was never one for hoarding keepsakes and cherished possessions.'

'Your books were your cherished possessions, sweetheart. You don't have to pretend you don't miss them. You'd spent years building up that collection, hadn't you?'

'True, and I'll admit there were a few valuable rare editions amongst them. But, as far as the content goes, well they're all up online, aren't they? You know, maybe I should take this is an opportunity and switch to reading electronic books...?'

'And at least you weren't in your flat when the bomb went off,' speaks up Trina. 'Cuz, y'know, you'd be dead if you had been.'

'A very good point, Trina,' says Mark. 'But I don't think I was meant to be in the flat when the bomb exploded. I think the perpetrator wanted me to be where I was, wanted me to see my home destroyed right in front of me.'

Dodo frowns. 'Who was it?' she demands. 'You sound like you know who did it.'

'Oh, I know damn well who did it,' affirms Mark, his voice betraying an edge of bitterness. He gives a brief *precis* of his encounter with Flat-Sol Park.

'That fucking bitch!' spits Dodo, amid similar exclamations from the other women.

'Seems like she wanted to put my unworldliness to the test,' says Mark, 'and perhaps also it was intended as payback for that trick I pulled on her people this morning.'

'Fucking bitch,' repeats Dodo. 'And I suppose there's going to be no way you can pin this crime on her...?'

Mark shakes his head. 'No way at all. It would be a complete waste of time to even try.' Mark drains his drink and inquires of the room at large: 'Could I have another one of these?'

Trina jumps up with alacrity to get him a refill.

'Ironic, isn't it...?' ruminates Mark, studying his glass. 'She would have spared my apartment if I'd agreed to sell out to her, but the truth is I didn't have anything to sell: I still don't know anything about Zero that she doesn't know herself. Apart from the outer space angle, of course, and if I'd told her about that she would probably have thought I was pulling her leg...'

'Yes, but there's also that girl you're still looking for,' Dodo reminds him. 'Flat-Sol probably doesn't know about her.'

'Yes, there's Amber... I'm not even sure if she's still alive. She never tried to pay Perfect a second visit, and I haven't heard a peep from the Cult Café, so it seems she hasn't been there, either...'

'How long will it take them to fix up your flat?' asks Trina.

'Oh, that's not going to happen in a hurry. I shall have to find somewhere else to live for the time being.'

'Well, you know you're welcome to stay here as long as you like,' says Dodo.

'Thank you. Although I wouldn't want to impose...'
'Don't be ridiculous, sweetheart. You would *not* be imposing, placing a hand on his shoulder,'

'Yes, I... Sorry...'

'And don't apologise either!'

Mark smiles at her gratefully. 'You know, since it happened, I keep thinking about Aldous Huxley. *He* lost everything when his house burnt down, didn't he? His library, his manuscripts... He said he'd become a man without a past, or something like that...'

'Your past is in there,' says Dodo, tapping Mark's temple. 'But we all form these sentimental attachments to possessions, things that remind us of a particular moment in time... And you, I'm sure you must have lost some tonight, some of those bridges to the past...'

'One or two,' admits Mark with a sigh. 'One or two...'

'Come here, you,' says Dodo, patting her lap. 'Lie down and relax.'

'Well, I... if you insist...'

'I *do*,' firmly.

Pulling off his shoes Mark lies down the sofa, pillowing his head on Dodo's warm and fragrant lap.

'You wanna borrow my ear-cleaning kit?' asks Mayumi. (For a Japanese woman, this reaction is instinctive: rest your head in a Japanese woman's lap and the first thing she will do is whip out her ear-cleaning kit and start doing your ears for you!)

'No, sweetheart, I don't think Mark wants his ears cleaning,' Dodo assures her. To Mark: 'Feeling comfortable?'

'Very.'

'More relaxed?'

'With every passing second.'

'Good...'

Dodo starts to slowly stroke his hair; the feeling is soothing. From his sideways perspective he sees the other four women; they are all smiling at him, Trina in that shy, uncertain way of hers, Mayumi glowingly, with all of her generous heart... Even Yuki and Shizuka, to women to whom he is virtually a stranger, look at him with warm smiles...

'Uprooted... that's what I feel like...' says Mark pensively. 'Like I've been set back to default... Like I've got to start something all over again... Sort of... empty... Still,' rallying himself; 'there's no future in dwelling on these things, is there? No point getting all maudlin. As a wise man once said: "The great thing in life is to keep your sense of humour. It isn't always easy—but if you lose it, you've had it chum."'

'Oh, yes? And who was the wise man that said that?' asks Dodo.

'Biggles.'

Dodo bursts into laughter. 'Biggles. Of course, you were raised on Biggles, weren't you? That's where you get all that silly stiff-upper-lippery of yours from, isn't it?' ruffling his hair affectionately. 'But look at you now: being comforted and coddled by a bunch of soppy women.'

'I know,' agrees Mark. 'Deplorable, isn't it? What would Biggles say if he could see me...?'

Comforted and coddled by a bunch of women...

There's one woman Mark remembers, and a bridge to the past has been burnt this night: it was just a book, one of the hundreds of books in his collection: no priceless first edition, just a mass-market paperback from the seventies of a book that is still in print and that these days would retail for about three quid in a charity shop—but irreplaceable to him because it had *her* name in it, *her* name, written in her own hand on the inside cover; the only memento of that long since vanished woman he ever had, the only proof he had been able to retain that she ever existed... And now it's gone, gone forever...

He'd been reading a Biggles book day... that that long ago day when he'd first met her...

Chapter Seventeen
The Spaceman Cometh

> ACE: What are we doing here?
> DOCTOR: Keeping an eye on Group Captain Chunky Gilmore. Although why his men call him Chunky, I've no idea.
> ACE: Maybe it's because he's got a big fat cock, Professor!
> -excerpt from *I'll Be in My Cabin if You Need Me*

'What about Ed Straker's exploding attaché case?'

'What *about* Ed Straker's exploding attaché case? We've *done* Ed Straker's exploding attaché case.'

'Yeah, but we've only done it *once*. I think that one's got wings!'

'I dunno...'

'I've got one, I've got one! You've got Wo Fat from *Hawaii-Five-0*...'

'Original or reboot?'

'The original one: Khigh Dhiegh.'

'It's pronounced "Kai Dee" not "Kigg Digg."'

'Is it? Well, him anyway. And since the series got cancelled, he's opened a Chinese takeaway, only he keeps attacking his customers, thinking they're Steve McGarrett in disguise!'

'Why would he do that?'

'Cuz he's got a complex about it, hasn't he? You know, after he got fooled by McGarrett's disguise in that last episode.'

'I dunno…'

'What was with that last episode anyway? Was it supposed to be a spoof or was it—?'

'Okay, how about this then? You've got *both* Wo Fats, the original and the reboot ones, and they've *both* opened up Chinese takeaways and they're right next door to each other, and they're business rivals! It'd be like *Never the Twain*, only with Chinese takeaways instead of antique shops! Yeah! We could line it up as the replacement serial for *Carry on Tenko*!'

'I'm not sure how much mileage we'd get out of that one…'

'Yeah, maybe we should just do it as a one-off…'

'Excuse me, gentlemen…?'

The three men look up. A man wearing a brown suit, affable-looking, coffee cup in hand, stands over their table.

'I wondered if I could have a word with you?' he continues.

'What about?'

'The proprietress tells me you are acquainted with a girl called Amber, a customer here…?'

'Amber? You mean Amber Windrush?'

'Amber *Windrush*? Is that actually her name?'

A shrug. 'It's the one she uses online.'

'Well, can I have a word with you about her? I should explain this is official and I'm not some stalker.' Putting his mug down the man reaches into his pocket and produces an ID card.

The three at the table lean forward to read it.

'MI5… Blimey, he's a spy! Is this for real?'

'Yes, my ID is genuine. You can ring this number and confirm it if you want to.'

'A real-life spy…!'

'Yeah… He looks like a spy, doesn't he…?'

'Do I?' says Mark with surprise. (He is more accustomed to hearing the contrary opinion.)

'Yeah, he does…! One of those lightweight spies like Noel Harrison in *The Girl from UNCLE,* or William Gaunt in *The Champions*…! Do you always wear that shirt?'

'This or one very much like it, yes.'

'Ever thought of switching to a polo-neck?' To his friends: 'Seriously: he should wear a polo-neck, shouldn't he?'

Noises of enthusiastic confirmation.

'May I take a seat?' inquires Mark.

'Sure.'

Mark sits himself down. The booth is the one with the *Earth Dies Screaming* poster Mark had noticed on his previous visit to the café.

'I'm Dave,' says the man beside Mark. 'This is Jimmy and this is Ken,' indicating the two seated opposite.

Pleasantries are exchanged.

'I'm thinking burgundy…' says Ken, studying Mark thoughtfully. 'Or maybe green…'

'Excuse me?' says Mark.

'For your polo-neck.'

'What about white?' suggests Jimmy.

'No, not with a brown suit! Burgundy or green.'

'What sort of green?'

'Olive green. Like the one Tony in *The Time Tunnel*'s got.'

'You mean Doug, don't you? Tony's the one in the tweed suit.'

'No, *Doug's* the one in the tweed suit! *Tony's* the one with the green jumper.'

'No, he isn't! Look, James Darren—!'

'Putting the matter of my wardrobe to one side for the moment,' interjects Mark. 'I understand that you three are with the *I'll Be in My Cabin if You Need Me* comedy team, is that right?'

'Yep, that's us! Writing and performing; ever watched the show?'

'I have seen it once or twice, but I'm not a big television watcher.'

'Yeah, too busy being a spy, eh? And you're on a case now, are you?'

'I am. That's why I wanted to know what you can tell me about that girl Amber Windrush.'

'Why, what's she done wrong?'

'Nothing, as far as I know,' says Mark, generously discounting one act of grievous bodily harm against himself. 'When did you last see her?'

'Not for a while…' Dave looks at his friends. 'When did we last see her? Must have been a couple of weeks ago…'

'At least,' says Ken. 'More like a month, I'd say…'

'Yeah, a month at least,' confirms Jimmy.

'And you only ever see her when she's in this café…?'

'Yes, only here. We don't know her that well. She's a quiet one; shy… We'd noticed her here lots of times before she even plucked up the courage to come up and say hello to us. You can't really help noticing her, with that Moonbase girl wig of hers.'

'Oh, so it is supposed to be a Moonbase girl wig, that wig of hers then? I wasn't sure.'

'Yes. She likes Dolores Mantez; you know, the black Moonbase girl.'

'Me too! I always liked her a lot more than Gabrielle Drake,' says Jimmy. 'Fills out her Moonbase uniform nicely, she does,' miming an hourglass.

'Yeah, I doubt that's why Amber likes her, Jimmy.'

'I know that! I was just saying—!'

'So, she comes and sits with you sometimes,' prompts Mark.

'Yeah, she's a fan of the show,' says Dave. 'She was much chattier once she got over being shy. She likes giving us ideas for skits.'

'And you know her online?'

'Yep. She follows our page. Shares a lot of her own stuff as well.'

'What sort of thing does she like to post messages about?'

'A lot of it's sci-fi stuff; things she's watched and all that; but she likes to talk about things happening in the news as well. Yeah, a lot of fans, they haven't got a clue when it comes to news and politics; completely socially unaware, most of 'em: but Amber's not like that. She's got opinions.'

'Any particular subjects she likes to talk about?'

'Oh, climate change; the rise of the far right; that sort of thing. How everything's basically going to hell in a handbasket… She can be very cynical, she can.'

'What about recently? Has she talked about anything online recently? Anything in particular?'

'Hm… Come to think of it, I don't think she's posted anything recently…' looking at his friends.

'No, I don't think she has…' confirms Ken. 'She's gone quiet…'

'Do you know where abouts Amber lives? What kind of work she does?'

'No idea where she lives; I assumed it was local, as she's always in here.'

'What about work? Has Amber said anything online about what she does for a living?'

'No… I don't think so…' Dave looks at Ken and Jimmy: they don't think so either.

Mark checks his wristwatch. 'Well, she should be here any minute…'

'Who should?' demands Dave. 'You mean Amber?'

'Yes, she's arranged to meet me here this evening.'

'Then why've you been asking us all this stuff about her? You could've just asked *her*!'

'I can ask her if she actually shows up,' answers Mark. 'But there's always the possibility that she won't...'

'What is it you want to see her about anyway?' questions Jimmy. 'You haven't told us that yet.'

'And I'm afraid I *can't* tell you; it's a rather delicate matter...'

'Ah! Official Secrets, and all that, eh?' surmises Dave.

'Something like that, yes,' agrees Mark.

With those Dalek doors the Cult Café has, no-one can walk into the place unnoticed. This evening, the café has a healthy turnout of customers, and as that familiar sound effect once again announces a new arrival, many pairs of eyes that turn doorwards to witness the entrance of the giant silver robot.

Silence descends on the café.

There it stands in the doorway: at least seven foot tall from the top of its cylindrical space helmet to the soles of its platform boots. The design is vintage: metallic arms, legs and torso that strangely resemble silver clothing, over which runs a complicated arrangement of wires and corrugated tubing; a smooth ovoid head with grille-like eyes, protected by a glass helmet with a snorkel arrangement that would seem at first glance superfluous for a creature innocent of any kind of respiratory system but which undoubtedly serves some important function. In short, the creature standing in the doorway is nothing less than an authentic reproduction of an alien robot from the 1964 feature film *The Earth Dies Screaming*.

After a brief stunned silence, the room erupts into cheers and applause.

'Do they have cosplay nights at this place then?' inquires Mark, puzzled.

'They *do*... But tonight's not supposed to be one,' replies Dave. Looking at his colleagues: 'Is it?'

Not that they've heard.

The robot, meanwhile, advances into the cafeteria. The applause subsides but not the curiosity of the customers, who continue to watch with interest, some of them addressing questions to it, others snapping pictures of it with their phones. Only the proprietress, the plus-sized Princess Leia, doesn't share the general enthusiasm. Stationed behind her counter, she observes the creature with puzzled concern.

The robot comes to a halt at the booth occupied by Mark and the three comedy performers. It turns to face them, towering over the table and its occupants.

'Hello, mate!' Jimmy greets it. 'Who's in there then? Anyone we know?'

'I'd think it was Amber, except it's way too big to be her,' says Dave.

'Amber?' Mark looks at him. 'Why would you think it would be her?'

'Cuz she loves that film,' says Dave. 'It's a robot from *The Earth Dies Screaming*. See? Same as the poster up there,' pointing towards the wall.

'I know. I've seen the film myself,' says Mark.

'You've got to admire the attention to detail,' says Jimmy, still looking up at the creature. 'The quilted jerkin; the phone cords attached to the eyes…'

'WHERE IS AMBER WINDRUSH?' grates the robot in a loud metallic voice.

This provokes a chorus of protest. 'No, no, *no*,' sighs Jimmy. 'The robots in that film don't *speak*. You've gone and spoilt the whole thing now!'

'What is that voice…?' wonders Ken. 'It's like a Cyberman, isn't it? How they spoke in The Invasion, wasn't it…?' Looking up at the robot: 'Go on: say it again!'

'WHERE IS AMBER WINDRUSH?' obliges the robot.

'Hmm…' ruminates Jimmy. 'No… I think it's more like the ambassadors from The Ambassadors of Death…'

'But they weren't even robots!' says Dave.

'No, but their speech was being translated through a machine, wasn't it? So it sounded robotic.'

Mark takes no part in this weighty dispute. He is by now very suspicious of this visitor.

'And why do you want to know where Amber Windrush is?' he inquires.

'WHERE IS AMBER WINDRUSH?' repeats the robot.

'Who are you and why do you want to find her?' demands Mark, standing up. 'In fact, would you mind removing your helmet? I'd like to see who I'm talking to here.'

'WHERE IS AMBER WINDRUSH?'

'I said: take your helmet off,' and to back up his request, he produces his Walther PPK and levels it at the robot's quilted jerkin.

Moving with surprising swiftness, the robot first swats the gun out of Mark's hand and then, grabbing him by the collar, lifts him high off the ground. The deceptively soft silver-gloved hand has a grip like a steel vice.

'WHERE IS AMBER WINDRUSH?'

Mark, his throat constricted by the robot's grip, would have had difficulty making any response even if he'd possessed the desired information and a willingness to share it.

It is this at juncture that the Dalek doors open and Dodo Dupont and Rick Bedford rush into the café from opposite directions, both of them weapons drawn. Assuming identical firing positions, they level their guns at the robot and cry 'Hold it!'

'Drop him!' snarls Bedford.

'Put him down!' shouts Dodo.

The robot, turning to face its new antagonists, does neither: instead, he throws Mark over his shoulder and sends him flying across the room, where he comes into violent contact with the opposite wall and slides to the floor (managing to avoid the broken neck a lesser person might have sustained.)

The robot now advances towards Dodo and Bedford.
'WHERE IS AMBER WINDRUSH?'
They both open fire. The bullets have no effect, the shots glancing off the protective helmet or penetrating the quilted jerkin without any apparent harm to the wearer.

By this time Mark has picked himself up and, regaining possession of his automatic (picked up and handed to him by the proprietress), fires on the monster from behind. It stops, spins round, looking from the antagonist behind to the antagonists at the door.

'Rush it!' yells Mark.

They charge the robot.

An excruciating sound of radio interference suddenly fills the air. The café patrons clamp hands over ears while Mark and his friends are brought up short in their charge. The sound emanates from the robot, who now starts to glow, its body becoming a swarm of monochrome dots and angry jagged lines, a robot-shaped doorway into a universe of static interference.

And then, in an instant the robot shrinks to a white dot and vanishes, like a cathode-ray television suddenly switched off.

Silence.

The café comes to life again, and Mark, with the help of the proprietress, calms the clientele. The proprietress departs and Mark turns to his two friends for an explanation as to their presence.

'I followed you here, man!' says Bedford.

'Any particular reason?'

'Because you've been holding back on me!'

Mark cannot deny the accusation. He'd been told to come alone, when Amber, speaking through the mouth of the café owner, had arranged this meeting, and as on the previous occasion, Mark had intuited the injunction to have been made with special reference to Rick Bedford.

'And what about you?' he asks Dodo.

'I also followed you, because I was worried about you,' replies Dodo. 'I thought you might be walking into a trap.'

'What if I was?' demands Mark, affronted. 'I've walked into lots of traps in my time. I'm very good at walking into traps.'

'I know, but you're not at your best right now, sweetheart. I don't think you've really recovered yet…'

'This is very sweet of you, Dodo but—'

'Hey, can we get back to what just happened here?' cuts in Bedford. 'What the hell was that thing and who the hell is Amber Windrush?'

'Amber Windrush is our elusive contact,' Mark tells him. 'I was supposed to be meeting her here tonight; and all things considered it's lucky for her that she didn't turn up—'

'Excuse me,' interjects the proprietress, coming back. 'But Amber *was* here. She got here before you did, and I let her hide in the back room,' indicating a door across the room labelled 'staff only.' 'She said she wanted to check you out before she showed herself, in case you brought anyone else with you.'

'You mean she was looking at me through that door the whole time…?'

'Yes.'

'You say she *was* here: you mean she's gone?'

'Yes, I just checked: she's gone; cleared off through the back door.'

'Well, that's just beautiful,' sighs Bedford, reaching for the cigarette he will have to go outside to smoke.

Chapter Eighteen
Through the Keyhole

The Earth Dies Screaming.

At the age of fifteen, Mark Hunter had stayed up late one night to watch this film on the portable telly in his bedroom, attracted by its title (which turned out to be the best thing about it.) That was over half a lifetime ago; and now, in the wake of last night's events at the Cult Café, Mark felt it was high time he gave the film a second viewing.

Released in 1964, *The Earth Dies Screaming* was one of the raft of low-budget science-fiction films produced during fifties and sixties which focused on the theme, pioneered by HG Wells' novel *The War of the Worlds*, of the invasion of Earth by extraterrestrials. And just as *The War of the Worlds* basically plays like 'The Martian Invasion of the Home Counties', *The Earth Dies Screaming* presented an even more localised extraterrestrial incursion, the invaders seeming to focus their attention exclusively on just one tiny village. The plot involves the decimation of the Earth's population by the release of a deadly gas. A small number of people who manage to survive this attack for various reasons, come together in the unnamed village (real name Critchlow), amongst them an airforce pilot (the lead, played by an imported American actor), a young pregnant woman, an alcoholic and a con-man. When the robots (never more than two of them at once) appear, they are at first mistaken for humans in protective suits (hence the robots' superfluous respirator helmets), but they soon learn to their cost that the creatures are mechanical and hostile. Several of the group are killed by the robots, who are armed with laser guns, and the remainder retreat to the shelter of the village pub (the alcoholic leading the way.) Here they come under siege from not just the robots but also by zombies, their recent companions amongst them, who have been reanimated by the robots. (It is unclear as to whether it is only people killed by the robots' laser guns, or also those who perished in the original gas attack, who come back as zombies—either way they are a rather sorry excuse for an army of the undead, as you only have to shoot one of them with a conventional firearm for it go straight back from being undead to just being dead.)

It is deduced that the robots are not the alien invaders themselves but merely their robotic vanguard, whose duty it is to neutralise the indigenous lifeforms and ready the planet for colonisation. Discovering that the robots are using a nearby transmission station to send out the signal guiding their alien masters to the Earth, the survivors, led by the gallant airforce pilot, escape from the village and, after arming themselves with guns and explosives from a local army base, launch an attack on the transmitter station and its one or two robot guardians; and it is the alcoholic who finally destroys the radio mast, gallantly sacrificing his life in the process (to atone for his having left his comrades in the lurch on more than one occasion earlier in the film.)

With the destruction of the radio mast the robots all fall lifeless to the ground (having in some mysterious fashion derived their motive power from the same signal they were sending into space), and the film then ends with the survivors leaving the British Isles by commercial airliner (stock footage) with the intention of linking up with other survivors around the world.

Having sat through the film Mark was left with pretty much the same impression it had left on him when he'd first watched it thirty-five years ago: that it was not a terribly good film. Not horrendously bad, but not particularly good either. Nor had this viewing of the film, closely as he had studied it, offered him anything in the way of an answer to the burning question: *what on earth could be the connection between the Zero campaign and a bargain-basement science-fiction film from the nineteen-sixties?*

This morning finds Mark Hunter standing before his apartment building. An eyepatch of taped down plastic sheeting marks the location of his gutted apartment.

Mark is not the only one who has been cast adrift. Amber Windrush has not returned to her apartment since the night of the break-in. And for a very good reason.

On the night of Mark's encounter with the robot at the cult café, a second incident had occurred at a bedsit in Islington. Two 'silver spacemen' were seen breaking into the bedsit; and were never seen to actually *leave* it—but when the police arrived the flat was empty: the intruders seemed to have vanished into thin air.

The tenant of the bedsit, not at home at the time of the break-in, was one Amber Windrush.

So Amber Windrush is now a fugitive.

But why? Why is she being hunted? What is it that she knows? Her social media accounts, of which Mark only learned the existence the other night, have suddenly been deleted. Deleted by Amber herself to stop anyone from contacting and possibly locating her? Or deleted by someone else? Perhaps there was something on one of those now-deleted posts that would have furnished Mark with a clue? Something perhaps entirely innocuous to most that might have provided the key to the mystery of how Amber came to find out about Zero, and/or to explain the apparent connection between Zero and *The Earth Dies Screaming*…

Where is she? Unless she has some friend she can turn to, who can shelter her, she's on her own. Surely by now she must realise that the best person she can turn to for protection is himself?

Locating Amber's family was easy enough to accomplish, but her family doesn't know anything. It seems that Amber and her parents had a falling out several years before and Amber had moved out of the family home and hadn't been in contact with them since.

It's so frustrating, knowing that all the time he was sat in the café talking to the *I'll Be in My Cabin* people, Amber had been watching him, hiding behind the door to the back of the premises! She was probably all set to come out and reveal herself the moment that robot turned up looking for her.

That she did a runner after this is understandable—but why hasn't she contacted Mark since then? She must have seen that Mark and her robot pursuers are not on the same side, and unless she destroyed that letter he wrote to her, she has his phone number—why doesn't she contact him?

He wants to help her, but he can't help her if he doesn't know where to find her…

There is always the option of making a public appeal, but for now at least, Mark doesn't want to resort to this, as there is the possibility of the publicity doing more harm than good.

'Could I trouble you for a light?'

The voice shakes Mark from his reverie. He turns to the speaker and the speaker is Flat-Sol Park. She stands, cigarette extended, just as she had that other evening.

'I think you've already troubled me more than enough already,' says Mark coldly; 'so I would prefer it if you could go and trouble someone else.'

Flat-Sol frowns. 'I am asking you for a light for my cigarette, Mark Hunter. It would be most ill-mannered of you to refuse.'

With a reluctance that suggests a lack of concern for the niceties of social etiquette in this particular instance, Mark produces his lighter and lights Flat-Sol's cigarette, and while he's at it lights one for himself.

'I was most distressed to learn about the explosion at your apartment,' says Flat-Sol.

'To *learn* about it?' from Mark, voice rising in disbelief. 'You were *here!* You must have seen it as you were walking away!'

'This is true; and I would have returned to offer assistance, but regrettably urgent business necessitated otherwise.'

'You don't even expect me to believe that, do you?' says Mark, with a weary smile.

'I see no reason why you should disbelieve me, Mark Hunter,' returns Flat-Sol equably. 'Untruths can be a necessary tool in business negotiations, but you and I are engaged in no business negotiations, therefore I have nothing to gain from telling untruths to you.'

'Oh, I'm sure you have something to gain,' says Mark. 'And no doubt sooner or later I'll find out what it is. So, what brings you here today? Or did you just "happen to be passing" like you were last time?'

'No, I came here seeking you on purpose,' is the reply. 'I have something I wish to show you. Come; my car is parked just here,' indicating a black Rolls Royce limousine parked at the curb nearby. 'Please step inside. I can take you there immediately.'

'I have no wish to be taken anywhere by you,' says Mark. 'I will have to decline your offer.'

'Really, Mark Hunter, I find your unfounded suspicions most offensive. This is no trap I can assure you; in fact, what I have to show you is something very much to your advantage.'

'Even so, I still have to decline,' says Mark and, wishing to terminate the interview, he turns his back on Flat-Sol, and starts walking away.

'And I really must insist, Mark Hunter.'

The tone of her voice stops Mark in his tracks and turns round. Flat-Sol has been joined by her chauffeuse, an immaculate blonde in a dark grey uniform with a peaked cap, Lady Penelope dressed as Parker. The woman's face is expressionless, and in one gloved hand she holds an automatic, pointed at Mark.

Mark smiles wryly. In the middle of a London street; Flat-Sol is nothing if not brazen. With a shrug, he climbs into the spacious interior of the Rolls, the door held courteously open by the armed chauffeuse, and sits himself on the back seat. The side seat already has one occupant, an Asian woman, short-haired like Flat-Sol, but smaller and chubbier, the skirt of her business suit of a more conservative length.

'My sister, Yu-Mi,' announces Flat-Sol, sliding onto the seat beside Mark.

Mark nods his head in greeting. Yu-Mi nods back at him.

The chauffeuse taking her place behind the wheel, the car joins the traffic flow.

'My sister is entirely innocent,' proceeds Flat-Sol. 'I have always done my best to protect her from many of the starker realities of life. Her presence here should serve to convince you I have no hostile intentions towards you. Would you care for a drink?' indicating the limousine's bar. 'I believe you prefer Scotch; I can offer you an excellent malt.'

'No thank you,' says Mark.

Flat-Sol shrugs and they set off, leaving the metropolitan area, heading north-west, where they finally come to a well-to-do residential area. The Rolls turns into the drive of a sizeable house with a mock-Tudor exterior: half-timbered walls, thatched roof, diamond-paned windows. The pleasant abode is surrounded by an extensive, park-like garden.

'We have arrived,' announces Flat-Sol, and waking her sister who has nodded off, they step out of the vehicle, the chauffeuse remaining behind the wheel.

Turning to Mark: 'I believe in this country there is a television quiz programme in which the contestants are shown around a house belonging to a notable person, and the object of the game is to deduce the identity of the owner; is that not so?'

'Yes, it's called *Through the Keyhole*.'

'Good. Then we shall play *Through the Keyhole*. I will show you around this house and you will endeavour to deduce to whom it belongs.'

'You brought me here for this?' says Mark, unimpressed. 'I'm not exactly in the mood for games.'

'Please indulge me in this, Mark Hunter. I can assure you that my motives will become clear.'

Mark shrugs. 'Very well. Lead the way…'

Producing a key, Flat-Sol opens the front door and they step into the hallway. The house's interior is in keeping with its *Olde Worlde* façade: wainscoted walls, beamed ceilings, delicately carved antique furniture. The walls are adorned with canvases, landscape paintings of the realist school, pastoral scenes, dense woodlands and spectacular mountain ranges.

They enter the living room, which runs almost the full length of the front of the house. Here there are more paintings, comfortable armchairs and sofas of antique design. A flatscreen television provides the only note of modernity. Mark is drawn to the farther end of the room which is fitted out as a library with floor-to-ceiling bookcases lined with finely-bound volumes. Inspecting some of the titles, he discovers the books to be a comprehensive collection of the classics. Recalling his own lost collection, he feels a pang.

'What do you deduce so far, Mark Hunter?' inquires Flat-Sol.

'Well, I'm fairly sure this isn't *your* house. This décor doesn't suit you at all. I see you living somewhere much more modern, much more spacious and angular. This place is too cramped and chintzy for a corporate highflyer like yourself. My guess would be that this house belongs to a scholar or a writer, probably middle-aged or elderly.'

'And does your middle-aged or elderly scholar or writer live here alone, or with his or her family?'

'I'm not sure… The house is rather big for just one individual, but on the other hand, a solitary person who could afford it, might choose to live in a place like this… I've seen nothing to indicate the presence of children, no toys lying around, so if our residents are a couple and they have any children living at home, they will be older children… I need to see more of the house…'

'Then let us proceed.'

A survey of the well-appointed kitchen reveals that the household is vegetarian in diet and that they do not stint when it comes to buying their groceries.

'And it's so immaculately clean,' observes Mark. 'Doesn't even look like it's been used recently. Are the owners away on holiday…? No, they can't be: there's fresh food in the fridge…'

'Perhaps they are about to return and supplies have been purchased in preparation for this,' suggests Flat-Sol.

'And put here by whom?'

'Servants, of course.'

They go upstairs. More landscape paintings on the landing. There are a number of bedrooms whose empty drawers and wardrobes suggest untenanted guest bedrooms. They move on to the bathroom which, like the kitchen, is necessarily more modern-looking in its fixtures and fittings. A beaker on the shelf above the wash basin contains two toothbrushes, but Mark observes a distinct lack of feminine products amongst the toiletries in the cabinet and on the shower rack.

'We now have only the master bedroom to view,' announces Flat-Sol.

They move onto the room in question, and the first thing to catch Mark's eye is the painting dominating the wall facing the bed: a full-size reproduction of Gustave Courbet's 'The Source,' the subject of which is a naked woman viewed from behind as she stands in an ankle-deep woodland pool, leaning forward towards the stream of spring water which, descending from the rocks above, feeds the pool. The sunlit paleness of the woman's body contrasts with the dark tones of the rocks, boughs and foliage encompassing the pool. (And if this description isn't good enough for you, then Google it.)

'I see you like the painting,' observes Flat-Sol.

'Well, one can't help but notice it,' replies Mark. 'It just seems a bit out of place. All the other paintings we've seen are landscapes; but this one, while it still belongs to the realist school, is a nude.'

'And what does this suggest to you?'

'I'm not sure…' Mark looks from the painting to the bed, a double bed on which Yu-Mi, having kicked off her shoes, is already making herself comfortable, stretching herself out on top of the counterpane. 'From the contents of the bathroom I was beginning to think that just a single man lived in this house, but here we have a double bed with the pillows arranged for two, suggesting a couple sleep here. Yet if a woman used this room, I'd expect there to be a dressing table…'

'Perhaps the occupants are a male homosexual couple?' suggests Flat-Sol.

'Yes, but in that case, I wouldn't have expected *that*,' indicating the painting with its unequivocally female subject.

'Then perhaps a confirmed bachelor who sometimes entertains a lover.'

'Yes, that might be it… Look, how about giving me a clue? I've still got absolutely no idea whose house this might be.'

'No clues, Mark Hunter, but I suggest you investigate the contents of the wardrobe. You might find your answer there.'

'Very well.'

Mark crosses to the antique wardrobe, opens one of the doors and is confronted by a row of identical brown suits—identical both to one another and to that which Mark currently has on his person. Taking out one of the suits, Mark turns to face Flat-Sol, offering her a tight smile and a pair of accusing, but enlightened, eyes.

'My size, I take it?' says he.

'Made to measure,' replies she.

'Really? I don't recall attending the fitting.'

'There was no necessity for that: we have all your measurements on file.'

'As well as everything else it seems, from my literary preferences to my taste in landscape painting. But why *that*?' pointing once again at the nude.

'Because according to our files you are a pygophiliac.'

'What?!' explodes Mark.

'The term refers to an excessive fondness for the buttocks,' replies Flat-Sol smoothly.

'I know what it *means*!' retorts Mark. 'But who says I've got it?'

'Our files do, and our files are never wrong. As evidence to support the truth of this, I have only to cite the fact that Professor Dupont, your closest friend, is notably well-endowed in this regard.'

'But that's not *why* she's my best friend!'

'I repeat: our files are never wrong. But as they then go on to say that sex does not play an important part in your life, we have only included this one canvas catering to your predilection.'

'Well, it wasn't necessary,' Mark tells her. He replaces the suit on the rack, closes the wardrobe door.

'Very well. I will have the painting removed if it causes you any embarrassment.'

'I don't mean the painting,' says Mark; 'I mean *all* of this was not necessary: this house you've furnished for me. I don't want it.'

Flat-Sol looks confused. 'Why would you not want it? This makes no sense: the house and its location have been carefully selected, the interior furnished and decorated to harmonise to the fullest with your personality, your preferences. No expense has been spared in achieving this and in the shortest possible time. There should be nothing in this domicile that you should find distasteful or displeasing; not a single thing.'

'What I find displeasing, Miss Park, is the very fact that you have offered me this house in the first place; the fact you seem to take it for granted that I would want to accept this gift from you.'

'I fail to see why you would reject it. You are presently homeless, are you not?'

'And whose *fault* is it that I'm homeless?' snaps Mark.

'Really, Mark Hunter, why do you insist on holding me responsible for the attack upon your apartment?' and, extending the flat of her hand to forestall Mark's angry response: 'Very well. Let us say for the sake of argument that it *was* myself who instigated the bombing: who then more fitting than myself to be the one to offer you this new accommodation, superior in every way to your previous accommodation, by way of atonement.'

A hollow, helpless laugh from Mark. 'I could almost think you actually believe what you're saying... And you think I should be grateful, don't you?'

'I fail to see why you should not feel gratitude. A great deal of money has been expended on your behalf. Your own meagre resources could never have encompassed this. And the government you so loyally serve: would they have provided you with accommodation such as this.'

'And of course money solves everything, doesn't it?'

'Of course it does, Mark Hunter. That money solves everything is a fundamental fact of life; and one that I had no choice but to accept a very long time ago. People like yourself who refuse to accept this basic truth are delusional; you live in denial of the reality around you, vainly striving to fight against it. And to fight against money and the power it commands is to be fighting a battle you can never hope to win. Yes, money solves everything, it achieves everything, it breaks down all barriers, it removes all obstacles, disarms all resistance. Witness how swiftly I was able to release my employees from police custody when you had them arrested the other day. Anyone can be bribed or coerced if the price is right; and as for those stubborn few who are not amenable to bribery, they can easily be removed and replaced by someone who will be amenable.'

'And in return for putting this roof over my head, you expect me to crawl meekly into your pocket, I suppose?'

'Your future cooperation would be a reasonable return, yes. However, it is not essential. Even if you do not wish to ally yourself with the Parkhurst Corporation you may keep the house. It can be fully signed over to yourself, no strings attached.'

'And why would you do that, Miss Park? To throw money away like that would be very bad business, wouldn't it?'

'It would be bad business practice, yes; but in that case I choose to consider the expenditure a personal indulgence: to lavish oneself with expensive trifles is a prerogative of wealth.'

'And how would giving me this "expensive trifle" gratify you?'

'Because you interest me, Mark Hunter; you interest me very much. Perhaps more than I care to confess,' replies Flat-Sol, making her way across the room towards him. 'By my own set of standards I should despise you, I *do* despise you, yet nevertheless I find myself inexplicably drawn towards you,' and, coming to stop before him: 'Perhaps you are feeling the same thing?'

'Oddly enough, I'm not,' replies Mark.

'No? Well, perhaps this will change in time. Perhaps I can accelerate the change.'

'How? By spending more money?'

Flat-Sol smiles. 'As you remain determined in your stance of unworldliness, I must resort to other means.'

She folds her arms around Mark's neck and, displaying considerable strength, she forces him back against the wardrobe, kissing him with her painted lips, Eastern kisses, delicate and fleeting butterfly kisses. Mark remains passive, unresponsive.

'Why do you resist me?' she breathes. 'That second toothbrush in the bathroom could be mine.'

'Like me file says: sex is not an important part of my life.'

Flat-Sol tightens her embrace, moving her body against his, her kisses becoming more fervid and continental. 'One part of you at least is starting to respond,' smiling triumphantly, grinding her crotch against his.

'A purely physical reaction. It doesn't mean I've fallen madly in love with you.'

'Then perhaps I can compel you to fall in love with me,' speaking between hungry kisses. 'Come, embrace me, Mark Hunter. Put your arms around me.'

And Mark does put his arms around her, he puts his arms around and gripping her firmly around the waist, he thrusts her away from him, wrenching her lips from his. Caught by surprise, Flat-Sol stumbles and falls backwards onto the bed (without disturbing its snoring occupant.)

'I have to decline your kind offer, Miss Park,' says Mark briskly, 'and I bid you good day.'

And he crosses the room to the door.

'Mark Hunter.'

Mark pauses with his hand on the door handle, looks round. Flat-Sol, on her feet again, glares at him, face as brittle as her voice.

'My chauffeuse will take you wherever you wish to go.'

Mark shakes his head. 'Thank you, but there's no need. I'll just catch the bus.'

And as Mark exits the room, the look on the face of Flat-Sol Park burns itself into his mind. He knows she is not going to forgive him for rejecting her anytime soon.

Chapter Nineteen
Three Strikes You're Dead?

'Hello?'

'Hello, is that Dodo Dupont?'

'Yes, it's me. Who's this?'

'You don't know me, but I've got some information you'll want to know.'

'Information about what?'

'About who's been trying to kill your girlfriend.'

'You're saying you know who they are? The people who killed Joanna Fairbright?'

'That was just an accident! It wasn't her they meant to kill! It was your girlfriend!'

'That's what I thought, but never mind that: who are they?'

'I can't tell you on the phone. Come to the—'

'*Why* can't you tell me on the phone? I mean—'

'Look, I just *can't*, okay?'

'I don't see why not. All you've got to do is—'

'Look, do you want to know who they are or not?'

'Yes, of course I do, but—'

'Then just fucking shut up and listen! Come to Plackett's scrapyard in Blackfriars this afternoon at three. I'll be waiting for you there. Got it?'

'Yes, I've got it. But why—'

'And it's gunna cost you, right? The information's gunna cost you.'

'How much?'

'Twenty pounds.'

'Twenty pounds? Yes, I think I can manage that. But where exactly—'

'Look, just go to the scrapyard and walk in through the gates, alright? I'll be waiting for you inside.'

A corrugated iron fence, rusting, topped with lengths of barbed wire, runs flush with the pavement, extending itself along the street. Although innocent of paint, the fence is plentifully adorned with graffiti, scrawled slogans and symbols. Close to its commencement the fence is interrupted by a pair of sagging wire mesh gates, also the worse for rust. Above the gates a wooden sign, its paintwork blistered and peeling, bearing the legend: S PLACKETT SCRAP MERCHANT. Beyond these portals can be seen the stacked corpses of hundreds and hundreds of motor cars. Above the fence a crane can be seen at work in the yard, lifting the gutted vehicles in its metal claw to be consigned to the crusher. On the nearside the yard is bordered by a row of terrace houses, and at the further end by an old factory building. Across the road from the yard, beyond a wasteland of scrubby vegetation looms the massive cylindrical form of a chemical storage tower. Aside from the methodical metal giant at work in the yard, the street, an urban photographer's delight, is quiet, dozing under the midday sun.

A car appears, driving slowly along the street towards the yard. The car is a stranger to the area; a four-seater Jaguar sports car, whose polished bright red bodywork stands starkly out from the much more modest automobiles parked along the street. The car, slowing as it approaches the scrapyard, drives on past the gates and then further along the fence pulls into the kerb, sliding in a vacant spot between two parked cars.

Dodo Dupont steps out of the driver's seat. Dressed all in figure-hugging black, her appearance is as vividly out of place in these surroundings as that of her vehicle: black polo-neck sweater, black PVC trousers and black boots form her ensemble. Raising her mirrored shades above her bangs, she surveys the down at heel exterior of the yard.

I'll be waiting for you inside, the caller had said.

Skirting round her vehicle, Dodo makes her way along the pavement towards the gates. The possibility that she might be walking into a trap has not escaped Dodo. And then there's also the possibility that she is being hoaxed. Since the incident at Television Centre there have been no further attempts on Mayumi's life; it appeared that the shock of killing the wrong person and the ensuing murder investigation had sent the perpetrators into hiding. But they might just be biding their time, waiting for the heat to cool off before making their next attempt. It all depends on how determined they are.

To Dodo it seems monstrous, completely insane, that anyone would target Mayumi, would want to take her life, just because they object to her photography. She knows full well there are no shortage of nutcases around, particularly in this day and age, but even so… They would have to be some seriously demented anti-porn activists who have decided that Mayumi's art is porn and that they are going to make an example of her. But for Christ's Sake…! If that's the bee they've got lodged in their bonnets, what about the *real* pornographers? But no, they target Mayumi: sweet, innocent, kind-hearted Mayumi, who would never hurt a fly. But then you have people doing the same thing all the time: ignoring the real enemy and choosing a nice soft target instead.

Well, whoever these people are, and whatever their motivations, Dodo isn't going to forgive them in a hurry.

Dodo loves Mayumi to distraction.

That day they had first met, it had been love at first sight. Dodo was in Japan making a documentary for which she wanted to interview the photographer whose work had come to her attention, and she had called on Mayumi by appointment in her studio. And it had been love at first sight. (The trite description is theirs not mine.) *Is* there such a thing as love at first sight, or is it only just the first sprouting of the seeds of love, seeds that then blossom with such fertile rapidity that in hindsight it just *seems* as though it was love at first sight? Either way, it was in a very short space of time from having first set eyes on each other that their fast-blooming love was consummated first in Mayumi's photographic studio and then in her bedroom.

And as they had begun, so they have continued, their flame burning continuously and as brightly as ever—and Dodo Dupont, take-charge, can-do, kick-ass, alpha-plus action heroine Dodo Dupont, is putty in the hands of the woman who calls her 'my master.' Dodo would do anything for Mayumi.

And when she gets her hands on the ones who are trying to extinguish that precious life—well, she won't take the law into her own hands, but she won't go easy on them either.

A head, with the upper part of a body attached to it, peaks out between the open gates of the yard, a cowled head with the face concealed behind sunglasses and a disposable facemask. The head looks first one the wrong way down the street and then the right way. Catching sight of Dodo, it quickly disappears.

Dodo, increasing her pace, reaches the gates and enters the yard. Directly before her is an expanse open ground, unsurfaced, rutted with fossilised tyre-tracks; on her left stands a substantial wooden hut, white-painted, flat-roofed; and on her right begin those serried ranks of piled up cars, the windowless, wheelless metal corpses. Just past the hut some of the more recent arrivals to the yard are gathered; fresh subjects waiting to be stripped and disembowelled.

A figure in blue jeans and a grey hoodie is running towards the rows of stacked up cars.

A girl, thinks Dodo. Definitely a girl: broad-framed, big-boned.

The voice on the phone had been a girl's voice; a Londoner. She had sounded young, nervous and agitated—and that demand for a laughable twenty pounds in return for her information had made her seem like a complete amateur. This must be her.

The masked girl turns and beckons to Dodo before disappearing behind the first row of stacked cars.

Dodo sets off after her. Who is she? Assuming that she's for real and that she knows the identities of the people trying to kill Mayumi, who is she? To Dodo the most likely explanation would be that the girl is a turncoat, a member of the group targeting Mayumi who has left them or else wants to leave. Those running figures caught by the CCTV camera outside Television Centre had looked like they might have been young people, and they had been wearing hoodies.

Strange that no-one has emerged from the hut to challenge either herself or the girl… But the crane is active so the yard is obviously open for business. Turning into the first avenue of stacked cars, Dodo regains sight of the girl, and she is still running. The girl turns and beckons again before disappearing round a corner.

Dodo runs to catch up with her. *How far is she planning to lead me into this maze?*

She reaches the corner. The girl is ahead of her, stationary now, standing at the further end of this second scrap-metal avenue, about fifty yards ahead. They are much closer to the crane now, sound of its engine, its gears and pistons, fills the air. Dodo, slowing to a fast walk, makes her way towards her. The girl just stands there, face still concealed behind mask and glasses, hands stuffed in the pockets of her hoodie. Dodo has closed the distance to twenty yards when the girl holds out her arm, displaying the flat of a gloved hand.

'Stop there!'

Dodo stops.

'You're the one who called me here?' shouts Dodo.

'Yes!' shouts back the girl.

'And you've got some information about who's been trying to kill Mayumi?'

'Yes, I have!'

'Look, can we stand a bit closer? I can barely hear you over all this noise!'

'No! Stay where you are!'

'Look, I'm not going to hurt, you for Christ's sake!'

'Just stay where you are! We can talk like this!'

The girl is looking up. Dodo looks up. She sees the underside of a car hanging high above her head—*directly* above her head.

Oh, not again!

The car drops, released by the crane's metal claw. Dodo runs, dives. The car hits the ground with a thunderous crash, raising a cloud of dirt. Dodo scrambles to her feet. The girl starts running.

'Oi, you little—!'

Dodo gives chase. A trap—and it's *her* they're after, not Mayumi! The possibility had occurred to Dodo right from the start, but up until this moment all the evidence had seemed to point to Mayumi being the intended target!

She chases the girl round another corner and they are in the centre of the maze: a square of open ground surrounded by stacks of flattened cars and in the middle of which stands the crane. (An old crane and one which looks about ready for the scrap heap itself.) The engine has been extinguished and the operator, masked and dressed in jeans and a hoodie identical to those of the girl, is climbing down from the cabin. A third person, identically dressed, stands waiting beside the crane.

'You missed her!' yells the girl, running towards the crane.

The announcement is somewhat superfluous as Dodo is already in full view of the fleeing girl's two cohorts. The one standing beside the vehicle starts running in circles, arms flailing.

The crane operator's reaction is much angrier. 'Why did you lead her straight to us, you stupid cow!'

The voice is female. Are they all girls? wonders Dodo.

The woman jumps down from the crane, grabs the headless chicken impersonator by the arm and starts running, the first girl falling in with them. There is another avenue of scrapped cars leading off from the far side of the open area, and the assassins flee down this, Dodo in hot pursuit.

No, they're not all women, decides Dodo. From the body-language, the panicky, uncoordinated one is male, a boy. But the crane driver, the tall one: her voice sounded more mature than the other girl's. She has to be the leader of the three.

The ground now opens out and before them the rear fence of the scrapyard stretches off in both directions. Piles of car tyres of varying heights have been stacked in front of the fence directly ahead, and Dodo, a much faster runner than her quarry, is closing on them fast as they start to scramble up the stacks of tyres, the highest of which reach almost to the top of the fence, where a thick blanket has been thrown over the barbed wire. Reaching the summit, first the girl, then the boy, climb over the blanket and drop down out of sight on the other side of the fence. Now only the erstwhile crane operator remains. She turns and seeing Dodo, kicks the stack of tyres below her feet, before scrambling over the fence. The stack overbalances, striking neighbouring stacks which also overbalance, precipitating an avalanche. Tyres come bouncing and rolling hither and thither and Dodo, swearing, is forced to take cover.

The avalanche subsiding, Dodo runs for the fence, jumps, grabs the end of the draped blanket and pulls herself up to the top. Beyond the fence, the ground slopes down to the river, and a small cabin cruiser, with three hooded occupants, is just pulling away from a jetty.

Chapter Twenty
Why Dodo Dupont Deserves to Die

These days it has become popular to say that the antithesis of love is not hate but indifference. Love is an active emotion, the loved one being always on the lover's mind. Indifference is a passive emotion, it is the dismissal of that person from your thoughts and to have no strong feelings either way about them. Hate, like love, is an active emotion, the hated one being the focus of the thoughts of the hater. Therefore, perhaps we could say that hate is not so much love's opposite number, as its evil twin.

Rajni Sunnybrook was once in love with Dodo Dupont, the woman she now hates so much that she is determined to kill.

It was at Cambridge that she had first met her, where they were both studying psychology. Like everyone else on the course, she had been magnetised by Dodo's alpha personality, and she had become one of the loyal circle of admiring friends who flocked around her. The eighteen-year-old Dodo was as physically fully grown (she'd attained her six-foot stature at the age of fifteen) as she is today, and her hair was cut short in more-or-less the same way. She was perhaps a little less robust and those androgynous lines of her face were still softened by the glow of youth. Her personality was at that time less evolved than her body, as she lacked the knowledge and the life experience that she was to gather over the next few years and which would serve to fill out and add the finishing touches to her character. The eighteen-year-old Dodo could be somewhat thoughtless of others at times and, it has to be confessed, she was just a tad full of herself.

But Rajni was only eighteen herself at that time, a shy, inexperienced girl; and to her Dodo had seemed like something entirely new: a paragon, someone she would have willingly followed to the ends of the earth. ('But I only live round the corner!') Yes, that was how Rajni had felt about Dodo Dupont—that is, until the day she found out that Dodo had slept with her boyfriend.

His name was Sheldon, a fellow student, and he was her first boyfriend, the first sexual partner she had ever had. And at the time their relationship had seemed very serious; at least it had seemed so to Rajni, and she had thought that Sheldon felt the same way.

It was a tale-teller who had brought the story to Rajni, one of those much-maligned individuals who of course only have your best interests at heart by bringing you the news they know you won't like hearing, and who really have no desire to just stir things up. Yes, the story came from a tale-teller, but the tale told was a truthful one, for all that, as Rajni found out when she had confronted Sheldon and he had shamefacedly confessed his guilt. But it was just a one-night stand! A moment of insanity! It had meant nothing, absolutely *nothing*, and it would never happen again! And *she* was the one who'd instigated it! *She* was the one who'd come after *him*!

And it turned out that Sheldon wasn't the only one. Not by a long chalk. The story soon began to come out, at first bit by bit, and then, when it formed into one cohesive truth, it was all over the campus: Dodo Dupont had systematically—and over the course of a mere two weeks!—bedded every male student in the psychology class!

And why had she done this? The immediate assumption was that Dodo must be clinically hypersexual; a nympho slut in lay terms. But this turned out not to be the case. And no, she hadn't done it for a bet, either. No, young Dodo had been motivated by only the loftiest of ideals when she bedded every boy in her class: it had been done in the name of science! Yes, it was an experiment, a research assignment of her own conceiving. She had done what she had done to see if it *could* be done, and to observe the responses of her male 'subjects' as well as her own thoughts and feelings. She had made copious notes and written a full report on her findings, which she even planned to submit to their professor.

It was like Dodo actually expected to be praised for what she'd done! Never mind that she'd ruined Rajni's relationship; no, never mind that! Because it had all been done in the name of science! (And the relationship *had* been ruined. She had refused to listen to Sheldon's snivelling apologies and she'd dumped him. For the remainder of the three-year course she had never spoken to him again.)

Naturally there'd been a furore; it was the talk of the college, it was the talk of *all* the colleges; and Dodo had been dragged before the faculty and there she had been officially reprimanded, and told in no uncertain terms to stick to the syllabus in future and to refrain from engaging in any unauthorised 'original research.'

And that was it! She should have been expelled! Thrown off the course! This was the outcome Rajni had confidently anticipated, and on hearing that the culprit had been let off with nothing more than a rap on the knuckles, her already simmering rage now boiled over completely. She wanted to go up to Dodo and tell her exactly what she thought of her, only she lacked the courage, the confidence, or whatever it was; so instead she had sent Dodo a blistering email telling her exactly what she thought of her. In response to this she had received an infuriatingly calm and composed response from Dodo in which she had apologised for her actions, gently advised Rajni not to let her negative emotions get the better of her, and suggested she give her relationship with Sheldon a second chance.

Of course this had just enraged Rajni all the more and she had sent Dodo a reply to her reply in which she had 'let her negative emotions get the better of her' with a vengeance, in a tirade of abuse and obscenity to which Dodo had replied by sending her link to the Samaritans website.

Rajni had assumed that popular feeling would be on her side and that Dodo would be sent to Coventry, ostracised by her fellow students; but no: in next to no time at all, all had been forgiven and Dodo was once again the centre of attention and everybody's friend! And Rajni wasn't the only one who'd had a boyfriend amongst the boys in the class; there had been several others, but those other girls: they'd all gone and forgiven Dodo! Just like that! And before you knew it, they were practically congratulating her for what she'd done! For Christ's sake! Give someone a charismatic personality and they can get away with murder!

So instead, it was Rajni herself who found herself being sent to Coventry; by refusing to associate with Dodo she sent herself there. She snubbed Dodo and continued to snub her until Dodo gave up and left her alone. And then the people around her just gradually stopped noticing her, because they were all flocking around Dodo and Rajni felt completely eclipsed by the other woman, neglected and undervalued. She tried to distract herself by throwing herself into her studies, but she would be plagued with wild fantasies about usurping Dodo's place, making herself the centre of attention, the one that everybody wanted to be with. And as there was no way the increasingly solitary Rajni could ever become as charismatic and popular as Dodo, these fantasies were really just a form of protracted self-torture. Result: she'd just become steadily more and more bitter and resentful.

But finally, the ordeal had come to an end, and Rajni had graduated and left Cambridge with every intention of just erasing Dodo Dupont from her mind and getting on with the rest of her life.

Fat chance of that.

Because very soon it was Dodo Dupont publishes her first book; Dodo Dupont appears on television programmes;

Dodo Dupont makes her *own* television programmes; Dodo Dupont publishes her first nudie photobook; Dodo Dupont, Dodo Dupont, Dodo Dupont.

All of Rajni's bottled-up resentment of Dodo, the wrongs she had suffered at her hands, started to foam back up to the surface.

The Chief-Inspector Dreyfus nervous tick started to manifest itself; whenever Dodo's name was mentioned in her presence, her face would start to twitch, all the more so when it was someone eulogising Dodo, singing her praises—and people were *always* eulogising her and singing her praises.

And while success just kept on following success for Dodo Dupont, everything just kept on going wrong for Rajni Sunnybrook. She couldn't get jobs; and the jobs she did get never lasted long; research projects would suddenly be cancelled; universities would suddenly institute staff cuts: always *something*. It seemed that while Dodo Dupont was leading a charmed life, Rajni Sunnybrook's was cursed.

And it was all wrong! It ought to be Dodo Dupont, that boyfriend-stealing, self-important con-artist Dodo Dupont: *she* was the one who deserved to fail! The woman was stealing all the fame and fortune that by rights should have been hers!

No! Dodo didn't just deserve to fail: she deserved to *die*. And if fate wasn't going to serve out this well-merited punishment, then somebody needed to lend fate a helping hand.

'"Twenty pounds." You and your stupid twenty pounds. Why couldn't you just stick to the script?'

'I thought it would sound more convincing if I asked for money!'

Rajni and Jenny are alone in the front room. Ian is asleep upstairs; Rajni has had to sedate him, after catching him in the act of trying to hang himself. Jenny sits on the sofa, chewing her nails; Rajni glares down at her, arms akimbo.

'Yes, but *twenty pounds*, for Christ's sake! For someone like Dodo Dupont, twenty quid isn't even pocket change! People with that kind of money use twenty-pound notes to roll their spliffs in! Or they did when they were still made of paper. No wonder she was suspicious!'

'She *wasn't* suspicious! You just dropped the car in the wrong place!'

'I did not drop the car in the wrong place: I dropped it in exactly the *right* place! She just got out of the way in time because she was *suspicious*!' Adopting a dopey voice: '"I want twenny pounds, see? Twenny big ones! And I want it in used, unmarked bills! Bring the money in a suitcase, and no funny business!"'

'Oh, fuck off,' says Jenny, half under breath.

'Don't you tell me to fuck off!' snaps back Rajni. 'Thanks to you we missed again and now Dodo knows it's her we want to kill! She'll be on the alert now!'

'So let's just get the fuck out of here while we still can!'

'What are you blathering on about? Why have we got to get out of here? You think the cops are on their way or something?'

'Yes!'

'Oh, for Christ's sake! Use what little brains you've got: Dodo didn't see us, did she? We had masks on! Nobody saw us and we all wore gloves, so there won't be any fingerprints for anyone to find. So will you just calm down and get a grip? It's bad enough I had to sedate Captain Useless upstairs, I don't want you flaking out on me as well! I thought you had more balls than that!'

'Yeah, alright,' mutters Jenny irritably. 'It's not Ian's fault, is it? You know what he's like. Why can't you leave him alone?' She reaches for her cigarettes.

'Yes, I know what Ian's like,' retorts Rajni. 'But he ought to show a bit blind more faith in *me*! That's what annoys me.

He ought to realise that whatever trouble I get him into I can get him out of as well! And you should remember that as well!'

Jenny lights her cigarette and following her example, Rajni lights up one of her cigars. She inhales and as usual starts coughing violently.

'Why do you keep smoking them things?' inquires Jenny irritably. 'You can't handle them.'

'Of course I can handle them!' wheezes Rajni, thumping her chest. 'I just went down the wrong way, that's all.'

'Every drag you take seems to go down the wrong way. Why don't you try vaping?'

'Why don't you try minding your own fucking business?' retorts Rajni. 'I don't go around telling you what to smoke, do I?' Jenny opens her mouth to speak, but Rajni holds out a silencing hand. 'Look, let's get this conversation back on topic: the point is Dodo knows now that it's her we're trying to kill, so she's going to be on her guard, and that means we've got to be even more careful from now on; we've got to plan our next move very carefully... I'm thinking if we could lure her onto a building site somewhere... We'd need a plausible pretext, of course, but if we could get her there and lure her to the right spot, we could drop one of those big girders on her; or maybe a whole load of big girders...'

'Why does it always have to be dropping things on her?' demands Jenny. 'There's other ways to kill someone, you know, besides dropping things on them!'

Rajni freezes, cigar halfway to her lips.

Other ways to kill someone besides dropping things on them... Other ways to kill someone... Well, well, well... She will have to give this some serious thought...

Chapter Twenty-One
Trina's Tribulations

*'Twenty-Eight More Days to Zero Day,
Zero Day, Zero Day,
Twenty-Eight More Days to Zero Day,
Zero Day, Zero Day,
Silver Spaceman!'*

Thus sings Trina Truelove, a very merry Trina Truelove, on her fourth gin and tonic.

'Silver spaceman?' The man sitting next to her, and who has paid for all but her first drink, asks the question.

'Yeah; didn't you hear the story? It's been all over the internet.'

'You mean those robot sightings? But weren't they supposed to be just people dressed up as the robots for some old film? What's that got to do with the Zero adverts?'

'Oh!' says Trina. It is the 'oh' of someone who belatedly realises they have been letting their mouth run away with them. 'No, I… No, it doesn't have anything… Like you say, they're just…' and then, more firmly: Well, it fits the lyrics, doesn't it? You know; Silver Spaceman instead of Silver Shamrock.'

'Oh, I see. I thought maybe you knew something I didn't…'

'No! No, no, no! I don't know *anything* you don't!' Trina assures him.

The man's name is Carl; he's a handsome hunk of guy in a sharp suit who runs his own company—and he actually knows who Trina is! He'd seen her when she walked into the pub, and he'd recognised her! He knew about her working for Mayumi Takahashi and that she'd been there when they'd tried to drop that piano on her!

Recognition at last!

Yes, Trina is very much taken by Carl. He's a good listener for one thing; not all men are, and that's a fact! Some of them they just go on and on about themselves all the time and you can't get a fucking word in edgewise! And then he looks hot, too: real male-model good looks. And from those clothes of his and that wristwatch he's got on, he must be totally loaded! Now Trina is not one to go around choosing her boyfriends based on the depth of their wallets, but it is always a bonus when the guy you've hooked up with is 'financially secure.'

But she can't shake the feeling that she's seen him before somewhere… Something about him rings a vague bell…

She looks at him. 'So, you're *sure* we haven't met before…?'

Trina had to just get out of the flat. Things have been a bit overcrowded of late.

Although the perfect hostess in every way, and never one to impose her opinions and preferences on others, one thing Dodo Dupont does not allow is the cooking of any meat products in her kitchen: hers is a vegetarian kitchen and she will not allow it to be contaminated with meat, nor let the atmosphere of her apartment be contaminated with the smell of cooking meat. Yuki Kinoshita, Mayumi Takahashi's competitive eating former schoolfriend, is especially fond of meat. In fact, meat is Yuki's favourite food, and the vegetarian diet imposed on her by staying with Dodo and Mayumi has been getting a bit much for her. After suffering in silence for as long as she possibly could, Yuki finally opened her heart to Mayumi, and Mayumi, ever sympathetic, generously arranged for Yuki to transfer her lodgings to the apartment of non-vegetarian Trina Truelove.

The first Trina hears of this arrangement is when she gets a call from Mayumi telling her that Yuki will be there in about an hour.

Her one hour's grace has allowed Trina time to gather up all the clothes strewn about her bedroom floor, sort out the sleeping arrangements, and then tidy up a bit in the kitchen.

Trina's is only a one-bedroom flat; one bedroom, one bed; but fortunately she also possesses a futon, on hand for those rare occasions when she is entertaining an overnight guest who won't actually be sharing her bed. And this works perfectly, doesn't it? Her unexpected guest is a Japanese woman, and a futon is a Japanese bed! Yes, they do also have beds with spring mattresses in Japan, but not everybody has one: a lot of people sleep on futons. So, while she's here, Yuki can sleep on the futon feeling right at home and Trina won't have to feel bad about keeping the big bed for herself!

A knock at the door. Flurried and breathless from the unaccustomed bout of housecleaning, Trina rushes to answer it. She hasn't had time to do anything about the front room which is still in its usual disorderly state.

Yuki stands smiling in the doorway.

'Hi!' Trina greets her.

Yuki bows. 'Thank you for having me!' she says.

'No probs,' says Trina. 'Come on in.'

Yuki, wheeling her suitcase, walks in.

'Sorry about the mess,' says Trina. 'I was just in the middle of cleaning up…'

Yuki takes in the living room, the clutter of art books, clothes, shoes, CDs, camera equipment, junk mail cluttering the carpet, the Argos furniture, the easel standing in one corner (our Trina is a budding artist as well as a shutterbug) and the framed posters on the walls: panda-eyed Kurt Cobain; the smiling faces of Japanese girl band No Tits…

(No Tits are a band whose music Mayumi, who of course went to school with them, has introduced Trina to.)

Yuki points at the poster. 'No Tits!' she enthuses, pronouncing the word 'teats.' 'I go to school with them!'

'Yeah, they're cool, aren't they?' says Trina.

'Kitchen is over there?' pointing to the open doorway across the room.

'Yep, that's it. Well, it's more of a kitchenette, really; it's not very big.'

'And you have meat in kitchen?' inquires Yuki.

'Yeah, I have meat in kitchen,' confirms Trina.

'Good!'

'Come on: I'll show you the bedroom and you can unpack your stuff.'

They enter the bedroom. Trina's double bed, which if it could speak could tell of many a night torrid of sex (and many a heated argument!) takes up most of the available space. The wall facing the bed is home to a framed enlargement of an example of her mentor's photography: a nude monochrome image of Dodo and Mayumi locked in a passionate lovers' embrace. (This strategically-placed image has fuelled many a bean-flicking session for Trina).

Trina has set the futon out along the wall next to the door, the only available space that won't obstruct access to any of her wardrobes or chest of drawers. A pillow (an English pillow, not one of those funny little Japanese ones) and a folded back duvet have been placed on the futon, in readiness for its occupant.

'Here we are!' says Trina, proudly indicating the futon.

Completely ignoring which, Yuki has jumped straight onto the bed. Stretched out full length, she bounces up and down on the spring mattress.

'Very nice bed!' she enthuses. 'I like!'

'Er...' says Trina. 'I've er, got a futon here... See? Futon: Japanese bed. Very nice, very comfortable.'

Yuki sits up, surveys the futon, nodding her approval. 'Yes! Futon very nice, very comfortable! You sleep well there!'

'Yeah...'

'…So, what can I do? I can't exactly tell her she's got it all arse backwards, can I? I can't just turf her out of my bed and tell her she's got to sleep on the futon!'

'No, I see your problem,' sympathises Carl. 'You didn't want to seem the ungenerous host, did you?'

'Exactly! But you haven't the worst of it, yet! Cuz I'd only just got used to the idea of having to rough it on a futon when there's another knock at the door…!'

Trina opens the door. Shizuka Todoroki, prim and bespectacled, stands on the threshold. At her side is a suitcase.

'Thank you,' she says and walks past Trina into the living room ('like I'm the bloody butler or something!' as she says to Carl.) She surveys the room critically.

'So, these are to be Miss Kinoshita's new quarters,' says she. 'Has Miss Kinoshita arrived yet?'

Yuki emerges from the bedroom, all smiles. The two Japanese women exchange rapid conversation in their own language.

'Excuse me,' interjects Trina pointedly. 'What's with the suitcase? I never said you could stay here as well.'

'Do you speak Japanese?' demands Shizuka.

'No, I don't,' says Trina.

'Precisely. And as Miss Kinoshita speaks very little English, I shall remain by her side as her interpreter.'

'But you can't stay here!' protests Trina. 'I've only got two beds! Look!' leading the way back to the bedroom.

'This will suffice,' declares Shizuka, having taken stock of the sleeping accommodation.

'Oh! You mean you're gunna sleep in the bed with Yuki? Oh! Well, that's fine then—'

'No, I shall sleep on the futon. It would be inappropriate for me share to a bed with my client.'

'Then where am I supposed to sleep!' explodes Trina.

Shizuka steps past her back into the living room. 'I see no reason why that settee cannot serve as a bed for yourself; indeed, it looks most comfortable.'

'…And that's how it's been, for the last three bloody days! Me having to crash on my own fucking sofa!'

'Is that so bad? It can't be any less comfortable than the futon would've been,' argues Carl. 'It's got padded cushions, hasn't it?'

'Oh yeah, it's got cushions alright, but it's not big enough! It's only two seats long, so I either have to lie on my side curled up, or if I lie on my back, I have to have my feet stuck out over the armrest! And there's not exactly much room for turning over, either! If you roll over in your sleep— bam! You're on the floor!'

'Well, I suppose it's only going to be for… how many more days, was it?'

'Ha! Well, that's something else, isn't it? How long *are* they gunna be there for? It might end up being ages now, cuz Yumi's got her modelling for her. We've been at the studio all week, doing pictures for this new project of hers called *Sexy Eatings*.'

'Sexy *Eatings*? That doesn't sound like good grammar.'

'It isn't good grammar, it's Japanese grammar,' says Trina. 'Well, Yumi always says "foods" instead of "food;" so I suppose for her, if "food" is "foods," then "eating" is "eatings." And Yumi's not only got Yuki stripping off, but she's even roped in the bloody interpreter as well! I totally do not get that woman! Not a word of protest; just does what Yumi tells her to: like she thinks it's just part of her job or something!'

'You mean the interpreter's in these pictures as well?'

'Yeah! And you should see what Yumi's got them doing! They're like eating food off each other! It's meant to be like this geisha thing, where one of the geishas lies there with food all over her, like she's a table; but when they do it, it's all little nibbles like sushi and stuff, stuff you can pick up with chopsticks; nothing messy. But what we're doing is like a piss-take version where it's all cakes and cream and puddings and stuff they've got all over them and they're like licking it off each other! And it's like you see them there and they're like totally lesboing it out those two, and I'm thinking "so you can eat chocolate cake off each other's arses for Yumi's pictures, but you can't even share a bed round mine so that at least I could have the fucking futon to sleep on?" I mean what's up with that for Christ's sake!

'And another thing: since she's been round mine Yuki's gone totally meat-mad! It's like she was suffering from major withdrawal from having to go without while she was round Dodo's, and now she's like making up for lost time! It's just meat, meat, meat! And you should see her when she's eating the stuff! The noises she makes! It's like she's having multiple orgasms…! Still, I will say one thing for her though, she's been buying all this meat herself, so it *is* cutting down on my grub bills…'

'…So, you're *sure* we haven't met before?'

'Positive,' replies Carl, giving her his best smile. 'Like I said, I'm not a regular here; I just happened to be in this part of town on business and decided to call in. And I'm very glad I did!'

'Me too!' says Trina.

They clink glasses.

'It must have been fate, mustn't it?'

'Yeah! Fate!'

Another clink.

'So, you've been doing all this photo work with Mayumi… Have there been any more attempts on her life recently? I haven't heard—'

'Oh God! You wouldn't know about that, would you? Well get this, then: turns out it wasn't Yumi they were trying to kill at all—it was Dodo! It's *her* they're after!'

'Really? Yes, she was there both times, wasn't she... Do they know who it is?'

'Not a fucking clue! Dodo's got no idea why someone would want to kill her. I mean, it's not like she's working with Mark—oop!' Trina clamps a hand over her mouth.

'"Working with Mark?" Who's this Mark?'

'Mark?' says blushing Trina, trying to sound inconsequential. 'Did I say Mark?'

'You *definitely* said Mark. Who is this Mark? Come on, now...! Not your boyfriend, I hope? You told me you hadn't got a boyfriend.'

'No, no! I *haven't* got a boyfriend!' insists Trina. 'Mark's just... he's just someone Dodo knows...'

'Just double-checking,' replies Carl; and then, with the air of someone having reached a decision, he picks up his glass, quickly drains it and puts it firmly back down on the table. 'Okay Trina, we can either go back to my place or else I'll just have to fuck you right here and now in the pub, because my cock's about to burst out of my trousers. What do you say?'

'Well...' says Trina, affecting a thoughtful tone. 'I wouldn't want to get banned from my local... So let's just go back to your place!'

And Carl, whose last name is Jensen, takes Trina out to his car.

Chapter Twenty-Two
A Bridge Too Far

'Hello?'

'Is that Mark Hunter...?'

'Yes... Who is this...?'

'It's me, Amber...'

'Amber! Thank goodness you're still alright! Where are you?'

'I'm in a phone box. I can't talk for a long; I haven't got much money. Can we meet up? I mean, right now?'

'Of course we can! Tell me where you are and I'll be there as soon as I can!'

'Okay; come to Blackfriars Bridge; I'll meet you in the middle of the bridge on the right side of the road.'

'The right side coming from which direction?'

'From the south side. Can you, can you help me? Can I trust you...?'

'Of course you can trust me, Amber! If you're in any danger I can help you! Are those people still after you?'

'I s'pose they are. I haven't seen anyone; I've been hiding... Just come to the bridge, alright? And come by yourself!'

'I will, I promise! I can be there in... half an hour; say nine o'clock, okay?'

'Okay. Nine o'clock.'

Click. Beep-beep-beep-beep...

Mark stands in the embrasure above the central pier of Blackfriars Bridge, looking out over the Thames. Night has fallen and the river's dark surface reflects the myriad lights of the city. Ahead is the railway bridge, that solar-panelled serpent spanning the river. Off to the left rises the illuminated dome St Paul's Cathedral (now repaired since being struck by a missile in a terrorist attack.)

Mark recalls a George WM Reynolds penny dreadful he once read, *The Young Duchess*, and an incident in that book that took place right where he now stands. Some of the characters had needed to dispose of an inconvenient corpse; and had attempted to do this by lowering it from the parapet of Blackfriars Bridge (the corpse having been dismembered and put in a sack.) 'Attempted to' because, alarmed by the sound of approaching footsteps, the conspirators had let go of the rope too soon, and the sack, instead dropping into the river, had come to rest on the abutment at the foot of the pier, and there it had been discovered the following day.

Good old clunky and verbose GWM: Those serial novels of his are a real eye-opener to anyone only familiar with the 'respectable' face of Victorian fiction!

Although now he comes to think of it, *was* it Blackfriars Bridge where that incident took place...? On reflection, it might actually have been the old Waterloo Bridge... (And of course, Mark can't just consult the book to check up on this, because his precious copy has gone up in smoke along with the rest of his collection.)

At this moment St Paul's and its numerous smaller brethren on both sides of the river break into simultaneous voice, tolling the hour. Nine o'clock.

Mark turns from the river prospect and now focuses his attention on the footpath stretching away towards the Southwark end of the bridge, the directions he assumes Amber to be coming from. The flow of traffic on the road is steady and continuous but there are comparatively few pedestrians crossing the bridge.

No sign of her yet.

Come on, Amber. Don't bail on me this time. Please.

In his mind he replays that terse telephone conversation, his first direct contact with that elusive girl in weeks and weeks and the first time he has spoken to her since that night at the Jolly Tar when he didn't even know who she was. She called him from a public phone box, which suggests she has either got rid of, or is wary of switching on, her mobile device. She sounded scared on the phone, desperate...

There have been no further sightings of those *Earth Dies Screaming* robots, but that doesn't mean that they, or whatever human agency might be directing them, have given up on their hunt for the girl. Amber obviously believes they're still out there, still searching for her, and so she has gone to ground somewhere. Just where has she been hiding herself? Is she alone, or with friends? She's been keeping clear of her apartment, and she's made no attempt to contact her family—who she's not on good terms with anyway. From all he has heard about her, Amber is a solitary, socially-awkward girl, perhaps even mildly autistic: does she even have any friends to turn to?

Still no sign of her.

Always just out of reach; that's how she's been; always just out of reach… First that night at the pub, hiding in plain sight, working the bar… Then in the hospital, when he'd chased her down to the carpark… Why hadn't she spoken to him there and then, for heaven's sake! Why clout him over the head and leave him a message it took him two days to find? (Mark looks forward to taking Amber to task for that one.)

Always just out of reach…

Oh, come on, Amber. Give me a chance; trust me; I can help you; I can protect you. Come on, don't be a no-show; not this time…

It was when she stopped believing in God: that's what got her in this mess. No. It wasn't because she stopped believing in God; it was because of that creep of an evangelist. Yeah, that was it, thinks Amber, as her life passes in rapid review: that was what started it all. Her not believing in God anymore; that would never have mattered if that evangelist hadn't come along and brainwashed her mum and her brother and sisters; cuz then Mum would never have chucked her out of the house in the first place.

They'd all been 'God-fearing Christians' in her family: her gran and grandad, Mum, even her deadbeat Dad; that was the way they'd been brought up; brought up to be God-fearing Christians. Going to church and to Sunday school was just a normal part of the week back then, and when she was a kid she'd believed it all cuz at that age you believed everything the grownups told you: and if they told you there's a God up there in the sky then there's a God up there in the sky; if they told you that Jesus rose up from the dead then that's what he did. She didn't question it, not back then: she probably *asked* questions about it, cuz kids are always asking questions—but she didn't question it. Back then when she was little, she'd just taken it all as... well, gospel!

But then, as she got older, she'd just sort of started to drift away from it... It had just started to seem less and less important... She didn't kick up a fuss, or anything; she still went to church every Sunday with Mum and her brother and sisters; but it didn't really *mean* anything anymore... The fact was she'd just stopped believing in God; and what's more, it didn't even bother her that she'd stopped believing in God! But she knew it would bother her family, so she kept quiet about it, so's not to rock the boat...

And things would have carried on fine like that, but then the creepy evangelist turned up. It was stupid Uncle Bob who came round one day, raving about the guy and how they all just *had* to go and see him; and they *had* gone to see him and it had been at the local community centre and to Amber it had just seemed more like a theatrical performance than a church service—but Mum and her brothers and sisters were all hooked: right from the start. They stopped going to normal church and joined the preacher's congregation instead. And the way Mum and Robbie, and Jemma and Denise, the way they were always quoting his sermons, and going on about how wonderful the guy was: it was just *creepy*; it was like they'd been brainwashed.

And the evangelist, he started coming round to the house, and Amber could tell from the way he looked at her that he knew she didn't like him. When he tried to talk to her, she'd just answered in monosyllables and he pretty soon stopped bothering.

But he must have said something to Mum when she wasn't around, cuz one day they confronted her, the whole family group, Mum and her brother and sisters, and they told her that she had to just do what the evangelist told her, cuz he was their spiritual advisor and he knew best. Amber tried to fob them off with vague promises, but they just wouldn't let it go and she tried and she tried to keep it all to herself, but they just kept on and on and they backed her into a corner and then she had flipped: she'd flipped out and she told them what she thought of their precious 'spiritual advisor' and she didn't mince her words.

And so they chucked her out. Just like that. It was like family ties suddenly didn't mean anything anymore; the only thing that mattered was doing what the evangelist said; and sixteen years of living with them, living in that house, just didn't mean anything. Amber was a heretic and they didn't want her under the same roof as them.

After that, Amber had buried herself more and more deeply in her fangirl interests. It was the only thing she had to turn to. She'd always been into sci-fi, but before she'd only really watched the new stuff; now she started looking more deeply and getting into some of the old stuff. First it was new *Doctor Who* leading her to old *Doctor Who*, and from that she started checking out some of the other sci-fi stuff from back then—all those old films; films like *The Earth Dies Screaming*.

And if she hadn't found out about *The Earth Dies Screaming*... You see? Cause and effect!

Why couldn't she have trusted that Mark Hunter guy sooner? Why did she have to be so suspicious? Maybe she wouldn't have been so suspicious if it hadn't been for that CIA guy. I mean, *nobody* trusts the fucking CIA, do they? If he hadn't brought that CIA guy along with him that night...

But he sounded so kind on the phone... He sounded like he really cared about her and he wanted to help her...

And she'd been holding onto that brief conversation, and she was on her way to see him and she was so close! She'd been so fucking *close*. She was nearly at the bridge, and she was already feeling like the weight of fear was starting to come off her shoulders at last, that there was someone who was going to help her and protect her and sort everything out for her—and *this* had to happen; she had to get grabbed and bundled into a car and it wasn't even any of the people who were *supposed* to be out to get her; it was just stupid gang and *they'd* got the wrong person as well and it was all to do with some stupid turf war, and she'd tried to tell them they'd got the wrong girl, she'd tried to tell them, but they wouldn't fucking listen would they, the stupid fucking morons and it was shut your fucking mouth bitch, don't fucking lie to us, bitch, we'll mess you up bad, bitch, and yeah bruv no bruv, it's her innit, it's D-Boy's bitch sure it is yeah bruv no bruv I'll go first bruv no *I'll* go first bruv and take it bitch take it bitch shuddup and take it bitch and then it finally sunk into their thick skulls that she *wasn't* D-Boy's bitch and they acted like it was *her* fucking fault for not telling her when she'd been telling them the whole fucking time but they were too stupid to listen and now they couldn't let her go now could they not after they'd messed her up this bad so they'd have to get rid of her and it was all so fucking *stupid* cuz she wasn't *supposed* to have landed in this mess, this wasn't *supposed* to have happened cuz she was supposed to be safe right now, safe with Mark Hunter safe where she wouldn't have to keep running…

But they couldn't let her go now, could they? They couldn't let her go now…

And Mark waits in vain for Amber Windrush on Blackfriars Bridge. The only time he will ever see Amber again will be eleven days from now, when he sees her lying on a mortuary slab, fished up from the Thames.

Chapter Twenty-Three
The Film-Tourist's Guide to the Galaxy

The road winds its way across the verdant landscape Surrey Hills, hugging the undulating gradients of the land. Along the road drives a pea-green Hilman Imp, at the wheel of which sits Rick Bedford, in the passenger seat Mark Hunter. Their destination is the village of Critchlow, the picture-postcard village featured in *The Earth Dies Screaming*.

The car is Bedford's own and for those of you who might be wondering why CIA agent Richard Bedford would choose to drive such an antiquated and downright unsexy car, then let me explain: Looks can be deceiving, because this Hilman Imp is no ordinary Hilman Imp. This Hilman Imp may look innocent enough but it actually anything but: under the bonnet (or hood as far as Bedford is concerned) is a turbo engine which activated can accelerate the car's speed to equal that of the fastest racing car; the car is equipped with a sophisticated security system which can detect any tracking and explosive devices; it is armed with concealed machineguns and both ground-to-ground and ground-to-air missiles; as well as featuring all the usual add-on extras like smokescreen generator, revolving numberplates, etc.

So, that should answer your question.
Actually, it *doesn't* answer it, does it? Because all of the above modifications could just have easily been installed in a much more modern and good-looking car.

Maybe the unassuming exterior is meant to be urban camouflage...

The Imp now slows as it enters the village of Critchlow, and as there is very little of this village, the car and its occupants very soon find themselves driving into the village square. The centre of the square is a war memorial surrounded by a grass plot. Amongst the buildings facing the square can be seen the village post office cum general store, a stable yard, and the village pub.

Bedford parks in front of the pub and the two men get out of the car.

They set off across the square, walking slowly.

'Just look at it,' says Mark admiringly, looking around. 'The pub, the houses... Just like they were in the film! It's amazing how little this place has changed in sixty years...'

'I'll take your word for that, buddy,' says Bedford.

'Well, *you* saw the film—'

'No, I did *not* see the film,' says Bedford.

'Why not? I thought you were—'

'Well, you thought wrong. I got better things to do with my time than watch some dumb British B-movie.'

'It was more of an Anglo-American job than a British production *per se*...'

'Alright, then I got better things to do than watch some dumb *Anglo-American* B-movie!' retorts Bedford.

'But you know the film has a strong connection with what we're investigating,' remonstrates Mark. 'I mean, that's the whole reason we're here. And it's only sixty-odd minutes long; it wouldn't have taken up that much of your valuable time, Rick.'

'Yeah, well *you* watched the movie; that's good enough for me,' says Bedford. 'So, now that we *are* here, where do we start looking? And where the hell is everyone? This place is like a ghost town!'

'Yes, funny isn't it? The absence of people: *that's* just like it was in the film, as well.'

'Why? What's happened to the people in the film?'

'Well, as you'd know if you'd taken the trouble to watch it, they're all dead. The protagonists arrive here and all they find is dead bodies. The telephones aren't working, there's no radio or television signals; there's not a sound to be heard or a living creature to be seen. And then, as they're standing here, wondering what could have happened, from around *that* corner, over there where that wall is,' pointing, 'comes this huge silver robot…'

And right on cue, a huge silver robot appears round the blind corner indicated by Mark: a platform-booted, quilted-jerkined *Earth Dies Screaming* robot!

Bedford has his gun out in an instant. Mark, just as quick to react, spoils Bedford's aim as he fires. The bullet ricochets off the wall.

Bedford turns on him. 'Whaddya do *that* for?' he snarls. 'It's one of those—!'

'It's *not* "one of those:" look!'

The robot, startled by the gunshot, has fallen to the ground, where it flails around in an undignified and un-robotlike manner and appears to be having a lot of difficulty in getting back up. And as Bedford now looks more closely, he sees that while this robot is identical in design to the robot encountered at the Cult Café, it's just not quite the same. The design is far less robust in its execution, less professional: like a flimsy, crudely put together imitation of the creature from before.

'Can we give you a hand?' inquires Mark.

'If you wouldn't mind,' replies the robot, in a muffled voice, *genus* human, gender male, accent home-counties. 'This thing's so deuced heavy; makes getting up rather difficult…'

Mark and Bedford take a hand each and pull the robot to its feet. The helmet and mask are removed by the wearer, now revealed to be a thirty-something Caucasian male. He looks accusingly at Bedford.

'You just shot at me!'

'Hey, I'm sorry, buddy; I just thought you were someone else.'

'Exactly what "someone else" did you take me for?' demands the man, indicating his costume. 'And even if I *was* "someone else," you can't just go around shooting at people!

It might be alright where you come from, but in this country—!'

'If I can just explain,' interpolates Mark; 'and I apologise for my trigger-happy friend, but we are both officials…'

MI5 and CIA identity cards are displayed for the man's inspection.

'We're here on official business,' proceeds Mark. 'Can I ask your name? I take it you're a visitor…?'

'You take it wrongly,' is the reply. 'I am a resident here. The name's Merrison.'

'If you're not a fanboy, then what's with the dumb costume?' demands Bedford.

'Well, I suppose I *am* a fanboy, really,' replies Merrison. 'Mind you, I don't much care for the term "fanboy." I prefer "film buff" or "enthusiast."'

'Look, if you dress up in dumb costumes, you're a fanboy,' insists Bedford.

'Well, I don't just wear this thing for the pure joy of dressing up in it,' says Merrison. 'It's sort of advertisement, really. For my shop.'

'What shop?' asks Mark.

'*The Earth Dies Screaming* memorabilia shop, obviously. Why else would I be togged up like this? I say, haven't you heard of my shop?'

'I'm afraid I hadn't,' confesses Mark. 'But now that we have, we'd be very interested to see it. Where is it?'

'Just over there,' pointing across the square. 'Next door but one to the post office.'

The building indicated is a tall narrow house with a bow window fronting the square. To the right of the window a door with a glass upper panel stands ajar.

'I know it doesn't look much like a shop from a distance,' says Merrison. 'But I couldn't really have a big garish signboard over the window saying *The Earth Dies Screaming*, could I? The neighbours would lynch me. Critchlow sells itself to tourists as the quintessential picture-postcard English village. You know, we get busloads of Chinese tourists coming here just to take pictures of the houses.'

'We'd like to have a look at this shop of yours if we may,' says Mark.

'Would we?' says Bedford.

'By all means,' says Merrison. 'Follow me.'

He leads the way to the shop. A discreet window display behind the square panes of the bow window displays some of the shop's wares: a t-shirt, a mug, a robot bust, the blu-ray release of the film…

The interior of the shop proves to be a single cramped room. The counter, with an old-fashioned cash register and new-fashioned card reader, sits at the back; the merchandise is arranged along the lefthand wall, while that on the right is adorned with a large framed poster, illustrated with stills from the film, which gives a potted account of Critchlow's association *The Earth Dies Screaming*. (Copies of which are available to purchase.)

'Well, well, well,' says Mark. 'You've got a nice little shop here.'

'Thank you,' replies Merrison, depositing his robot helmet on the counter. 'It's all official; the merchandise, I mean; all above-board. I have a licensing agreement with the copyright holder.'

'You can't be making much dough from this place,' remarks Bedford.

'Oh, of course not,' is the ready reply. 'There's no profit in it at all, really. I just run the place as a hobby.'

'Then how'd you even pay the rent?'

'I don't have to,' says Merrison. 'I own the place. I live up there,' pointing to the ceiling.

'And are your customers mostly those general sightseers?' says Mark. 'What about the sci-fi fans, the film tourists; do you get many of them?'

'Well, they don't exactly come in droves, but yes, I get some, every now and then.'

'And I suppose you get chatting with some of them?'

'Oh, yes. I'll happily chat with the ones who want to chat.'

'My friend and I, we're looking for someone, a fan of *The Earth Dies Screaming*. We think she may have come here quite recently. Perhaps you'll remember her: a young black girl, with or without a purple wig. Her name's Amber, Amber Windrush.'

They both see it: the look of surprise on Merrison's face. It quickly vanishes, and now he stands rigid, affecting insouciance. 'Er… No… no, I don't recall anyone of that name…'

Says Bedford, smiling wryly: 'You know, pal, you're a pretty lousy liar.'

'Which is to your credit,' Mark assures him. 'As it carries with it the implication that you're not someone who's accustomed to lying. She was here, wasn't she? Amber was here. Look, we only want to help the girl. You know who we are…'

'Yes, and I know that people like you aren't always to be trusted,' retorts Merrison, regarding them with suspicious eyes.

'Look, buddy, you can trust us.'

'Says the man who just nearly killed me!'

'That was a misunderstanding, for crying out loud! How many more times do I have to tell you?'

Says Mark: 'I can only assure you we don't mean Amber any harm. We only want to know when it was Amber came here and anything she might have said to you… Why are you so defensive, Mr Merrison? Is this just a general distrust of the intelligence community, or is there something else…?'

'Alright,' says Merrison, sighing. 'Yes, she was here; and the last time she was here she asked me if anyone had been asking questions about her. She seemed to think it was likely to happen. And now here are you two, asking questions about her.'

'The *last time* she was here?' echoes Mark. 'You mean Amber's been here more than once?'

'She's been here twice. And that second time she looked very worried; frightened about something. What it was, I don't know: she wouldn't tell me.'

'And it was on this second occasion she wanted to know if anyone had been asking questions about her? How recently was this? Are we talking within the last few days?'

'No, not that recently… It was, let me see… two, maybe three weeks ago…'

'And what about the first time she came? When was that?'

'Oh, that was back in March, I think… Yes, around then…'

'And what happened on that occasion? Did you speak to her?'

'Yes, I spoke to her. She was just here doing the usual film tourist thing. She came into the shop and we had a natter about the film. That was it, really.'

'Was she by herself that time?'

'Yes.'

'And she seemed okay?'

'She seemed fine that time.'

'But not the second time. What did she say then, when she came back the second time? I mean, apart from asking if anyone had been inquiring about her. Was there anything else? Did she say why she'd come back again so soon?'

'No, like I said, she was scared; keyed up, like a cat on hot bricks. I asked her what was wrong but she wouldn't tell me. The last thing she said was "if anyone asks, tell them you haven't seen me, okay?" And then she took off.'

'And that was the last you saw of her?'

'Yes. And now I've gone and broken my promise to her,' says Merrison wretchedly. 'I've told *you*.'

'I can assure you, Mr Merrison, that we don't mean Amber any harm. In fact we want to find her so we can protect her from people who *do* mean her harm.'

'So, someone *is* after her then? But what's this fangirl done that MI5 and the CIA should be interested in her? And what's it got to do with Critchlow?'

'I can't go into details, but Amber discovered something, something that other people don't want her talking about, and all the evidence points to her having made this discovery while she was here in Critchlow.'

'In *Critchlow*? But what could she have seen around here that was so important it would endanger her life?'

'I was hoping you might be able to shed some light on that one. Has anything strange happened around here lately? Anything suspicious, or out of the ordinary? Any strange people?'

'No... nothing like that.'

'When Amber was here the first time, doing her film tourist sight-seeing, where would she have gone? Most of the location scenes in *The Earth Dies Screaming* were right out there in the square as I recall.'

'That's right. The square and a couple of the streets leading off it; the stable yard, the pub, of course... They didn't film inside it, though: the interiors were all studio sets.'

'So,' says Mark, looking out into the square, 'whatever Amber saw or heard, it must have happened somewhere around here...'

'Yes. Unless it was out at the radio station.'

Mark turns back to Merrison, surprised. 'The radio station?'

'Yes, the one from the end of the film. Don't you remember it?'

'Yes, I do remember it; but you mean it's actually *here*? I'd always assumed the radio station was somewhere else; a building on the film studio lot or something. And you're telling me it's actually *here*, near the village, just as it was supposed to be in the film?'

'Yes, it is; at least if you call a couple of miles away near. Place is abandoned now; the radio station closed years ago; but the building's still there.'

Mark looks at Bedford. 'We need to check this building out.' To Merrison: 'It's two miles away, you say?'

'Yes, you just take the Lipcot Road out of town...'

'We've picked up a tail,' announces Bedford. They are driving down the Lipcot Road.

'I've seen them,' says Mark. 'Ever since we left the village. Of course, they could just be going the same way as us.'

'The road's clear and I'm only doing forty; they could pass us if they wanted to.'

'Well, let's see what happens when we get to where we're going.'

Their destination soon appears ahead on their left: a flat-roofed, brick-built structure set well back from the road. The transmitter mast which once stood on the roof now lies rusting and broken-backed, half on the roof, half on the ground.

Bedford pulls over to the side of the road. The car behind overtakes them. There are two men in the car, both of them wearing dark glasses. Rapidly accelerating, the car soon disappears from view.

'And suddenly they're in a big hurry,' comments Bedford.

'I'll admit its suspicious,' agrees Mark.

'Shall we wait and see if they come back?'

'No, let's not hang around. I'd like to check out the building now that we're here.'

'What're you expecting to find in there, man? Look at the place: there's no way in hell this is where the Zero guys are sending out their commercials!'

'It doesn't look like it is, I know; but Amber saw *something* when she was here doing her fangirl tour, and it might have been in that building. Come on.'

They get out of the car and make their way towards the derelict building. In the film there had been an access road stretching from the road to the building, but this has long since disappeared beneath the encroaching weeds and grass.

The building's main entrance is a pair of double doors, their once glass upper panels now boarded over. Mark tries the door, finds that it opens. Pushing it open, he is about to step inside, but then common sense intervenes, and he turns to Bedford.

'After you.'

Bedford shrugs, walks past him and through the door. After he doesn't get hit over the head, Mark follows him. They are in what was once the reception area. A counter still runs along the far wall, but apart from this the room is empty, cobwebbed and stripped bare. As they make their way inside, the rest of the building proves to be the same, everything empty and neglected, save by the passage of time.

'So much for your idea,' says Bedford. 'Nobody's been near this place for years.'

'Which is rather strange in itself,' replies Mark. 'An abandoned building like this: you'd expect kids to have been hanging out here; you'd expect homeless people to have used it as a squat. But look: there's no sign of either; no refuse, no graffiti on the walls…'

'So what?' says Bedford, unimpressed.

'Well, I'm just saying it's odd… You know, there's something about this place… A kind of atmosphere… Don't you feel it?'

'No,' definitely.

'Well, I do… Maybe somebody *is* here… hidden somewhere…'

'Right. And I suppose when it's time for the next Zero commercial to air, that antenna lying on its back out there just climbs back up on its feet and starts pumping out signals. Come on, man! Let's get out of here. I wanna see if those bozos who were tailing us are still hanging around.'

The bozos are still around. Returning to the reception area, they see them through the open doors: two men with dark glasses advancing towards the building, their car parked beside the Imp.

Says Mark, dropping his voice: 'Let's keep out of sight until they get here; then we can—'

But Bedford is already outside, gun levelled at the two approaching men.

'Okay, you turkeys, reach for the sky!'

Preferring cold steel to thin air, the two men reach for their guns instead. Bedford shoots them both.

'Well, that's just marvellous,' says Mark, joining him. 'They could have told us something!'

'I was out of my hands, man,' says Bedford.

They walk over to the two fallen men. Bedford is a good shot and they are both quite dead.

'Well, lookee here,' says Bedford, standing over one of the corpses, whose glasses have fallen off. 'I've seen this guy before and so've you: he was one of the fake ambulance crew who grabbed you that day.'

'You're right...' says Mark.

'Sure I am. And now we know what the Parkhurst Corporation's deal is. They don't want in on Zero: they're the guys *running* Zero!'

'But they can't be...'

'Why not? Because that boss lady, the same chick who firebombed your apartment, told you they weren't? Man, I wouldn't take her word for *anything*.'

'But even so—'

'Then what about these two jokers? How come they showed up here? You think they tailed us all the way from

London without us getting wise to it? Forget it, man: they were here before us! They were already here and they work for Parkhurst, so Parkhurst are the guys behind Zero!'

'But it just doesn't make sense...' protests Mark.

'The hell it doesn't!' snarls Bedford, working himself into a frenzy. 'They knew we were on the case, so they make like they're just as fired up as everyone else to find out who's running the show; but it was all a smokescreen, man! I'm telling you: it's Parkhurst who're behind the whole damn business, and that Flat-sol Park bitch has just been giving us the runaround the whole time! *Jesus!*'

And he vents his frustration by kicking one of the corpses in the ribs.

PART TWO - ZERO HOUR

Chapter Twenty-Four
The End of the World as We Know it?

It is on Zero minus Twenty, with Zero Day just under three weeks away, that it really hits the fan. Somehow word has got out that aliens come into the picture and anticipation quickly turns to panic: Zero isn't a *thing*, it isn't a product at all! Zero means nothing and nothing can't be something! Zero is a negative quantity. Zero means null, nada, nothing, oblivion; and on Zero Day everything will become nothing.

In other words, Zero Day equals Doomsday! The end of all things!

The rumours spread like a pandemic. Something cataclysmic is going to happen on Zero Day, and the aliens are trying to warn us of our impending doom! The adverts were never meant to be a promotional campaign at all; that was just the way our primitive Earth brains interpreted them: they are a warning.

Numerous theories are propounded as to the precise nature of the impending disaster.

Some kind of cosmic disaster is about to strike the Earth: an asteroid, like the one that killed the dinosaurs, will smash into the planet and choke us all with the dust cloud it raises; or a huge solar flare will scorch the Earth and turn us all to ash; something cataclysmic that will result in instant global extinction. And somehow the aliens can see this disaster coming and in their unfathomable alien way they are trying to warn us about it.

Or perhaps the disaster won't be coming from outer space at all; perhaps climate change will suddenly accelerate to terminal levels. But climate change doesn't work that way! It can't just change that much overnight! Oh yes it can; it can if something unprecedented occurs, like a sudden chain-reaction of seismic activity, a chain-reaction of such intensity that the planet will shift on its axis; only ever so slightly, but enough to cause disastrous change: temperatures will increase to above human tolerances, and the accelerated melting of the icepacks will cause the oceans to flood the land...

Or perhaps the disaster about to strike us is not any natural disaster at all: perhaps Zero Day is Zero Hour for an alien invasion: the day aliens will arrive in force to either enslave us, kill us or eat us. (As to whether the invading aliens are the same one's sending the signals, or some second set of aliens, opinion is divided.)

So, take your pick; but whichever way you slice it, we're all Private Frazered. And what can we do to avert disaster? Absolutely nothing. Time to start resigning yourselves to doomsday, folks.

But as thesis must always give way to antithesis in the inevitable line of succession, a ray of hope is just around the corner.

Not many more days have passed before word starts to circulate of an entirely different school of thought; one that says that, far from being the end of the world, Zero Day will actually be the day of our salvation—because Zero Day marks nothing less than the Second Coming: the day when the Lord will return to the Earth in human form or otherwise to reward the righteous and punish the wicked.

Yes, this is what it is actually all about. God, seeing the fine mess the human race is making of things, has decided it's time to take a hand, to drop his whole non-interventionist policy and get down to some serious intervening.

Oh, yeah? say the sceptics and nonbelievers. But where's the connection? If Zero Day is the Second Coming, then why call it Zero Day? What the hell has 'Zero' got to do with 'God'?

Well, actually it's got everything to do with it. Zero is God because God is infinite, and zero is infinity! It's obvious! What else is the infinity symbol but the numeral zero lying on its side and twisted round in the middle?

Do the Math! It's a simple enough equation:

$$0 = \infty = \text{God}$$

Well, you can't argue with the exact sciences, can you?

But why is God announcing his returns to Earth by means of a television and internet advertising campaign? Because God likes to keep up with modern technology, of course, and also to demonstrate that even these inherently evil forms of mass-communication can be used for good.

But why such an ambiguous advertising campaign? Why couldn't God announce his plans more clearly? Because the message already *is* clear! Clear to the righteous at any rate. Only the heretics and the sinners see Zero Day as Doomsday—and for those poor souls it *will* be Doomsday!

So says the evangelist leader of the newly-formed Church of Zero, who, being a completely certifiable megalomaniac, very quickly gathers a large and fiercely devoted following. (Coincidentally this religious dignitary happens to be the very same evangelist who took such a disliking to Amber Windrush and got her family to chuck her out in the street.)

The remainder of the population, those not subscribing to either of the above schools of thought, are nonetheless very concerned. That Zero is going to turn out to be just a new range of toiletries or a sugar-free energy drink, as had been speculated in the early days of the campaign, nobody can any longer believe. The conviction seems to be that Zero is an event, and that *something* is going to happen on Zero Day. They just don't know what.

The Zero commercials have started counting down the days themselves. Commencing with 'Twenty Days to Go,' a new announcement appears every day, marking the progress of the Countdown to Zero. Many people are starting to develop a phobia of those commercials, a powerful aversion to them. They dread the moment when the next commercial will suddenly take over their television and computer screens; they begin to fear the very sight of the Zero logo.

People are angry and scared and they are demanding answers from their governing bodies; they are demanding action. And those governing bodies don't have any answers to give them, but *are* taking action: they are mobilising their security services, readying them to cope not with any extraterrestrial or environmental threat, but with the threat posed by their own increasingly frantic and unstable populations.

And as if just to exacerbate the problem, the Met Office has issued a severe weather warning for the end of May, forecasting a protracted heatwave for the last ten days of the month, with temperatures steadily climbing into the high thirties and set to peak on the thirty-first of May, Zero minus One. Of course, the advocates of a climate-change disaster leap on this as proof of their predictions; but whether significant or pure coincidence, the soaring temperatures are not going to do anything to improve the temper of an already agitated population.

Mark Hunter is under pressure to wrap the case up, to find and expose the instigators of the Zero campaign, so that these alarmist rumours about space aliens and doomsday can be quashed once and for all. And this is much easier said than done, especially when there is a very good chance that the identifying of the culprits will only serve to *confirm* those rumours.

Mark does not share Rick Bedford's conviction that the Parkhurst Corporation are the ones behind Zero. Too many things just don't add up for that to be true. However, it *is* puzzling that they seem to know Mark and Bedford's every move. What happened at Critchlow was only the beginning. Two days later they had paid a visit to Shepperton Studios (where *The Earth Dies Screaming* was filmed) and there they had run into Parkhurst goons. (The ensuing gun battle on the studio lot had been witnessed and applauded by a passing tour party.) Everywhere they go it seems that Parkhurst is either right behind them or there before them. (They tailed Mark the day he visited the Marine Policing Unit morgue to look at a particular body that had been fished from the Thames.)

Mark has set his grunts Daisy Fontaine and Mike Collins to Critchlow to keep an eye on things there—and so far, all they have been able to observe is themselves being observed in turn by spies from Parkhurst. Both sides seem to know of the connection between Critchlow and Zero, but neither knows what they are looking for; just what that connection *is*. Mark still considers the abandoned radio station to be a place of interest, but more detailed searches have so-far turned up nothing. Bedford's suspicions at first fixed themselves on Merrison, the proprietor of the *Earth Dies Screaming* giftshop, and Merrison's house cum giftshop were thoroughly searched, but the search revealed nothing. The CIA man has now turned his attention to the Parkhurst's corporate headquarters, playing a hunch that the building itself might be the location of the transmitter sending out the Zero adverts.

Mark still thinks he's wrong. He firmly believes that it is in the vicinity of Critchlow that the answers are to be found.

Meanwhile Dodo Dupont is not as concerned with the possible impending extinction of all life on Earth as she is with the mysterious antagonist who seems so determined to ensure she won't be around to enjoy it.

But who is it who is so persistently trying to kill her? Who are those assailants, two female, one male? Since the incident at the scrapyard that revealed it was indeed herself and not Mayumi they were after, she has come no closer to actually collaring the culprits. In fact, being able to lay her hands on them has become more difficult, because now they have diversified their attacks; planting bombs, setting traps, sending booby-trapped parcels... When they'd just been dropping things on her, the culprits were always there in the immediate vicinity of the attack, and it was possible for her to give chase; but now...

If only she could find out who they are! If she could just get some clue as to their identities...! And Christ knows these people need to be stopped and as soon as humanly possible; not just for her sake, but for the sake of the general public. The death toll of innocent victims just keeps piling up. Take the most recent incident: Dodo had been driving home one afternoon when the car behind her had suddenly blown up. At first Dodo thought her attackers had lobbed a bomb at her and missed their target: but no, CCTV footage revealed that the bomb had in fact been attached to the underside of her car—only it hadn't been attached very well, because it had fallen off onto the road just before the timer was due to detonate and the unfortunate car behind had received the full charge.

These people are inept, but they are *dangerously* inept!

But who the hell are they? This is still the burning question. Dodo has been wracking her brains looking for the answer, but she still can't figure it out.

One possibility: could the attempts be connected to her association with Mark Hunter? True, she has not been actively assisting Mark on his current assignment, which might seem to negate that possibility—but then there's that Flat-sol Park creature to be factored into the equation. The woman seems hell-bent on tormenting Mark: could she be trying to kill *her* as a way of getting at *him*? From Dodo's own assessment of the woman, it would be entirely in character for Flat-Sol Park to do something like this. That woman seems to have developed a very unhealthy interest in Mark, by turns tempting and tormenting him. (Although Dodo did have to laugh when Mark had told her about the

Courbet painting and Flat-Sol's assertion that Mark's strong bond with herself was proof positive of his pygophilia. It *was* true that Mark's first sight of Dodo, the day he had burst into her hotel room, had been of her bending over in the act of putting on a pair of knickers—perhaps she *had* somehow imprinted herself on him posteriorly!)

The main argument against Flat-Sol Park being behind the attempts on her life is that Dodo would have expected Flat-Sol to have more competent assassins on her payroll. In fact, Dodo would have considered their ineptitude to be proof positive that her assailants were amateurs and not professional assassins—except that, like Mark, Dodo has long since stopped being surprised at how many people there are out there who just aren't very good at their jobs.

Yes, Flat-sol Park should not be dismissed entirely as a suspect... But if it isn't her, and if the attacks on herself have no connection with her friendship with Mark Hunter, then she needs to be looking closer to home, looking for someone with a much more personal motive for wanting to kill her, someone with a grudge or a grievance...

Dodo is a media celebrity, and media celebrities attract stalkers. The culprit could be some deranged obsessive fan, a fan whose adoration for her has turned to an intense hatred, fuelled perhaps by an entirely imaginary grievance.

But if it's not a stranger; if the culprit is actually someone she knows, a friend or acquaintance, then who could it be? Dodo has always gone through life doing her best not to make enemies, not to cause friction, to be always mindful of other people's feelings... It has always been her way to state her case, to set forth her opinions, her observations, her ideals, in a calm and reasonable way, and never to launch personal attacks against individuals in the process. So if ever she does offend anyone, it will not have been done intentionally; but with some people just giving voice to an opinion that is contrary to a cherished one of their own can be enough to incur that person's undying wrath... Who could she have offended or pissed off in that way recently? What feathers might she have unwittingly ruffled...? She can't think of anyone. And it would have to be something that happened fairly recently, wouldn't it? If it was anything she'd said or done a long time ago, the offended party wouldn't have waited this long to come back and settle their score...

Oh, *Dodo*! And you call yourself a psychologist!

Mayumi Takahashi meanwhile has not been spending as much time as usual in the company of her goddess of late, because her goddess doesn't want Mayumi becoming the victim of any cack-handed assassination attempt upon herself. Personally, this possibility would not deter Mayumi one jot from remaining at Dodo's side; indeed she would consider it both an honour and a duty to stand—well, not shoulder-to-shoulder, the height discrepancy precluding this—but side-by-side with her, sharing in her danger.

But Dodo commands and Mayumi obeys.

And anyway, Mayumi has her *Sexy Eatings* photo project to keep her occupied. She had soon convinced Yuki Kinoshita to agree to model for her; indeed, it was primarily with this in mind that Mayumi had invited her friend to the UK in the first place. (You Machiavellian manipulator, Mayumi Takahashi!) And as a bonus, she has an additional model in the shapely form of interpreter Shizuka Todoroki! Like everyone else, Mayumi has no idea why Shizuka is actually even there; but she *is* there, and she seems to consider it her duty to cooperate in every way with the photo project, and this is enough for Mayumi! The woman is an interesting subject: her personality, very different to that of the principal model, provides a stimulating contrast.

Sexy Eatings has taken a turn to the dark side. From the innocent, carefree world of whipped cream and chocolate gateau being licked from intimate body parts, the project has now entered the taboo world of carnivorism, the consumption of the flesh of living creatures. No taboo at all for her model: Yuki Kinoshita is an avid meat-eater, her canines much sharper than her sweet tooth; but Mayumi, a proud vegetarian since hooking up with Dodo, has come to look upon the eating of meat as another pornographic excess to be ranked alongside graphic the excesses of sex and violence; its depiction in art a guilty pleasure, a trip to the dark side.

And so, for this new phase of *Sexy Eatings*, Mayumi has posed her models first against harsh concrete angles suggestive of the slaughterhouse, tearing into hunks of raw meat in a blood-drenched gastro-sexual orgy; and then against sylvan landscapes, habitat of the natural woman of yore: the hunter-gatherer, painted and adorned, at one with nature, joyfully devouring the fruits of the chase.

But beware, Mayumi Takahashi! Gaze too long through your viewfinder into the abyss, and you may have a dizzy spell and fall in.

None of the above photography could have possibly been accomplished without the assistance of Trina Truelove, Mayumi's invaluable apprentice. Now Trina is probably far too modest to tell you this herself: others must sing her praises for her. Trina has been enjoying *Sexy Eatings* immensely, but the highpoint of her days is always when she returns to the arms of Carl (Jensen to us, but Trina's on first name terms), her corporate boyfriend. She's been spending most of her nights with him, which is good because it stops her from going stir-crazy stuck in that overcrowded apartment of hers. Carl is loaded of course—drives an expensive car, and you should see his pad: almost as swanky as Dodo's!—but Carl is also loaded where it *really* counts, cuz boy can he fuck! And it's not just the quality, either; it's the quantity as well. It's like having a stonker is Carl's natural state, and he only goes flaccid when he needs to put his trousers on.

Yeah, he's good is Carl, but he knows it and he really fancies himself. Why is it always the self-satisfied egotists who are the best in the sack? (But then, maybe it's because they're good in the sack that they *are* self-satisfied egotists.)

Still, he has made this one thoughtful gesture: it was not long after they first got together; he'd given her this lovely gold bracelet.

And the way he'd presented it to her was so sweet! He told her to kneel down and close her eyes, because he had a present for her and he wanted it to be a surprise. So Trina had knelt down and closed her eyes; and then, when he'd told her to open them again, she'd opened them and, lo and behold, there was the business-end of Carl's stonker right in front of her face. Which was all very nice and all that, but Trina had already had *that* present from him and lots of times! so she couldn't help feeling just a tad disappointed. But then Carl had drawn her attention to the gold bracelet, parked there at the other end of his cock: *that* was the present! And so, she'd blown Carl off and transferred the prize to her wrist.

Yes, it was a thoughtful gesture (and a very expensive piece of jewellery!) but even so, Trina knows that this relationship with Carl isn't going to last forever. Trina knows Carl's type, knows that he's a player not a stayer. Sooner or later he'll be off.

Well, she'll just have to make the most of him while she's still got him!

Chapter Twenty-Five
You Just Can't Get the Help These Days!

'I think I've got ADHD...'

'Oh, shut up. *Everyone's* got ADHD these days! That's the main reason I quit working at the clinic: I was getting sick to death of hearing about AD-bloody-HD all the time!'

The speakers are Jenny and Rajni, the place the living room of the latter's house. They are watching the morning television. Jenny is chain-smoking cigarettes as per usual, and the Professor has been choking on her morning cigar (also as per usual.)

Proceeds Rajni: 'ADHD. Autism. Manic depression. Personality disorders... People like you are proliferating all over the place,' throwing a sour look at Jenny. 'A hundred years from now, if we haven't globally-warmed ourselves into extinction—'

'Or if the world doesn't end on Zero Day,' interjects Jenny.

'The world is *not* going to end on Zero Day,' says Rajni. 'Zero Day is just a stupendous hoax; somebody's idea of a practical joke. Anyone with sense can see that. Where was I? Oh, yes: a hundred years from now, if the human race is still around, half the population of the planet are going to be mental health cases and the other half will be their therapists. Yes, half the population: walking car-crashes like *you*,' glaring at Jenny.

'Well, pardon me for being alive,' says Jenny sulkily.

'I'll think about it,' replies Rajni. 'And speaking of walking car-crashes, where's Ian got to?'

'Oh, he's off sulking somewhere,' says Jenny.

'What?!' Rajni jumps to her feet. 'And you let him? Last time you said he was "off sulking," we found him in the attic hanging himself! Go and find him!'

'I'm not his bloody keeper, am I?' snaps Jenny.

'Actually, that is precisely what you are!' retorts Rajni.

'Hang on a minute! I'm—!'

'Listen, freeloader,' says Rajni. 'As long as you're living under my roof, you'll bloody well make yourself useful! And one of your uses is to keep an eye on Ian: you know what he's like half the time. Or don't you mind if he goes and tops himself?'

Jenny's careless shrug seems to indicate that no, she doesn't particularly mind.

Rajni looks at her. 'Yes, I know he's been giving you the cold treatment recently, but I'm sure it's nothing personal; it'll just be one of his mood-swings.'

'Like I care, anyway,' mutters Jenny, stubbing out her cigarette with unnecessary force.

Rajni points to the hallway door. 'Look, whether you care or not, just shift your arse and go and find him, will you? And if he's still breathing, bring him back here. I want to give you both a final briefing about tomorrow's operation.'

Jenny departs on her errand.

Alone, Rajni smiles to herself, and it's not a nice smile, either. She knows full well the cause of the rift that has developed between Ian and Jenny, the antipathy of the former for the latter. The cause was a letter: a letter written by Ian to Jenny, and in which he declared his love for her. Too bashful to actually place the letter directly in Jenny's hand, he had left the missive on the coffee table in the front room for her to find. Unfortunately for him Rajni found it first. She had had absolutely no qualms about opening it and reading it, and so she opened it and read it. It was a surprisingly eloquent confession of love: with the written word, the shy and silent young man had found an outlet, a means of communicating all those thoughts and feelings he felt unable to express verbally; yes, it was a touching, heartfelt letter—and it seriously pissed Rajni off. Back when she had first met Ian, when she had started counselling him at the clinic, the boy had—predictably—started to develop a crush on herself; this usually happened in the case of needy young men like Ian. But even so, he'd never sent *her* a letter like this one!

In fact, *nobody* had ever sent her a letter like this one!

And so, she destroyed the letter. She tore it up into little pieces and consigned it to the bin and after that she felt a lot better.

And here's the best bit: Ian, seeing the letter gone from the coffee table, had assumed it had been picked up and read by the person to whom it was addressed. Eagerly, fearfully, he had awaited her response. And finally, when that response was not forthcoming, when it became clear to him that no response ever would be forthcoming, and Jenny continued to behave towards him as though no such letter had been sent, he assumed that his confession of love had been rejected, rejected with contempt, deemed not even worthy of an acknowledgement. Feeling the full sting of this apparent rejection, Ian's love for Jenny has now turned into the deepest and bitterest resentment.

Just as Rajni expected it would.

And now Ian has retaliated the only way he knows how: by snubbing her; by matching rejection with rejection; responding to her rejection of him with an even more crushing rejection of his own. making no reply to any words Jenny addresses to him; looking away whenever her eyes happen to meet his…

The power of the snub. It is the only power the Ians of this world possess, the only weapon they know how to use.

And this is how things have been going for over a week now, and Rajni has looked on at the results of her handiwork with a fierce sense of satisfaction. She considers it a punishment well-deserved by both of them. Before the letter incident, they had been starting to get far too chummy, those two. Jenny (who, it will be remembered, herself has—or *had*—feelings for Ian) had actually succeeded in starting to coax Ian out of his shell, encouraging him to be more forthcoming in his interaction with herself—and who knows where it all might have ended? If those two had ended up coming to an understanding, and actually getting together, becoming girlfriend and boyfriend, who knows what might have happened? They might have started to think they didn't need her, Rajni, anymore! Might have started to think they would be better off without her!

Then where would she be? Where would all her plans for revenge on Dodo Dupont be, if she lost the services of her minions?

No. No fraternising between the house-slaves. Not on Rajni's watch. Far better for them to be not on speaking terms with each other at all, just so long as they remain obedient to *her*.

Jenny and Ian now come trooping into the room, Jenny looking even more sullen than when she left on her errand, Ian looking furtive, head bent, eyes cast down.

'Where was he?' inquires Rajni.

'In the kitchen,' says Jenny.

'The kitchen?' cries Rajni, alarmed. 'What were you doing in there, Ian?'

'Nothing,' mumbles Ian.

'Well, don't go in there when I'm not around,' Rajni tells him. 'It's dangerous.'

Rajni's kitchen, in addition to still serving its usual function, has been turned into a miniature bomb-making factory. Neither Rajni or either of her assistants had any previous knowledge of bomb-making; but you can find out anything online; and what's more, you can also *buy* anything.

'Sit down, you two,' says Rajni, pointing at the settee just vacated by herself.

Ian and Jenny sit, placing as much distance between each other as possible. Jenny lights another cigarette, Ian, hunched forward, pigeon-toed, studies the carpet.

'Right. I want to take you through tomorrow's operation one more time,' begins Rajni.

'What's the point?' mutters Jenny.

'What do you mean "what's the point"?' demands Rajni.

'It's only gunna go wrong, innit? Just like every other one's gone wrong.'

'Not this time!' snaps Rajni. 'This plan is going to succeed!'

'Yeah, that's what you say every time!' snaps back Jenny. 'But they still always go wrong! Like that parcel that squirted acid when you opened it: you go and send it to the wrong address and it was some old lady who gets her face burnt off!'

'I did *not* send it to the wrong address! The postman *delivered* it to the wrong address!'

'Well, whatever. Alright: what about the catapult that was supposed to lob a bomb into her box at the opera? It misses, bounces off the box, lands on the stage and kills the soprano!'

'Yes, but—'

'And that trap with the ten-ton weight: doesn't drop down when *she* walks under it, but nearly gets *us* when we go back to see what went wrong!'

'Well, that—'

'Then there was the model plane with the explosives in it: it goes off course and dive-bombs a school playground!'

'Yes, but—'

'And the *last* one! You stick a bomb under her car and the bomb falls off and blows up the next car that's got a married couple and their kids in it! At this rate you're gunna waste half the people in London and *still* not get Dodo Dupont!'

'Now, don't be—'

'It's like she's got a charmed life or something!'

Rajni's face, which has been twitching intermittently during this recital of their failures, now goes into twitching overdrive. 'Don't be *silly*, Jenny. We've just been *unlucky*, that's all. Dodo doesn't have a charmed life…'

'She *does*!' insists Jenny. 'I'm tellin' you: you just can't kill that woman! She's indestructible!'

'Dodo Dupont is *not* indestructible!' thunders Rajni. '*Never* say that Dodo Dupont is indestructible! Never! Do you hear me?' Her face isn't twitching now: it is a mask of undiluted fury. 'She can be killed just like any other flesh and blood human being! Do you hear? It's just *your* negative attitude that keeps holding us back! Now, I do not want to hear another word about that woman having a charmed life! And not a single syllable about her being indestructible!' stamping her foot for emphasis. 'Now, do you hear me? DO YOU HEAR ME?'

Jenny hears her. Goggle-eyed, she nods her head in mute acquiescence. For the first time in her life, Jenny actually looks scared of Rajni.

Ian, unaffected by the storm, continues to study the carpet.

Rajni sighs deeply, collects herself and her face resumes its normal configuration. 'Good. I'm glad we've got that one cleared up.' Clapping her hands: 'Right! Back to tomorrow's operation…'

Suspended from hydraulic davits, the window cleaning gondola hangs at the eleventh floor of the twenty-storey high-rise. Three window cleaners are at work in the gondola. They are dressed in beige overalls and baseball caps both of which are emblazoned with the company logo. Positioned at intervals along the length of the twenty-foot gondola, the three men are working industriously with their mops, sponges and scrapers, soaping and rinsing the windows. Above them is a cloudless blue firmament, while below is a busy thoroughfare, the noise of its motor traffic rising into the air.

A window at the right-hand end of the platform slides open and from it emerges a beckoning hand. Catching sight of this hand, the nearest window cleaner goes to investigate. As he reaches the open window, the hand reappears, seizes him by the collar and before he can utter a sound drags him bodily into the building. The window slides shut. So quickly does all this take place that the man's two colleagues, eyes on their work, do not even notice.

The window opens again and the same beckoning hand emerges, this time accompanied by a sharp whistle. Attracted by the sound, the remaining two window cleaners turn and see both the beckoning hand and also that their colleague has mysteriously deserted his post. They go to investigate. The first man reaches the open window and a hand shoots out, grabs him by the collar and yanks him into the building. Voicing a sharp exclamation, the remaining window cleaner rushers to his friend's assistance, only to suffer the same fate. Having devoured its victims, the window slides shut, and the gondola is left vacant. The sun continues to shine, the traffic continues to flow.

A minute passes, another, and then the window opens once more and three window cleaners climb out onto the platform, or rather three people wearing the same beige caps and overalls, but now two of the window cleaners are women and all three have their faces concealed behind dark glasses and facemasks. The tallest of the trio, one of the women, also has a backpack. Turning to the controls operating the winch, she now pulls the main lever and the gondola begins to ascend.

'Oh my Gawd,' says Jenny, peering over the edge of the gondola into the street far below. 'Look how high up we are! You sure this thing's safe?'

'Of course it's safe!' snaps Rajni.

'But what if the cable breaks?'

'Steel cables don't just break! What's the matter with you? Are you scared of heights or something?'

'Yes, I am!'

'Well, you could have mentioned it before! And anyway, you were alright when we were up on that catwalk in the TV studio!'

'That weren't as high up as this!'

'Look, just get a grip, will you! And focus, girl! Focus on what we're here to accomplish! Look at Ian: you don't hear him complaining, do you?'

You don't. Ian stands there silent, inscrutable behind shades and mask.

Smoothly and steadily the gondola ascends, scaling the glazed façade of the high-rise. Reaching the top floor, Rajni pulls the lever, and they come to a halt. Before them a full-length window wall looks into the living room of a penthouse apartment—a penthouse apartment very familiar to the reader.

At last! thinks Rajni. Dodo Dupont's apartment! Just look at it! It's disgusting! She's just flaunting her wealth, living in a place like this! My whole house could fit in her living room! A status-symbol apartment; that's what it is!

Well, it won't be looking so pretty after today—and it will be in need of a new owner.

Rajni turns to the avoidants. 'Alright, you two: stop gawping like idiots and start cleaning windows.'

'What for?' demands Jenny.

'In case she's *in*, stupid! We've got to act like we're genuine window cleaners, or she'll get suspicious, won't she? Now pick up those mops and start cleaning!'

Rajni's precaution proves a wise one. One of the doors across the room (the door to the bathroom) opens and Dodo Dupont emerges, clad in shorts and t-shirt. Espying the window cleaners at work, she directs a broad smile and cheery wave towards the window as she walks barefoot across the room. The lips behind her mask puckering with disdain, Rajni observes her enemy until she disappears through another door. (The study.)

Oh, look at me: I'm Dodo Dupont! And even though I'm disgustingly rich, I'm friends with *everyone*! I even have time to wave at the peasants who clean my windows for me! It's because I'm *such* a nice person! And that's why *everyone* adores me!

Well, just you wait, Dodo Dupont; by the end of today you won't be preening yourself about how popular you think you are—because you'll be too busy being dead; that's why! In fact, because you've been considerate enough to be at home this morning, you won't even live to see this afternoon! We can put the plan into operation immediately!

Rajni's plan is this: under cover of cleaning the windows she is going to attach an explosive device fitted with a remote-control detonator to one of them. Having done this, they will return the way they came, make their way to the roof of a high-rise a few blocks away, which vantagepoint will, with the aid of a telescope, afford them a clear view of Dodo's apartment. Rajni will then place a call to Dodo's landline, advising her that if she were to walk up to her window she will see something to advantage. And *then*, once the target is standing right in front of the window, Rajni will press the button on the remote-control unit and *boom!* the esteemed Professor will be blown to kingdom come!

And what is so much better about this plan, in contrast to all the previous attempts, what makes this one so much more satisfying, is that by being in direct telephone contact with her victim, Rajni will have the opportunity to unmask herself, to reveal her identity to Dodo Dupont, remind her of the crimes she has committed and the lives she has ruined, and generally get to savour the moment and exalt in her triumph before pressing the button and blowing the bitch to smithereens!

Oh, joyous, perfect plan! It just can't go wrong!

Rajni shucks off her backpack and hunkers down to open it. 'Alright, you two. I'm going to attach the bomb now. You just keep working.'

'It'll probably just fall off like the last one did,' says Jenny.

'It will *not* fall off,' says Rajni firmly. 'Not this time. I've brought better tape this time.'

From the backpack she extracts the Ryvita tin containing the bomb—or at least it *should* contain the bomb; but the tin feels alarmingly light in her hands. Her heart springboarding, she lifts the lid.

Empty! No! How can this be! She put it in there herself—!

'The bomb!' Leaping to her feet, she pulls off her glasses and facemask and turns on her minions, giving them the full benefit of her furious, accusing stare. 'Where's the bloody bomb? Which of you two took the bloody bomb out of the box?'

'Well, I didn't nick it!' retorts Jenny, pulling down her mask. 'Why would I?'

Rajni looks at Ian. 'Ian?'

For a moment, Ian just stands there, motionless, silent. But then his shoulders start to shake and from behind the mask comes a strange high-pitched sound neither Rajni or Jenny has ever heard before...

At first Rajni thinks the boy is crying; but then she realises that no, no it isn't *crying*: it's *laughing*. Ian is actually *laughing*.

The atmosphere on this hydraulic window-cleaning gondola has suddenly changed: The two women both feel it, and they exchange anxious, questioning looks.

'Ian...' says Rajni cautiously. 'If you've taken the bomb, just tell me what you've done with it. I won't be angry with you if you just tell me where it is... Come on now. Don't be silly...'

Ian stops laughing. 'You want the bomb?'

The voice that utters the words is shrill and quivering, not at all like Ian's usual mumbling baritone.

'Ian...?'

You want the bomb?' he repeats, louder this time. 'You want the bomb? *I'll* give you a bomb!'

Ian pulls down his mask, flings off his glasses, exposing wild, bulging eyes and a rictus smile of insane fury. Now he unzips the front of his boilersuit, and pulls it wide.

'Here's a bomb!' he screeches. 'Here's a bomb!'

Ian has an explosive belt strapped around his middle.

'Jesus fucking Christ!' exclaims Jenny, leaping backwards into Rajni.

Ian now takes out a detonator device—Rajni's detonator device—and he holds it aloft, his thumb hovering over the button.

'Don't come near me!' he cries.

'Ian!' snaps Rajni, adopting the authoritative 'angry mother' tone that in the past has never failed to quail the boy. 'Put that down! That's very dangerous! Do you want to blow us all up?'

'*Yes!*' says Ian, his voice an insane banshee screech. 'Yes, I do! I'm going to blow *her* up!' His face a mask of demented fury, he glares at Jenny.

Oh God, thinks Rajni.

'*Me?*' protests Jenny. 'What have *I* done?'

'You *know* what you've done!' rages Ian.

'I fucking *don't*!'

'*Liar!*' screeches Ian. '*Liar!* I told you how I felt! I told you how I felt! I poured out my heart to you and you threw it back in my face! You didn't even bother to reply!'

'Now, Ian—' begins Rajni.

'What are you *on* about?' says Jenny. 'You never said *anything* like that to me!'

'The letter! It was in the letter I sent you!'

'Ian—'

'What letter, for fuck's sake? I never got any letter from you!'

'Liar! You *did* get the letter! You did! You just didn't bother to reply! You didn't care about my feelings at all! You were laughing at me and treating me like dirt and now I'm going to make you pay!'

'I never got any fucking letter from you!' insists Jenny desperately. 'I swear it! Christ, if I had, I'dve *replied* to it! I would've!'

'Liar! You're just saying that! You're just saying that to try and stop me from blowing up the bomb! Well, it won't work, because I'm going to blow us both to smithereens and it'll serve you right!'

I'm out of here, thinks Rajni and, jumping onto the edge of the gondola, she grabs hold of the cable and starts shinning up it. Catching sight of her, Jenny makes a grab for her leg.

'Oi!' Rajni kicks her in the face and Jenny is pitched backwards into Ian, who, losing his balance—

With a sound like thunder, the explosion rips through the penthouse apartment.

Dodo, at work on the computer in her study, leaps to her feet screeching 'What the fucking hell—!?'

(Yes, even the iron nerves of a Dodo Dupont can be shaken by these sudden occurrences.)

She bursts into the living room to find it a shambles. Most of the window wall has burst inwards, projecting a hailstorm of glass splinters across the room. The floor is scorched; furniture lies overturned, upholstery ripped to shreds; the air is thick with acrid smoke. A cacophony of fire alarms, car horns and screaming rises up from the street.

Oh my God! The window cleaners! thinks Dodo.

Through the dissipating haze Dodo descries an object swinging back and forth outside the window, an object that looks very much like a human body. At first she thinks it is a corpse, a corpse hanging by the neck, but then, as she approaches nearer, she sees that the person, although smoke-blackened, is still very much alive, and clinging for dear life to a swinging steel cable.

Dodo rushes to the window. With smoke rising from scorched overalls, the figure swings helplessly, and a terrified pair of eyes stare at Dodo from a blackened face. One of the window cleaners! And it's a woman! Dodo can't help but feel momentarily surprised (while silently acknowledging that there's no reason at all why women shouldn't be window cleaners.)

'Hang on!' cries Dodo.

Standing perilously on the brink of the abyss, she attempts to reach out to the woman…

'I can't reach you! Can you try swinging in towards me? If you can do that, I can grab you and pull you in!'

Making no verbal reply, the woman, by exerting her legs, succeeds in turning the direction of the cable's pendulum movement towards the apartment.

'That's it! Just a bit closer…!'

The woman swings towards her, and Dodo grabs her round the waist. Shouting: 'Now! Let go!' she falls backwards into the room with her burden, and lands heavily on her back, the rescued woman on top of her. For a moment the two women lie there, nose to nose, both panting with exertion, the rescued woman staring into the face of her rescuer with bulging eyes.

'Phew!' says Dodo, breaking into a smile. 'Thank God for that!' Rolling from underneath her, she gently lays the woman down on the floor. 'Are you hurt? What happened? You were cleaning the windows, weren't you?'

The woman nods her head, never taking her eyes off Dodo.

'But what happened…?' Dodo crawls back to the window, peers out, down into the street.

The street below is a scene of carnage. The flaming wreckage of the gondola has plunged into the road, smashing at least two cars under its weight and causing an horrendous pile-up. Several of the cars are in flames, thick petroleum smoke rising from their engines.

'My God...' Dragging her eyes from the sight, Dodo returns to the woman. 'It was a bomb, wasn't it? That platform you were on: it exploded, didn't it?' The staring woman nods. 'And your two friends? Did they...?' Another nod. 'Jesus Christ... You're lucky to be alive. Oh, Jesus... Those *maniacs!* Those fucking maniacs! Christ, they've really done it this time! God knows how many people are dead down there...! Those stupid, fucking maniacs!' She stands up, rubbing her frustrated forehead. 'Okay, look, you just lie there and don't move; I'll go'n call an ambulance.'

Dodo runs back to the study, scoops up the phone and dials 999. She tersely explains the situation and ending the call rushes back to the living room.

She pulls up short. The woman she rescued has vanished.

Chapter Twenty-Six
Forced into Liquidation

Mark Hunter has been tied to many a chair over the course of his illustrious career. In fact, being tied to chairs is one of those frequently-occurring situations to which spies are prone, alongside such things as getting hit over the head, being lured into bullrings, and finding that your brakes have been cut and it's downhill all the way to the quarry.

Sometimes a spy can be compelled, through threats or force, to submit to the process of being tied to the chair while fully conscious; and sometimes he can be tied to his chair while out for the count.

The present occasion is one of the latter for Mark. He has awoken from oblivion to find himself tied to a chair.

Actually, *manacled* to a chair in this case. And manacled to a very solid chair, made of steel and either bolted or welded to the floor. The manacles restraining his arms and legs are also of solid construction and are welded to the chair's framework: the wrist manacles, placed at the bottom of the chair-back, pin his arms to his sides; while the manacles around his ankles, fixed to the front two chair-legs, force him to sit with legs apart, his feet flat on the ground.

The chair is solid and unyielding, the manacles likewise.

A steel chair in a steel room; windowless, cylindrical in shape, burnished steel from floor to ceiling, lit by strip-lighting endlessly reflected and re-reflected from its surfaces. The room is utterly devoid of furniture save for the chair itself, which is placed in the exact centre of the floorspace. A pair of steel doors, facing the chair and its occupant, form its only entrance and egress.

Mark is completely helpless.

And he is also completely naked.

Naked and helpless, one flesh and blood man, manacled to a steel chair in a steel room, a chair made for interrogation.

Well, it could be worse, thinks Mark. At least the chair hasn't got a hole in the seat for his testicles to hang through.

But where is he? Who are his captors? The room itself offers no clue, and neither do the circumstances of his capture.

He had been at Dodo's place when he got the call; an urgent phone call from the code-breakers at Turing Grange: they were under attack! Silver robots had suddenly appeared inside the building! As is only to be expected in these situations, Mark's caller had been cut off midsentence. Bedford was absent, Dodo had tossed him her car keys and Mark had driven to the scene as fast as he could. He arrived too late, of course. There were no fatalities, but the code-breaking machinery had been destroyed by the attacking robots. The code-breakers had been on the edge of a breakthrough, and now all their work was destroyed, lost forever. After they had done their work the silver robots had vanished into thin air in the same spectacular fashion as that which Mark had witnessed in the cult café. That was that. There was nothing Mark could do.

And then, as he was leaving, and when the last thing he had been expecting was trouble, someone had clobbered him over the head!

So, just who are his captors? The silver robots? Well, they had definitely been around and Mark's present location does look as though it might be part of some futuristic installation or spacecraft… But hiding behind doors and coshing people on the head? This seems a rather prosaic method for alien robots to employ…

Mark's speculation is interrupted when the metal doors in front of him slide open, to reveal a section of carpeted executive corridor and the identity of Mark's captor.

Flat-Sol Park.

She enters the room, the doors sliding closed behind her. She is dressed in her usual immaculate corporate grey plumage and her trademark loafers. Her legs are bare.

Walking up to him, she stands before him, narrow eyes behind designer frames coolly appraising the naked prisoner. 'Good afternoon, Mark Hunter,' she says, offering him a brief smile. 'I am pleased to see that you have recovered. I trust you are feeling no ill-effects?'

'No, I tend to recover from these blows to the head very quickly,' replies Mark. 'I must have built up a tolerance over the years. You said "good afternoon": how long have I been unconscious?'

'For two hours. You were brought here directly from Turing Grange.'

'"Here" being the Parkhurst Building?'

'Correct.'

'And is there any particular reason you've got me manacled to a chair like this?'

'Yes. It is for interrogation purposes.'

'And who is going to conduct this interrogation?'

'*I* am conducting the interrogation, and it has already begun. My first question regards the Turning Grange establishment: what work is being conducted there?'

'You mean you don't know?'

'I was unaware that the establishment had any bearing on the situation until this morning,' replies Flat-Sol.

'So, you weren't behind the attack?'

'My organisation had no hand in the incident. I know that your colleague Richard Bedford stubbornly maintains the belief that we at Parkhurst are the instigators of Zero, but he is in error.'

'And how did you come to find out about Turing Grange?'

'Through the same means by which we have been apprised of many of your recent activities: we have an inside source of information.'

Mark looks at her.

'Yes... I thought it had to be that... But who...?'

'I see no reason for my divulging the identity of our informant—and may I remind you, Mark Hunter, that this is an interrogation and that is *I* who am asking the questions. You will confine your speech to your responses to those questions. So, to repeat my first question: what work was being conducted at Turing Grange and how does it relate to the Zero campaign?'

'The people there were attempting to decipher a coded message transmitted to Earth from the Vega system that was picked up by one of our radio observatories.'

'From the Vega system? Am I to understand that all of these rumours in circulation claiming the Zero commercials are messages from outer space are actually true?'

'Yes, it is true. At least that is what we suspect. What the commercials are actually supposed to *be*; that we still don't know. We were hoping to learn more from the coded transmission they were working on at Turning Grange. They were close to cracking the code and obviously someone didn't want them doing that, so they made sure that they couldn't, by destroying all their work.'

'And just who is this enemy? Who are these so-called silver spacemen? Robots from a motion picture over half a century old? Are *these* your aliens? Your Vegans?'

'Well, I'm still a bit fuzzy as to how those robots fit into the picture and why they look the way they do.'

'But what *is* Zero?' demands Flat-Sol. 'You say you still don't know. It has to be something, either a commodity or an event.'

'Personally, I think it's neither.'

'You cling to the idea that the Zero campaign is a joke?'

'I do.'

'And this connection with the village of Critchlow? Why do you attach so much importance to the place?'

'Because it was where the film with those silver robots was made, and because we know that a girl called Amber Windrush, who had discovered something about Zero, visited the place, and I believe it was there she made her discovery.'

'But what do you hope to find in Critchlow? My own people have studied the area and have found nothing; neither have your people.'

'Well, we're hoping to find Zero's base of operations, the place they're sending out the adverts from.'

'You contradict yourself, Mark Hunter. You just told me the commercials are coming from outer space.'

'We think they are; but not *directly* from outer space. We think the signals are being received and then relayed from a location here in England. Perhaps the signals have to go through some kind of decryption process before they can be re-transmitted.'

'Perhaps. You think. We have returned to baseless speculation when I asked for facts. It seems you really do not have much to tell me, Mark Hunter.'

'I'm afraid I don't and I'm very sorry to disappoint you. You might as well just let me go, hadn't you?' says Mark, smiling up at her hopefully.

'I shall do nothing of the kind, Mark Hunter,' is the crisp reply. 'I have a secondary reason for having you placed in the position in which you find yourself. Perhaps, if I am honest with myself, it is my *primary* reason, and the interrogation nothing more than a preliminary.'

'And what would that reason be?' inquires Mark politely.

'Revenge, Mark Hunter. You may recall that day I showed you round the house I had made ready for you, to replace your fire-gutted apartment. You not only refused my generous offer, but you also rejected me personally. You pushed me away, Mark Hunter, and that is an offence I can never forgive—at least not until I have satisfactorily revenged myself.'

'I see…' says Mark. 'And what form precisely is this revenge of yours going to take?'

'Can you not guess? I am going to take by force that which you would not grant me of your own volition: I'm going to rape you, Mark Hunter.'

'I see…' says Mark. 'Could I ask you to reconsider this?'

'You do not find the prospect of sexual congress with myself appealing?'

'I do not.'

'Good. Then my revenge will be all the more satisfactory. You must realise that if I choose to couple with you, there is absolutely nothing you can do to prevent it. You are completely helpless in that chair. You have no freedom to move your arms or your legs and your genitalia is completely exposed. You have a very good body, Mark

Hunter…' cooly appraising him once more. 'If only you would make the effort to develop your musculature. This could be easily achieved through a course of bodybuilding and with musclebuilding protein supplements to facilitate the process… Yes, if you were to improve your physique… It is only a shame you could not have been a few centimetres taller…'

'Ah! Well, no amount of food supplements are going to do anything about *that*.'

'No matter. I shall take you as you are now.'

'Are you sure about that?' cautions Mark. 'Wouldn't it be better to wait until I've buffed myself up a bit? How about you let me go and I'll nip down to the gym and start on that bodybuilding programme? Then, when I've done that, I'll come straight back here and you can manacle me to the chair again! How about that? Sounds like a plan?' hopefully.

'You are very amusing, Mark Hunter. I will keep you while I have you.'

'And have me while you keep me. Would it help if were to say I'm sincerely sorry for pushing you away that day?'

'I accept your apology and I believe in its sincerity; but even so, it will not save you. We shall begin immediately. Excuse me while I disrobe.'

She slips off her jacket and throws it aside. And then, loosening the belt, she unzips her skirt. It falls to the ground.

'They say,' begins Flat-Sol as she unbuttons her blouse, 'that we never forget our first sexual experience, do they not? Perhaps this is true of most people, but for myself I have no recollection at all of my deflowering, for the simple reason I was unconscious at the time. It happened at a party in Seoul. An exclusive party for the wealthy: the media celebrities, the business executives. I was only a junior data analyst at the time, and I was very lucky to be invited, or so I thought. However, I was unaware at the time that there was a practice at these parties of men acquiring female sexual partners by means of soporific drugs.'

Her blouse unbuttoned, she slips out of it, drops it on top of the skirt. She is not wearing a bra. (She never does, disdaining them as a meaningless superfluity for women with no breasts to speak of such as herself.)

'If a female partygoer caught the eye of one of these men, he would have her given a doctored beverage and, upon its taking effect, the unconsciousness subject would be carried to a bedroom where the man who selected her would be free to undress her and have his way with her inert body at his pleasure. These unconscious subjects were referred to as "corpses."'

Off come her knickers, and now she is naked except for her flat-soled shoes. Keeping these on, she approaches Mark and stands before him, and Mark cannot help but take in the sight of her nudity: the dark honey of her flawless skin; the rugged *mesa*s of nipple and aureole; the dense undergrowth of her pubic hair.

'Needless to say,' continues Flat-Sol, 'I myself caught the eye of one of these men; I was given a doctored drink and I was rendered a "corpse." I awoke to find myself in an unfamiliar room, deflowered and inseminated. And so, Mark Hunter, I have no recollection of my inaugural sexual experience, and to this day I remain ignorant of the man's identity. Very likely I snored my way through the entire procedure. Most unladylike, wouldn't you agree?'

Mark looks up at her.

'I'm sorry,' he says.

'Do not be. I consider the incident to have been a valuable life experience; it taught me much. But I see you are not yet aroused. I will remedy the situation.' Squatting on her haunches, she takes hold of Mark's flaccid penis, and with a practiced hand, soon brings it to full tumescence. Her eyes lighting up, Flat-Sol explores it with her hands, caressing the glans, the shaft, the testicles.

'Ah... Very handsome... You are admirably endowed, Mark Hunter.' (Well, of course he is! How could he be 'the thinking woman's James Bond' otherwise?) 'But this I already knew: we have your measurements on file... Yes, the shape, the dimensions, are perfect. And complete firmness. When I exert pressure with my fingers, I feel not the faintest suggestion of softness; it is as though I were attempting to squeeze granite... Yes, I have you now, Mark Hunter: you are completely physically aroused. Your body is as impatient for this consummation as my own.' Pulling it towards her, she takes the glans in her mouth, savours the taste of it with her tongue. And then: 'But your state of arousal does not mean that you have fallen in love with me? That was what you said on that other occasion, yes? You were speaking of romantic love, I think. Personally, I have never experienced the emotion; but you: yes, I think you would be the type to experience romantic love. Well, let us see if I can compel you to fall romantically in love with me, Mark Hunter.'

Flat-Sol stands, straddles the chair with first one leg then the other, and then she slowly lowers herself onto him, guiding him in until he is entirely consumed, and she has him held fast inside her. Closing her legs around Mark's hips, she begins to move up and down on top of him, building up a slow, steady rhythm.

Mark is silent, his face averted.

'You look away,' says Flat-Sol. 'It is not very polite to look away from a lady when she is raping you.' She takes his jaw in her hand, turns his head to face her. Reluctantly, his eyes meet hers. She sees pain in them. 'What are you thinking, Mark Hunter? What are your feelings for me now? Do you wish to tell me you despise me? Or that you pity me?'

Mark remains silent.

'You will not speak. No matter. Let us say this: let us say that I shall have succeeded in compelling you to fall romantically in love with me, when I succeed in causing you to discharge inside me. And if you do not wish for this to happen, if you wish to deny my victory, then you must prevent yourself from reaching that crisis.'

And Flat-Sol now sets about her task in deadly earnest. Slowly at first, but then with increasing speed, increasing force does Flat-Sol pound into Mark, loudly giving voice to the giddy ecstasy of battle. And ultimately, inevitably, flesh triumphs over flesh and the floodgates are opened.

'Ah...' sighs Flat-Sol. Inundated, satiated, her body soaked with sweat, she subsides against Mark. She folds her arms around his neck, feels his fast-beating heart against her own. 'I have triumphed...' she gasps. 'I have made you fall in love with me, Mark Hunter... Or perhaps you will argue the contest was unfair...? Yes...? Perhaps you would rather we were to look upon this as a business transaction...? Very well... Then let us say that I have executed a hostile takeover upon your person... Yes, I have seized your assets and I have forced you into liquidation...

'So you see, Mark Hunter... whichever way you choose to regard it, the result is the same... You are mine...'

Chapter Twenty-Seven
Variation on Some Lousy Luck, Part One

Richard Bedford is on the warpath.

It is late afternoon and the plaza fronting the polished obsidian tower that is the Parkhurst Corporation's headquarters is thronged with office workers coming and going; but all of them make way for the burly man with prematurely grey hair, the scowling face, and the cigarette jammed in the corner of his mouth. And when he reaches the main entrance, even the automatic doors seem to slide open with more alacrity than usual.

He marches across the stadium-sized foyer to a space-age reception desk, at which sit two immaculate women in air stewardess uniforms, caps at rakish angles. A matching pair, one blonde, one brunette. Behind the reception desk rises a black marble monolith emblazoned with the Parkhurst logo.

Bedford walks up to the blonde receptionist.

'Good morning how can I help you sir I'm afraid this is a non-smoking area so I will have to ask you to extinguish your cigarette,' says she in one smooth breath.

'Never mind the cigarette. The name's Bedford and I'm here to see the boss lady.'

'I'm sorry sir but Miss Park cannot be seen without an appointment and I'm afraid this is a non-smoking area so I will have to ask you to extinguish your cigarette.'

'Look sister, you just get on the horn, and you call up the boss lady and you tell her that Rick Bedford is here to see her. You tell her that; she'll see me alright.'

'I'm sorry sir but Miss Park cannot be seen without an appointment and I'm afraid this is a non-smoking area so I will have to ask you to extinguish your cigarette.'

'I'm telling you, she'll see *me*, with or without an appointment. Just get her on the horn, will you?'

'I'm sorry sir but Miss Park cannot be seen without an appointment and I'm afraid this is a non-smoking area so I will have to ask you to extinguish your cigarette.'

'Look sister, we can do this the easy way, or we can do this the hard way. So do yourself a favour and just forget the protocol, get the boss lady on the horn, and—'

'I'm sorry sir but Miss Park cannot be seen without an appointment and I'm afraid this is a non-smoking area so I will have to ask you to extinguish your cigarette.'

'Jesus Christ, I can't even finish a goddamn *sentence* around here!' flares up Bedford, slamming his fist down on the counter. 'Now you just get on the horn and call up the boss lady before I start getting *really angry!*'

'I'm sorry sir but Miss Park cannot be seen without an appointment and I'm afraid—'

'Look, I'm gunna give you one last chance, sister! Either you get the boss lady on the horn and tell her that—'

'I'm sorry, sir but—'

'Will you just stop saying *the same Goddamn thing?*' snarls Bedford. 'Jesus Christ Almighty! The same damn thing, over and over! Just the same Goddamned thing! This is just so *senseless*! Are you a goddamn robot or something?'

'I'm sorry sir—' begins the flesh and blood automaton.

'Alright, *forget it!* Just *forget it!*'

Fuming, Bedford turns from the reception desk and stalks off towards the bank of elevators. One of those lifts, a lift with golden doors and a more imposing façade than its fellows, Bedford correctly determines to be the executive lift. Making this his target, he heads towards it.

A squad of uniformed security guards, armed with batons, suddenly appear in his path.

'You are creating a disturbance, sir,' says the guard captain. 'I am going to have to ask you to leave the building.'

'Oh yeah? Just you try and make me, buddy,' growls Bedford.

And now it's straight into the fight scene as Bedford presses forward, the guard captain raises his baton, and Bedford floors him with a swift uppercut. The other guards pile in and Bedford lashes out, slugging left and right. The guards have their batons but Bedford his own big stick in the shape of his anger, and he wields it to good effect. And when he resumes his course towards the lifts the guards are all out for the count and Bedford doesn't have so much as a dent in the cigarette in his mouth.

A woman approaches the doors of the executive lift, presents her security pass to the scanner. The doors open and the woman steps into the lift car.

Bedford slips in through the doors just as they are closing.

'Don't mind if I join you, lady?'

Apparently, the lady doesn't mind. As the lift begins to climb, she regards the intruder with a curiosity so mild as to border on complete indifference. The woman is Asian and for a moment Bedford wonders if he has actually collared the boss-lady herself: but no; a quick glance at the snapshot of Flat-Sol Park stashed in his breast pocket disproves this. This woman is stockier, no glasses, different haircut, different expression... Still, there is some resemblance there in the features... Of course: the sister! The sister Dodo's friend picked up by mistake at the airport that day! Yeah, this has got to be her.

Yu-Mi Park (for it is indeed that worthy) having completed her survey of the newcomer, has now turned her attention to the burnished lift doors in front of her.

'You the boss lady's sister?' asks Bedford.

Yu-Mi looks at him again.

'I said, are you the boss lady's sister?'

No response.

'Sister?' more loudly, stabbing a finger at her.

'Sister...' slowly nodding her head.

'Good,' says Bedford. 'Well sister, I wanna see *your* sister, okay? So, when we get to the top floor, you just show me right on in. You got that honey? You got that?'

But Bedford has already lost his audience, Yu-Mi's vacant gaze having drifted back to the lift doors.

The lift arrives at its destination, pings and opens its doors.

'Okay, sister,' taking Yu-Mi by the arm. 'Let's go.'

They step out of the lift and are then brought to a halt by the Korean woman's passive resistance.

'C'mon, lady,' urges Bedford, tugging her arm. 'Quit dragging your heels. Which way do we go?' Yu-Mi just looks at him blankly. 'Which... *way*?' slowly and with emphasis, pointing in the three available directions: left, right and straight ahead. 'C'mon, I wanna meet the boss lady!'

'Meet!' echoes Yu-Mi, latching onto a word she recognises. 'You go meeting…?'

'Yeah, that's right! I wanna have a meeting with the boss lady! You got it now? Which way?'

'Meeting: this way!' declares Yu-Mi, pointing down the lefthand corridor.

They set off, Yu-Mi leading the way. She walks with the confident tread of someone who now feels they are on firm ground, and brings them to a halt before a pair of double doors.

'Okay, sister,' says Bedford, relinquishing his hold on the woman's arm. 'I can take it from here.'

Taking the handles of both doors, Bedford thrusts them open and erupts into the room.

'Okay, boss lady—!' He stops. He is in a boardroom, an *empty* boardroom.

Bedford is back out in the corridor in a twinkling, and Yu-Mi, who hasn't moved, finds her upper arm once more in a tight embrace. 'Okay, sister: what's going on here?' pointing through the open doors. 'There's no-one in there! D'you hear me: no-one in there!'

'Meeting room!' says Yu-Mi, pointing with her free arm.

'I can *see* it's a meeting room, but it's a Goddamn *empty* meeting room! Now, where's the Goddamn boss lady, for Christ's sake?' shaking her for emphasis. 'Take me to her *office*, you hear me? Her *office!*'

'Ah! Office! Office!' smiling and nodding her understanding.

'Yeah, you got it! Her *office!*' nodding and smiling in turn.

'Office this way!' announces Yu-Mi.

They set off back the way they came, past the lift and stop before a door, which Yu-Mi opens and ushers Bedford inside.

'Office!' declares Yu-Mi, indicating the room with a proprietary sweep of the arm.

It is indeed an office and a well-appointed and important-looking office—but there is no-one in it.

'Well, where is she then?' demands Bedford. 'Where... is... she?' pointing at the vacant desk.

'Office, office!' enthuses Yu-Mi.

'I can *see* it's a Goddamn office! But where's the boss lady? *The boss lady!*' Espying a name plaque on the desk, Bedford strides across the room and snatches it up. Yu-Mi Park. Yu-Mi Park; not the name he was expecting. 'This is *you*, isn't it?' thrusting the name plaque under her nose. 'This is *you!*'

'Yu-*Mi!*' pointing at herself. 'Yu-*Mi!*'

'Lady, I don't want *your* office, I want your *sister's* Goddamn office!' now taking her by both arms. 'Your *sister!* YOUR SISTER!!!'

And to cut a long story short and after more shouting and shaking and broken English, Yu-Mi finally takes Bedford down the correct corridor and to the doors of the office of Flat-Sol Park.

The doors open and there is Flat-Sol herself, seated calmly behind her desk at the far end of the room.

'I am glad you have at last found your way here, Mr Bedford,' says she.

'You tellin' me you knew I was here?'

'Of course. I have been observing your progress on the monitor, and I must inform you I do not care for the way you have been manhandling my sister, Mr Bedford. You have been treating her with scant respect.'

'Yeah, well that's too bad, lady,' says Bedford, squaring his shoulders and walking into the room. Jensen, hiding behind the door with reversed gun in hand, moves in to administer the immobilising blow to the head, but Bedford, catching sight of him out of the corner of his eye, swings round and drives a fist into the man's stomach.

Jensen goes 'Oomph!' and falls to the floor, and Bedford turns back to Flat-Sol, who still sits calmly at her desk. 'Nice try, lady. But did you really think I'd fall for that old trick?'

Yu-Mi, suddenly armed with a life preserver, now moves in behind Bedford and clubs him smartly over the head.

'Son of a—!'

And his cigarette drops from the corner of his mouth as he collapses to the ground.

Chapter Twenty-Eight
Variation on Some Lousy Luck, Part Two

'Rick, Rick…'

The face of the Oriental beauty swims into soft focus, a look of profound sorrow written in her mascaraed eyes, the arch of her overbite.

Taiko…!

'You must not go, Rick! I beg of you… When Max was dying, he had you to crawl to you… But you, you will be all alone in a strange place: who will you crawl to? Where will you go…?'

Taiko…

Bedford's eyes open on a bare concrete ceiling. He is lying on a cot in a small windowless room, lit by a bare electric bulb, a chair and a wash-basin the only other furniture. His head hurts. (Bedford never seems to recover from these blows to the head with as much ease as Mark Hunter does.)

Taiko… Taiko Yani, the Japanese vedette he'd met in that Parisian nightclub all those years ago. The most warm and compassionate woman he'd ever met… Their eyes had met, something had passed between them, and she had come and joined him at his table after her show…How long since he'd thought of Taiko...? He'd locked her away, locked away her memory... What made him remember her now of all times...?

And who the hell was that *Max* she was talking about? Far as he can recollect, he's never even *known* anyone called Max, let alone a guy called Max who'd crawled to him when he was dying...! Dammit, he'd *remember* something like that!

Bedford sits up on the cot and lights a cigarette, still searching his memory for possible Maxes. The headache isn't helping.

The sound of a bolt being drawn back and the door opens. There stands Jensen, and in his hand the same automatic he'd failed to hit Bedford over the head with.

'Okay, get up,' he says. 'Miss Park wants to see you.'

'Oh, she does, does she?' Bedford rises from the bed, his temper rising with him. 'So, Miss Park wants to see me, huh? Well, that's just BEAUTIFUL! Seeing her's what I came here for in the first place! Why the hell couldn't she just see me while I was there in her office, for Christ's sake?'

'Yes, but you forced your way in and caused a scene, and Miss Park doesn't like that. They don't like scenes, you know, these East Asians.'

'Yeah, I know that,' says Bedford. 'But I wasn't exactly in the mood for observing the social niceties.'

'Are you ever?'

'Listen, wise guy—!'

Jensen raises his gun. 'Can we just get a move on? Miss Park's waiting.'

'Yeah, let's get outta here...'

Shrugging, Bedford straightens his jacket, and steps out into a spartan corridor, Jensen close behind, covering him with the gun.

'Where is this place, anyway?'

'Basement. This way.'

Two corridors and a pair of doors bring them to an underground carpark where a black Rolls Royce limousine awaits them, a uniformed chauffeuse standing at its side. She opens the rear door for the newcomers.

'Please enter, Mr Bedford,' invites a voice from within.

Bedford leans into the car. Flat-Sol Park sits on the side seat, sipping a glass of Chateau Lafitte. 'What gives, lady? I thought you wanted to talk? You planning on taking me someplace?'

'Yes, Mr Bedford. I'm taking you home; back to your hotel. We can have our discussion on the way.'

Bedford shrugs, climbs into the car, sliding onto the back seat. Jensen follows and sits beside him.

'You may put the gun away, Mr Jensen,' says Flat-Sol.

The car sets off. The time is nine o'clock and the sun has just set.

'I really have just one thing I would like to say to you, Mr Bedford, before we part company,' begins Flat-Sol. 'And that is my earnest wish that you would disabuse yourself of this notion you persist in clinging to, that we of the Parkhurst Corporation are the ones behind the Zero campaign. We are not. It's as simple as that.'

'Uh-huh. And I'm supposed to just take your word for that?'

'My word, and the application of your own common sense, if you happen to possess any of that commodity.'

Jensen sniggers.

'Oh, I get it,' says Bedford. 'I'm a dummy if I think it's you guys who're behind Zero, right? Well then, this dummy would like to know what you've done with Mark Hunter. Because he disappeared from Turing Grange just after those silver robots of yours had come along and trashed the place.'

'Once again you are in error, Mister Bedford. The Parkhurst Corporation has no silver robots in its employ and the attack on the codebreaking facility was none of our doing. And as for Mark Hunter, he is presently staying as a guest at my villa, where he is unharmed and perfectly safe.'

'Yeah? Well, I sure as hell know Mark would never stay as *your* guest, lady, not if he had any choice about it. So how about we all just drive on to this villa of yours so that I can see for myself that he's okay?'

'I'm afraid that will not be possible, Mister Bedford'

'Then you better *make* it possible, sister! Cuz I ain't goin' nowhere till I've seen Mark Hunter and I've seen that he's still in one piece! You hear me, sister? You hear me?'

Flat-Sol turns to Jensen. 'Mr Bedford seems to be getting somewhat overwrought; I think he requires some fresh air. Please see to it.'

'My pleasure.'

Jensen drives his fist into Bedford's stomach, drags him bodily from his seat and, opening the door, pitches him out of the car.

Beford hits the asphalt, smashes his knee, tumbles into the kerb. The limousine, accelerating fast, is soon out of sight.

Those sons of bitches...!

Bedford staggers to his feet. His knee hurts like hell. Where is he? Some side-street. No traffic, no people around... He starts limping down the street.

Gotta find me a taxi... Fat chance of one showing up around here...

He comes to a corner, sees a signpost on the wall of the building: Bedford Road. A good omen or bad? Doesn't help him any: he's never heard of any Bedford Road in London before...

Round the corner he sees a man walking down the street in front of him.

'Hey, mister! I'm kind of lost here! Which way's the nearest—?'

The man ignores him, keeps on walking.

'Hey! I'm talkin' to you, buddy!'

Still ignoring him, the man vanishes round a corner.

Muttering, Bedford continues on his limping way. He soon discovers he's in a maze of Bedfords: Bedford Avenue, Bedford Lane, Bedford Square, Bedford Way... A labyrinth of lookalike streets, all spiked railings and looming smoke-blackened housefronts.

He catches sight of another solitary pedestrian.

'Hey, buddy! Can you tell me—?'

Galvanised, the man crosses the road and ducks down an alleyway.

'Son of a—!'

And then it happens again. And again. Every time he tries to ask someone for directions, they just split as fast as they can! What the hell is wrong with the British anyway? So goddamned antisocial!

He sees a cat regarding him from the top of a wall. He smiles. He kind of likes cats.

'Hey there, buddy! Don't suppose you can steer me out of this neighbourhood...?'

The cat's response is as swift as it is unexpected. It springs from the wall and onto his face, raking it with its claws and squealing what sounds like a torrent of feline verbal abuse. Caught off guard by the sudden attack, Bedford staggers across the pavement. He grabs hold of the flailing animal, prises it off his face and hurls it away.

'Son of a goddamn bitch!' roars Bedford, slumping against the wall. 'What the *hell* is going on around here? Jesus Christ Almighty!'

He feels his face and his hand comes off wet with blood. Jesus! That cat's really gone to work with its claws!

Round the next corner he sees a woman coming towards him. She looks friendly. Maybe his luck's about to change.

'Hey, lady! Can you please just tell me how to get out of this crazy neighbourhood? All I want is to find a main road...'

The woman sprays him in the face with an aerosol.

Bedford screams.

'For Christ's—!'

Following up her attack, she knees him in the crotch.

Bedford jackknifes, hands clutching the violated zone, mouth wide with voiceless agony. Dimly, through the tidal wave of pain, he hears the sound of the woman's fleeing footsteps.

Son of a goddamn motherfucking *bitch!* This is fucking *insane!*

Obeying some impulse of movement, he staggers blindly on, still clutching his groin, eyes streaming, the wounds on his face shrill razors of pain.

'WE HAVE YOU SURROUNDED! SURRENDER PEACEFULLY!'

The order, shouted through a bullhorn, stops Bedford in his tracks.

Now what?

'SURRENDER NOW, OR WE WILL BE FORCED TO OPEN FIRE!'

Bedford raises his hands, blinking his eyes madly. 'Now, hold it! I'm unarmed! Just hold it, will you?'

His vision clears. He has wandered out onto a wider street. He's standing in the middle of the road and in front of him is a row of police cars parked bumper to bumper, and behind the cars a squad of armed police officers, all with guns pointing in Bedford's direction.

'Now, let's just take it easy, guys—'

'DROP YOUR WEAPONS AND COME OUT WITH YOUR HANDS UP!'

It now occurs to Bedford that he may not be the one they're shouting their orders at here; especially as one of the officers is urgently waving his arm in what are clearly 'get out of the way, you idiot' gestures. He looks behind him. A shuttered shopfront and above it a signboard reading 'Men's Hairdressing and Vaping.'

Say, wasn't there something on the news about those places…? Something about them being fronts for hood activity…?

The click of safety catches being released. Bedford looks to the floor above the signboard, sees open windows bristling with gun muzzles.

Son of a—!

All hell breaks loose. A rapid fire of bullets rains down on the police cars, the armed officers return fire and Bedford is right in the middle of it. Running for cover, he catches a bullet in the ribs. Smoke bombs are thrown as the police prepare to charge. Clutching the bleeding wound in his side, Bedford staggers on through thick clouds of choking smoke.

Something he's gotta do… Someplace he needs to be…

He staggers on…

He makes it to another side street. He feels dizzy… He's losing blood fast…

Mark… Gotta let them know… Tell 'em where they've got Mark… His old buddy Mark…

A car skids round the corner. It drives past at speed and a voice calls through the passenger window: 'This is for you, Mariocki!'

The glint of metal in the air and a knife, thrown with precision, buries itself in Bedford's shoulder.

Bedford screams, staggers back against area railings.

'You crazy idiot!' he yells at the retreating taillights. 'My name's…! My name's… Bedford…'

The face of Taiko Tani appears before him again. Taiko… Taiko… So kind… So beautiful…

'When Max was dying, he had you to crawl to you… When *you* are dying, who will you crawl to, Rick? Where will you go?'

Taiko…

Where… Where is he…? Gotta get to someplace… Gotta to warn somebody… Who is it…? What is it he has to to…?

His vision settles on a woman hurrying along the opposite sidewalk. Something about her… He tries to focus… Taiko! It's Taiko! It's her!

Taiko! Taiko!

He tries to call her name; but the words won't come.

She doesn't see him! She walks on down the street.

Taiko!

Fighting the pain, he propels himself from the railings, lurches across the street. His legs are so weak…

Gotta get after Taiko… Can't lose her… Not again; not like before… Can't lose her this time…

He follows her, desperate to catch up… She's way ahead of him… She turns a corner. He hurries after her, stumbles, falls, picks himself up again… He makes the corner just in time to see her disappear into an apartment building down the street. He knows that building…

In Dodo's apartment, the girls are all gathered: Mayumi Takahashi, Trina Truelove, Yuki Kinoshita and Shizuka Todoroki, the latter just now returned from a visit to her embassy building. Of the recent bombing there is no sign; everything has been repaired reglazed, the replaced, resurfaced, redecorated. When you command as much money as Dodo Dupont, you can make sure things get done quickly.

There comes a volley of knocks at the door and Dodo runs to answer it.

She opens the door and there stands Bedford; Bedford, his face covered with scratches, a knife-hilt sticking out his shoulder, shirt and jacket completely soaked with blood. He stands there for a moment, mouthing wordlessly and pitches forward into Dodo's arms.

'They got Mark…' he gasps. 'Flat-Sol Park, at her place… A villa…'

Gently, Dodo sets him down on the floor.

'One of you call an ambulance!'

'I'm on it!'

Trina picks up her phone while the three Japanese women join Dodo.

Bedford's eyes focus on Shizuka. He smiles.

'Taiko...! I made it, Taiko...! I made it...!' he winces, struggles against the darkness closing in on him. 'Taiko... Still... still can't figure out who the hell Max is...'

His eyes glaze over, his breathing stops.

Dodo checks for a pulse. 'He's dead,' she says.

And the odd thing is Shizuka doesn't look a bit like Taiko Tani.

Chapter Twenty-Nine
A Fine Upstanding Citizen

Jensen is annoyed. Very annoyed. He can't seem to get Trina Truelove off his mind, and it bothers him that he can't get her off his mind. I mean what's so special about her anyway? Yeah, she's young and she's a good lay; but so are a lot of girls Jensen has biblically known in his time, girls he has loved and left without a second thought; nary the smallest pang of regret. So what the hell is so special about Trina Truelove? True, he can't actually do the leaving part of loving and leaving her, not just yet: she's too valuable a source of intel, and if he were to stop seeing her that source might suddenly dry up; especially if the split proved to be an acrimonious one. So, he can't just end things with Trina Truelove right now: it would be bad business.

But why can't he treat the whole relationship like that: a business arrangement, plain and simple? Why can't he just put the girl out of his mind when he's not actually with her? What is it that's so great about her that he can't seem to do that? The sex? Well, yes, the sex is good: for one thing, she makes a lot of noise, which is always gratifying to the male ego; and when it comes to variety, she's up for pretty much anything, which again is a quality highly esteemed by men. So yes, the sex is good; more than good, it's great; but even so, it's not like it's the best he's ever had.

And then there's her looks. For Jensen such details as personality and intellect come a poor second to looks and Trina's are nothing to write home about. She's not ugly or fat or anything, but she's nothing special either. For one thing she's covered with tattoos, and Jensen's never been a fan of tattooed women. For another, she dyes her hair stupid dayglo colours, something else that clashes with Jensen's aesthetic sense. Altogether, she's not exactly the most drop-dead gorgeous woman he's ever laid.

Then there's her lifestyle and her values; her counterculture aesthetics, her charity shop clothes and accessories, her woke, lefty politics. (She even calls herself a feminist; the last thing Jensen would have expected from a woman who took dirty pictures for a living.)

And that *car* of hers…!

So to sum up, she's a good lay and nice enough to be around; but she's no great looker, her bank balance is a joke, her car an even worse one, and in terms of ethics, ambition and lifestyle they're poles apart.

So just *why* can't he get the bitch out of his mind? It's been really pissing Jensen off.

It's still pissing him off now, as he steps out of the air-cooled interior of his Mercedes sports car and into the stifling hot night (the predicted end-of-May global heatwave has well and truly kicked in) and walks up to the porch of Flat-Sol Park's riverside villa: angular, and ultramodern in design; flat-roofed, more windows than walls. A maid opens the door, and curtsies Jensen into the air-conditioned hallway.

'Please make yourself at home, Mr Jensen,' says the maid. 'Miss Park will be with you shortly.'

Jensen goes into the living room, heads straight for the bar, fixes himself a generous scotch on the rocks. Armed with this, he paces the room restlessly.

For Christ's sake, what is *wrong* with me tonight? Just because I'm not seeing... No! It's *not* that! I'm *fine* with not seeing Trina Truelove for one night! Totally fine! Couldn't care less. In fact, it's a relief to have her out of my hair for once!

But he continues to pace.

Flat-Sol is keeping him waiting, and while Jensen is perfectly aware that as the president and CEO it is Flat-Sol's prerogative to keep him, a mere personal assistant, waiting as long as she pleases, tonight he finds himself very ill-stocked with patience, and overflowing with its opposite number, irritability.

His patience exhausted, he slams his glass down on the bar counter, exits the living room and mounts the open staircase to the upstairs floor. Well, why not? He was told he could make himself at home, wasn't he? He makes straight for Flat-Sol's bedroom and is surprised to see the door ajar and the room beyond in darkness.

She's not in her room...? He pushes open the door. No: she *is* in her room! In the uncertain light he can discern a naked female form stretched out on the empress-sized round bed in the middle of the room. From the way the woman is lying there on top of the sheets, she has the appearance of someone who, having just laid down for a rest, has fallen asleep.

Is she asleep?

'Miss Park...?'

No response.

Jensen advances further into the room.

'Miss Park...?'

Still no response. He approaches the foot of the bed. There she reposes, her tanned body stark against white satin sheets, the darker loci of the nipples and pubic hair picked out against the skin. She lies on her back, one forearm resting on her forehead, the other arm thrown limply across the sheets. As he watches she murmurs in her sleep, in what sounds like her native tongue. She looks so peaceful lying there; so unlike the ruthless acquisitive businesswoman she usually is; so innocent and vulnerable...

Oh, fuck it, thinks Jensen; and pulling out his raging hard-on, he climbs onto the bed and with scant ceremony mounts the sleeping woman. And her awakening is not a gentle one, as Jensen proceeds to work out all his pent-up frustration on the woman beneath him, as though by so doing he can expunge the image of Trina Truelove from his mind for good and all. And he pursues his objective with an energy and determination worthy of a better cause. The fact that Flat-Sol might fire him—at the very least—as punishment for taking this liberty is something he just doesn't care about right now.

This is the first time Jensen has actually had sex with his boss since the berserker session on the boardroom table on that memorable day of his promotion—and this time it's different, very different. Then Flat-Sol was like a wild animal, loud and furiously energetic; but this time she is passive, inert, her vocal responses limited to soft grunts.

And then the lights come on and Jensen turns to see the woman he thought he was fucking standing there in the doorway. Hands on hips, she regards him with a rare ironic smile, like a strict schoolmarm showing an unexpectedly indulgent side when she catches one of her boys masturbating over a dirty magazine in the stationary cupboard.

Jensen looks at Flat-Sol in astonishment and then he looks down to see just who it is he's got on the end of his dick.

It's Flat-Sol's sister, Yu-Mi Park.

She returns his gaze with a mildly questioning look, as though to say 'So, are you going to finish this, or what?'

It is Flat-Sol who breaks the silence. 'I had not realised you had feelings for my sister, Mr Jensen,' she says.

'I thought it was you,' confesses Jensen bleakly, stuck for a plausible cover story.

'Then be grateful that it wasn't,' says Flat-Sol. Switching to Korean, she addresses her sister. Her sister replies with a monosyllable.

Says Flat-Sol: 'You may proceed, Mr Jensen. Finish what you have started.'

Jensen complies; and the second half of his performance is much more restrained than the first.

'Perhaps you can spare me the time to furnish me with your report, Mr Jensen, now that you have finished deflowering my sister.'

Jensen freezes in the act of returning his spent penis to its berth. 'Deflowered! You mean she…? At her age…?'

'Yes. Yu-Mi has led a very quiet and uneventful life,' explains Flat-Sol.

Jensen looks down at Yu-Mi with renewed interest—only to find she has already gone back to sleep.

'Your report, Mr Jensen,' prompts Flat-Sol.

'Oh, yeah. The latest is that Dodo Dupont is planning to pay headquarters a visit sometime tonight.' He grins. 'She thinks that's where we've got Mark Hunter locked away. I've alerted security.'

'Good. Then if she believes her friend is to be found there, she will not be troubling us here, will she?'

If you were to step out onto the rear terrace of Flat-Sol Park's villa you would find a swimming pool of some size, with all the usual paraphernalia of deckchairs, recliners, tables with parasols on the tiles surrounding it. The swimming pool, lit from within, throws an aurora of blue-tinted light over its surroundings. Beyond the pool are the flower gardens, and beyond them, more park-like terrain, dotted with a number of venerable trees, extends itself towards the riverbank.

Here, on the margin of the river, you will find a boathouse and jetty, with a river yacht berthed in the former and a small motorboat moored to the latter. The quiet waters of the nocturnal Thames lap against the riverbank.

But now the surface of the river disturbed as a pale human figure, hitherto submerged, breaks the surface and, taking hold of the ladder, climbs onto the jetty.

A tall, strongly-built woman with an hourglass figure and short black hair, she wears a red two-piece swimming costume and has a sheathed knife strapped to her thigh.

The woman is Dodo Dupont and twenty or so miles further down the river, in a building on Canary Wharf, people are still vainly awaiting her appearance.

Hunkered down on the jetty Dodo surveys the terrain ahead, running a hand through her wet hair to expel some of the moisture. Through the trees she can see the lights of the villa and the terrace swimming pool. There is no sound or sign of movement.

Unsheathing her knife, she makes her way towards the villa, keeping low and moving from cover to cover.

Dodo knows that it is here that she will find Mark Hunter. Rick Bedford had told her as much when he collapsed in her arms. But the others had been too far away to hear, and Dodo hasn't told them. Not all of it. She told them Bedford had told her Parkhurst had Mark, but not that he'd also told her where. This is a precaution she has taken reluctantly, but it has been necessary.

Information has been getting out; and it has been getting out from her apartment.

She comes to the extremity of the trees with their deep shadows and before her is the open lawn with its shrubberies and flowerbeds. Veering away from the glare of the villa and the swimming pool, Dodo makes a dash for a belt of shrubbery towards the edge of the garden. Gaining this cover and keeping low, she makes her way towards the rear of the garage adjoining the villa. She hears voices coming from the villa. She stops and peering through the foliage sees two people stepping out through the French windows onto the patio. The woman she recognises as Flat-Sol Park, and the man as one of the male employees who had accompanied her the day she had turned up at Dodo's flat. Flat-Sol is wearing bikini shorts, the man a suit *sans* jacket and tie. Both carrying iced drinks, they seat themselves on two of the poolside deckchairs.

Flat-Sol is speaking. 'There is no reason why Zero should not after all prove to be a product or a service. The rumours of the commercials being warnings from extraterrestrials of impending doom are internet hysteria; they have no foundation in fact.'

'Yes, but all this internet hysteria was caused by the adverts being there in the first place,' says Jensen. 'And maybe that's what they were designed to do. These riots that are breaking out all over the world; maybe that's what somebody wants.'

'But why? There is little profit to be made from short-term social unrest which will pass as soon as Zero Day has passed and we are all still here.'

'*If* we're all still here.'

'You are a pessimist, Mr Jensen. You seem determined to subscribe to the predictions of the Doomsday Prophets.'

'Well, I've got a right to be worried, haven't I? I mean, if there really *is* going to be some serious shit going down... It's alright for *you* to be so calm about it. *You* don't have to worry, do you? You've got your cabin on the Floating Island all booked and waiting for you; you can just ride out the end of the world, while the rest of us burn up or drown or whatever it's going to be.'

'I do not believe that Zero Day will bring any catastrophe of that nature, Mr Jensen.'

'Still, I bet they're making sure the Island is all ready to go, just in case.'

'The Floating Island is always "ready to go," Mr Jensen.'

The Floating Island! Dodo can hardly believe her ears. She has heard of this Floating Island, a self-propelled sanctuary for the oligarchs and the elite, waiting to be put into use in the event of some global catastrophe, but she had always assumed it to be nothing more than a wild conspiracy theory…!

Inspired by Jules Verne's novel of the same and several other names, the Floating Island is reputed to be a scientific wonder; the size of a small island and powered by turbines enabling it to sail the seas—with the key difference from its prototype in the Jules Verne novel, that this Floating Island has got a lid on it. An impenetrable metal dome is said to cover the island, rendering it a self-contained, self-sustaining ecosphere, its inhabitants protected from whatever hostile conditions may exist without: extreme temperatures, a contaminated or poisoned atmosphere… In short, the Floating Island is a lifeboat enabling its inhabitants, as Jensen has so aptly put it, 'to ride out the end of the world.'

'Thought about who your plus-one's going to be…?' ventures Jensen.

'I'm afraid that it will not be you, Mr Jensen,' is the frank reply. 'But perhaps I can obtain you passage as a crewmember.'

'Better than nothing,' says Jensen philosophically. 'I suppose you'd make that new toy of yours your plus-one, wouldn't you?'

'Perhaps I would, although I doubt that he would accompany me willingly.'

'How much longer are you going to keep that guy?' inquires Jensen, irritability creeping into his voice.

'That is none of your concern Mr Jensen.'

'I'm surprised he hasn't escaped. I mean, he's a spy, isn't he? They're supposed to be good at that sort of thing.'

'That he hasn't escaped is not for want of trying on his part. In fact, his repeated attempts have necessitated my having to place additional restraints upon his movements.'

That's Mark they're talking about, thinks Dodo. And it sounds like they've got him locked up somewhere inside the house. Although she's tempted to stay and continue listening to their conversation (they might say something to reveal the identity of their informant) she knows that now, while the coast is clear, is the best time to go into the house and look for Mark.

She makes her way to the end of the shrubbery and keeping low, crosses the remaining space to the rear of the garage. Here she is beyond the reach of the lights of the patio. Between the garage and the villa, there is a gateway giving access to a narrow pathway between the two buildings. The gate is ajar and Dodo slips through it into the shadowy passageway. She comes to a glass-panelled side door to the villa. Through the door is a lighted corridor. The door is unlocked and Dodo steps inside, carefully closing the door behind. The sound of female voices issues from an open doorway further along the corridor. Dodo creeps noiselessly up to the doorway.

'And did you remember to wash beneath the foreskin, Third Maid?'

'Yes, First Maid; I did indeed remember to wash beneath the foreskin.'

'And did you remember to shampoo and rinse the pubic hair, Third Maid?'

'Yes, First Maid: I did indeed remember to shampoo and rinse the pubic hair.'

'And did you remember to moisturise the scrotum, Third Maid?'

'Yes, First Maid; I did indeed remember to moisturise the scrotum.'

'Excellent work, Third Maid. Second Maid: I believe it is your duty to administer the next sponge bath, is it not?'

'That is so, First Maid; and I shall endeavour to discharge my duties to the best of my ability.'

'As indeed you must, Second Maid.'

Her curiosity by now piqued beyond all bounds of human endurance, Dodo risks a peak through the half-open door. She sees a room that appears to be a sort of servants' parlour and three women dressed in the full-skirted uniform of Victorian maids seated at a table. On the table stands a China tea-service, and the three maids sit primly sipping their cups of tea. They are a matching set, virtually identical in appearance, faces as perfect and as expressionless as their voices. (Apparently Flat-Sol Park gets her house servants from the same production line as her front-desk receptionists.)

A buzzer rings and one of the lights on a control board fixed to the wall lights up.

'A summons from the mistress,' says First Maid. 'You are on duty, Second Maid. Make haste.'

'Yes, First Maid; I shall indeed make haste.'

Dodo retreats from the doorway as Second Maid rises from her chair. Moments later she comes out into the corridor, closing the parlour door behind her. Dodo pounces. She clamps one hand over the woman's mouth and, forcing her head back, presses the blade of her knife against the exposed throat.

'One sound and I'll slit your fucking throat,' hisses Dodo. 'You are going to take me to wherever it is you've got Mark Hunter, and you're going to take me straight there. Any noise, any sign of stalling and you're dead. Understood?'

The maid, terrified, nods her head.

They proceed along the corridor, Dodo pinioning the maid's right arm, and keeping the knife close to her throat. Through the door at the end, they emerge into the main hallway.

'Which way?' hisses Dodo.

The maid points to the stairs. They mount the staircase, and the maid leads Dodo along the righthand corridor. They stop before a closed door. The maid unhooks a bunch of keys from her belt and unlocks the door.

The room is a sumptuous bedroom, with suggestively-subdued lighting and a naked man lying spreadeagled on a luxury four-poster bed, wrists and ankles manacled to the four posts. His erection, perpendicular to his supine body, stares hard at the ceiling.

The manacled man is Mark Hunter.

'You took your time,' says he, regarding Dodo without surprise.

'Well, I don't have to ask whether you're pleased to see me,' grins Dodo.

'I *knew* you were going to say that.'

Pushing the maid before her, Dodo crosses the room to the bed.

'What you see is priapism rather than actual arousal,' explains Mark. 'A result of the diet they've had me on here.'

'What: spinach and Viagra, three meals a day?'

'Pretty much.'

Dodo shakes the maid. 'Alright, Miss Sponge-bath. Unlock those manacles, and don't waste your breath telling me you haven't got the keys.'

The maid doesn't waste her breath and Mark is soon on his feet.

'Where are your clothes?' asks Dodo.

'Missing in action. Last seen two days ago.'

'Then I'll have to just take you as you are.' To the maid: 'Okay, you. Lie down on the bed.'

The maid complies and Mark and Dodo secure the manacles to her wrists and ankles. Dodo takes off the maid's lace cap and ties it round her mouth as a gag.

'So, how did you know I was here?' inquires Mark. 'Definite information or a matter of deduction?'

'Ah,' says Dodo, her face falling. 'It was Rick Bedford who told me, and I'm afraid I've got some bad news—'

'Yes, I've heard about Rick's death,' Mark tells her. 'My hostess informed me.'

'Oh, did she? Well, that's interesting, because Bedford died in my flat, and including myself there were only five witnesses to the event, which has *not* been officially announced yet. We've got a problem, Mark.'

Mark meets her gaze. 'I'd come to the same conclusion.'

'Well, let's focus on getting out of here first. Come on.'

Leaving the maid they exit the bedroom, Dodo locking the door behind them. They make their way along the corridor to the main staircase, Dodo leading the way, her knife at the ready.

'What's our escape route?' asks Mark, keeping his voice low.

'The river. I got here by swimming, but as there happens to be a speedboat moored to the jetty, we can borrow that for our getaway. Then it's just down the river to where I parked my car.'

'Do you know if the mistress of the house is around?'

'She is. When I left her, she was out by the swimming pool with a man called Jensen. I haven't seen anyone else.'

'Let's get a move on, then,' says Mark. 'And, erm… Dodo…?'

'Yes?'

'You can let go of me, you know…'

Dodo looks down and discovers that all the time she has been walking along the corridor she has had Mark's tumescent penis firmly clasped in her hand.

'Oh, sorry, sweetheart!' relinquishing her hold. 'I didn't realise I was doing it…! Pure female instinct; beautiful in its way.'

'Quite so. Shall we proceed?'

They reach the top of the stairs. Voices in the hallway below.

'...I don't see what you're making such a fuss about,' comes Jensen's voice. 'She's probably just gone to the bog.'

'When she should have been responding to a summons from her mistress? No servant of mine would dare do such a thing.'

They come into view at the foot of the stairs: Flat-Sol, Jensen and maids number one and three. Mark and Dodo quickly retreat out of sight.

'Come on,' breathes Dodo. 'This way.'

They hurry down the lefthand corridor.

'What's the plan now?' asks Mark.

'There's a garage right next to the house this side. We can climb out a window onto the garage roof and then get down to the garden.'

At the end of the corridor, they find the window they want. Dodo opens the sash. The passageway is directly below and on the other side and at a slightly lower elevation, the flat roof of the garage.

Says Mark: 'When you said the garage was right next to the house, I'd thought you meant *right* next to.'

'What are you complaining about? We can jump it easily enough,' says Dodo, and stepping onto the ledge, leads by example, leaping effortlessly over the intervening space and landing safely on the garage roof.

Mark follows, clears the gap, grunting with pain as he lands. 'Although it might be an easy distance to clear, you could try and remember that in my present physical state violent movements like this can cause considerable discomfort.'

'Sorry, darling,' apologises Dodo.

They cross to the rear of the roof and drop down into the garden, Dodo assisting Mark.

Dodo throws the maid's keys into the bushes. 'There,' she says. 'We managed that without serious injury to your manhood.'

'Yes, but unfortunately we had an audience,' says Mark, inclining his head.

Dodo swings round. She freezes in the act of reaching for her sheathed knife. Flat-Sol Park's blonde chauffeuse, Lady Penelope Parker, stands before them, the automatic pistol in her gloved hand pointed squarely at her. Composed and expressionless as always (another production line model?) she doesn't even spare Mark's priapism a second glance.

'Ah!' says Dodo, clapping her hands and affecting an embarrassed laugh. 'Now you're probably wondering what we're doing here, right? Well, my friend and I were just enjoying a moonlight skinny-dip when would you believe it? we got caught in the current and swept downstream, and—'

'She's not buying it, Dodo,' Mark tells her wearily. 'You're overdressed for skinny-dipping and she knows who I am.'

The chauffeuse makes an upward jerking motion with her gun-hand, unmistakable in its meaning.

Mark and Dodo raise their hands.

'Doesn't say much, does she?' remarks Dodo.

'She's a nonspeaking chauffeur,' says Mark.

Which, as she now reveals, in no way inhibits her ability to raise the alarm. Reaching into her hip pocket with her free hand, she produces a silver whistle and applies it to her mouth. Its shrill blast rips through the nocturnal stillness and is immediately answered by voices inside in the villa.

One last chance, thinks Dodo. She looks suddenly and pointedly at Mark's crotch.

'Oh, *Mark!*' she exclaims in her best how-could-you tone. 'You've just *come!*'

It works. The chauffeuse's gaze flickers downwards; only for an instant, but instant is all Dodo needs. She strikes with cobra-swiftness, a straight-legged kick to the woman's face, which she follows up with a vicious chop to the side of the neck. Stunned, the chauffeuse collapses, Dodo snatching the gun from her hand as she falls.

She throws the gun to Mark. 'Here you go, sweetheart. Now you can feel like a real man again.'

'Very amusing,' says Mark. 'But why don't reserve the glib one-liners until we're safely out of here?'

They set off across the garden at a run. Shouts from the patio; they have been seen. Sounds of pursuit. They make it to the riverbank. Dodo jumps into the speedboat and pulls the cord on the outboard motor, while Mark unties the painter. He jumps into the passenger seat and the speedboat pulls away from the jetty, curving out into the river just as the pursuing party appears: Flat-Sol, Jensen, and the two maids. (The third maid is still chained to the four-poster and likely to remain that way for the rest of the night.)

Flat-Sol, enraged at this theft of her property (and I don't mean the boat), runs out onto the jetty, and taking aim with the SA-80 machine gun she has mysteriously acquired, opens fire at the retreating vessel. Bullets peppers the surface of the water around the speedboat, throwing up angry bee-stings of water; but the distance is already too great for effective shooting, and no bullet finds its home in either the the boat or its passengers.

But it does succeed in making the escape look more dramatic.

Chapter Thirty
A Rift in the Shamisen

'Well, that's it then,' says Mark, switching off the device. 'I've swept every room; your apartment is *not* bugged, my dear.'

Dodo pulls a face. 'I was actually hoping it *would* be.'

'I know what you mean. It would have been nice, wouldn't it? Flat-Sol Park would be our only culprit and we would have deduced that either she planted the bug herself that day she was here, or *had it* planted subsequently by one of her agents. Yes, it would have been all very nice, neat and tidy…'

They re-enter the living room.

'How about a cold beer?' offers Dodo.

'A cold beer sounds very nice,' says Mark.

While Dodo goes to the kitchen, Mark seats himself in an armchair. Recovered from his abduction ordeal, he is back in his usual brown suit and able to zip up the trousers. Depositing his bug detector on the coffee table, he lights himself a cigarette.

Dodo returns with two chilled bottles of beer. She hands one to Mark.

'Thank you, my dear.'

Dodo seats herself on one of the settees. She takes a swig of the beverage, then morosely examines the label on the bottle.

'So, now we know for sure it has to be one of the girls,' she says.

'Yes, that would appear to be the case,' agrees Mark, tapping the ash from his cigarette. 'We have four suspects, four people who were all here on those occasions when information was leaked back to the Parkhurst Corporation. Four people, two of whom we know well, and two of whom we don't: Mayumi and Trina, Yuki and Shizuka.'

'And one of them's a traitor,' says Dodo glumly.

'Not necessarily,' says Mark.

Dodo looks at him. 'What do you mean "not necessarily"? If the flat isn't bugged—'

'The *flat* isn't bugged; but what if one of the people who happens to be in it at the time *is*?'

'One of the people...?' Dodo pauses, ruminating. 'Carrying a bug without knowing it... I dunno... I mean, where would this bug *be*? When you consider all the different times over the last few weeks that things that have been said in this room have leaked back to the Parkhurst people, it would need to be in something they had on them every time... That would rule out most clothing, wouldn't it?'

'Yes, but there are other things that people have on them or with them all the time. Phones are the obvious suspect; most people carry their smartphones around all the time, and it's the easiest thing in the world to put a bug in one. Then you've got things like hair brushes, accessories, pens, lighters... Any of the bits and pieces women carry around in their handbags or shoulder bags—and the bag itself for that matter.'

'Okay, I'll accept that,' says Dodo. 'One of the girls might be carrying a bug around not knowing it. But let's just say we get all the girls over here, you give them the once over with that gadget of yours, and they all come up clean: none of them is bugged. Then we're back to what I said before: we've got a traitor on our hands.'

'You seem determined to dwell on the worst-case scenario, Dodo. Is there a reason for this? Is there someone in particular you suspect?'

'Yes...' answers Dodo, looking away from Mark. 'There is someone...'

'Well, come on, then!' urges Mark. 'Don't keep me in suspense. Who is it?'

A pause. And then:

'Yumi…'

'*Mayumi?*' blurts Mark, incredulous. Mayumi! The very last name he was expecting her to utter. 'Why on earth do you suspect *her?*'

Dodo continues to stare at her beer bottle. 'She's… she's been acting suspiciously lately…'

'Suspiciously? In what way?'

'Like she's got something on her mind… Something she doesn't want to tell me about…'

'Well, that could be anything, couldn't it? Haven't you even asked her what's wrong? If there was something on her mind she wanted to talk about?'

'Yes, I *asked* her; but she just laughed it off and said that everything was fine… But she was *lying*. I *know* she was…!'

'Well, did you tell her *that*? Did you tell her you knew she was holding something back?'

'No…'

'No? Why on earth not? I thought you two shared *everything*; complete empathy; all cards on the table…'

'Look, it's *difficult*, Mark…' Dodo looks at him now. Her expression is pained; sorrowful to the verge of tears. Mark has never seen Dodo like this before.

'I see… Well, I still think you're being unduly pessimistic here. Even if it turns out that she *is* the cause of the leak, that she *is* consciously passing on information to the Parkhurst Corporation, she won't have been doing it by choice, will she? They'd have to have some kind of hold over her; some way of forcing her to do what they want…'

'What sort of hold could they have over Yumi?' Dodo sounds sceptical.

'Well, how about threats? Threats against you?'

'I don't see how that would work; Yumi knows I can take care of myself. Christ, she practically thinks I'm indestructible.'

'Well, alright: what *do* you think her motive could be?'

'I *don't know*,' says Dodo wretchedly. 'I think… I think I almost want it to be this… to be this that's on her mind… Passing on information… Because if it's *not* that, if it's something else she's been hiding from me, the only explanation I can think of is that it's another person… that she's found somebody else and she… she doesn't love me any more…'

'I can't pretend to know Mayumi better than you do, Dodo,' says Mark. 'But I find it very hard to believe that she would be deceiving you in that way.' He takes a swig of beer. 'No, the one I would consider the most likely suspect is Shizuka Todoroki. She's the only one none of us knows very well. And the inexplicable way she's attached herself to Yuki that we've all been treating as a joke, as an endearing eccentricity on Shizuka's part: what if she had some other reason for sticking around?'

'Yes, I had thought of her,' replies Dodo. 'And yes, I agree she's the obvious suspect… But Yumi's still hiding something from me. I *know* she is… And I'm *scared*, Mark…'

Well, here's a turn up. A rift in the lute—or perhaps we should say shamisen in this particular case: Mayumi Takahashi hiding a guilty secret and Dodo Dupont too scared of rocking the boat to have the matter out with her.

Yes, Dodo Dupont, the paragon, the eminent psychologist, with all her knowledge and understanding of human beings and of what makes them tick; Dodo Dupont now shows herself completely incapable of applying that knowledge and understanding when it comes to dealing with a problem in her own personal life!

But then the situation is an all too common one, and one which applies equally to both mental health professionals and creative writers, so perhaps we shouldn't be surprised at all.

'Sit down girls, I want to have a word with you. You too, Yumi.'

Obeying Dodo's request, Trina, Yuki and Shizuka, just arrived from Trina's flat where the two Japanese women are still lodging and Trina has been staying away from as much as she can, sit themselves down. Mayumi is seated in her usual chair, and Mark Hunter is present as well. Dodo is on her feet, and she stands facing her auditors, the window wall behind her, with the air of someone who has an important announcement to make.

'Now, you know there are only two more days to Zero Day,' she begins, 'and you know about the disturbances in the streets; and it's safe to say things are only going to get worse. What I want to suggest to you is this: that the three of you come and stay here in my apartment for the next couple of days: I suggest this because I think you'll be safer here and that it'll be a good idea for us all to be here together in the same place until this all blows over.'

Dodo raises a hand as Trina opens her mouth to speak. 'Let me finish please, Trina. You can ask your questions in a minute. Now I've made out a list of some of the things we need to consider in order to make ourselves safe, which I'm now going to hand out and you can glance over.'

Dodo hands out four folded sheets of A4 printer paper. Trina opens hers. The message, and it is a message, not the advertised list, handwritten in large, urgent letters, reads:

READ THIS MESSAGE BUT DO NOT MAKE ANY VERBAL RESPONSE TO IT. This room is BUGGED. Mark is going to sweep the room for bugs. While he does this, DO NOT SAY ANYTHING. Listen to me and act like Mark isn't here.

The letters handed to Mayumi, Yuki and Shizuka contain the same message in Japanese.

'As you can see,' proceeds Dodo, 'it's mainly a list of the things you'll need to bring with you when you come over. That is, if you decide you *do* decide to come over. I strongly advise you to, but obviously the final decision will be up to you...'

Trina, goggle-eyed, looks first at Dodo, then at the other recipients of the letter, and then at Mark. Mark smiles at her, puts his finger to his lips.

'...We've seen the clashes between the Doomsday Prophets and the Church of Zero; the demonstrations that have turned into full-scale riots: but that's just the beginning...'

Mark picks up the bug detector, which has been lying unremarked on the coffee table. He shows it to Mayumi and puts his finger to his lips. Mayumi nods her head. Activating the device, Mark makes a show of running it over the sofa Mayumi is seated on, before scanning the woman herself. The needle of the dial remains motionless: Mayumi is clean.

'...all the rape gangs, looters and arsonists will be crawling out of the woodwork. Now of course, in the case of the looters, the decline of high-street shopping will somewhat limit their options...'

Mark approaches Trina's chair. Trina, attentive to her instructions to act like Mark isn't there, freezes and, sitting awkwardly upright, stares with intent interest at Dodo as she waffles on. Mark sweeps the scanner over her. As he runs it down the length of her left arm, the needle suddenly slews from one end of the dial to the other.

Trina is bugged.

Trina is in the shower in Dodo's bathroom. She hears somebody enter the room and through the frosted glass recognises the naked body of her hostess, who now steps into the cubicle and joins her.

And for the first time in her life Trina doesn't seem to be pleased at being up-close and naked with Dodo. In fact, she glares at her. 'Come to check up on me, have you? Well, here I am! I've got the shower going full blast and I'm using the soap and I'm getting all nice and clean and I don't need you here to supervise me or to scrub my back for me and I'm *really sorry* if I happened to be a bit sweaty and if my body odour was offending your delicate sensibilities but it is thirty-six fucking degrees outside and anyway I really don't think I was any more stinky than anyone else in the room was so I don't see why I should be the one who gets singled out for—'

'TRINA,' cuts in Dodo loudly, silencing the shower for emphasis.

'What?' testily.

'Shut up, sweetheart.'

'But—'

'Shut up. And *listen*. You were *not* stinky and you were not offending my delicate sensibilities with your body odour at all, okay? What I said was just a pretext, so that we could have this conversation we're having without being overheard.'

Trina's anger has evaporated. 'Oh,' she says. 'You mean because of the bug? Oh, okay. What did you want to talk to me about?'

'I want to ask you about that gold bracelet of yours, Trina.'

'My bracelet? What's my bracelet got to do with anything?'

'It's got a great deal to do with everything, Trina: *the bug is in your bracelet.*'

'The bug is in my bracelet…?' repeats Trina stupidly.

'Yes, darling, it is. You can't see it, but there's a radio transmitter built into it. Now, where did you get that bracelet, Trina? Did someone give it to you?'

'Carl gave it to me…'

'And who is Carl, Trina?'

'He's my boyfriend…'

'And does Carl have a surname?'

'It's Jensen…'

'Jensen! As in the Jensen who works for the Parkhurst Corporation?'

Trina looks confused. 'No; who's he? Carl's got his own company, Jensen Enterprises.'

'And what does he look like, this Carl Jensen of Jensen Enterprises? Describe him to me.'

'Well, he's in his twenties, about six foot two; very fit; y'know, muscular but not too chunky; more like a boxer than a wrestler. And he's really good-looking: thinnish face, but not too thin; chiselled cheekbones and jawline; brown eyes, sort of golden-browny hair in a swept-up undercut…'

'And he basically looks like he's just walked off a catwalk in a Milan? Like he's hot stuff and he knows it and he's really pleased with himself about it?'

'Yeah, that's him! You know him, then?'

'Yes, I do know him, Trina; because that's the Jensen who works for the Parkhurst Corporation. You know: the villains of the piece? You saw him yourself once: that day Flat-Sol Park paid us a visit after you'd picked up her sister from the airport? He was *there*, remember? He was one of her entourage.'

'I *thought* I'd seen him somewhere before! When I first met him…!'

'Where did you meet him? How did it happen?'

'About a month ago… It was at my local, the Red Lion. He was just there one evening, and we got talking…' She looks up into Dodo's face, tears gathering in her eyes. 'You mean he only hooked up with me cuz he knew I knew you and Mark…? And he only gave me the bracelet just so he could…?'

Dodo nods her head. 'I'm afraid so. I'm sorry, Trina.'

'Then he was…' sobs Trina. 'He was just… All the time… And I've been, I've been wearing that bracelet and…'

She dissolves into tears.

Dodo hugs her close.

Chapter Thirty-One
The Return of a Silver Nemesis

'*...And I repeat, nothing is going to happen tomorrow; there is going to be no global disaster. No asteroid or comet is going to collide with the Earth; as we have said repeatedly, no astral body of that size could possibly approach the Earth without being detected well in advance; and the same applies to that even more ridiculous notion of an attack by a fleet of alien invaders...*'

'You've got *that* wrong mate. Meteors and comets, yeah: you can see them coming through a telescope; but your alien invaders: *they* can just pop up out of nowhere.'

'Wormholes.'

'You what?'

'Wormholes: that's what they call them. They're like these shortcuts in space, so you can get from one place to another in next to no time.'

The place is the living space of a campervan, the speakers are a man and a woman. The man, dressed in jeans and t-shirt, reclines on a sofa, watching the morning news on a laptop computer. The woman, fresh from the shower, stands towelling her hair. The man is in his forties, tall and thickset, weatherbeaten, square-jawed. The woman is younger, petite and sinewy, dark tousled hair cut short. The man's name is Mike Collins, the woman's Daisy Fontaine, and they work for Mark Hunter, presently assigned to keep an eye on the village of Critchlow and its environs. The campervan, parked in a woodland clearing not far from the village, is their mobile base of operations. And I hasten to add, they have been cohabiting very chastely, as Collins and Fontaine are strictly a buddy duo, and that's not buddies-with-benefits, either. (And quite rightly so. We don't want any touching below the waist in *this* book, thank you very much!)

Outside, the morning is already blazing hot, and they have the portable AC unit switched on. Daisy, having donned a khaki crop top with knickers to match (Daisy is ex-Army and retains a fondness for khaki and olive drab) joins Collins in the seating area.

'What's happening in the news, then?' she inquires, pouring herself some coffee.

'Not much, yet,' says Collins. 'They've got the defence secretary on; he's been telling us that nothing's going to happen tomorrow and we should all just go about our usual business like it's just another normal day.'

'*...the more people panic and take to the streets, the more they are playing into the hands of the perpetrators. The people behind Zero want to cause a panic; that has been their objective from the start.*'

'*So you keep saying; but you seem to be no closer to apprehending these perpetrators.*'

'*Ah, now that just isn't true. We are very close to apprehending them. Naturally, I cannot go into any details and risk compromising an ongoing operation, but what I can say is that the suspects have been identified and even as we speak, our security forces have them under close surveillance.*'

Collins laughs. 'You hear that? "Our security forces have them under close surveillance." That's *us* he's talking about: you and me! Oh yeah, we've got 'em under close surveillance alright: we dunno who they are or where they're hanging out, but "we've got them under close surveillance."'

'The guv'nor still thinks that radio station's got something to do with it,' says Daisy. (The 'guv'nor' being Mark Hunter, who does not care for the appellation.)

'I know what he thinks and he's farting in the breeze,' returns Collins (whatever that's supposed to mean.) 'If there is any secret base under that building, then the way in and out of it must be bloody well-hidden cuz we haven't found any sign of it, and we've searched every inch of the place.

Well-hidden and well-shielded an' all, cuz we haven't detected any heat sources, radio emissions or anything like that. And all the time we've been watching the place the only people we've seen going in or out are the Parkhurst lot and those other spies we've got hanging around here—and *they're* only interested in the place cuz they know that *we* are!'

On the laptop, the television interview suddenly cuts off and the Zero logo fills the screen.

'Hello!' says Collins. 'Here we go!'

Daisy jumps to her feet. 'Shall I try and trace it?'

'Don't bother. We've been trying nearly every day for the last two weeks and coming up with squat.'

Comes the familiar ominous sting that reminds you of the intro to *Lost*, and a second message materialises:

ZERO
Arriving Tonight
01/07 0:00 BST

The music expiring, the message lingers for a few moments and then suddenly the newsreader is back on screen, finger to her earpiece. She starts, turns to the camera.

'Ah! It appears we're back on air…!'

'So now we know,' says Collins. 'Whatever it is, it's happening tonight at midnight local time.'

'Midnight tonight,' says Daisy. 'You know what? That just makes me think of midnight openings. Wouldn't it be funny if it turned out that Zero is just some new energy drink and it's going on sale at midnight.'

'Don't be daft,' scoffs Collins. 'Midnight openings are for Harry Potter books and new video games. No-one's gunna stay up till midnight queueing up to buy some new energy drink that'll probably taste like cat piss anyway.'

'Well then maybe it *is* a new video game,' argues Daisy. 'Yeah! Maybe it's a sci-fi video game where you have to stop these silver robots from blowing up the world or something…!'

Collins favours her with a considering look. 'You know, in your blundering, half-arsed way you may have just stumbled on the truth there… A video game… Yeah, it'd make sense, wouldn't it? The signals from space, the robots: it could all be a put-up job, a publicity stunt… And those codebreakers: maybe what they'd got hold of was an encrypted copy of the game; and they had to stop them decoding it otherwise it might've got leaked and copied by a rival company… Yeah, a new video game…! And who's the company who'll be putting out this video game? Parkhurst; that's who!'

Daisy looks doubtful. 'But Parkhurst's not a video game company…'

'Yeah, but you can bet your arse they *own* video game companies! Outfits like Parkhurst own *millions* of other companies—officially and not-so-officially!'

'But still…' says Trina. 'Why Zero? What's the Zero about?'

'It's the name of the video game, isn't it?'

'But shouldn't the game be called *The Earth Dies Screaming* if it's from the film?'

'Well, maybe it's both: *The Earth Dies Screaming* dot dot Gunna *Zero*.'

'Or *Zero* dot dot *The Earth Dies Screaming*.'

'Yeah! Either'll do.'

'What do you think then…? Should we get the guvnor on the blower? Tell him about it?'

'Nah… Let him work it out for himself; he's supposed to be so bloody clever, isn't he? Besides, we might be wrong…'

'Yeah, let's look on the bright side,' agrees Daisy, grinning. 'Maybe it *is* just the end of the world that's happening tonight and not a video game going on sale!'

'Well, I'll tell you one thing,' says Collins. 'That stuff about Zero Day being the end of the world makes a lot more sense than it being the Second bloody Coming. I mean: zero equals nothing as in nothing left of us when we all get wiped out; you can see the logic in that. But that Church of Zero with their zero equals infinity which equals God; that's bullshit; that's just twisting things around!'

'Well, yeah, they *are* twisting things around: they're twisting the zero round in the middle to make it look like the infinity sign!' chuckles Daisy.

Collins gives her a sour look. 'Ha, ha; very bloody funny.'

Suddenly Daisy's cheeky grin vanishes. She is staring past Collins and through the window behind him, surprised and incredulous.

'What's that?' she exclaims.

'What's what?'

'Out there! Look!'

Collins looks. Across the glade a figure has emerged from the border of the woods and is walking towards their van; a tall, silver figure.

'It's one of those robots!'

'Maybe it's just that pillock from the shop in the village...' ventures Collins.

'No, it doesn't look right,' argues Daisy. 'The costume looks too good... Now there's another one!'

A second robot, identical to the first, has emerged from the treeline. Both are now lumbering purposefully across the glade, their sunbathed silver bodies vivid against the surrounding greenery.

An idea striking her, Daisy runs to the back of the van, looks out the furthermost window. 'Shit! There's two more of them over there!' she reports. 'They've got us surrounded and they don't look like they're handing out fliers!'

Trina, standing outside Dodo's apartment building in the shade of the entrance portico, is waiting for her dear sweet boyfriend Carl Jensen. She is wearing plastic sandals, a denim micro-mini and a one of her own patented 'Get Your Penis Out of My Vagina I Was Kissing You Goodbye' t-shirts (available on eBay, size S to XXL) which she has modified by tearing off the sleeves and shortening the length in the same rough and ready way to give the garment more of a punk look. In the street in front of her there are people walking past and there are cars on the road, but less than you'd normally expect to see. As per Dodo's instructions, Trina has vacated her own apartment, and is staying round Dodo's with the others. (And now that she's finally got Yuki and Shizuka out of her flat, she's going to make bloody sure they don't go back there!)

    She catches sight of Jensen, immaculate as ever in spite of the broiling sun, eyes hidden behind mirrored wraparounds. A look of lip-curling contempt appears on Trina's face, which, remembering her instructions, she quickly suppresses and by the time Jensen joins her under the portico has turned into a welcoming smile. With a 'Good to see you, babe!' Jensen takes her in his arms. Trina responds to his embrace, to his kisses; she responds because she knows she has to; any sign of reluctance or aversion on her part and he will get suspicious; and Trina doesn't want him getting suspicious: she has a part to play. She's like a proper spy today! doing spy-work for Mark Hunter; and sometimes spies have to sleep with the enemy. No, Jensen mustn't start to suspect; and so Trina lets him grab her arse, rub his raging hard-on against her crotch and she returns his kiss, resisting the urge to sink her teeth into that intrusive tongue of his. (She's never actually done that to a guy before: bitten down on his tongue while he's trying to give her a Frenchie. Bet it hurts like fuck!)

    'So, is the coast still clear?' asks Jensen.

'Yeah; they're still out,' replies Trina.

'Come on, then,' and he takes Trina by the arm and guides her up the steps and through the sliding doors and into the foyer.

'Say, what happened to that bracelet I gave you?' says Jensen casually.

'What are you on about?' says Trina. 'Nothing's happened to it. I've got it on.'

And she holds out her left arm, with the gold bracelet in its usual place on her wrist.

'Oh…' says Jensen, perplexed. He takes hold of Trina's wrist, studies the bracelet, tapping it experimentally.

'Must've packed up…'

'You what?'

'Oh, nothing, nothing…'

They step into the lift.

'So, what do you think, then?' she asks Jensen. 'To think that all the time Dodo was the one behind Zero! I still can't believe it!'

'I know, I know,' says Jensen. 'All the way here I've been trying to work it out… I mean, it seems impossible that it's her who's the one behind it all… But then, maybe it *isn't*, maybe it *does* make a kind of sense… I'll know when I have a look at this file you saw. You're sure it was an official Zero document, and not just something she'd written about Zero?'

'Yeah, I'm sure it was. That's what it looked like.'

'Hm. I suppose it's possible she might've just hacked into Zero's computer…'

'Yeah, but if it was that she'd have said something, wouldn't she? She would have told the rest of us about it!'

'Yes… Whatever it is, if she's kept quiet about it, then she must have something to hide…'

The lift reaches the top floor and the doors open. They step out and walk down the corridor to the door of Dodo's apartment. Trina produces a key and unlocks the door.

She opens the door and walks in. Jensen follows. The door slams violently shut; simultaneously Jensen is grabbed from behind and pushed face-first against the wall.

'Legs spread and hands against the wall,' orders a voice Jensen recognises as Dodo's. He is briskly searched and relieved of his gun. 'Alright. Into the room.'

Jensen walks into the room, Dodo urging him forward with gun-muzzle prods in the back.

They're all here, Jensen now sees. Mark Hunter, Mayumi Takahashi, the other two Japanese women; all of them. He has been led into a trap.

'You can stop here,' says Dodo. She snatches off his Ray Bans and throws them aside.

Mark now approaches, followed by Mayumi. Yuki and Shizuka remain seated, but interested, spectators.

Jensen turns to Trina, smiling grimly. 'You sneaky bitch,' he says.

'It's called payback you fucking piece of shit!' snarls Trina, her expression suddenly furious. She yanks the bracelet from her wrist and throws it in his face.

Mark picks it up from the floor. 'Yes, we found and neutralised the built-in micro-transmitter yesterday. Better late than never.'

Jenkins shrugs. 'So you found it. What now? You going to charge me with industrial espionage? Or,' sneering at Trina, 'have you retrospectively decided you're a rape victim?'

Dodo slaps him in the face. 'No, we're not going to indict you for rape. It's not the sex that bothers Trina. You may have concealed your real intentions from her, but she never had any illusions about the kind of person you really are. So no, as far as the sex goes, you and her are quits. It's bugging her and duping her and making her into your spy: *that's* the thing she never agreed to; *that's* what she's never going to forgive you for.'

'He *did* rape Yuki,' speaks up Mayumi. 'In the back of his car at the airport.'

'That was consensual!' protests Jensen. 'More or less…'

'Yeah, but she thought you were a friend of mine,' argues Mayumi.

A humourless laugh from Jensen. 'Oh, so it was alright for me to jump her if I'm a pal of yours, but it wasn't if I'm not? Well, that makes a lot of sense, doesn't it?'

'There are other things we could easily charge you with,' says Dodo. 'Violation of privacy, industrial espionage, unauthorised use of surveillance equipment, possession of firearms… But we're not planning to bring the police into this.'

'Then why did you set up this trap for me?'

'Ah, yes: why did we…?' affecting a musing tone. 'Well, maybe we lured you here for some personal payback…'

'What kind of payback?' warily.

'Oh, let's see… Well, I could beat the crap out of you. That would be pretty damaging to your masculinity, wouldn't it? Getting beaten up by a woman in front of women. Or we could even perform an impromptu castration: that would be *even more* damaging to your masculinity.'

'You wouldn't dare…' alarmed now.

'Or maybe we could just make you disappear completely. I'm sure Mark here could smooth things out for us; couldn't you, sweetheart? Write him off in your report as unavoidable collateral damage. Especially on a day like this, with people going off the rails all over the place. Yes, it would be easy enough to cover up your disappearance…'

'Dodo…' cautions Mark.

Jensen, conscious of the ease with which Flat-Sol was able to cover up Brunner's disappearance, makes a break for the door, but is intercepted by Dodo's fist. She slams him back against the wall.

'Dodo, if you've finished torturing the man, I would like to ask him a few questions,' says Mark.

'He's all yours, sweetheart.'

'Thank you.' To Jensen: 'Your employer, Flat-Sol Park: what does she have planned for today?'

'Why should I tell you?'

'It would be in your best interests.'

A shrug. 'She's just waiting to see what *you'll* do.'

'She hasn't learnt anything new? She doesn't have any new leads about Zero?'

'No. She's still convinced there has to be money in it somewhere; she doesn't buy your practical joke theory. She's sitting tight waiting for you to come up with a lead.'

'Which you would have picked up on that electronic eavesdropper of yours and reported back to her, yes?'

'That's what *would've* happened, yeah.'

'I see...' He looks at Dodo. 'Well, that seems to be about that.'

'What shall we do with him now?' asks Dodo.

'I was going to say we should just let him go, but on reflection I think it might be a wiser course of action if we were to keep him on ice for the time being...'

Dodo Dupont was right when she speculated that her would-be assassin would be lying low after the window-cleaning debacle: Rajni Sunnybrook *has* been lying low. But today she has come out of hiding, because today seems like the perfect day for killing Dodo Dupont and getting clean away with it.

Of course Rajni knows the world is not going to end at midnight tonight; she has scorned the idea from the start, and the rational part of her mind still scorns the idea; and while it is true that the rational part of Rajni's mind has been getting increasingly less screentime of late, being shunted off-camera by that scenery-chewing drama queen, the *ir*rational part of her mind, she nonetheless remains sceptical of the Doomsday Prophets' predictions that Zero Day is going to bring with it the instant annihilation of the Earth.

But the point is that there are a lot of other people who *do* believe it—and these people are conducting themselves accordingly.

Already they've been pouring out of the woodwork: the psychos and sickos, the suicide-bombers and spree-killers; the looters, the rioters and rapists—and tonight they will be out in force, convinced that as there's going to be no tomorrow, they can do whatever they want because they won't be around to face the consequences of their actions.

And it is *this* that is going to provide the perfect cover for the consummation of Rajni's vendetta against Dodo Dupont; Dodo Dupont will be written off as just another one of the casualties of the general insanity; and then, when it has all blown over, a brave new world will be ushered in, a world in which Rajni will no longer be eclipsed by her rival and in which she will at last achieve all the wealth and renown that are rightfully hers.

Sounds like a plan!

And the great thing about this plan, compared to all her previous plans, is that she doesn't really have a plan at all; this time she's just going to wing it, play it by ear and seize opportunity when it arises. Come to think of it, maybe this is the very reason why all those other plans backfired: just too much *planning* had gone into them; the more detailed the plan, the more windows you open for things to go wrong.

Yes, that's it: don't plan; just *do*. Action is better than talk.

Oh, and work alone; that's the other thing to remember. Don't rely on other people for support, because other people will always let you down in the end, no matter how well-trained you think you've got them. This is another valuable lesson Rajni has learned.

At first, after that window-cleaning near-death experience and her subsequent escape from Dodo's apartment, Rajni had been thrown into a complete panic, expecting the police to come knocking at her door at any moment. She was ready to run for the hills, because she knew it was only a matter of time before the real window-cleaning crew, who they'd left tied-up in that empty apartment, would be found and Dodo would realise that the three people in the gondola, the survivor as well as the two victims, were actually the bombers themselves. Right so far: this is precisely what happened. But Rajni had thought it would also only be a matter of time before Dodo remembered who the apparent window-cleaner she had rescued actually *was*.

Here she was wrong, because staggeringly, this had *not* happened.

That Dodo had not recognised Rajni right away had been apparent; this was understandable given the circumstances and Rajni's singed and smoke-blackened appearance; but Rajni could not but believe it would only be a matter of time before Dodo's memory would supply her with the name that went with that face that had been so close to her own for those brief seconds after she had pulled her into the apartment. But as things transpired, not only had Dodo failed to remember Rajni, but the identikit photo released to the media, and which must have been put together from Dodo's own verbal description, had looked absolutely nothing like her!

Now, on the one hand this came as a tremendous relief, because it meant that after all the cops were *not* looking for her, they were *not* about to come knocking on her door—but at the same time it had really pissed her off. How could Dodo Dupont have stared straight into Rajni's face and not remember who she was? How could she not remember the woman she'd been at uni with, the woman whose boyfriend she had stolen, whose whole life she had ruined?

Well, today, that is going to change; because today, before she finishes her off for good, Rajni is going to make damn sure that Dodo Dupont remembers who Rajni Sunnybrook is.

'You look troubled, Mark darling.'

'I am troubled. I can't get through to Collins and Fontaine in Critchlow. I've tried several times now, by phone and by radio, and neither of them is answering.'

'When did you last hear for them?'

'Last night.'

'And?'

'Same as usual: nothing to report.'

'And today they've gone silent... Do you think they could have finally tracked down Zero's HQ and...'

'...And gotten themselves captured or killed for their troubles; yes, that is one possibility. Another is...' Mark inclines his head towards the door to Dodo's study.

'...A run-in with the Parkhurst people.'

'Or one of the other interested parties lurking in the area. I think we should have a word with our guest.'

Mark and Dodo walk into the study. Here sits Jensen handcuffed to a straight-backed chair.

'How about a drink?' are Jensen's first words. 'I'm dehydrating here.'

'In a minute,' replies Mark. 'Answer some questions first. Have you ordered your people at Critchlow to take any hostile action against *my* people at Critchlow?'

'No. Why would I do that?'

'Could Flat-Sol have ordered them to do that?'

'She *might* have; but I don't see why. Why, what's happened?'

'I've lost contact with them. When did you last contact your people out there?'

'First thing this morning.'

'And they had nothing to report?'

'No, nothing.'

Mark moves over to Dodo's desk, where the contents of Jensen's pockets have been deposited. He picks up the smartphone.

'I want you to call them up right now.'

'Alright, but I'll need my hands free.'

Mark takes out his automatic from its shoulder holster and passes it to Dodo, who trains the weapon on Jensen. Mark moves round behind Jensen's chair.

'I'm going to unlock the handcuffs now and give you your phone. Put it on speaker mode and keep the screen where I can see it. If you try to contact anyone else or make any attempt to escape, Dodo will shoot you.' To Dodo: 'Aim for the lower body if you can, we don't want to kill him.'

Mark unlocks the handcuffs and hands Jensen his smartphone. Standing behind the chair he watches as Jensen unlocks the device and places the call. The call connects.

'They're not picking up…'

'Do they usually answer promptly?'

'Yes, always—it's gone to voicemail now.' He ends the call. 'Want me to ring up Flat-Sol Park and see if she knows anything?'

'That won't be necessary,' Mark takes the phone from him.

'What now?' asks Dodo, handing Mark his pistol.

'I think a trip to Critchlow might be in order,' says Mark, holstering the weapon.

On the day of that last disastrous attempt to kill Dodo Dupont, Rajni's plan had been, after having successfully planted the explosives, to retire to a rooftop a couple of blocks away which would—with the aid of a telescope—afford her a clear view into Dodo's apartment. She would then have made her phone call to Dodo, instructing her to come to the window and would have been able to see when Dodo came into position for the bomb to be detonated.

It is this rooftop Rajni has chosen as her vantagepoint today, and with her telescope set up on its tripod stand, she has been surveying the apartment. Rajni, clad in halter top, shorts and sandals, is sporting a bobbed blonde wig with a straight fringe, which, in addition to a pair of dark glasses, form a partial disguise. She has taken this precaution to avoid being spotted by the authorities because, and in spite of that insultingly inaccurate identikit picture, Rajni has found herself starting to develop a Richard Kimble phobia to the sight of police cars and uniforms, and so, out in the open she feels safer disguised. (And unlike Richard Kimble, Rajni doesn't have a pair of huge, sticking-out ears to act as a dead giveaway and render any attempts at disguise a complete waste of time.)

So here she sits, looking through her telescope and waiting for that opportunity for her to move in and finish off her hated rival—and that opportunity is a long time coming. For one thing, Dodo is entertaining an unexpected and inconvenient number of guests today: Mayumi Takahashi she had expected; as far Rajni knows they share the apartment, or if they don't actually cohabit, Takahashi is always staying over. But as well as her, there are also three other women; two Asian and one white; *and* one man, also white. These guests have been there all day and none of them show any sign of leaving. The Asian women are probably Japanese and friends of Takahashi, the white woman Rajni thinks is that Trina Truelove, Takahashi's assistant, the girl she spoke to that night at the Elysium Gallery. But who is the man? He doesn't seem to fit in at all. He's wearing a brown suit and he looks official. Could Dodo have hired herself a bodyguard? Is that what he is?

But that doesn't make sense. If Dodo felt she needed a bodyguard to protect her from the attempts on her life, she would have hired one long before now...

But *something's* going on over there; that's for sure. First Truelove had gone out and then come back with some man, another guy in a suit; and then Dodo jumped the guy when he walked in! And then it looked like they were interrogating him and Dodo had even slugged the guy a couple of times. After this interrogation, Dodo and Mr Brownsuit had taken the man into one of the other rooms and then came out without him. That was several hours ago, so presumably he's still in there. Dodo and the man have just been back into that room again now.

What the bloody hell is going on?

It suddenly occurs to Rajni that she is broiling to death. The ambient temperature is at its midafternoon maximum and Rajni, sitting on the baking tray flat roof of a twenty-storey building, is completely exposed to the full force of the sun's baleful ultraviolet gaze. She now knows how David Balfour and Alan Breck must have felt in chapter seventeen of *Kidnapped.*

But *unlike* David Balfour and Alan Breck, Rajni doesn't have any searching redcoats to prevent her from vacating her current position and seeking shelter; and deciding she's endured all that she can for the time being, she now deserts her post and makes a beeline for the blessed shade of the leeside of the stairwell entrance housing.

Gaining this cover, she throws herself down, and, sitting back against the wall she reaches into her rucksack which she has been keeping here out of the sun, takes from it a plastic bottle of no-longer-chilled but still cool H_2O, and gulps down half its contents.

She heaves a grateful sigh.

What to do? she wonders. Her plan (or rather her nonplan) of playing it by ear really boils down to her either waiting till Dodo leaves her apartment and making her move then or, failing that to just go up to the door and knock—but both of these scenarios really require Dodo to be alone, or at least only accompanied by her girlfriend. Mayumi Takahashi Rajni has taken into account, and she does not consider her to be much of an obstacle, and if she is present when Rajni strikes and tries to obstruct the course of justice or even if she is just an inconvenient eyewitness, Rajni has no qualms about killing her along with the primary target.

That steady stream of collateral damage, that rollcall of incidental fatalities, that has accompanied her efforts to exterminate Dodo Dupont has rendered Rajni somewhat callous when it comes to respecting the sanctity of human life; and considering how many people have perished as a result of her actions who she didn't know from Adam and therefore had no feelings about either way, she has no qualms at all about purposefully and with malice aforethought killing someone she *does* know and *does* have good reason to dislike.

Yes, Rajni holds a grudge against poor unsuspecting Mayumi Takahashi, a woman she has never even met face-to-face; a minor grudge compared to her grudge against Dodo herself, but a grudge nonetheless. The reason for this grudge amounts to this: if Dodo Dupont had never met Mayumi Takahashi, then Dodo would (most likely) never have branched out into the arena of nudie modelling, and if Dodo Dupont had never branched out into the arena of nudie modelling, she, Rajni Sunnybrook, would never have got the idea that branching out into the arena of nudie modelling might also be a wise career move for herself, and if Rajni had never decided that branching out into the arena of nudie modelling might be a wise career move for herself, she would never have hooked up with that seemingly respectable erotic photographer who turned out to be anything but, because when Rajni had arrived at her studio she had found the cameras ready for motion picture rather than still photography, and that in addition to herself also present were three well-endowed male participants with whom she would be sharing the set, and as contracts had been signed and doors locked, she couldn't really back out, she—

Well, Rajni prefers to draw a blackout curtain over what happened after that. (But if the reader is sufficiently interested, you can probably find what you're looking for on Pornhub.)

So, yes, if it had just been Mayumi Takahashi likely to get in the way, Rajni would have been quite happy to terminate her along with her primary target; but it's not just Takahashi, because there are all those other people who are in the way as well: the three other woman and the man. The man in particular bothers Rajni. Mr Brownsuit. Who is he?

If Dodo's not going out at all, and those friends of hers are staying for the duration, then what she needs to do is find some way of luring her out of her apartment. She's got Dodo's home telephone number, so...

Christ, I need a pee.

First the heat, now her bladder. All these bodily functions getting in the way!

But where to go to relieve herself...? Discounting the time-consuming and possibly risky option of a descent into the building below in search of the nearest office staff facilities, the obvious alternative would be to just nip inside the doorway and go on the landing at the top of the stairs... But then why even do that? Why not just have her pee out here *alfresco*? From where she is now there are no nearby tall buildings from which she might be seen... Anyway, it's not her neighbourhood, is it?

Yes, why not?

Feeling reckless and just a little bit horny, Rajni pulls down her shorts and knickers and hunkers down on the margin of her shadowy haven for a one-woman pissing contest, watching with justifiable pride as the floodgates open and her golden waterfall arcs gracefully across the concrete surface of the roof, shimmering and sparkling in the sunlight.

Yes, it really is the little things in life that count; these fleeting moments of escape from the hurly-burly of life, oases of calm briefly visited where one can just switch off and mellow out...

And being switched off and mellowed out as she is, Rajni doesn't really register the sound of the approaching helicopter until it's almost on top of her.

And now the hurly-burly of life is back with a vengeance in whirly-bird form, and Rajni, trying simultaneously to pull up her shorts and to retreat further back into the shadows, falls over on her side, still in full flow. The imperative sound of the helicopter's rotor-blades fills the air as it flies low over the rooftop.

Shit! Shit, shit, shit! Who was it: the fuzz? The BBC? And more importantly, did they see her? Are they going to turn round and come back…?

Peering round the corner of the entrance housing, Rajni sees that the chopper is hovering over Dodo Dupont's apartment building. It looks like it's going to land there.

Something's happening.

Quickly making herself decent, Rajni runs sticky-legged back to her telescope and applies her eye to the eyepiece in time to see the helicopter's skids come to rest on the flat roof. And there's Mr Brownsuit, standing out on the roof, waiting for it! The door of the helicopter opens and the pilot jumps down. He joins Mark and they both disappear through the doorway into the stairwell.

Now what? wonders Rajni. It looks like Mr Brownsuit summoned the helicopter; or at least, he was expecting it. Are they planning to evacuate? To flee to some location less dangerous than London is likely to be tonight? No! She can't let Dodo Dupont slip through her fingers now! It has to be today that she kills her!

She readjusts the telescope to look into Dodo's apartment. They're all still there, Dodo and her friends. And they're just sitting around, chatting and watching TV like they've been doing all day; they don't look like they're about to head off anywhere… Come to think of it, the helicopter doesn't even look big enough for what, six passengers. So, what's it there for…? Now Mr Brownsuit has walked into the apartment; and he's alone! What's happened to the helicopter pilot? She looks at the rooftop again. The helicopter sits motionless. No sign of the pilot. Where is he?

Had he just landed there to deliver something to Mr Brownsuit? Then why bother leaving the rooftop at all? Why not just take off again?

What is going on here...?

She has to find out.

'Hello?'

'Oh, hello. Am I speaking to Professor Dupont?'

'You are indeed. Who is this?'

'I'm Raj-Rachel Summerhouse from *The Day Today*. I'm glad I caught you, because I was wondering if you were free to do a quick interview for tonight's show? You know, about Zero Day and—'

'I'm sorry Rachel, and normally I would've said yes, but I'm afraid I'm *rather* busy right now. I have to go somewhere rather urgently and I'm heading off in just a few minutes. It's a shame you didn't ring me earlier: I've been free pretty much all day, but now this thing's come up and I have to leave town for a while.'

'I see. Will this business take very long? I mean, if you'll be back home later this evening—?'

'Well, that's the trouble, you see: I don't know how long this business is likely to take. I *might* be back in an hour or two, but on the other hand I might be away a lot longer. So you see, I really can't promise to be around for you any time this evening. I'm very sorry. Perhaps tomorrow, if we're still here tomorrow, of course! Which incidentally I'm sure we will be...!'

'Tomorrow? Yes, yes, that would be fine.'

'Good! Then we'll leave it at that, shall we? And you know where to get hold of me. Nice talking to you, Rachel!'

'Yes, thank you for your time, Professor. Goodbye...'

'Bye!'

Click.

Dodo replaces the handset. Dodo Dupont, dressed for action in form-hugging black: matt black from neck to waist, glossy black from hips to feet. She looks at Mayumi; Mayumi in indoor casual; baggy t-shirt, Bermuda shorts, barefoot.

Dodo is about to set off. Mark wants to find out what's happening in Critchlow, why his agents there have gone radio silent; he has requisitioned a helicopter for the purpose, and Dodo is going with him. Mayumi is not going; Mayumi will be staying here with the others and 'holding down the fort.'

Dodo and Mayumi look at each other, not saying anything. There has been a lot of this not saying anything going on between these two people recently. Both of them are painfully aware of the fact.

Mayumi breaks the silent moment. 'I will go up to the roof with you!' she says.

Dodo smiles. 'Good idea: you can wave me off!'

'Can't we *all* go and see you off?' asks Trina.

Says Dodo: 'Sure. Why not?'

'Yes, I think we can safely leave our guest unattended for a minute or two,' agrees Mark.

Leaving Mayumi and the girls with custody of Jensen (still cuffed to his chair in the study, now with the addition of a gag on account of his increasingly distracting complaints) had momentarily presented something of a problem, it being deemed necessary that a gun would be required by his guardians in order to discourage escape attempts. (There would be times when it would become necessary to unhandcuff Jensen, the only other alternative being a bucket in the room with him, and this would require intimate physical contact with Jensen to ensure that his aim was true, and which was something the women, especially Trina, would rather be spared.) They had Jensen's own handgun and it could be left with Yumi; but Yumi doesn't really know how to use one, and neither does Trina—but then it transpired that Shizuka *does* know how to use one (apparently the Japanese like their embassy interpreters to be proficient in the use of firearms) and so the problem has been resolved.

The six of them now exit Dodo's apartment, and take the flight of concrete stairs which bring them to the rooftop. The sun is now declining towards the western horizon and there is that first suggestion of dusk shading the blue of the sky. The heat remains intense, the humidity oppressive.

Dodo turns to Mayumi. 'Well, hopefully this won't take too long, and we should be back long before midnight. It just all depends on what we find. Anyway, I've got my phone with me,' tapping her hip pocket, 'so I'll call you if we're likely to be held up, and you can call me if anything comes up here. Okay?'

'Okay!' affirms Mayumi with energy.

Dodo grins. 'Good! Now, I'm leaving you in charge, sweetheart. So just make sure everyone stays in the flat. We've got plenty of booze in, so have a party, and you just make sure it's in full swing by the time we get back, okay?' wagging a finger for emphasis.

Mayumi salutes. 'Loger!' (*anglice*: roger.)

At this display of innocent enthusiasm Dodo's heart melts. She takes Mayumi in her arms and hugs her tightly. Mayumi responds to the hug without hesitation. Clasping around the waist, she buries her face in Dodo's chest, and Dodo buries her face in Mayumi's hair, inhaling the comfortable, familiar scent. This is how they have always embraced, thinks Dodo. Nothing feels different. If they can hug like this, then surely nothing can have changed between them, nothing can have gone wrong, can it…?

Mayumi looks up at her, tears streaming from her yearning eyes.

'My master…'

And there are tears in Dodo's eyes as well as she gives her a parting kiss.

Dodo joins Mark and they board the helicopter, taking the pilot's seat. Mark makes the usual 'Let's go, Worrals" joke he rolls out whenever Dodo is at the controls of an aircraft and they lift off.

As the helicopter ascends Dodo sees Mayumi, her hair wild in the slipstream, waving madly with both arms. The others also wave, Trina and Yuki energetically, Shizuka with more decorum. Dodo feels a stab of annoyance at seeing Yuki Kinoshita's enthusiastic waving.

Is she leaving the field clear for her rival…?

Mayumi and the others have only just returned to the apartment when there comes a knock on the door; the peremptory knock of a caller who expects to be admitted and admitted promptly. They exchange looks. They are not expecting callers.

'Maybe it's one of the neighbours, wondering about the helicopter…' suggest Trina tentatively.

'I will go and see,' declares Mayumi.

Mayumi goes to the door. The door has a spyhole but having been installed at Dodo eye-level it is useless to Mayumi unless she brings a chair with her. So perforce, she just opens the door.

'Thank you,' says Flat-Sol Park pushing past Mayumi into the flat, her sister and her chauffeuse following in her wake.

'Hey!' protests Mayumi.

Shizuka produces her handgun. 'Halt!'

Instantly, the chauffeuse has her own gun in her hand and aimed at Shizuka.

'Put your gun away,' orders Flat-Sol.

The chauffeuse re-holsters her gun.

'There is no need for any hostility,' says Flat-Sol, cooly surveying the room and its occupants. 'I come here only to inquire after Mark Hunter. Where is he?'

'He's not here,' replies Mayumi, standing before the intruder, arms folded.

'Then I will speak with Professor Dupont.'

'*She's* not here, also.'

'They are both absent? When will they return?'

'None of your business,' says Trina.

'I think perhaps they were aboard the helicopter which just lifted off from the roof of this building…?'

'Think what you like,' says Trina.

'And what is their destination?'

'None of your business.'

The sound of a heavy thump comes from the closed door of the study.

'What was that sound?' demands Flat-Sol. 'There is somebody in that room.'

'There is nobody,' says Mayumi. 'You may leave now.'

'Thank you, but I prefer to discover what it is you are attempting to conceal from me.'

Followed by her entourage, Flat-Sol crosses the room to the door of the study. Shizuka steps in front of her, gun raised.

'Halt!'

Flat-Sol turns to Mayumi. 'Who is this person?'

'Her name is Shizuka. She works for the Japanese embassy.'

'Ah yes, the interpreter.' To Shizuka: 'Please step aside, unless you deem whatever it is you have concealed behind that door worth the sacrifice of your life. My chauffeur has her gun trained on you and she is certain to be a more accomplished markswoman than yourself.'

'Yeah, forget it,' advises Trina. 'Just let her look if she wants to. He's not worth getting killed over, is he?'

'She's right,' says Mayumi.

'Very well,' says Shizuka. She steps aside.

Flat-Sol thanks her and enters the study and here she is greeted by the sight of her personal assistant lying on the floor handcuffed to an overturned chair. At a signal from Flat-Sol the chauffeuse stands the chair back on its legs and removes the gag from Jensen's mouth.

'Whew!' says he. 'I'm glad you showed up! I—'

'And why do I find you in this unseemly predicament, Mr Jensen?' cuts in Flat-Sol.

'They found the bug in her bracelet, somehow,' says Jensen, nodding towards Trina, who has entered the room with the others. 'They set a trap for me.'

'And you walked into it. How very unprofessional of you.'

'Okay, so I messed up. But now that you're here—'

'I did not come here in search of you, Mr Jensen; it is Mark Hunter I seek. Do you know where he is?'

'Yes, him and the Dupont woman just took off for Critchlow. Hunter's lost contact with his people out there and wants to find out what's happened to them. And by the way, our own people—'

'I am aware that our operatives in Critchlow are not responding to calls. So, Mark Hunter thinks there may be something afoot in Critchlow. I shall follow him there.'

'Great! I'll come with you! One of that lot's got the keys to these handcuffs, so if you just—'

'Return the gag to his mouth,' orders Flat-Sol.

'Hey, wait a minute—!'

The chauffeuse forces the gag into Jensen's mouth and ties it firmly in place.

'You're not going to take him with you?' asks Mayumi.

'No, I prefer to leave this man in your custody for the present,' replies Flat-Sol. 'I require time to consider his future as an employee of the Parkhurst Corporation. I apologise for the inconvenience and promise that you will be fully reimbursed for it.'

Flat-Sol turns away from Jensen and Jensen launches into frantic speech, his words so muffled into incomprehensibility by the gag in his mouth that it's difficult to determine whether he is imploring his employer or hurling abuse at her.

Flat-Sol takes no notice. 'We will take our leave of you now,' she tells Mayumi. 'My apologies for the intrusion.'

Pity, thinks Trina, who had been hoping they would have Jensen out of their hair. There is a general move to vacate the room, and Trina turns the door. A stranger is standing there, just outside the room: a brown-skinned woman with a blonde bob and a pair of shades.

'Oi!' exclaims Trina.

The woman disappears.

Mark and Dodo are flying over Hampton Court Palace on a sou-south-westerly course. Off to the right a bloated orange sun sinks heavily towards the horizon. The two friends have been enjoying one of their companionable silences, Mark cogitating his problems and Dodo her own. Shortly after they had taken off Mark had asked her whether she has managed to have her 'little chat' with Mayumi today; Dodo had replied that the right moment had not presented itself, and Mark had said fair enough and dropped the subject.

Yuki Kinoshita. If there is another person in Mayumi's life, some undisclosed intimacy behind all those expressions of guilt and reserve she has demonstrated recently, Dodo feels sure that it can only be her. Has she really lost Mayumi's love for her to another woman, or has that love merely become divided?

Christ, that look Yumi had given her when they parted— Dodo just *couldn't* have lost her love! She just couldn't have! It was there, written loud in her eyes, in her words, in her tears; every iota of that all-consuming slavish adoration but makes Dodo just as much Yumi's slave. That wasn't something that could just be faked; no diminution or loss of affection could be dissimulated as compellingly as that—not by Mayumi. Mayumi is no actress; Mayumi is only ever herself, her adorable, perfect self.

But if there has been another woman in Mayumi's life, it can only be Yuki Kinoshita. Yuki is an old schoolfriend, they go back a long way, and they have been spending a great deal of time together, at Yumi's studio working on the *Sexy Eatings* photo-project, very intimate erotic photography. But then over the years Yumi has worked with dozens of other women, a great many of them old schoolfriends, engaged on equally intimate erotic photography projects, and nothing has occurred before… But even so, something *might* have occurred this time. Perhaps it was only once, just one moment of weakness… But if it was just that, Dodo would have expected Mayumi to have confessed. She can even picture her, throwing herself in floods of tears at Dodo's feet, confessing her crime, begging for forgiveness, insisting on punishment… So why hasn't she just *done* that? Why all those nights returning late to the apartment, saying she has been 'eating out' with Yuki and Shizuka? Why does she look so guilty, if all they've been doing is eating out…?

She *has* to have it out with Yumi. The moment they return from this trip (and dependent on what external events might be transpiring at the time) she has to have it out with Yumi; they have to confront the issue instead of avoiding it as they have been.

That look Yumi gave her just before they took off: she could *never* have looked at Dodo the way she did if she had any thoughts of leaving her, leaving her for somebody else. No way! Not in a million years!

So, stop being a coward, Dodo Dupont, and just *talk* to her!

'I'll try the shortwave one more time,' announces Mark, reaching for the radio headset. 'Mark Hunter to Collins and Fontaine. Are you receiving me? Are you receiving me, over…?' He frowns. 'That's odd…'

'What is?' asks Dodo.

'I'm picking up a strange interference pattern…'

'The same as before?'

'No, before they just weren't answering. This is something new...'

More companionable silence. They are over the Surrey Hills now, the green hills now bleached yellow by the heatwave. They will soon be within sight of Critchlow.

'Take her down a bit, Dodo,' requests Mark. 'I want to have a look at things through the glasses.'

Dodo reduces altitude. Mark raises the field-glasses to his eyes, scanning the terrain below.

And then something like a lightning bolt hits the helicopter; a blinding light that shoots shockwaves of agony through their bodies. Dodo falls forward over the controls and the stricken helicopter plunges from the sky.

Chapter Thirty-Two
Zero Hour

'Planet Earth is finished. It was a nice place but then human beings came along and ruined it. Even the aliens from the X-Files *have changed their minds about coming back to colonise the planet; we've ruined it for them, as well. We've polluted the oceans and we've poisoned the atmosphere. We've systematically destroyed our own environment and ignored all the warnings till it's too late. After going around killing each other for centuries and centuries, now we've committed this final act of genocide against ourselves—and we didn't even do it on purpose: we did it because we were fucking stupid.'*

Stars. A clear night sky, free from light pollution, the stars sharply defined. And there is Vega, pinnacle of the Summer Triangle and one of the brightest stars in the Northern Hemisphere. Forming part of the constellation Lyra, Vega is a mere twenty-five lightyears from Earth's sun and more than twice its size. A relatively young star, it is not even known for sure if it has any planets in its orbit, nor whether the dust cloud that encircles the star is the remains of disintegrated planets or the raw material from which they will someday be formed. But *something* is out there in the Vega system, something that has been transmitting signals to Earth... And perhaps something else is coming from Vega, something that is set to arrive at midnight tonight...

Smells of the countryside. Grass. Mark is lying on grass, lying on his back on a hillside looking up at the sky.

The helicopter! They were in the helicopter—!

Mark sits up. Unfolding in every direction a moonlit vista of meadow and woodland, the sculpted landscape of the Surrey Hills. No sign of human habitation; not a light to be seen.

And there, just off to the right, the helicopter. It lies prone and mangled on the hillside, tail twisted, a single warped rotor blade reaching feebly into the sky. It seems strangely peaceful, this aftermath of tumult and carnage.

Next to the wreckage lies a motionless body.

Dodo!

Mark scrambles to his feet, noting with surprise that he feels completely uninjured, and rushes to Dodo's side. She is lying on her back, just as he was. No twisted limbs, no torn clothes are abrasions to the skin. He presses a hand to her chest. Heartbeat regular. He begins a careful inspection for broken bones; arms, torso, legs...

'You enjoying yourself, feeling me up?' murmurs a voice.

Mark turns. Dodo, sleepy-eyed, smiles at him.

'Were you awake the whole time?' he asks accusingly.

'Nope,' answers Dodo. 'Not even sure if I'm awake now. Where are we?'

'Lying on a hillside beside the wreckage of our crashed helicopter,' says Mark. 'What's the last thing you remember?'

'I remember being hit by that light, whatever it was… and the pain: it was like being electrocuted… And then we went into a nosedive… and that's it: I don't remember the crash… I must have blacked out… What about you?'

'The same. So, we get zapped by a laser beam or whatever it was, the helicopter goes down and crashes on this hillside and we are both miraculously thrown clear, unconscious but uninjured. It feels choreographed, doesn't it? Like this whole thing has been staged by someone well up on the conventions of the genre…'

Dodo sits up. 'Hang on a minute! It's pitch dark! It was still daylight when we got hit! What time is it?'

They both look at their watches.

'Five to ten! Christ, we've been out for hours!'

'I want *meat!*'

Oh, for fuck's sake change the channel already! What is it with that woman? Two days on a vegetarian diet and she's like a junkie eating cold turkey! (Actually, that's not a very good simile in this particular case: Yuki would murder for some cold turkey right now!)

'No meat!' spits out Mayumi.

Yeah, you tell her, girl! Yuki ought to show a bit more consideration: Yumi's got other things on her mind. It's nearly ten and Mark and Dodo haven't come back yet; and they haven't sent word, either. Yumi's tried calling Dodo, but she can't get through; the calls just aren't connecting, like Dodo's out of range or something.

Still, they did say they might be gone for longer than this, and it's not like those two can't take care of themselves… Too soon to be assuming the worst, but Yumi's bound to be worried, with tonight being what it is… And here's Yuki going on about wanting meat every five minutes—that's enough to drive anyone up the wall!

As instructed, the girls are having a party; a fairly subdued party so far, just chilling out on the sofas, drinking and eating and listening to music. Trina as she sips her Bacardi and Coke, sprawled on the sofa, scratching her feet, watching the television screen, swaying her head to the music (from Mayumi's J-rock girl bands collection naturally.)

Mayumi sits in her usual place, the sofa she always shares with Dodo. She's completely in the buff, and Yuki and Shizuka have stripped to their undies (white and black respectively), but Trina's only taken her skirt off so far. She still can't forget that Jensen's still here, tied to a chair in the study... So she keeps her t-shirt on, her t-shirt with its talismanic slogan. Shizuka sits sipping her drink sedately (Trina's never seen that woman get so drunk that she's lost that 'cool, professional' demeanour of hers. Does she ever lose it?)

They've got the telly switched on as well, muted, tuned to one of the news channels, just to see what's happening, or if anything *does* happen... At the moment is just the anticipated disruption; reckless people taking the streets with their well-what-the-hell-if-the-world's-going-to-end-anyway-we-might-as-well-cut-loose-and-have-some-fun mentality; it's happening in cities all over the country, all over the world... For half the world it's already June the first, but everyone knows that Z-Day doesn't officially kick in till 0:00 British Summer Time, and that if anything's going to happen it's going to happen *then*.

'We could borrow meat from one of neighbours,' persists Yuki, still standing over Mayumi, and still speaking in English. (Mayumi has issued the injunction that out of consideration for Trina only English should be spoken.)

'No, that's still going out,' replies Mayumi. 'And anyhow, Dodo doesn't like the cooking of meat in her apartment.'

And now, Yuki proceeds to really put her foot in it.

'But Dodo's not here—!'

'Dodo will be here!' explodes Mayumi. 'Dodo will be here anytime now! You want meat: eat tofu and make pretend!'

(They have the eatables set out on the kitchen table: a generous selection of nibbles and cold snacks, both Japanese and English: sarnies, sushi, cakes (rice and sponge), crisps, etc, into which, and in spite of her complaints about the menu, Yuki has already made deep inroads.)

Chastened, Yuki returns to her seat beside Shizuka, Trina observing her without sympathy.

What is it about that woman and meat? As a competitive eater she'll eat pretty much anything that *can* be eaten, but when it comes to meat, it's like a total mania with her—and a *sex* mania, at that! Christ, when she has on one of her meat-eating binges: it's like she's having multiple orgasms! Trina, she's no veggie herself, but she can survive on a meat-free diet for a few days without going stir crazy.

'Hey! Look at that!'

The exclamation comes from Mayumi. She's looking at the television.

Trina looks. The News 24 studio has disappeared and the Zero logo has appeared and with it a message:

ZERO
Midnight Tonight (1/6/202- 0:00 BST)

And beneath the message is a digital display counting down the seconds. It has just hit ten o'clock and the digital display is counting down the remaining one hundred and twenty minutes to midnight.

To Zero Hour.

Trina grabs the remote and switches off the mute. An electronic beeping sound marks the passing of the seconds on the screen.

'Let's see what the other channels are saying,' says Trina, holding out the remote.

The other channels are not saying anything—the same countdown has hijacked all of them; every single television channel, terrestrial, cable or satellite, domestic or foreign.

And now it all suddenly seems much more urgent, more ominous. The countdown has started: the countdown to *what?*

The Spirit of Ecstasy, the winged goddess who isn't actually winged but is just wearing loose sleeves, has been driven face first into a tree and is now bent sadly out of shape. Tire-marks tell the story: the loss of control, the slip-sliding across the macadam and then leaving the road and into the venerable oak. An expensive car expensively wrecked.

'This is Flat-Sol Park's Rolls,' says Mark.

They stand surveying the wreck: the front of the car, broken and buckled, wrapped around the tree, the rest of the vehicle undamaged. As with their own helicopter there seems something posed and artificial about the crash. The vehicle is empty.

'What would Flat-Sol Park be doing in this neighbourhood?' wonders Dodo.

'Probably the same thing we are,' replies Mark. 'Checking up on the agents she's lost contact with. And from the looks of things she may have run into the same hostile reception as us.'

'Yes, but why come here herself? She's the CEO; wouldn't she normally delegate a job like this?'

'You have a point,' says Mark. 'True we do have her righthand man on ice, but he's not the only person on her staff… Yes, Flat-Sol would only have come in person if she considered it profitable to herself to come in person…'

Mark and Dodo resume their progress along the road which winds its way through dense woodland. All is quiet and still, the overheated air enervating.

Dodo checks her smartphone.

'Still no signal,' she reports.

Presently, they leave the surfaced road, follow a track through the trees and emerge into a glade where a campervan is parked.

'Ah! It's still here!'

'Yes, but no sign of life,' says Dodo. 'And look: they've left the door wide open.'

They approach the campervan. Mark's foot strikes something. He picks it up. A handgun, a Glock.

'This is Mike or Daisy's,' says Mark. 'And the clip's empty.'

'They came under attack then,' surmises Dodo.

'Yes, but from whom? Look at the campervan: not a bullet-hole in sight.'

They enter the van. Mark turns on the light. Everything is in its place; the living area looks like it might have been vacated only a moment before, except that the coffee in the mugs and the pot on the table is stagnant, its surface filmed.

'This coffee's been sitting here since this morning,' declares Mark, inspecting the glass coffee pot. 'So, Mike and Daisy came under attack from someone who couldn't be stopped by a whole clip of bullets and who didn't return their fire, at least not with any conventional weapon. Who does that bring to mind?'

'Those silver robots,' says Dodo.

'Yes. Let's head to the village.'

Another car come to grief. This one lies flipped on its back in the middle of the road. The door opens and a woman crawls out, a tall Indian woman with short dark hair, dragging a rucksack with her. Tentatively, she rises to her feet, checks herself for damage and is pleasantly surprised to find none. Patting the top of her bare head reminds her of something. She crawls back into the car and reappears with a blonde wig which she now carefully arranges on her head.

Circling the vehicle, she observes that it appears as inexplicably undamaged as herself; flipped over on its back, but otherwise completely intact; not a dent or a scratch to be seen.

What the hell happened? wonders Rajni. She casts her mind back... She was driving along, following the Rolls— no, she'd *lost* the Rolls, hadn't she? Yes, and her satnav had packed up, so she was having to find her way to Critchlow via the old-fashioned method of following road signs... And then, that sudden blinding light, searing pain, losing control of the wheel...

After which, oblivion; until a few moments ago when she had awakened to find herself seated upside down at the wheel of a car that had turned turtle.

And it's night, as well! When the accident happened, the sun had only just been setting...! She has been unconscious for over an hour...

Over an hour...

What the crap? Out cold in a car lying on its back in the middle of the road for over an hour and during that time no-one has stopped to help her...!? Surely there must have been *some* traffic on the road during all that time! Did they all just drive round her, without even bothering to stop? Talk about selfish motorists!

She surveys her surroundings. Open countryside, hills and trees, a belt of woodland further down the road... How far was she from Critchlow when it happened?

Phone! She can use her location finder!

No, she can't. Extracting the device from the pocket of her shorts, she discovers she can't get a signal.

Shouldering her rucksack, she sets off along the road at a brisk walk. What can be going on in Critchlow? It's just a poky little village. But *something* is going on: and must be something big as everyone seems so anxious to get there.

After her phone call to Dodo, her one idea had been to get to the helicopter before it took off, but she hadn't made it in time. The helicopter had taken off just as she made it to the top floor of the apartment building. She'd nearly run into Mayumi Takahashi, Trina Truelove and those other women as they'd been coming down the stairs from the roof. And then, while she was still beating her brains about what to do next, out of one of the lifts had stepped Flat-Sol Park. Rajni knew the woman by sight because she had once applied for the post of recruitment advisor at the Parkhurst Corporation. These big corporations often like to have a headshrinker on their staff to a analyse job applicants and promotion candidates; and the salary they were offering was insane! (Naturally, Rajni's usual bad luck had ensured that she had failed to get the position.)

She had watched as Flat-Sol Park and her entourage had gone straight to Dodo's apartment. When they were let in, the front door had been left conveniently ajar and Rajni had crept up to it and listened in. There seemed to be some sort of confrontation going on. Dodo's name had been mentioned. Then they had all gone into a room at the other end of the apartment. Rajni had waited for a bit, and when they hadn't come out, she had risked entering the apartment and going up to the door of the room for some more earwigging. And there was that man she'd seen them shut up in this room earlier and they'd actually got him tied to a chair! And she had heard them talking about Zero and about a place called Critchlow, and how it was to this Critchlow that Dodo and her friend had flown—and then Trina Truelove had spotted and she'd had to make tracks.

But she had heard more than enough! All this talk about Zero could only add up to one thing: Dodo Dupont is actually the mastermind behind Zero! Now that she knows this, Rajni wonders why the possibility hadn't occurred to her before. It was just the kind of thing that woman would do: orchestrating this whole elaborate advertising campaign, triggering this global hysteria! And why? Another one of her psychological experiments, that's what! Another one of her reckless, grandstanding, psychological experiments!

All this panic, all this social disorder... And Dodo Dupont the evil mastermind behind it all! Oh yes, she'd do it alright. Anyone who could systematically steal all of her classmates' boyfriends and then have the nerve to say it was all done in the name of science is capable of any iniquity!

Mayumi stands at the window wall, gazing past her own phantom reflection into the night sky of the city. Behind her comes the monotonous electronic tick-tock of the countdown to Zero.

They haven't been able to turn it off. First, Trina discovered she couldn't put the sound back on mute; and then she found out she couldn't switch off the television at all—not even when they unplugged it at the mains! It's like the television set has been possessed; taken over by Zero. Trina has cranked up the volume of the music to try and smother the electronic clock sound, but there it still is, persistently audible. Mayumi can see the same countdown displayed on a billboard across the city. She wonders if the normally mute billboards are likewise projecting that digital ticking sound. (They are.)

She can also the light of several conflagrations flickering in the night sky, signposts of riot and carnage hotspots.

But Mayumi's gaze focuses more on the sky than the streets. She is desperately hoping to see the approaching aircraft lights that will announce the safe return of her beloved Dodo. She still can't contact her; phone calls, text messages, emails: none of them are getting through.

Her beloved. Yes, Dodo suspicions are wrong. Mayumi's love has not been transferred to another; it still belongs to Dodo.

But Mayumi *does* have a guilty secret. Dodo was right about that. A guilty secret she has been keeping from her lover and now, when perhaps it is already too late, she wants desperately to confess it. She despises herself for having avoided the confession before now, despises herself for a coward. She has betrayed her lover's trust. Worse, she has repeated the offense, betrayed her not once but repeatedly. Yes, she could say that it was a moment of weakness that first led her astray; but that moment of weakness has been followed by numerous other moments of weakness, days and consecutive days of moments of weakness. She could put the blame on another; she could put the blame on Yuki Kinoshita for having led her astray; but that would be unfair. Yes, it was Yuki who had first presented the temptation, and it is with Yuki that she has been committing her sin; but she could have resisted; if she had displayed more fortitude, if she had been mindful of the debt of loyalty she owed to Dodo, she would not have fallen into sin.

So yes, Dodo Dupont was right in linking Yuki Kinoshita with Mayumi's guilty secret—but she is wrong about the crime. Mayumi's betrayal of her lover has not taken the form of any sexual infidelity, but a dietary one: for Mayumi Takahashi has abandoned her pledge of vegetarianism and succumbed to the temptation of eating meat!

Lots of meat. Lots and lots of meat.

It was to please her lover rather than anything else that Mayumi had first adopted a vegetarian diet. Mayumi would do *anything* to please Dodo Dupont, and the sacrifice and the pangs that had at first accompanied giving up meat had been a pleasure in themselves. But she had come to accept and embrace Dodo's ethical perspective on the subject, and she had never experienced any regrets, or felt any desire to return to a carnivore diet. And indeed, it was her perceiving the consumption of animal flesh as being a pornographic excess akin to violence and torture and unbridled sexuality that had inspired the meat-eating segment of the *Sexy Eatings* project.

But then Yuki Kinoshita, Yuki who had chosen to move from Dodo's apartment to other lodgings on account of the impost on cooking or eating meat, had started to tempt her old schoolfellow into joining her in her evening meat-eating orgies. Yuki hadn't done this maliciously; she hadn't done it with any cruel desire to drive a wedge between Mayumi and her *Gaijin* lover; and to the ethical arguments she was completely oblivious: she just thought it was very silly for people to go around being vegetarian when there was so much lovely, mouth-watering meat around for people to eat!

Mayumi, in her defence, had not only at first refused point-blank, she had put forward all the moral arguments against meat-eating; but from Yuki Kinoshita such arguments slid like water from the duck's back. She acknowledged that yes, all those poor animals had to suffer and die in order to provide her with their lovely flesh for her to devour; she acknowledged and she respected them for their noble (and completely involuntary) sacrifice. She wept for all the cows and pigs, the sheep and horses that had to die; for all the cute little lambs and piglets that had to be wrenched from their mother's teats; all the ducks and geese that had to be stuffed full of corn until they couldn't stand up—she wept oceans of tears for them all. But alas, this just had to be! These poor defenceless creatures just *had* to be slaughtered in their millions so that people like her (and especially her) could experience the pure, sensuous joy of consuming their flesh (which by the way is also an important source of protein) each and every day of their lives! It just had to be! It was the curse humanity was compelled to endure for having been placed at the pinnacle of the food chain! We did not ask for this! No, we did not ask for it, but it was nonetheless so, and we had no choice but to endure it. And as thus she unburdened her soul, Yuki *did* cry; she cried and Mayumi cried too and they wept in each other's arms.

The outcome was inevitable. Such was Mayumi's profound grief for all the poor slaughtered animals, naturally she had to start eating them. (Well, what else could she do? Otherwise their sacrifice would have been in vain!)

And once that first succulent slice of meat had passed her lips and collided with her taste buds, there was just no turning back.

The first of these meat-eating orgies had taken place at Trina's flat, the food being prepared by Yuki herself; but then they had spread their wings and then they started dining out; sampling the fare of eating establishments all around the capital, from exclusive French restaurants to Japanese sushi bars, sampling the meat dishes from nations all around the world. (Well, travel does broaden the mind!)

And this is why Mayumi has been 'eating out' so very often of late; eating out and then returning to the arms of her lover with guilt in her heart and mint on her breath.

But no more! Now it must end! When Dodo returns and she throws herself at her feet (Mayumi has pictured the scene identically to Dodo) and confessed all, she will renew her vow of vegetarianism, never to break it again!

When Dodo returns...

Oh, please, my love, my master; please come back to me...

Trina Truelove's smiling reflection appears next to her own, a drink in each hand.

'Here, get this inside you,' says the owner of the reflection, passing a glass to Mayumi.

'Thank you,' says Mayumi, taking the glass. Mayumi feels well-disposed towards Trina. Due to being out with her boyfriend, Trina was absent from her flat on the occasion of those first meat-orgies, nor has she been present at any of the subsequent restaurant trips. Trina has no knowledge of Mayumi's fall from grace and no complicity in the concealing of her guilty secret from Dodo.

'Y'know, you shouldn't stand here moping,' advises Trina. 'Dodo'll come back. And she did order you to keep the party going, didn't she? Just think if she comes back now and sees you letting it fizzle out!'

The words hit home. Trina is right! The party doesn't truly begin until her beloved Dodo returns, and it is her bounden duty to keep said party in a fit state of readiness for her. It was the last promise she made, and she will not further disgrace herself by breaking it!

'Yes!' affirms Mayumi. 'It is our duty to keep this party in progress!'

She clinks glasses with Trina.

'Something feels odd about this place,' says Dodo.

They have just arrived in Critchlow and are walking along the street towards the village square.

'Something *is* odd,' says Mark. 'Look at the houses: not a light to be seen. I can't believe that tonight of all nights everyone would've just gone to bed early. Let's check out the pub; it ought to still be open at this time.'

When they reach the square and the first thing they see are two figures, one tall, one small, standing in the street in front of the *Earth Dies Screaming* memorabilia shop.

'I think I know those two profiles,' says Mark. Dodo at his side, he walks up to the two figures, calling out.

'Collins? Fontaine? Is that you?'

They make no reply. They remain standing motionless.

It *is* Mike Collins and Daisy Fontaine: Mike wearing jeans, t-shirt and trainers; Daisy barefoot in her khaki underwear. Side-by-side they stand, expressionless faces staring straight ahead, straight through Mark and Dodo, who now stand before them.

Mark takes Collins's arm, shakes it. 'Hey! Collins! Collins!' Collins remains silent, inert.

'They're in some kind of trance,' says Dodo, looking into Daisy's unblinking eyes.

'Shh! Someone coming!'

Lots of someones. They start to pour into the square from every street, a silent lumbering crowd, men and women in civilian clothes and varying states of dress. They advance towards Mark and Dodo, the separate groups merging together. Mark recognises Merrison, proprietor of the memorabilia shop, amongst the front ranks.

As the crowd closes in on Mark and Dodo, they raise their arms before them in one simultaneous motion. At the same time, Collins and Daisy come to life, raising their own arms. Mark and Dodo back away from them.

'Of course!' cries Mark. 'They've been turned into zombies! Just like in the film!'

'Very warm-blooded zombies,' remarks Dodo.

'Yes, and if we don't want to have to start shooting them, I suggest we beat an orderly retreat.'

And they turn and run, cutting across the grass plot around the war memorial. On their left now is the village pub and a light is visible through the curtained ground floor windows.

They sprint for the pub, and the zombies, arms outstretched, lumber after them. (Modern-day zombies have been known to run and run very fast, but the traditional zombie only lumbers, and being loyal to the mid-twentieth century source material, these zombies are adhering to the traditional style.)

Mark and Dodo rush into the pub and, securing the door, they enter the saloon. The lighted room has just three occupants: Flat-Sol Park and Yu-Mi Park seated at one of the tables and, behind the counter serving as bartender, Penelope Parker the chauffeuse.

None of them show any surprise at the appearance of the newcomers.

'You are tardy, Mark Hunter,' says Flat-Sol. 'I was beginning to believe I had been misinformed as to your being in Critchlow at all.'

Rajni had always planned to kill Dodo covertly, to let her death be blamed on the general violence and unrest of the build-up to Zero Hour; but if Dodo herself is the mastermind behind the whole thing, then Rajni can just kill her openly and everyone will thank her for it, won't they? She would be ridding the world of its greatest menace! They'd probably give her a medal! Maybe even a knighthood! Yes: Dame Rajni Sunnybrook, DBE! She likes the sound of that.

But what about the academic title she already possesses? With the knighthood would she be Dame Professor or Professor Dame...?

Rajni, following the road, has entered the woods and she now comes upon the crashed Rolls Royce limousine. She checks the car, finds it empty. It must have been hit by the same thing that hit me, she decides. She had been following this car all the way from London, but then, after leaving the motorway, she had lost it. She is still unsure as to whether her losing the Rolls had just been bad luck or if she had been spotted and deliberately shaken off. Speculating as to Flat-Sol Park's interest in all this, Rajni has come to the conclusion she must be either Dodo Dupont's financial backer or else a business rival.

She moves on. How far to the village now...?

Two figures step out of the woods further down the road, two very tall figures wearing bulky suits and helmets. As they step clear of the shadows of the trees overhanging the road, the moonlight illumines the metallic silver of their bodies.

Rajni freezes. The silver figures, coming to a halt in the middle of the road, turn to face her and the faces behind the glass helmets are definitely not human.

Robots!

Rajni runs for the cover of the woods and she keeps running.

Robots? What the crap? How do robots come into this? She knows there had been talk online about silver robots being sighted, but Rajni had dismissed the story as hysteria. Could the story about Zero Day being an alien invasion actually be *true*? But *Dodo* is the one behind Zero! How can alien robots come into it? As she runs through the woods, crashing through the tinder-dry bracken, her mind tries desperately to make sense of these seemingly irreconcilable facts.

One theory that pops into her mind is that Dodo is really an amateur spy and that that Mark Hunter is the professional spy she works with and that together they save the world from extraterrestrial threats—she quickly dismisses the notion as preposterous.

Out of breath Rajni comes to a stop and, taking cover behind some ferns, looks for signs of pursuit. She sees nothing, hears nothing. If the robots have pursued into the woods at all, she has lost them.

She also may have lost herself.

'I NEED *MEAT!*'

Yuki throws herself on Shizuka, locking her hands round the woman's throat. Instantly Shizuka has her gun (which incidentally there is no way she could have had concealed anywhere about her nearly-naked person) pressed against her attacker's forehead.

'Cease and desist!' she orders. 'You are a representative of the Japanese nation on foreign soil and as such you will deport yourself with modesty and decorum at all times!'

Yuki subsides, abashed.

Mayumi and Trina both burst into peals of merry laughter.

'Serves you right!' declares Mayumi.

'Yeah! Chill out, sister!' says Trina. 'Have a toke!'

Mayumi and Trina are stoned. The other two women had looked askance when the narcotic had been produced, and have declined to partake. (They're not very big on street-drugs in Japan. The major syndicates have pretty much written the country off as a lost cause.)

'Don't want to,' sulks Yuki. 'Want meat. Have been deprived for two whole days now. My shits smell funny…'

'Then don't smell them!' replies Mayumi.

'Yeah, you can last one more night, can't you?' urges Trina. 'You could even kick the habit and become a fulltime veggie like Yumi here!'

This rouses Yuki. 'Ha!' she says sarcastically. '*She* not vegetarian!' pointing an accusing finger at Mayumi. 'She been eating meat all the time!'

'Blabbermouth!' spits Mayumi. 'Traitor!'

Trina looks at her, bewildered. 'Eating meat? What's she on about? Have you stopped being a veggie?'

Mayumi makes no reply; instead, she gets up and walks purposefully over to Yuki. Taking her by the hair she pulls her friend from her sofa and drags her across the room. 'Whose fault is it I started eating meat again? Yours!' She now throws Yuki facedown onto the seat of her own sofa (and why it had to be this sofa and not the sofa Yuki was already sitting on, I really couldn't say.) 'Time for your punishment!'

And so saying, Mayumi pulls down Yuki's knickers and proceeds to administer a furious spanking, punctuating the blows with cries of 'Take that…! And that…! And that…!' The unfortunate victim wails under the onslaught and sheds oceans of tears. Her pleas for clemency go ignored. Shizuka observes the proceedings calmly and impassively, Trina with undisguised relish.

'Your fault…! Your fault…! Take that…! Take that…!'

'They're just standing there at the entrance to the yard,' reports Mark. The curtain dropping back into place he turns from the window. Flat-Sol Park and her sister are still seated at their table, and Dodo leans against the wall near the vestibule, surveying them suspiciously, casting frequent glances to behind the bar where the chauffeuse stands endlessly polishing the same glass.

'Once again this is just like the film,' proceeds Mark. 'They were holed up in the pub, as well…'

Says Dodo: 'We came here to find out what happened to your agents and now we know what's happened to them. What are we going to do about it?'

'Well, they seem to be under some hypnotic influence. We need to find out how they're being controlled. The logical place to look would be that radio station...'

'Ah, yes. This is the location you have always believed to be the centre of operations for Zero,' says Flat-Sol. 'Is it there that the product will be found?'

'What "product"?' inquires Dodo derisively.

'I refer to Zero. What else?'

'I don't know if it *is* a product,' says Mark. 'I have no idea what it might be.'

'You mean to say you still have not ascertained the truth?' demands Flat-Sol. 'Really, Mark Hunter, I am beginning to believe that you are a bad investment.'

'Look, Mark isn't your "investment,"' says Dodo, glaring at Flat-Sol. 'And as for what Zero is, maybe we're seeing that outside right now.'

Mark looks at her. 'You mean it's Zero that turns people into zombies? I hadn't thought of that... But Zero's only supposed to come into effect at midnight, isn't it?'

'Well, maybe the locals have been treated to an advance trial of the product,' suggests Dodo.

'Hmm... Well, first we need to work out how we're going to get there... There must be a way we can slip past those zombies unless they've actually got us completely surrounded...' He returns to the window, lifts the curtain. 'Hello! They're moving! They're all just walking away; it's like they've been called off!'

'Did *that* happen in the film?' asks Dodo.

'No, it didn't; but let's make the most of it, shall we?' To Flat-Sol. 'Are you coming with us or staying here?'

Flat-Sol rises from her seat. 'We shall be coming with you, naturally.' She signals to the chauffeuse who puts down her glass and dishcloth.

They exit the pub. The zombie villagers have crossed to the far side of the square and are now pouring into one of the streets.

'I wonder where they're all suddenly going...?' says Dodo.

'Perhaps to this radio station to prevent us gaining admittance,' suggests Flat-Sol.

'No, it's the wrong direction,' replies Mark. Pointing: '*That's* the way to the radio station; and they're giving us a clear field, so let's go.'

After blundering about in the woods for a frustrating length of time, Rajni finally strikes a footpath which takes her out of the woods and out onto a road, and there before her is Critchlow. The continuous stream of obscenities Rajni has been giving muttered voice to finally comes to an end.

She enters the village, surprised by its peaceful aspect. Where is Dodo Dupont? Isn't this village supposed to be her base of operations? That is if she is the one behind Zero and it's not those silver robots. Well, whichever it turns out to be and even if the human race *is* about to be wiped out by alien invaders, Rajni has still got to find and kill Dodo Dupont before that happens! *That* is all that matters! She can't just let her enemy die along with everybody else: she has to have her revenge first.

The road now brings her to the village square. She stops in her tracks. A huge crowd of people is gathered there. But it's a bloody *strange* crowd of people! They're all just standing there completely still and not saying a single word to each other. It's weird. Are they praying, or something? Holding some sort of Zero Hour vigil? Yes! Maybe they're all Church of Zero followers in this village. Wait a minute. Could that mean that Dodo Dupont is behind the Church of Zero, as well? Yes...! Yes, that would make sense! She's going to announce herself as God Almighty returned to

Earth! *That's* why she started this Zero thing! Yes, it's just the kind of thing that egomaniac would do!

She approaches the rear of the crowd. She clears her throat loudly. Nobody looks round. She clears her throat even more loudly.

'Erm... excuse me...?'

Still nobody looks round.

She taps a man on the shoulder. Slowly the man turns round. He stares at Rajni with glassy, vacant eyes.

'Hi! I'm sorry to disturb you... your... whatever you're doing...'

Other people now turn round. The people standing in front of them start to turn round. The people standing in front of *them* start to turn round. And soon the whole crowd has turned round and Rajni finds herself under the intense gaze of dozens and dozens of pairs of glassy, vacant eyes.

'So... I was just passing through and I was wondering...?'

And now the crowd starts moving towards her arms outstretched...

Rajni turns and legs it.

Jensen has started kicking on the door; kicking very insistently; and Mayumi is finding this very annoying. True it has been a while now since they have allowed him a trip to the toilet... A *long* while, come to think of it... But even so, the bastard has to remember he's a prisoner, not a guest; no room service on demand!

The digital clock on the television is still electronically ticking away. Less than an hour to midnight, and still no Dodo. Outside, the fires are still raging.

The spanking administered to Yuki seems to have left that worthy in a heightened state of sexual arousal. It's as though her libido having been stimulated but not satiated by the spanking itself. And what she still craves is not further chastisement, but the very thing that led to her being spanked in the first place: meat. It is meat she still craves, only the craving has turned from an angry obsession to an overwhelming sexual desire. Stretched out on the sofa, on her front of course ('Tell me, Doctor, will I ever be able to sit down again?') she repeats the word over and over to herself as she twists and squirms, swivelling her red-raw buttocks, an out-of-sight hand busy between her legs.

'Meat... Meat... Meat...'

The kicking on the study door persists. Mayumi scowls. This is going to ruin her buzz in a minute!

She stands up. 'Come, Shizuka; we'll see what he wants.'

Shizuka takes up the gun and the two women cross the room to the study door. Another barrage of angry kicks.

'Okay, okay!' snaps Mayumi. She pushes the door open with force and it comes into violent contact with an obstacle: Jensen and his chair, both lying on their sides on the floor.

With Shizuka covering her, Mayumi squats down and roughly pulls the gag out of his mouth. 'What do you want? You're making too much noise.'

'Then how about letting me go? What time is it, anyway?'

Mayumi tells him.

'You see? It's nearly midnight and Hunter and Dupont aren't back, are they? Something must have happened to them!'

'Something has *not* happened to them!'

'How do you know? Have they called you?'

'No... There's no signal...'

Jensen pounces on this. 'You see! Something *must* have gone wrong, or they'd have called or they'd have come back!'

'Not true!'

'And I say it is! Face it: they're probably both dead!'

Mayumi springs upright. 'Shoot him!' she snarls.

Shizuka takes aim at the helpless man.

'Hey, wait a minute! Wait a minute! You can't just shoot me for saying something you don't like hearing! But you've got to face facts! Something's going down in Critchlow, your friends have got to be in trouble, and God knows what's going to happen when it turns midnight! So how about letting me go? There's no point you keeping me on ice *now*, is there? I can't do any harm now! So why don't you just untie me and let me go and then I can be out of your hair? Come on! I don't want to be stuck in here tied to this chair when it turns midnight and whatever's going to happen happens!'

Mayumi appears to consider this. She turns to Shizuka. 'What do you think...?'

There follows a rapid colloquy in Japanese, and then Mayumi squats down again to address Jensen. 'Okay, we let you go. But we keep your gun and any funny business and we shoot you.'

'Fine with me!' accedes Jensen eagerly. 'Keep the gun; just let me have my car keys, my phone and my freedom and I'll be out of your hair.'

Mayumi goes back to the living room for the key to the handcuffs. She informs Trina and Yuki of what they are doing.

'Good,' is Trina's verdict. 'I'd prefer it with him gone.'

Mayumi returns to the study. The chair is set upright and Jensen is freed from his restraints. From the desk he collects his belongings and slips them into his pockets.

He turns to the two women in the doorway. 'Erm... there is just one more thing...'

'You want to talk to me?' says Trina coldly.

'Yes, I want to talk to you, Trina,' says Jensen. 'And can't we talk in private? Just give me five minutes; five minutes and then I walk out of your life forever.'

Trina turns to Mayumi and Shizuka. 'Go on. You can leave us. I'll be okay.'

'You sure?' questions Mayumi.

'Yeah...'

'Take this,' invites Shizuka, holding out the gun.
'Nah, I'll be okay.'
'Just call out if you want us,' says Mayumi.

The two women depart and Trina and Jensen are left alone in the study.

'Go on then,' says Trina, still icy. 'What do you want to talk about?'

'Oh, don't be like that. I just want to try and explain things—'

'I don't really want to hear your lame excuses.'

'Look, I know there's no excuse for what I did, with the bracelet and everything... But in the world I live in, we're always playing dirty tricks like that on each other, and the way we look at it is that the victim's the one to blame for being stupid enough to fall for the trick.'

Trina laughs a bitter one. 'So I'm the idiot for actually believing the bracelet you gave me was a sincere token of your affection? Well, yeah, I suppose I *was*, really; cuz I knew what kind of bloke you were; the love 'em and leave 'em type...'

'Yes, I am that type; I admit it; *usually* I am... But with you... it was *different*... I'm just trying to say that there's something about you, Trina... I don't know... I mean you're not the best-looking woman I ever went out with—'

'Oh, thanks!'

'...And you live in a completely different world to me, and we don't really have any interests in common... In normal circumstances we'd probably never even have met...'

'Yeah, but you went out of your way to meet me, didn't you? Cuz you wanted to use me.'

'That was the original reason, yes. I'm not denying that... But, like I say, there was just something about you; I can't explain it in words; there was just something about *being* with you; it was like I could never get enough of you...!'

'Because I was a good lay?' sarcastically.

324

'Well, why not?' demands Jensen. 'That's what it was about, wasn't it? For both of us! That was what our relationship was about; it was the sex; it was always the sex; we were good together…!'

Trina smiles in spite of herself. 'Well, yeah… It was pretty good.'

'There! You see? Well, look, I'm getting out of here now. And you; well, your friends aren't coming back because they're probably dead, and Christ knows what's going to happen at midnight… So why don't you come with me?'

'What!? Are you serious?'

'Yes, I am! Look, we may all only have less than an hour to live and I want to make the most of it, if that's all I've got. I want to be with you. So come on; come with me, Trina.'

Trina shakes her head, slowly, sadly. No, the attraction has gone; the connection has been severed; she just doesn't want this man any more… 'No… No, I'm sorry. It's sweet of you to ask and everything, but I want to stay here with Yumi; she's my friend…'

'Yeah, but what can you do with her?' demands Jensen. 'She hasn't got what *I've* got, has she?' He grabs Trina's arms. 'Come on, baby; you and me, just you and me…'

Trina pulls herself from his embrace. 'Read the t-shirt, arsehole! It's over between us! Just get out of here!'

And she turns to leave the room.

She never makes it. Jensen pounces on her, twisted handkerchief held thug-like, forcing it into her mouth, knotting it tightly round her head.

'If I'm going to die tonight, I'm going to die fucking you,' hisses Jensen.

Trina, with muffled screams and furious eyes, struggles with all her might, but Jensen, much less gentle than the Jensen of yore, throws her violently to the floor and comes down on top of her, pinning her down and pulling out his violent erection.

The struggle is still going on when the door opens. Mayumi and Shizuka charge into the room, the latter armed. She reverses the gun and brings it down on the crown of Jensen's head. Jensen collapses on top of Trina.

With Mayumi's help, Trina frees herself from under him. She pulls the gag from her mouth. She is flushed and gasping for breath. 'Bastard!' she spits.

'Maybe dead bastard,' says Mayumi. She shows her palm, wet with blood from the back of Jensen's head. Shizuka examines her gun; it too has blood on it.

Yuki has appeared. 'He's dead? He's really dead?' she inquires eagerly.

'Looks like it,' says Mayumi, standing up.

Yuki studies the prostrate man, assessing him with hungry eyes.

'Conference!' she cries, and grabbing Mayumi by the arm, propels her out of the room.

Trina and Shizuka exchange puzzled looks and follow their friends out of the room. The door closes behind them.

And Jensen is left alone, his body sprawled on the floor under bright electric light, motionless and to all appearances dead. He lies close to the rear wall where the window, concealed behind vertical blinds, runs its entire length. To the right, against the wall closest to Jensen's expensively-shod feet stands the tall bookcase containing Professor Dupont's library of scholarly works (her own included.) Infront of the bookcase stands the straight-backed wooden chair to which Jensen has spent a large part of the day uncomfortably handcuffed, the handcuffs now lying on the seat. On the other side of the room, and close to Jensen's battered and bloody head, is Dodo's desk on which her computer, printer, pen-holder and letter trays are all neatly arranged. In pride of place on the wall above the desk hangs a framed photographic enlargement, a self-portrait of Mayumi Takahashi, topless, grinning, her hand raised in what for her is a variant of the peace sign, but for an English observer would be an invitation to go forth and multiply. All is silent in this room, all is still, like the eye of the hurricane, undisturbed by all the turmoil boiling and seething beyond its four walls, outside the window with its drawn blinds, outside the closed door.

Jensen looks a sorry sight, lying there. Not nearly as battered and bloody as his friend Brunner had looked that day Jensen had kicked him to death, but still the worse for wear, still far from his usual immaculate state. His face is marred by scratches and a bloody noise, sustained in his thwarted attempt to rape Trina Truelove. His hair is a mess, greased tufts of it sticking out in all directions; and round the back where it rests on the floor, it is matted with blood, blood which has spilled onto and soaked into the carpet around it. There are further indications of the struggle in Jensen's clothing: the disarranged collar and tie, the shirt-front partially torn open. And there, lolling from the open trouser fly is Jensen's flaccid penis. Formerly its owner's pride and joy, his whole *raison d'être*, it hangs there a sorry sight, frustrated of its last moment of glory. An observer might have wondered why the penis hasn't remained in the tumescent state it was in at the moment the blow fell on Jensen's skull; they might have argued that if the heart has ceased to beat and the blood to circulate, then surely it should have remained as it was…?

But there is a good reason for this: it is because the heart has *not* ceased to beat. Jensen is not actually dead. For some minutes now he has *appeared* as one dead—but now he starts to stir. His lips move, mumbling incoherencies. The head moves, the eyelids twitch and then open, as slowly, painfully, consciousness starts to return.

No, Jensen is *not* dead—but when the door opens and the four naked women come slinking into the room with claws unsheathed, they are just way too far gone to be taking such trivial details as this into consideration.

First Yu-Mi complained that her feet were hurting, and Flat-Sol had consoled her by pointing out that they would have been hurting a lot more if she hadn't been wearing the regulation flat-soled shoes instituted by herself; then Yu-Mi complained that she was tired and her legs were aching; then Yu-Mi started to lag behind the rest of the group; then she disappeared completely and they had to retrace their steps, where they discovered her lying on the grass verge fast asleep; now she is being carried on the chauffeuse's back, still fast asleep.

A light has become visible on the horizon, a finger of light reaching into the sky.

'That light is coming from where the radio station is,' declares Mark.

'Then it looks like we're on the right track,' says Dodo.

As they draw nearer to their destination it becomes clear that the finger of light isn't just a light; it is a *radio mast*, surrounded by an aureole of luminance; the radio mast that was lying toppled on its side... Mark recalls the day he came here with Rick Bedford and the CIA man's sarcastic suggestion about the mast just climbing back up on its legs whenever it needed to start transmitting. Well, it looks like it has done just that.

The radio station comes into sight. It isn't just the antenna but the whole building that is radiating ethereal light. It is as though the building has been rejuvenated; the doors and windows are now glazed; the brickwork has recovered its freshness; even the access road stretching across the field from building to road has reappeared. The station looks just as it had looked in *The Earth Dies Screaming* over half a century ago.

The building is just as aglow with light within as without; it shines from the windows, from the glass panels of the entrance doors. But there is something unreal about it all, something ghostlike and insubstantial. There is no movement, no sign of life.

'So you were right, Mark Hunter,' says Flat-Sol Park. 'This building *is* Zero's corporate headquarters after all.'

'It's where the transmissions have been coming from, yes,' says Mark.

'And it looks like they're transmitting right now,' says Dodo.

'Well, let's find out.'

The gravel of the phantom road crunches underfoot as they approach the building's entrance. As they reach it, the double doors swing open, inviting them into the shimmering interior.

Mark turns to Dodo. 'Well, shall we go in?'

'We might not have much choice,' says Dodo, nodding over her shoulder.

Four silver robots have silently materialised behind them; identical, standing in a perfect line.

Yu-Mi Park finds herself rudely awakened as the chauffeuse drops her without ceremony from her back, unholsters her gun and levels it at the robots.

'Hey, what's going on?' mutters Yu-Mi in Korean.

'We have arrived at our destination,' explains Flat-Sol, helping her to her feet. 'Compose yourself.' Switching back to English, she addresses the robots. 'Are you the controllers and originators of Zero?'

'PROCEED.' The voice, metallic, imperative, booms from the mouth grille of one of the robots.

'Are you authorised to speak on behalf of the controllers and originators of Zero?'

'PROCEED.'

'Please respond to my questions. I wish to enter into negotiations with you. I am Flat-Sol Park, chief executive—'

'PROCEED.'

'Let's just do what they want and go inside,' advises Mark. 'It's what we were about to do anyway. And you can tell your chauffeur to put the gun away: those creatures are bullet-proof.'

Followed by the robots, they enter the building and pass along corridors hazy and intangible; a light-saturated an impressionist dream of the building's interior as it once was. A feeling of unreality assails Mark, a feeling that was there, vague but persistent, tugging at the edges of his mind when he was here before, a feeling to which pragmatic Rick Bedford had been insensible, but which had convinced Mark that there was more to this place than met the eye.

And now they step through an open doorway into a much larger chamber. They have arrived. The master control room, the hub of the operation.

'HALT.'

This room is in much sharper focus, everything is solid and real, from the antiseptic walls, floor and ceiling to the electronic equipment lining the walls: control desks with their dials and levers and switchboard displays of bleeping flashing lights; locker-sized computer banks with spinning tape spools, spewing out streamers of punched paper tape.

Four more of the robots are seated at these control desks, aesthetically in harmony with the equipment they are operating. On the wall to the left of the door, is a huge display screen with the Zero logo and the digital timer ticking off the counting down the now less than twenty remaining minutes to Zero Hour.

But in the centre of the room stands something of an anomaly: a huge metal container, rivetted, reinforced, rectangular in shape, whose purpose Mark cannot fathom. Windowless, it has but one visible means of access, a heavy door like the hatch of a ship or submarine, opened and closed by a wheel. A metal rod or cylinder extends from the roof of the tank disappears into the ceiling.

The spokesman of their four robot conductors now stands in front of them, while the other three move to various positions around the control room.

Here we are, thinks Mark. The hero and heroine confronting the real villains of the piece in their secret nerve centre as the clock ticks down to Zero. The stage is set for the dramatic finale.

'Now,' begins Flat-Sol Park. 'If we may commence negotiations—'

Make that the hero and the heroine plus some of the comedy secondary villains.

'Before you begin your negotiations,' says Mark; 'don't you think it would be a good idea to find out just who you are negotiating *with* and precisely what it is you will be negotiating *for*?'

'Why? Are you authorised by your government to bid against me?'

'No, I'm not here to bid for anything. I am here to find out just what's going on and to prevent from happening anything that needs to be prevented from happening.'

'In other words, shut your fucking gob and let Mark do the talking,' says Dodo.

Mark addresses the robot leader. 'Are you prepared to answer some questions?'

'SPEAK.'

'Thank you. First of all, who are you? What form of life are you?'

'WE ARE SYNTHETIC LIFEFORMS.'

'Mechanical?'

'SYNTHETIC.'

'Do you originate here on Earth?'

'NEGATIVE.'

'So where do you come from? Vega?'

'WE COME FROM ANOTHER DIMENSION. THE STAR YOU CALL VEGA IS THE NEXUS POINT.'

'And why have you come to Earth?'

'THOSE WERE OUR INSTRUCTIONS.'

'Whose instructions?'

'OUR CREATORS. THE ONES WE SERVE.'

'And who are you creators?'
'THE ONES WE SERVE.'
'Yes, but what are they called?'
'THE ONES WE SERVE.'

Abandoning this line of questioning: 'Then *why* were you sent to Earth? What is your purpose here?'

'TO MAKE THINGS READY FOR THE ARRIVAL OF ZERO.'

'But *what* is it?' demands Flat-Sol impatiently. 'What is Zero?'

'ZERO IS ZERO.'

'That does not explain! Please clarify.'

'ZERO IS ZERO.'

'That is not enough! Be specific!'

'ZERO IS ZERO.'

'Is it Zero that has turned the local population into zombies?' asks Mark.

'NEGATIVE. THE HUMANS ARE UNDER OUR DIRECT CONTROL.'

'Why?'

'IT WAS NECESSARY. THE CONDITION IS TEMPORARY. THEY WILL NOT BE HARMED.'

'So, what has happened to them isn't going to happen to the whole world at midnight?'

'NEGATIVE.'

'Then what is going to happen at midnight?'

'ZERO WILL ARRIVE.'

'How will it arrive, exactly? Will it appear everywhere?'

'IT WILL ARRIVE AT THIS LOCATION.'

'Here? You mean in this building?'

'AFFIRMATIVE. IT WILL MATERIALISE IN THE CONTAINMENT TANK.'

'The containment tank being that object in the middle of the room?'

'AFFIRMATIVE.'

'So, Zero is being transmitted electronically?'

'AFFIRMATIVE.'

'But what *is* it?' demands Flat-Sol. 'Precisely what will materialise in that container?'

'ZERO WILL ARRIVE.'

'And what is Zero? What does it do?'

'ZERO IS ZERO.'

'That is still not an answer! Clarify!'

'ZERO IS ZERO.'

'Foolish automaton!'

Says Mark: 'And when Zero arrives, what will be the immediate effect? What will happen?'

'NOTHING WILL HAPPEN.'

'Nothing. And is that a good kind of nothing, or a bad kind of nothing? Is Zero is dangerous?'

'ZERO IS ZERO.'

'So you keep saying. Is there any way to prevent Zero's arrival?'

'AFFIRMATIVE. THERE IS AN ABORT MECHANISM WHICH WILL PREVENT THE SIGNAL FROM BEING RECEIVED.'

'Is there, now? And how would one activate this abort mechanism?'

'THE ABORT SWITCH IS LOCATED ON THE CONSOLE BELOW THE DISPLAY UNIT.'

Mark looks. On the console below the monitor there is a big red button.

The big red button. Mark has a long association with big red buttons.

He smiles.

Somebody is seriously taking the piss out of Rajni Sunnybrook and she does *not* appreciate it.

First that death ray, or whatever it was, that had flipped her car on its back, then those silver robots chasing her into the woods, and now these zombie villagers coming after her! All she wants to do is find Dodo Dupont and kill her, but fate keeps throwing these increasingly ridiculous roadblocks in her way!

She has had to take to the countryside once more. The pursuing zombies had shown no sign of increasing their speed to match hers, but there were a lot of them and they were annoyingly persistent, and if she hadn't left the road and taken to the wooded slopes, she would have had them following her around all night.

She has to focus! All these robots, zombies and death rays are just a distraction. She has to focus on what is real and important: and what is real and important is finding Dodo Dupont and killing her! *That* makes sense. The robots, zombies and death rays *don't* make sense. She must not clutter up her mind worrying about things that do not make sense; not until she has killed Dodo Dupont. When that has been done, *then* she can start worrying about everything else. Think about your target. Think about all her crimes. Think about where it all started…

In one of her books (academic rather than photographic), Dodo had actually written about her boyfriend-stealing 'experiment' at university, and she had the nerve to say that she 'felt bad about it now'! Oh, well that's alright then? Never mind that she acted like a complete whore and ruined people's lives in the process; as long as she 'felt bad about it now'! But it didn't stop her capitalising on it by writing about it in her stupid book, did it? (And not a *mention* of Rajni, either!)

Well, soon Rajni will be publishing her own book about that little incident, a book giving *her* side of the story, in other words, the *true* story! As matter of fact, she has already written this book, but her attempts to get it published have been unsuccessful. They'd actually claimed it was libellous! How can the truth be libellous? The truth is the truth, isn't it? (And anyway, it won't matter after tonight: the libel laws don't apply to dead people.)

Reaching the crest of a hill, Rajni sees a light shining into the sky somewhere ahead. She turns her steps towards it. They might be the lights of a helicopter landing pad, and if they are then Dodo Dupont's helicopter must be there, and if Dodo herself happens to be there with it, Rajni can kill her, and if she isn't there then all Rajni has to do is wait for her to come back and kill her then.

But the light isn't a helipad, as Rajni discovers when she emerges from the trees: it is a glowing building with a big glowing aerial on its roof standing in the middle of a field. For a moment Rajni is disappointed, but then it occurs to her that this building must be the transmission centre that all those Zero commercials are being sent out from, the place the whole world has been looking for (although it does seem a bit odd that nobody's found the place before now, what with it being lit up like a Christmas tree); and as Dodo Dupont is (probably) the evil mastermind behind Zero, then this is where she will be!

The helicopter's probably parked round the front.

The helicopter isn't parked round the front as she soon discovers, but the main entrance is there and when she stealthily sidles up to it, the doors swing wide to admit her. She looks inside. The foyer is empty. She enters, crosses the foyer and advances along a corridor, and the corridor obligingly leads her straight to the control centre.

It's her! There she is. She pauses on the threshold and takes in the tableau: a room full of retro-futuristic robots and retro-futuristic equipment and directly in front of her, five human beings. They are standing with their backs to her, but Dodo Dupont is someone Rajni can recognise from any angle, from any isolated body-part—and those buttocks she would recognise anywhere! Look at them: they seem to be jeering her, sneering at her, inviting her to give it her best shot. Go ahead, come and get me, but you're doomed to failure, because I always win and you always lose! those buttocks seem to say.

We'll see about that!

There are four other people present, that Mark Whatshisname, and Flat-Sol Park and her entourage, but *they* are unimportant; *they* are just bystanders...

Mark Whatshisname is talking to one of the robots. He's asking them why they look like the robots from some old B-movie...

'THIS IS THE FORM WE HAVE ASSUMED ON EARTH.'

'Yes, but *why* have you assumed this form?'

'IT WAS HOW WE WERE PERCEIVED BY THE FIRST EARTHLING TO SEE US.'

'You mean Amber Windrush, don't you?'

'AFFIRMATIVE.'

'And she saw you here, didn't she? Here in this building.'

'AFFIRMATIVE.'

'And so, her seeing you influenced your appearance... But I think she's done more than just influence your appearance, hasn't she? She's been influencing the way you've carried out your instructions.'

'WE FOLLOW OUR PROGRAMMING.'

'Yes, but I think she's still been influencing you... I doubt she even knew it herself, but when you and she crossed paths that day... some sort of connection was made between you...'

'AMBER WINDRUSH NO LONGER EXISTS IN LINEAR TIME.'

'She was killed, yes. But even so, I think she's still having an effect on you, isn't she...?'

'All this talk concerning a deceased female is irrelevant,' cuts in Flat-Sol Park. 'We have still to reach any agreement regarding distribution rights for Zero.'

'Oh, for Christ's sake!' says Dodo wearily. 'Haven't you got it yet? There's nothing *to* distribute! Zero is nothing! As the name implies, it is a negative quantity: it is the absence of form, substance, light, sound, taste, odour: everything! Don't you get it? We're the victims of a great big cosmic practical joke here—and you're one of the idiots who has been taken in by it!'

Mark addresses the robot. 'Is she right? Why are you bringing Zero to Earth? Why have you been sending out those broadcasts?'

'WE FOLLOW OUR PROGRAMMING.'

'But the beings who programmed you, the ones you serve: what are *their* motives? Why are *they* sending Zero to Earth?'

'UNKNOWN. THAT INFORMATION IS NOT IN OUR PROGRAMMING.'

'You see?' says Dodo. 'Even they don't know. It's like they're being had, along with the rest of us. Face it, sweetheart: we're heading towards another one of our anticlimactic endings.'

Mark indicates the screen on the wall. 'What, in spite of the dramatic countdown?'

'In spite of the dramatic countdown.'

'So you want a dramatic ending do you, Dodo Dupont?' comes a new voice, shrill and maniacal. 'Well, *I'll* give you a dramatic ending!'

Dodo swings round. A woman, brown-skinned, blonde-haired, dressed in shorts, t-shirt and trainers, is charging across the room at her, a kitchen knife in her raised right arm.

'Time to die, Dodo Dupont!' she cries. '*Your* countdown is ending right now because I'm—!'

The report of a gunshot. The woman spins, falls backwards, the knife clattering to the ground beside her.

The chauffeuse, calm and expressionless, returns her gun to its holster.

'You didn't have to do that!' snarls Dodo.

She goes to the stricken woman, kneels down beside. A widening pool of blood seeps from the wound in her side, but the woman is still alive, gasping with pain. The blonde wig has slipped from her head, revealing short black hair.

'You...!' exclaims Dodo.

The woman smiles through her pain. 'So... you finally recognise me, do you...?'

'Of course I recognise you. From the day you tried to blow up my apartment. You're the one who's been trying to kill me all this time, aren't you? But why—?'

'You know me from before that day... We go back much further than that, you and I... Look at me closely...'

Dodo looks. 'I'm sorry; I don't—'

The woman winces. 'It was a long time ago... Perhaps... Perhaps, I've changed too much... But you'll remember... you'll remember when I tell you my name...' Making a supreme effort, the woman stares deep into Dodo's eyes. 'Rajni... Sunnybrook...!'

Dodo's eyes widen. 'Rajni Sunnybrook?' Her lips form a reflective moue. 'Rajni Sunnybrook... Rajni Sunnybrook... Sunnybrook...' She shakes her head. 'Nope. Doesn't ring any bells...'

'What!?' Wild fury overwrites the expression of pain on the dying woman's face. 'You don't *remember me*? You don't even *remember me*?' left eyelid and mouth corner twitching epileptically; 'You... You... *bitch*! You fucking *bitch*! You're doing this on *purpose*! I swear you are! You... You...!' Eyes glaring pure hatred, her arms, with clawed hands, reach for Dodo's throat... But the effort is too much; the eyes glaze over and the arms fall limply at her sides.

And Rajni Sunnybrook dies as she has lived: thwarted, frustrated and completely exasperated by that insufferably successful, seemingly indestructible, boyfriend-stealing bitch, Dodo Dupont!

'ZERO MINUS ONE-HUNDRED AND TWENTY SECONDS,' announces the robot.

Dismissing Rajni from her mind, Dodo gets quickly to her feet. All eyes are turned to the countdown display: two minutes and counting to Zero Hour.

Mark comes up beside Dodo, and, speaking in an undertone: 'You *may* be right about Zero being literally nothing, but I just can't take the risk. I'm going for that abort button and I need you to make a distraction.'

'Okay, but what do you want me to do?'

'Pick a fight with the chauffeur; you've got a good pretext for doing that.'

'Alright, I'll do that and you can go and press your big red button.'

Dodo strides up to the chauffeur and shoves her. 'That woman's dead because of you! You had no right to interfere! I didn't ask for your help, did I?'

The chauffeuse of course says nothing. Her employer speaks up on her behalf.

'Why do you complain?' demands she. 'She saved your life, did she not?'

'I didn't need saving!' retorts Dodo. 'I could have disarmed her myself, and I could have done it without killing her!'

'As if such trivialities can matter at a time like this,' retorts Flat-Sol. 'If that woman was the perpetrator behind all those recent attempts on your life, then there are a considerable number of incidental deaths to be laid at her door. I see no reason for this discussion.'

Dodo smiles tightly. Now, picking a fight with Flat-Sol Park is *much more* to her taste than picking a fight with her chauffeur. 'Oh, don't you? Well, I don't recall asking for your opinion.'

And Dodo slaps her round the face. Flat-Sol staggers.

'You will regret that,' tightly. She takes a flying kick at Dodo; Dodo parries and retaliates and a full-on no holds barred fight is soon underway.

'STOP THIS DISTURBANCE!' booms the robot leader.

Meanwhile Mark moves backwards towards the control console with the big red button.

A countdown and a big red button. A familiar situation for Mark Hunter. When the big red button does something bad, then his job is to prevent it from being pressed, and when, as in this case, the big red button *stops* something bad from happening, then his job is to press the button or see that it gets pressed.

Why do the robots even have a big red button? Why would they have installed an abort function that would prevent them from completing the task they have been programmed to carry out? Perhaps he has the unseen influence of Amber Windrush to thank for the abort switch… Yes, Amber, with her specialist knowledge would be up on all these cliches…

The console with the big red button, conveniently enough, is not one of the consoles with a robot operator seated in front of it; but there *is* a robot operator seated at the next console but one. The four standing robots are now moving in to break up the fight, but those at the control desks have remained seated and undistracted and continue to work at their consoles. He looks up at the countdown: sixty seconds to go. Now or never.

He makes a run for the console. He throws himself at the switch. A metal hand closes round his forearm like a vice. Mark screams. The robot swings him away from the console and forces him to his knees.

'REPORT,' calls out the robot leader.

'THIS HUMAN ATTEMPTED TO ABORT THE COUNTDOWN,' replies Mark's captor.

'FIFTY SECONDS TO ZERO,' announces a third robot.

'Let go of him!' shouts Dodo.

'THERE MUST BE NO INTERFERENCE.'

'FORTY SECONDS…'

Dodo unholsters her gun and, knowing it is useless, empties the clip into the robot leader. The bullets have no effect.

'RESISTANCE IS USELESS.'

'THIRTY SECONDS...'

The robot leader takes the gun from Dodo's hand and crushes it to a ball in its fist.

'TWENTY SECONDS...'

'PREPARE TO RECEIVE SHIPMENT.'

'CIRCUITS ACTIVATED.'

'TEN SECONDS... NINE... EIGHT... SEVEN... SIX... FIVE... FOUR... THREE... TWO... ONE... ZERO.'

A pregnant pause.

And then, from inside the containment tank comes a deep metal thud like the impact of something very large; the sound reverberates around the control room.

And then silence once more. All eyes are fixed on the containment tank. The red light above the hatch turns from red to green.

'SHIPMENT RECEIVED.'

The robot pinioning Mark's arm now releases him. He staggers to his feet, wincing as he flexes his hand. Dodo comes towards him, smiling.

'You okay?'

'I'll live.'

'Well, it's gone twelve and we're all still here.'

'But *something* happened, didn't it?' says Mark. 'We all heard that sound: something has materialised inside that tank.'

Dodo shrugs. 'Something called Zero. We seem to be heading into paradoxes here. How can nothing be something?'

Flat-Sol Park now speaks. 'What has happened? What has been introduced into that container?'

'ZERO,' replies the robot leader.

'It is in there?' pointing at the tank. 'The thing you call Zero is actually within that container?'

'AFFIRMATIVE.'

'How much is it worth? What is its market value?'

'UNKNOWN. IT IS FOR HUMANS TO ASSESS ITS VALUE.'

'Yes, but how much do you want for it?' insists Flat-Sol. 'For how much are you willing to sell it to the Parkhurst Corporation? Name your price.'

Dodo rolls her eyes. 'Oh, for God's sake—'

'IT IS NOT FOR SALE. IT IS A GIFT.'

'You mean to say it is *worthless*?'

(To Flat-Sol Park, if something is being offered gratis there are either strings attached or it's just not worth having in the first place.)

'IT IS FOR HUMANS TO ASSESS ITS VALUE.'

'But what is it? What is the product—?'

'NO MORE QUESTIONS. WE HAVE PERFORMED OUR DESIGNATED TASK. OUR PRESENCE IS NO LONGER REQUIRED.'

'You mean you're leaving?' asks Mark. 'You're going back to those "ones you serve"?'

'OUR PRESENCE IS NO LONGER REQUIRED. INITIATING DEACTIVATION…'

And so saying, the robot leader staggers, its legs give way and it collapses. This seems to precipitate a chain reaction: one by one, the other robots collapse; those on their feet falling like puppets with their strings cut, those seated at the equipment slumping forward over their consoles.

'They're just switched themselves off…' says Dodo.

'More than just that…' Mark points to the prone body of the robot leader. It seems to be deflating, the arms, legs and torso caving in on themselves. The same thing is happening to the other robots, the seated ones sliding limply from their chairs.

And then it is done and all that is left are just eight empty silver costumes with hollow metal heads in glass helmets at one end and pairs of empty boots at the other.

Mark and Dodo crouch down to examine the robot leader. Mark lifts one of the limp arms.

He looks at Dodo. 'Well, they did say they weren't actually robots...' He stands up, turns to Flat-Sol Park and her entourage. 'Well, now that that's—'

He stops. The chauffeuse is covering them with her gun.

'Both of you raise your hands,' instructs Flat-Sol crisply.

'Oh, what do you think you're playing at now?' says Dodo wearily.

'I am not "playing" at anything, Professor Dupont,' responds Flat-Sol. 'Raise your hands.'

Mark and Dodo raise their hands.

'I am taking possession of Zero in the name of the Parkhurst Corporation,' announces Flat-Sol, indicating the containment unit. 'You will neither of you attempt to interfere. If you do you will be shot.'

'Oh, for God's sake—! There's nothing to take possession *of!* It's just an empty metal tank, you stupid bitch! Zero is Zero, remember? And zero means nothing!'

'That remains to be seen,' replies Flat-Sol. 'I shall examine the merchandise myself.'

'You mean you're going to open that hatch?' says Mark, alarmed. 'I wouldn't do that, Flat-Sol. If there *is* something in there, it might be better if it's *left* in there.'

'Mark Hunter, the only way to determine if there is anything in the container is to examine the contents.'

'But it might be something *dangerous*!' insists Mark. 'And if you open that hatch you might be letting it out!'

'You talk as though there is a wild animal in there,' says Flat-Sol. 'The mechanical creature said that it was for us to assess its value, did it not? For that assessment to be conducted, the product must be examined.' To the chauffeur:

'Keep them covered. If either of them makes the slightest move to interfere, shoot them.'

Accompanied by her sister, Flat-Sol walks up to the hatch door of the containment unit. She takes hold of the wheel and turns it. The mechanism clicks as the lock is released.

'Don't open that door, Flat-Sol!' calls out Mark.

'There won't be anything in there,' opines Dodo. 'This whole thing's just been one big joke with a mare's nest for the punchline.'

'I wish I could share your optimism,' says Mark glumly.

Flat-Sol pulls open the hatch. Inside is darkness. She looks inside.

'What is this? It is empty! *Empty*!'

'You see?' says Dodo. 'Nothing in there.'

'This cannot be!' fumes Flat-Sol Park. She steps into the tank. 'This cannot—'

Like the springing of a trap, the hatch swings shut with impossible force and speed. From within the tank comes a piercing, protracted scream.

Apparently 'nothing' can be very scary.

Epilogue
The Earth Sighs Dreaming

The countdown is over; Zero has ceased transmission and normal service has been resumed. And as the population of Critchlow comes out of its zombie trances, people all around the world likewise start to come to their own senses; they look around them and they see that no catastrophe has occurred, everything is still as it was before. The world has not ended: it has been reprieved. The locked-down start to come out of hiding, and some of the people involved in the disturbances start to feel rather foolish, and they wonder whether the CCTV cameras have got any clear shots of them engaged in their foolishness… And as for those who preferred to meet doomsday halfway and end their own lives before the countdown reached zero: well, they will never know by how much they have jumped the gun.

As dawn breaks a helicopter flies low over central London and sets down on the roof of a particular apartment building. Mark Hunter and Dodo Dupont emerge from the aircraft, which immediately takes off again, and head for the stairs.

They enter Dodo's apartment and are greeted by silence. A powerful odour hangs in the air.

Dodo sniffs it. 'That smells like meat…!'

Mark inhales a sample. 'Could be one of those meat-substitutes…'

'It had bloody better be…!'

They advance into the living room. And there they are: Mayumi Takahashi, Trina Truelove, Yuki Kinoshita and Shizuka Todoroki, all sprawled naked on the furniture, and all fast asleep. The coffee table is littered with empty plates and glasses, the detritus of a midnight feast.

Dodo can't help smiling at the sight. 'Ah, look at them. Don't they look sweet?'

Mark accepts the invitation. 'Yes; in a debauched kind of way…'

'But what have they been eating…?' Dodo, still troubled by the prevailing odour, picks up one of the plates. She examines the fragments of food dried to its surface. She puts one in her mouth. 'It *is* bloody meat!' spitting it out. 'It's pork! I'd swear it's pork! The moment my back's turned, and they start cooking meat in *my* house.'

'Well, they didn't know if they were going to live to see another day,' answers Mark diplomatically. 'Maybe Mayumi thought the others deserved a treat.'

'Yes, I suppose she… Wait a minute! Look: four plates and they've *all* had meat on them…!'

She looks down at Mayumi, sprawled on the sofa, innocently asleep. Her hands are resting on her tummy, as though arrested in the act of rubbing it contentedly after an enjoyable but very filling meal.

She looks at Mark.

'Maybe you've just discovered that deep, dark secret she's been keeping from you,' he suggests, smiling wryly.

'You mean she—?'

'Could have been a lot worse, couldn't it?' says Mark. 'I'll just go'n check on our friend Mr Jensen.'

Mark heads for the study and Dodo looks back down at Mayumi. She sneezes in her sleep and Dodo's heart melts. Dropping to her knees beside the sofa she gently strokes Mayumi's long, thick tresses.

Mayumi's eyes open, focus on Dodo. She smiles.

And then they open wide.

'You're okay…!' she breathes.

'Yes, sweetheart; I'm okay. Mark as well. We're both okay.'

Mayumi springs from the sofa and Dodo lifting her off the ground, they embrace wildly, joyously, Mayumi wrapping her arms and legs around Dodo.

Aroused by the noise, the other three women begin to awaken. Trina farts, sits up, rubbing her hair.

'Huh…?' looking around her groggily. 'Wassappened…?'

'Nothing,' Dodo tells her. 'The world hasn't ended, we're all still here.' She sets Mayumi down on her feet. 'And now, young woman, I think you've got some explaining to do.'

She points to the table with its incriminating crockery.

Mayumi looks first confused and then distressed. She drops to the floor in the very same supplicating posture both women had envisioned for this moment.

'I'm sorry, I'm sorry, I'm sorry! I confess! I confess! started eating meat again!' And she looks up at Dodo, the tears streaming down her cheeks.

Dodo sighs. 'You silly thing... Why didn't you just *tell* me?'

(Trina, with the horror-stricken expression of someone remembering something she really wishes had just been a dream, sees Mark emerge from the study and make his way towards the kitchen. Galvanised, she leaps from her chair and races to intercept him.)

'Surely you didn't think I was going to throw you out bag and baggage, just for that?' proceeds Dodo. 'Your being vegetarian was never a condition of our relationship, silly!'

(Trina, arms outstretched, bars the way to the kitchen, blocking Mark's progress as he tries to get past her.)

'I was too ashamed to tell you!' wails Mayumi. 'I betrayed you!'

(Mark lifts Trina gently but firmly in his arms, puts her to one side and enters the kitchen.)

'You haven't betrayed me, silly. Yes, I was pleased when you turned vegetarian; I was touched because I knew you'd done it mainly for my sake, but if you've decided to start eating meat again—'

'No! I stop! From today, I go back to being vegetarian! I swear!'

(Mark comes out of the kitchen. His face is pale and rigid. Absently patting Trina on the head as he passes her, he makes his way across the room at a fast walk, heading for the door.)

Dodo lifts Mayumi to her feet. 'If that's your decision, then thank you, sweetheart. But from now on, no secrets, okay? You had me really worried, you know.'

Mayumi salutes. 'Yes, master! I promise! No secrets!'

They embrace. And then:

'One thing I *am* annoyed about, though! To get this meat you had last night, you must have—Hey! Where are you going?'

This is directed at Mark Hunter, who, caught in the act of surreptitiously opening the front door, momentarily freezes, before turning to face his questioner with a bleak imitation of an insouciant smile 'Ah! Well, you see, I just remembered I've got a report to write about this whole business, and a very long report it's going to be! So I thought I'd just toddle on off to the office and get it out of the way…'

'But can't it wait till tomorrow? You've been on your feet all night!'

'No, no; best to do it now while it's all still fresh in my mind…! And anyway, I really think it would be for the best if I were to make myself scarce and leave you to clear up the little mess that needs to be cleared up here… So, yes: I'll be off!'

And Mark is gone.

Dodo, confused, turns back to the others. Mayumi looks very uncomfortable. Trina looks a lot more than very uncomfortable, and so do Yuki and Shizuka.

'What's he talking about? What "little mess"?' and then, suddenly remembering: 'And where's Jensen…?'

***

If you are wondering what happened to Zero, I'm afraid I can't tell you. The containment tank in which it materialised was taken away and it's probably now gathering dust in the same subterranean vault you will find the Roswell flying saucer and the Ark of the Covenant. But if you're wondering what happened to the woman who went into that containment tank and sampled Zero firsthand, there I can help you. So just follow me while I take you to a Georgian manor house in the heart of leafy Buckinghamshire. It was once the country seat of a titled family, but it now serves as a private mental asylum. An exclusive institution, affordable to only the wealthiest of the wealthy, it is somewhat unorthodox in some of its practices, but the staff and directors, who know what they're about, have always been successful in concealing these things from the annual inspectors.

If you were an authorised visitor and you had all the right credentials, you would be shown to a particular room on the second floor, a room unoccupied for much of the time, but equipped with a large one-way mirror, by means of which you would be able to see into the adjoining room, the adjoining room being a gilt-panelled drawing room supplied with antique furniture.

The room has two inhabitants and they are a curious couple: one an old man, a cackling, liver spotted, wizened imp, with sightless eyes concealed behind black glasses and dressed in a Victorian nightshirt and bobble hat; the second a beautiful Asian woman, short-haired, whom you will recognise as Flat-Sol Park. Flat-Sol has changed a great deal since her experience in the Zero chamber. No longer obsessed with financial gain, now her main object in life is self-effacement; to make herself as small as possible, and endeavour to remain unnoticed. Permanently terrified, she is usually to be found huddled in corners, hiding her face and shaking with fear; and when she does have to move, she much prefers to crawl along the ground than walk upright.

Her companion, the old man, likes nothing more than to tease and torment Flat-Sol, to aggravate and take advantage of her permanently terrified state. As we look in now, he is engaged in one of his favourite occupations: he has fitted Flat-Sol with a saddle and bridle designed for the human steed (available from all good BDSM retailers) and he rides on her back as, terrified and tearful but obedient, she crawls around the room, he urging her forward with cries of 'giddy-up!' and resounding slaps to her naked buttocks.

The old man is Jaundyce Hurst, formerly Jaundyce Parkhurst, and formerly CEO of the Parkhurst Corporation, until Flat-Sol Park had come along and introduced him to her spiked heels. The room with the one-way mirror is here for the benefit of Parkhurst executives who like to come and amuse themselves watching the antics of their two fallen leaders. Yes, the Parkhurst Corporation did not collapse along with the mind of its incumbent CEO: the corporation is still up and running and a new president has been installed. And the new president is none other than Flat-Sol's younger sister, Yu-Mi Park—but although she is ostensibly the CEO, in actuality her role is more that of a sleeping partner.

Printed in Dunstable, United Kingdom